I ATE IT COLD

I ATE IT COLD

IVAN DE NEMETHY

PENNILESS PRESS PUBLICATIONS

Website :www. pennilesspress. co. uk/books

First published May 2019

ISBN

Cover by Ivan de Nemethy

IN MEMORY OF
John Bull
Ron Budge
Dave Phillips
Colin Elmore
Mike Taylor

With help from,
Lez,
Tors,
And Ken

CONTENTS

Hors d'oeuvre   9

Warming the plates   25

What's on the menu?   31

Chew slowly   46

Pepper and salt?   59

Clear your palette with this cheeky red wine   64

Ready for dessert?   70

Coffee with Pálinka?   82

Clear the table   110

Who spilt the wine?   129

Leftovers   142

Your bill, Sir   175

They've loaded my bill!   195

Pay up!   209

HORS D'OEUVRE

Xabia was dying.　　The usual neon signs outlined Death's shadow;

Tea like mum makes
English Pub
Beans (Heinz)
Fish and Chips

Not much left of the proud little fishing village that used to live here. Distracted as I drove past the picturesque harbour, I had to brake hard to avoid a gang of drunks Congaing down the road. Acknowledged the oaths and knee jerk v signs with a "Sorry. My fault" wave. The drunks threw bottles and cans.

Mow them down next time?

Startled by a double bang and whoosh of foam spray showering the screen and bonnet as I parked at the kerb. Stretched back wearily in my seat, waiting for the spray to stop. It had been a long drive.

Swung the door open, looked back as I unfolded my body out of the car, smiled as the drunks melted away, afraid I had stopped to discuss it – too tired, and, anyway more important things on my mind. A front wheel had squashed a couple of full lager cans, the plastic noose held another two, the missing two were swilling around inside the drunks and would end up in some local garden. Picked the cans up…. not a waste bin in sight…apart from Xabia.

Shook the cans in the direction of Alicante, fifty miles along the beleaguered Spanish coast. Alicante airport was the primary node for this cancer, spewing it out by the plane load for about a hundred cans per lager lout. Hasta la vista Espana, forget about the viva bit, it's been flushed, untreated, straight into the Med.

Drank the evening away at a Tapas bar hanging precariously over the harbour, tossed morsels over the rail for the fish. The fish didn't care either, they fought for the cooked bits of their brethren and shat in the water, just like the humans. The Spanish owner was, regretfully, going to have the bar converted to an English pub. He couldn't afford to buck the trend any longer. In a year or two, when he was that much richer, he wouldn't give a toss either. He had his price.

9

At least he had waited a little before giving in, which meant his price had been that little bit higher, or, maybe, not quite so low. Anyway, he was selling out. Listened sympathetically to his chest beating until the second bottle of Rioja did its work, dimming the life in my eyes and brain. But the anger and pain remained.

Slept fitfully in a small family run hotel hidden away in a side road, re-dreaming the same dream throughout the night. Woken early by the warmth of the sun through the open window. It was going to be a blisteringly hot day. As a hot blooded Hungarian I prefer the cold. Out before breakfast, strolled down to the harbour, taking photographs with my empty Pentax, pretending to be on holiday, embarrassed at the thought of adding to Xabia's discomfort, consoling myself that it was not my fault I was here.

Looking for a medium-sized stinkpot (a diesel engined cabin cruiser. If you were travelling with the wind behind you the exhaust fumes clung to the boat like nautical body odour). I was hoping that the main season was not yet underway and that all the hire boats weren't taken up, I had to get back before Jozsef Huszár was missed.

Soon found what I was looking for, an old fashioned twenty-four foot-er, teak decks, leather upholstery, brass fittings. In its day, even more reassuringly expensive than Stella lager. Like all truly classy things, it still had class in spite of the crazed varnish and dried up leather, the sort of class you were born with and no amount of money could stick on later. Reminded me of my Jag, still looking good after twenty-three years.

Paid for a week's hire and an extra large deposit, in dollars. The boat made me feel better, it felt good to do it in style. Lesley deserved that. The owner had insisted on the extra large deposit and on keeping my car keys, he was worried because I claimed to have lost my passport. This trip wasn't happening. József Huszár was still back in Budapest, on a drunken, memory-proof bender, his Jaguar in the garage.

Made a point of asking the owner to demonstrate the SatNav in case I lost sight of land on my way up the coast to Valencia, my alibi for the next leg of the trip.

József Huszár wasn't going to Ibiza, either.

Having struck the deal I loaded a basket at the tiny supermarket and was on my way after a quick breakfast, studying the chart from the boat as I ate. Xabia was the nearest mainland point to Ibiza, that's why I was here. I am no sailor and now was not the time to learn, not sailing.

The map told a simple story. Ibiza town was about seventy miles away, due East, as near as made no difference. The boat was capable of twenty knots so I would easily get there before nightfall. Never been out on a boat alone, apart from once, in a tiny scull on the Thames when I capsized and decided eights were safer. The area should be full of small boats and the ferry route from Alicante came up from the south, swinging up to join my route about half way to Ibiza. Wasn't like I was crossing the Atlantic. Due East would take me to the southern tip of Ibiza. If I drifted South a little I would land at La Sabina Island. Drift North and I would strike Ibiza Island itself. Anywhere between 76^0 and 98^0 would see me striking land. Could hardly miss, even if there was a cross current, or continental drift, or exceptional gravitational pull from the moon or the hard up Spaniards had sold Ibiza to McDonald's who had had it reshaped to match their dog ugly Logo.

Folded the map and gunned the engine, going cautiously past the other boats. It had all seemed a lot easier in theory, back in the familiar surroundings of József Huszár's flat, watching the boats casually cruising up and down the Danube. Dead easy, from a sixth floor balcony with a Pálinka in your hand.

Headed East and as the coast line sank noticeably below the horizon, switched off the navigator. The sea suddenly looked bigger, a hell of a lot bigger than the three hundred metre wide Danube, but I couldn't risk the navigator telling any one where it had been. Clever little bastards, these navigators. The weather looked good, slight breeze from the port side so no stinkpot fumes. The sun was set on frying my brain, and I was squinting, struggling with the reflected glare off the sea. Thought of my aviator shades left behind in the glove compartment of the Jag and my Magellan GPS – should have brought them both. Left in a hurry, never had been good at packing. Lesley used to do it for me.

Checked the dials, the engine looked happy. Opened the throttle wide, the big diesel clattered and the tired old hull vibrated in sympathy with the engine, fighting the resonance from its own bow waves as the speedo touched 22 knots. Eased back until, at fifteen knots, the boat was in easy harmony with the sea, the engine and waves singing the same tune. The throbbing from beneath the teak decking gently massaged my feet, eased my tightened leg muscles, helped take the edge off my tension. Looked again and again at the compass, nervously remembering that there was a significant difference between true north and magnetic north. Wasn't magnetic north at about two minutes to twelve, or two minutes past twelve, instead of twelve? Not knowing whether to add or subtract the 12^0, or should that be 6^0, from my course, decided it was best to ignore it, just aim due East, easiest on the brain.

Bigger things to worry about than yet another of God's mistakes.

Now, if only God had been a Physicist, everything would add up. No North that wasn't North.

No need for this trip that Huszár wasn't making.

Looked scornfully at the empty sky. If there was a God who knew and saw everything, the shyster already knew that I had him sussed. Knew that I knew that God was just another pyramid salesman, flogging self-cleaning consciences. God was fly, he did not ask for money, all he asked was that you promised him your redundant soul after you died and your conscience was wiped clean on the spot. It was guaranteed to work every time because it was your own conscience that did the cleaning.

God's scam fooled billions, some dyslexics even built real pyramids. Well…. . their slaves built them for them and their God was so impressed with the pyramids that he forgave them for using slaves. I accept that everybody is entitled to their own God, just like I accept that everybody is entitled to their own arsehole. Difference is, everybody needs their own arsehole.

Grinned broadly as I scanned the horizon, no giant hand to smite me, no lightning bolt burning me to a crisp.

But God had been sloppy, hadn't done the maths. For the scam to thrive, God needed exponentially more people to sign up at the bottom, else the pyramid would collapse – that's why Popes had to take such a hard line on contraception – desperate for new recruits.

What if someone wouldn't join the scam, refused to give up his soul? What if someone knew about the syphilitic portraits in the attics? What would membership of God's cosy little club be worth then?

Locked in my thoughts I was relieved, after three tense hours, to spot the Alicante ferry coming up from the South East and joining my path, ending up three kilometres or so dead ahead.

Just follow the wake, could have thought of that earlier, might have saved a few anxious heartbeats, saved a few microns of fat furring up my arteries. The ferry was clipping along at a good rate and I had to speed up slightly to stay with it. As my grip loosened on the wheel, the knotted muscles in my arms lost some of their definition, my shoulders felt a little less broad. Breathed deeply, exhaling slowly, aware of the hint of lingering diesel fumes from the ferry ahead. Liked the smell, it meant I was on the right track. After trailing the ferry for over an hour I could see Ibiza Island to port and La Sabina to starboard. A half hour later the ferry veered off to starboard. Could see both islands clearly now, exactly as the map had promised. Headed round the headland, Ibiza town was visible straight ahead. Under six hours. Stood up, leaned forward as I pulled the throttle to the end stop, patted the dials smiling back at me from the teak dashboard, flashing their pearly white needles in unison. Never been to Ibiza before but I watched TV so I knew what to expect. Visualised the occasional shot of what looked like a sizeable Marina carpeted wall to wall with hundreds of boats. The programmes usually concentrated on the night life, the bars, the clubs, the pavements littered with comatose lager louts.

Brains in neutral, loins in overdrive top.

As I came closer I could see that Ibiza town was long dead, deader even than Xabia. Shiny white holiday blocks pointed to the sky from out of its rotted corpse like barbed spears saw toothed with balconies. Breeding grounds for the maggots crawling all over town.

Stomach rumbled, complaining that it was hungry because I'd forgotten to feed it. Slid easily past the jetty walls and soon spotted an empty berth in the outer harbour. Parked successfully at my first attempt, with only a mild bump as the boat hit the tyres hanging from the side, Allowed myself a faint smile. At the quayside bar I went through it all in my mind, a well-worn route, been dreaming about it for months. John Bull had owned a flat in Ibiza and had given me the phone number one time when he was off on holiday and the hotel project was at a critical stage. Hadn't rung the number until January, wanted to see if it was answered, desperate to know if Bull still owned the flat. Eighty-seven calls later, three days ago and six hundred miles up the road, it had been answered. BY BULL!

Came straight here, having hired the Merc and using my Hungarian passport. That's how Hungarian born English raised Jozsef Huszár wasn't making this trip. Fortunately, all bearded men looked the same to the clean shaven, just like all Westerners look the same to the Orientals.

Bull had been able to keep his flat out of the hands of the liquidators. BASTARD! Must have lied about it. Had Bull managed to keep his boat as well? Bull had referred to his boat as Maggie (the name of his mistress), that was the only clue. That and also that it was a twenty footer with wooden decking. Bull had often complained that his holidays at his Ibiza flat were fully taken up with maintaining his flat and his boat, especially the teak decking on the boat. Unlike most people, Bull's complaining wasn't a device to let people know that he had a flat and a teak decked boat in Spain. Bull really was moaning about the responsibility of having a flat and a boat in Spain. Should have read the signs and run when I had the chance.

Should have read the signs, they were there all along. Sorry, Lesley.

That was three years ago, Bull might have sold the boat since then or lost it when he went bust four months ago. The flat had been in a modern condominium not far from the Marina, Bull had bragged that he could see his boat from the balcony. Looked around from my table on the pavement. The place was one bloody great condominium, there must be thousands of flats fitting the description of Bull's flat. Somebody should have shot the architect. Bull used to be an architect. Toyed with the idea of ringing the number again. This was Easter Saturday, surely Bull would be here staying over the Easter weekend? At least until Monday or Tuesday? Best not to ring, no point. I was here now and I would either find Bull or I wouldn't find Bull. Yes?. . . . No?. . . Yes?. . . No? Got tired of trying to guess the answer from the expressions of the passers-by and ordered another beer.

The frosted bottle slipped out of my hand, a million splinters over the tiles, all from such a tiny, tiny bottle. Looked down at the bubbling, glass decorated beer. Suddenly, this trip seemed like a wild goose chase, a waste of time. Bull used to come out for a fortnight at a time, but he might have been here for weeks already, been out the times I had rung the number each and every day for eighty-eight days.

Bull would surely be here over Easter, surely Bull wouldn't have left since he had answered Huszár's call, not just days before Easter? Left an extra tip at the bar for the breakage, noting in the bar mirror how different I looked with a beard. Still found it disconcerting to catch sight of myself, hadn't grown used to being bearded again. Strolled towards the Marina, taking the scene in, counting the pontoons, trying to look casual. Must be at least three hundred, maybe even four hundred boats. Fifteen, twenty seconds per boat, it would take an hour and a half to check them all.

Narrowed it down to two possibles. Both in a mild state of disrepair, May Dancer and Go Lightly. Maybe Rod Stewart's Maggie May? but

Bull had had no discernible interest in any kind of music, except the music of a cash register ching chinging. Maybe Huszár had misunderstood the Maggie reference? At least wooden decks were few and far between in this plastic Marina. These two were the only boats that fitted the description, except for a couple of others that were in pristine condition and looked seriously expensive. Bull was certainly too lazy to have done the maintenance himself and too broke to have bought and paid for that sort of level of care. Retired back to the bar.

Bull had always fancied himself as a gourmet and food here was cheap, everything here was cheap. Asked at the bar for likely upmarket restaurants near the Marina. The barman didn't understand and just gestured towards the main drag. Ambled around the streets until midnight, eating a take-away pizza on the hoof, got to keep moving. No luck. Ignored the glad looks from the dolly birds and even from the dolly men, out on the prowl, out for their definition of a good time. Well, it wasn't mine, either way round, whichever way or wherever they wanted to put it.

Came dejectedly back to the Marina, quite a few boats had cabin lights on. Ibiza town was at least five times bigger than I had imagined, Bull could be here all year and I might never catch sight of his stubby, short-limbed body. Cursed under my breath, I might have missed a chance already.

Should have stayed at the Marina to watch the boats. Go Lightly had a group of young couples drinking on deck. May Dancer was unlit, as were the two other wooden decked boats. So, either it was May Dancer, or Bull had gone up in the world, or there was no boat at all and I was wasting my time. Or, might have to trace the flat, if I could work out a way to do it without attracting attention. Sleepless night on the stinkpot. The bunk had been tailor made for a legless dwarf with no arms. It was airless and stiflingly hot in the cabin because the decimated dwarf obviously had no need of lungs. Wondered what it must be like in mid summer. Had never seen the point of boating, could see even less point to it at four thirty when I finally gave up trying to sleep. My stomach was complaining, made it happy with a seriously greasy breakfast of choritzo and eggs, enough fuel for the whole of the day ahead.

As I drank my third coffee I wondered if there was a more scientific way of tracking Bull down. Since I wasn't supposed to be here, I couldn't just ask around openly, couldn't attract attention. Anyway, who could I ask? No point in phoning the bastard, might tip him off.

Why not phone the bastard? Bull would never dream that Huszár would have come all this way on the off chance. One voiceless wrong number four days ago, Bull would not have connected that with anybody. No breathing even, Huszár had held his breath just in case, didn't want to put Bull on his guard. Wrong numbers must be a regular pain in the arse at a seaside resort cum knocking shop like Ibiza. All those young girls spread-eagled on a plate, handing out their phone numbers to young swains both willing and eager to gobble them up. All stumblingly drunk on the triple measures of cheap booze, inhibitions mislaid back home in the ruts of their daily lives. They were here for a different kind of rut. Wrong numbers must outnumber regular calls by about two to one.

Looked at the map for something to do. Bull had mentioned sailing round the island once, to......Fomentera! It was there! North end of Sabina Island. Finding Fomentera made it feel much more tangible again. Touched the spot on the map for reassurance, I WOULD find Bull! Encouraged, decided to ring the flat after all, say nothing, just listen to his voice. Just check to see if Bull was still here, Couldn't stand not knowing if Bull was still here.

Locked up the cabin and headed for a breakfast bar with a phone booth. "Hello?..... . Hello?" Bull was still here! Slightly falsetto voice roughened by having been woken abruptly from his sleep. Put the receiver back on the hook. BULL WAS STILL HERE!

But where, where was he? Looked up at the blocks. Somewhere in one of those rabbit hutches, Bull was cradling the receiver, unaware that I had come all this way just to see him, unaware that I was actually looking at his flat. Harvey Oswald could probably shoot Bull from here, but there was never a bloody sniper around when you needed one!

Closed my eyes and slowly clenched my fists until my knuckles hurt. Recalled, vividly, the strong smell of nasal irritant after shave when Huszár had first met Bull, wearing his natty overcoat with the velvet collar and racy little toy Toyota car, rear spoiler almost as big as he was. Focused on one of the windows, four stories up, "Hello John, surprise! Surprise!" No response from the window as I turned away and had to consciously unclench my fists because of the pain. My knuckles still hurt when I got back to the Marina. I could smell Bull, my nostrils filled with his stench and it wasn't his after shave, the hate must have shown in my face because a passer-by moved to the other side of the pavement as I approached.

Cleared my thoughts, seven thirty, early yet. Walked slowly past May Dancer, examining it carefully but not letting it show. The sails were tightly furled, the dirty water marks and salt stains on the covers told me they had been untouched for months. Walked around the Marina again, keeping a weather eye on May Dancer, re-checking for other likely boats.

Better see about paying for the berth, stopped at the pierside office. The faded, sun-baked paint seemed to be all that was keeping it upright. One good breeze and it would be matchwood. Tried the door gently in case it came away in my hand, still locked up. There were a few scruffy for sale sheets stuck inside the window glass, curled and yellowed by the sun, ink only two shades darker than the yellowed paper they were written on. A couple of photos, the images relying more on memory than the silver oxide of the film, the bright blue sky faded to white. Looked closely, nothing that seemed to fit the description of Bull's boat as far as I could tell, no six metre boats. Walked aimlessly around the Marina until, eventually, saw the elderly Spaniard opening up the office. The sun had baked him just like the shed, only in his case it had made him darker, he had what looked like real mahogany head and hands. He was anywhere between sixty and a hundred years old.

My Spanish was even poorer than the Spaniard's English but paying for the berth was easy. The Spaniard had made to fill in a form but he readily recognised the sweep of my palm as I handed over the money. This was a cash deal in exchange for a small discount, hence no record of my having been here. It took several attempts, pointing at the for sale notices, before the Spaniard understood that I wanted to buy a small yacht. Wrote down, May Dancer, on the back of my phrase book and pointed towards the boat. Rubbing my thumb and forefinger in the internationally accepted sign denoting, Pesetas, Francs, Drachma, Dollarrrrrr.

You name it, everybody wanted some. Flashed a wad of dollars. Mañana. Gave the Spaniard a ten dollar note, making sure that he saw and appreciated the size of the wad. Mañana, Pointed to my watch, indicating the same time the next day. The Spaniard seemed to understand well enough so I walked off to find a bar. Wait and see what pink and slimy creature came crawling out of the woodwork.

Always the best bait, money. Just show them the money and all language barriers disappear behind a green-backed cloud of greed.

17

From a vantage point at a first floor restaurant I spotted Bull two hours later heading, or rather, waddling, towards the Marina. Bull was about a hundred metres away on the other side of the road. God, he'd put on some weight, he looked like an imminent heart attack. Bull was short, about five foot four and must be the wrong side of a hundred kilos. Eating for comfort? Couldn't be comfortable carrying that wobbly blubber around all day, comfort didn't come into it. Watched Bull pass and then went downstairs to follow as Bull went straight to the pier side office.

Bull came out a minute later and headed from the pier office. . . . straight to May Dancer! I had guessed right, almost cheered out loud with the relief. Made my way to the stinkpot, passing within fifty metres of Bull on his yacht, not daring to even glance in Bull's direction. Instantly sweating with the excitement of having found Bull, dried my face with a tissue and carried on sweating from pores I didn't even know I had. Popping out of my brow and filling my eyes, dripping from my nose, soaking my clothes. Gave up trying to dry myself, may as well enjoy the shower. Drank a warm beer as I watched Bull uncovering the sails. Bull was preparing the boat for an inspection, raising the sails to unfurl them. It was getting even hotter and stickier in the cabin but I couldn't risk being seen. Stayed inside and drank another, even warmer beer, tasted like piss. Nine out of ten people can't tell the difference between warm Spanish lager and piss. I am one of the nine. Missed Bull's return to the pier office, spotting him waddling back out of the Marina and towards town. The sails were still raised, Bull must be coming back.

Decided to wait, too risky to trail Bull round the harbour, no point, anyway. Spotted Bull a half hour later with a young man in a monkey suit following behind, a mechanic? The mechanic was struggling with an oversize marine battery strung with a short rope round his neck. Bull was going to take the boat out? Minutes later, I could make out the distressed sound of a clapped-out diesel engine turning over incessantly, pointlessly. It was not about to start, I could tell.

I had once owned a clapped-out diesel truck. Bull's engine was so worn that it didn't have sufficient compression to fire, it needed a cold start spray immediately, followed by a full engine rebuild later. The mechanic came out of the boat and despite Bull's entreaties strolled off at a leisurely pace. Siesta time, always siesta time – in Spain. Bull stayed and hosed the decks and sails with a hose pipe from the quay side. An hour passed before the mechanic returned, apparently empty handed, hands in pockets with the swinging gait of an evening sea front prowler out to pull the birds, or more accurately, he wasn't going to run away from them. He'd had a couple of beers and was looking forward to the evening hunt, easy meat. Minutes later, a huge belch of blue white smoke rose into the air as the engine fired first time, the smoke floating off in the breeze like a hot air balloon. The mechanic had brought the cold start spray. The mechanic emerged triumphant and looked very angry when Bull made it clear that the bill should be added to his account. Bull hadn't changed. The mechanic kicked the side of the boat, contemplated further action and, thinking better of it, went off scowling and muttering under his breath, the bounce gone from his walk. His boss had warned him to make sure he collected the money, he would have to tell his boss to collect it himself.

Bloody Englishmen! Hello, English girls.

As the mechanic disappeared into the crowds on the pavement Bull quickly cast off and headed out of the Marina. He didn't want to get caught by the chandler's proprietor who would be mad as hell. Bull had told him his money was on the boat and he would pay when the engine started up. Still, maybe he would have plenty of cash tomorrow, Julio had been very specific about a large wedge of dollars. He headed out to sea for a run, blow away the cobwebs, from the boat and from his mind. Bull was not coping well with his new-found poverty. His uncle's empire, built up over forty years, had crumbled to nothing in his hands. No empire, no money, no fancy expensive dinners out at the Randolph, no fancy cars. Bull didn't fancy it. He was a qualified architect but he was a crap architect, even he could see that. His future looked bleak. For a while, he had had it made, had it made really big. This was much harder than if he hadn't tasted success at all. He knew what he was missing. It had felt good to be a millionaire, on paper, but then the magic ink had disappeared and the paper was worthless without it.

Forced myself to wait, willing my watch to go faster and then I slipped out of the Marina, turning in a wide arc before I went after the yacht. Couldn't be too careful and, anyway, I would have no difficulty catching up with the little twenty footer. Could tell from the sound of the engine that it was only fitted with a tiny diesel, intended solely for manoeuvring round Marinas, not for serious trips. This was a little toy yacht for little toy sailors. It fitted Bull's image perfectly. Toy developer but not, unfortunately, for toy money.

Huszár's money!

It was Bull's incompetent handling of the Hotel project that had led to Huszár's losing Lesley. Time to pay up, no need for a receipt and we'll forget all about the VAT, shall we? Amused by my VAT analogy as I opened the throttle wide and the boat surged forward, the bow rising satisfyingly high in the water. It was Huszár's creative VAT returns that had kept the project alive, propping up Bull's expensive changes of mind until Huszár couldn't stall VAT man any longer and VAT man decided forty thousand of missing VAT warranted a spell in jail – the Judge had concurred. Huszár had tried to get his money by suing Bull, but Bull had finally gone bankrupt. In the words of a disgruntled contractor who had chased Huszár with a kitchen cleaver to ensure he had his attention, "Either I get all my money, or, I'll write it off. "

Bull had no money left, so I had come to write it off.

Hadn't formulated a plan, in Huszar's dreams he always woke when he caught up with Bull, so what was I to do now, now that it was happening and I was wide awake?

 Ram the bastard? Just follow Bull's wake, see what came up? Even if Bull saw me in the distance, Bull wouldn't recognise me with a beard, especially as he expected me to be eleven hundred miles away in England. Bull would never dream that it was me in the stinkpot trailing a couple of miles or so behind. I had stopped sweating and the cooling breeze from the boat's motion dried me surprisingly fast. Felt cool and in control as I deftly turned the wheel, aiming towards the little boat, the sharp bow lined up with Bull's dyed blond hair, an easy target against the blue of the sea.

Bull was heading for Eulària, ten miles East along the coast. He owed the chandler too much money to risk his interfering with a possible sale. He would meet the buyer in the morning and bring him round to the boat. He rubbed his hands together at the prospect of some real cash. The boat was probably worth twenty-five thousand if he was lucky.

He would gladly let it go for twenty or even fifteen. Fifteen was too good a deal for the buyer to pass up and Julio had been very specific about the thick wedge of dollars. Bull was desperate. Fifteen thousand! He looked around the boat, with the sails up in the light breeze, it looked all right. It looked all right! He didn't notice the stinkpot bearing down on him, now less than a mile away. Now he could hold on for a better price for the flat. He was set. The boat sale would set him up on the road to recovery, maybe even get sixty thousand for the flat.

The boat sale would give him the time he needed to wait for the selling season, hold out for a good price. The boat sale would save Bull.

Less than a hundred metres behind when I throttled back so I could be heard. Cupped my hands. "Ahoy, Sailor. " Bull's head snapped round, he recognised that voice, but it couldn't possibly be! He looked hard and long. IT WAS! "Joe? Joe, what brings you out here?" Bull's voice lost its power by the end of the sentence and the last word came out as a strangled squeak as the enormity of Joe's turning up forced its way through the fear clogging his brain. He stared back at the boat, transfixed like Lot's wife as the stinkpot came closer, now less than forty metres behind. Bull knew what had brought me out here. Unfinished business! Bull had left a trail of dissatisfied business partners and the odd irate husband in his wake over the last twenty years and he recognised the signs.

My motionless stance, my fixed stare, gave every impression that I was looking at a helpless quarry that I had cornered and was about to eat. Bull had been surprised not to have heard from me before, but back in England, not here in the middle of the Mediterranean. Bull recalled the two recent phone calls and the now ominous silences at the end of the line. He cast his mind back, the first was three or four days ago, the second was that morning. Huszár had come all this way just to see him, having first checked that he was here. This was not an accidental meeting…. . HUSZÁR WAS THE MYSTERY BUYER! Huszár had lured him out onto the sea on his own. Should have been more careful but the prospect of selling the boat had allowed Bull to drop his guard. Bull looked around. He had taken a wide sweep out from the island, now at least four miles north. There were a couple of small boats about two miles ahead, also heading for Eulària. Bull started the diesel, partially warmed up from its short run earlier it fired up instantly. Thank God for that! Bull pushed the throttle wide open, holding the lever hard against its stop, willing it to go faster, his body rocking backwards and forwards, mouth wide open in a soundless scream of terror.

Huszár had smashed a new wall down once, when Bull had changed his mind. Huszár had taken a running jump at it and it was more than three metres high. Bull had been terrified at the intensity of Huszár's rage at the time, remembered the wall crumbling, taking several seconds to fall as Huszár walked away from it, satisfied that he had made his point. Bull had been relieved at the time that the wall was there to be kicked down, it might easily have been him.

Saw the puff of smoke as Bull's engine started and, opening my own throttle wide again, I easily caught up and swept past the toy boat on its starboard side, the wake from the stinkpot rocking the yacht wildly from side to side. Bull, rigid with fear, kept his eyes fixed on the boats ahead, clutching the tiller with one hand and holding the throttle lever down with the other, his mouth still wide open in terror. I turned to port, cutting across Bull's bow and headed away to come back in a wide sweeping arc. Did some mental calculations as the boat turned. The stinkpot must be twice as heavy as the toy boat, it had a much larger super structure and a five litre diesel engine, at least four hundred kilos of engine plus about four hundred litres of fuel for it to drink. The toy boat had a sewing machine for an engine and a yoghurt carton for a fuel tank. Plenty of mass on my side, there was no substitute, when it came to the crunch, for sheer unadulterated mass. Even Einstein could have told you that double the mass meant double the energy, double the heat, double the destruction, double the pain.

More pain, even more pain. The sun caught the twin hinged claws of the shiny zinc anchor on the fore deck, they looked very painful. More speed! Energy obeys a square law, double the speed gives four times the energy, four times the pain. Left the throttle wide open and went to the bow, collecting the anchor, must weigh twenty kilos, nearly half a hundredweight in old money. Took the wheel again and turned full circle. Heading back towards the yacht, anchor on my left.

Bull had been watching, mind numbed but his steering had not wavered. He tried calling out but his voice, totally drained by the fear gripping at his chest and freezing his diaphragm muscles, was easily drowned out by the noise of both engines at full throttle. His despairing shout for life came out a stage whisper. The stinkpot was bearing down on Bull on the port bow, surely Joe didn't mean to actually ram him? Watched the bow of Bull's boat, approaching at a relative speed of twenty five knots. Bull waited until the boats came to within thirty metres and then turned hard to starboard, underneath the path of the looming bows rushing towards him. Bull was an experienced sailor and he knew that I would not be able to turn in as sharply as he could, my boat was too heavy and going far too fast. Bull would scrape past on the inside and head for the safety of the boats ahead. The little boat, its horizon filled by the stinkpot, seemed suddenly to be going ten times faster.

Bull was going to make it.

I had also been waiting and once Bull was committed to the turn I picked up the anchor, flexed my shoulder muscles and hefted it with all my strength, swinging my arms and body round, using the discus throwing technique I had learnt at school. With pure adrenaline flooding my heart, I aimed at the mast of the yacht, knowing that with Bull's forward speed the anchor would miss the mast and go in front of Bull's head. Bull, concentrating on avoiding a collision had been looking at the stinkpot's bow. He had done it, Joe had missed! The other boats were noticeably closer. By the time Joe turned round again and caught up Bull would be safe. Joe wouldn't dare attack him in front of witnesses. From the corner of his right eye, Bull saw a shiny bird, trailing what looked like a streak of light, flying past his head. Involuntarily, his eyes followed and he turned his head to see the shiny bird suddenly bank towards him. His hands flew up instinctively to protect his face.

The chain caught Bull's wrists, clamping them to his throat, making him look like the say no evil monkey. The anchor, pivoted at his neck, swung round in a short arc and after one and a half turns, with the chain choking him and breaking his neck as the stinkpot pulled it tight, the flat anchor claw pierced through Bull's left ear cavity, cutting off the front of his face just as his body was yanked out of the back of the boat like a rag doll's. Bull's face flew upwards and landed in the water a full second after his body and already five metres behind it. Bull's shape and bulk dragging through the water at twenty knots was too much for his neck, and with his spinal cord already severed, the chain cut off his head and both hands like a cheese cutter through a round of Brie. The stinkpot lurched forward as Bull's body floated free. Looked back in time to see Bull's floating face, empty eye sockets looking up at the deep blue Mediterranean sky, his body floating five metres closer and his bloody, faceless head, just sinking out of sight, streaming a trail of blood and hands behind it. I calmly closed the throttle and hauled in the anchor. The anchor and chain were clean and totally unmarked, the side of the boat had suffered a little but there were other, older marks already on the hull. Nothing to show.

Pictured Bull's head spiralling slowly to the bottom as I urinated from the stern of the boat, aiming the thick yellow stream of recycled coffees and Spanish beer in a high arc at Bull's floating face.

"See you in Hell, John!" Looked around the horizon as I zipped my fly with a flourish. Bull's boat was heading straight on towards the other two boats, his body looked like a piece of flotsam even from this close up and the boats were over a mile away. Even with binoculars they would not suspect that the flotsam was a headless body, it looked like a bundle of clothing.

Just another bit of human waste clogging up the Med.

It was the Italians, probably the Sicilian Mafia, who said revenge was a dish best served cold. The Italians were right.

This was just the hors d'oeuvre.

Appetite whetted for the next course.

St Matthias clock tower struck midnight just as I closed the door and flopped fully clothed onto my bed. Slept through till noon when I was woken by my telephone ringing. Wasn't sure in my half sleep if I should answer but couldn't resist the temptation, never could. Can't stand secrets. The receiver went down at the other end just as I picked up the phone. Must have been a wrong number, the girls weren't expecting me back yet.

Rang Zsu after three at her office. "Hi, I'm back. Any news?"

"No. Did you have a good time?"

"Boring really, came back early. It's not the same, on your own. Heard from Zsofi?" Didn't need to feign my sadness, it was boring and depressing on my own. Missed Lesley, badly.

"Zsofi rang last week, day after you left. She might be changing jobs, she's applied to the BBC. "

"Sounds exciting, I'll ring her tonight. Fancy dinner out later this week, your turn to choose?"

"Saturday?"

"Aren't you free before then?"

"It's only a few days, it's my Hun classes tonight and Thursdays and Fridays are always busy, I have to work late. "

"Saturday then. " Lost track of time. It was Wednesday, thought it was Monday. Went back to bed. Dreamt of Bull's faceless head at the bottom of the Med, open, full of crabs, all looking straight at me. Woke in a cold sweat the next afternoon. The sheets were wringing wet, streaked with my salt. Only just beginning to face up to what I had done. I had murdered John Bull! I closed my eyes and relived the moments in graphic detail. KILL THEM ALL, LET GOD SORT THEM OUT! Evening, time to show my face at the local bar, my local alibi. Came back late, happy drunk. The locals had taken a shine to the returned Hungarian prodigal, back in Budapest having grown up in England. They all but poured the drinks down my throat. Settling in the chair, I poured himself another Pálinka and toasted a framed photograph on the mantle, "Miss you. "

Woke with my head pounding, but not too badly, I felt too good for it to hurt much. Unpacking my case I came across the Spanish phrase book, returned it to the shelf. Hesitated and half pulled it out again. 'May Dancer' still on the back, nearly missed it. Burnt it in the stove along with the food wrappings from the Spanish supermarket.

The next month went without incident. Integrating well with the locals and they appeared to accept me seamlessly as one of them. It was my impeccable old-fashioned Hungarian that did the trick. The Hungarians were so used to foreigners butchering their tongue, just as they were famous for butchering everybody else's tongue almost as if in retaliation, that it was out of the question that I was anything other than a home-bred Hungarian.

Not surprisingly, I heard nothing about John Bull. Not that I would have expected to hear about a boating accident to a British citizen in Spain, in the Budapest press. Didn't dare ask Zsofi for any Oxford papers or news items. I would find out eventually, could always check the papers when I went back to Britain. Time for a trip to London, Zsofi had been on her own for too long. Hadn't even seen her new flat. Rang. "Zsofi. I fancy coming back to civilisation for a couple of weeks. When are you free?

"Friday, five forty five. Bring duty frees dad, the blue gin. It tastes much better when it's duty free. "

This was Wednesday. "I'll pick you up from work. Set off Thursday morning in the Jag. " Joszef Huszár's English passport this time. This trip was on the record. Stopped for the night at Cologne and arrived in Bloomsbury at five, buying a special bouquet at a flower shop near Covent Garden. Amazing what they could do for fifteen pounds. Zsofi would love them. She almost walked past me at the door, she still didn't think of me as being bearded.

The air was noticeably cleaner in London. Budapest was being smothered by two stroke Trabants. Impressed with the air in London. A lot of the locals didn't share my opinion, they cycled round with Japanese style face masks which didn't work but it made them feel better. Realised that after less than nine months in Hungary, I was thinking in Hungarian. It took me the whole of Saturday to re-programme my brain, by which time I was in full Anglophile mode, at least, as full as I had ever been considering I am Hungarian.

Zsofi was shocked to hear that I had been held up at Dover customs whilst they checked my passport in a private office. I guessed it must have been my record that gave them food for thought. Polite enough, but they had to check it out. Couldn't get a straight answer when I asked if there had been any question of my not being allowed back in.

Who knew? It had served to remind me of something that I had forgotten all about, my fingerprints and DNA were on file with the police, fancy that. Didn't fancy that at all. Hadn't thought of my VAT escapade as criminal, more of a temporary loan. I thought of John Bull, just a sort of watery road traffic accident? A driving mishap? "I put the anchor on, hard as I could but I still hit him, officer. He got it in the neck".

Dropped Zsofi off at work on Monday morning, promised to be back for a meal by seven. Back to Oxford, could hardly wait to check the news. Interested to see how people had reacted, the English normally go soft on someone once they are disadvantaged, doubly soft if they are dead. Even the biggest arsehole was, suddenly, a bosom pal, salt of the earth, but only once he was definitely dead. And Bull was definitely dead! Wanted to find out if Bull had been canonised.

Drove straight to Jude the Obscure, the local near The Standard in Jericho, our favourite restaurant. The owner knew me well. I hadn't been there for the best part of a year. "Huszár! Long time no see. Kronenberg? On the house. Where you been?"

I smiled. "Ford open prison for a short while, and don't tell me you didn't know. "

Michael grimaced. "Sorry Huszár. I'm too used to being polite, comes with being a landlord. How was it?"

"It was just five months, boring. Losing Lesley in the accident is what sealed it for me. I sold up and buggered off to Hungary. I'm based there now, bought a massive flat for the price of one of your pints. Like the people, makes a change from dealing with whinging pommes and ex potato-picking Irish pub landlords. "

"What, whinging Hungarians instead?"

"Yeah, but they're professional whingers, they actually train for it. They could all whinge for their country at the Olympics. How are you guys getting on without me then? What's been happening?"

Michael looked at the ceiling. "What's been happening?" Always a difficult question to answer. "OH! YES! Your mate Bull, the developer? Died in a boating accident in Spain. The local paper made a big thing out of it, local lad made it big, then lost it in the property crash. Tragic boating accident, what a nice man etc etc. "

"That what people thought, nice man?" I couldn't conceal the anger and hatred I felt at the thought. "Nice man?"

"Jacking Off, was more like it. A few letters from the locals complaining that he was being whitewashed. He screwed a lot of people for a lot of money. Got you big, didn't he?"

"Too big, it hurt, it still hurts. " I thought of Lesley. "What sort of boating accident?"

"He fell off a boat apparently and his head and hands got chopped off by a passing propeller, probably his own propeller. His boat sailed into harbour all on its own, spooky. "

"Suicide?"

"The question was asked because he'd just gone bust, but nobody knew. There was an inquest held here in Oxford. I think the verdict was accidental death. "

"When did it happen?"

"Around Easter. There were a few jokes about where were you at the time. Got a good alibi?"

Found I was laughing, quite naturally. "Easter? Yeah, as Maggie Thatcher used to say, *'I was on holiday at the time. '*Have one with me, Michael, this deserves a drink! Fuck John Bull, may he stay dead a lot longer than he was tall. "

After a couple of pints I moved on. Things to do. Went to Osney, the Oxford Mail had their offices there. It was interesting and peculiarly satisfying to read about Bull's death in print. They had printed a wedding picture. The silly prat had married in a white suit! If I'd known that at the time I wouldn't have touched him with a barge pole. A five foot four prat, in a white suit, and a mousey moustache that looked like a shadow under his nose.

"Tough titty, JB, tough titty. " Another reader looked across the desk at me. Had been talking to myself out loud. Looked back at the man, studious, with half rimmed glasses. Gestured towards the paper. "Just expiating a grudge, I hated the bastard. Travelled twelve hundred miles to gloat. " The man tried not to look worried and returned to his studies. That was stupid. Wasn't supposed to have known about Bull's death so I couldn't have travelled twelve hundred miles to gloat. It was that sort of smart crack that gave you away. Have to be more careful, wasn't accustomed to having something to hide. Better get used to it or I would end up with nothing to hide except my arse in the prison showers. Grimaced, remembering a Clint Eastwood film.

Went round to BT headquarters in Paradise Street and scrounged a telephone directory, saying I was back in the area, lots of friends to look up. The girl was very sweet and dug out an old copy as well in case my friends had moved since I was here. Taylor wasn't in the latest book but I recognised his voice when I rang his number, still there then, just gone ex-directory. Too many cover ups, or should it be covers up? Have to check the Black Hand Dictionary. Elmore was still at the same number but Budge was no longer listed. Tried Budge's original Oxford number. Mrs Humphries was very helpful, the Budges had sold up two years earlier and moved out of the area. She thought Budge had retired, somewhere on the south coast. She gave me the number. Retired? Budge must been older than he looked. Retired, and forgotten all about it? I hadn't forgotten, remembered well enough for both of us, for all of them – never forget – never forgive.

Rang a Hounslow number, disguised my voice. "Dave Phillips please. " "Putting you through, Sir. "

"Phillips!" It was him, Jesus, it was him! Put the phone down, hands trembling. Leaned against the booth, remembering.

Drove past our old house, choked at the memories.

We had been happy here. The prim new owners had scythed down the trees and the shrubbery, the house looked naked and vulnerable. . Philistines! One of our ex-neighbours recognised the car, it had been the only white seventy-three XJ in Oxford, and waved. Waved back but didn't stop. Nothing to say, got to keep moving. Can't afford to let the bastards take aim. What was that First World War rule? The third one to light up a cigarette from a light got hit, the sniper had time to take aim for the third light. Need more matches.

Headed back to Zsofi's flat. It was only five and she was due after six so I cooked dinner, using up the fresh leché peppers I had brought, easy on the paprika, she didn't like things too spicy, even weak Hungarian spicy. Zsofi was the English Rose of the Huszár family - somebody had to do it. On my third drink when she turned up a little late, having stopped off at the supermarket for more gin. Perfect timing, I'd just finished the bottle. It was very pleasant, getting drunk with my own daughter We toasted Lesley. Absent mums.

Zsofi was twenty-four, rising twenty-five. "Now you have your own flat does that qualify you as a spinster of this parish?" This was an old joke of mine, worn thin after six years or so, mainly because the six years were added to her original eighteen. It had been a much more amusing crack all round, when Zsofi was eighteen.

"I've been busy. Anyway, there's no hurry, I'll know when I meet the right man, you wouldn't want me to repeat mum's mistake, would you?" Huszár had met and married Lesley within six months in his final year at Oxford, Lesley's one and only mistake, according to Zsu and Zsofi.

"Don't forget, CV in triplicate, in my FAX. Not later than the third date, followed by an in depth interview and bank references shortly afterwards. "

"Mind your own business. I'll let you know. " She smiled to herself as she cuffed me on the head.

Stayed another week, aimlessly drumming up contacts for possible business connections with Hungary, except that I wasn't. I had other things on my mind. Anyway, having sold the house in Oxford and bought a flat in Budapest, I was loaded, by Hungarian standards.

Made a half day of it at Watford Electronics. I'd done my homework with the nerdy computer mags and bought the fanciest Fax modem available as a present for my computer, plus, some useful software. Hopefully, some very useful software.

Set off back to Budapest after dropping Zsofi off at work. Straight through customs at Dover, but then I was leaving, maybe they were glad to see the back of me. My police record put a whole new slant on life, hadn't felt self conscious about who or what I was since I was five. We had been the only Hungarians at the refugee camp and I got stick for it, but only until the day I lost my temper and throttled a kid with his own scarf. I could still picture the kid's eyes bulging as I was finally pulled off him by the teacher. Nobody picked on me after that.

Lately, I had simply been Huszár, some people liked me, some didn't, and, it hadn't mattered to me either way. Now I was one of the criminal classes, double checked by customs as I came in to Britain. For only the second time in my life I had an inkling of what it was like to suffer from prejudice. Well, I was extremely prejudiced against a handful of local bastards who had gone out of their way to fuck me.

Held my hand up, examining my palm and fingers, thoughtfully.

A whole handful?

WHAT'S ON THE MENU?

Applied for a freelance job writing articles for an English-speaking Ex Pats magazine. Foreigners were coming over in droves since Hungary had finally blown the Russians out, hoping to be in on the ground floor with the most Westernised of the Communist Block countries. I could bring the Ex pats up to speed in their new jobs by giving them an outsider's slant from an insider's point of view, help them understand the mind set of a nation whose people had suffered thirty years of Communist rule. Surprised to get the job, thinking a local with good English would be better suited but the magazine had had enough of trying to get sense from the usual applicants, mind fucked by Communism and on a mission to prove otherwise. They needed a more balanced, down to earth view and my draft article, written live at the interview was what they were looking for. Hadn't expected this, hadn't attempted proper joined up sentences since the fifth form at school, after which I concentrated on illiterate sciences. Amazed to find I could write, it was just like speaking, only the mechanics of using a keyboard made it slower. The pay was good too, not by Western standards, but at least I was more than able to pay my way. By local standards I was well off and I was paid in inflation proofed dollars. The local economy was inflating at over thirty per cent per year. Gave them my Hungarian name and Zsu's address. The only reason I had a Hungarian passport was to give Zsu moral support when she had applied for hers. In her case it was to please Big George Soros's foundation. Big S was a very charismatic man, in spite of being a billionaire, so it had been a pleasure pleasing him and his foundation.

Had settled for my mother's maiden name on the Hungarian passport because my father's paperwork was incomplete and the Huns had been very fussy about it. Now I had a good use for a Hungarian passport, my Ibiza trip had been as a full blown Hungarian, Joszef Lévai. Joszef Huszár had stayed in Budapest that Easter.

In my free time I got to serious grips with the computer. Relentless, pedantic, unforgiving, liked its style. It just never gave an inch and if it didn't like what you were doing it gave you the sack by sulking and crashing out. Played around with some of the system files so that when it crashed the screen was emblazoned with SodOff in seventy-two point letters. It was worth the hassle of the occasional crash just for the satisfaction of seeing this line come up. Found myself arguing with it when

I couldn't get it to do what I wanted. Had the ultimate sanction if it really pissed me off, just pulled the plug on it. Made me feel good.

The Fax modem was state of the art, at least for a month or so till some nerd doubled the speed yet again just to make me feel inferior. After a month, I could page it, call it, FAX with it, it would even forward calls for me. Over the next three months I spent hundreds of hours mastering the intricacies of the programmes. Nicknamed the computer Paraszt, Hungarian for peasant because it carried out my orders to the letter, but only when it wanted to, just like a real peasant. Paraszt was a very, very rude term in class ridden Hungary, so had to be careful when referring to the computer. The Huns were very touchy about matters of class and Paraszt could invite a knife fight, if you were in the right sort of bar, a knife throwing bar.

October came and I thought of going back to London for my birthday. Bought an oldish Mercedes registered in my name as József Lévai at Zsu's address. Did the same with a new Hungarian registered mobile phone connected to the Panon network. My Hungarian identity was complete, a passport, a job, a car, a mobile phone, a spare address, and, I was fluent in an impossible language. Even paid tax at forty-six per cent. Reading and writing was poor but improving daily. Moustache-dominated beard, now full grown but trimmed short, icing on the cake. I passed for Hungarian.

Packing, ready for the trip and taking stock. Bad mistake to have been ringing Spain for all those months before the trip Huszár didn't make to Ibiza. Only actually got one reply, but had just read that the Hungarian telephone system had been brought up to date with full call logging available but as yet unreleased to the punters. Bad news if the phone company records covered that last call to Bull's flat, just days before Bull's accident. Checked the WinFax phonebook, changed Bull's Ibiza number to his English number and changed Zsofi's entry to BaBa, her childhood nickname.

Set up the computer to receive and then forward messages to any one of three computer MailBoxes, if I added an extra code. Coded incoming calls would be passed onto one of the MailBoxes and then forwarded on to Zsofi's number, Zsu's number or to Zsu's mobile. Tried it live for the first time, ringing my number with the new mobile, adding the extra digit to access Zsofi's MailBox, and then watched the computer dial Zsofi's number and replay my message. Only it didn't replay my message! After some experimenting found that the computer was in fact trying to forward a FAX confirming a message had been received.

When it didn't get a FAX response it gave up and automatically redialled. So the phone records would show that I had just rung London from Budapest on my flat phone in Hungary, except that it kept doing it every two minutes and stopped after about thirty two seconds, every time.

Just like a real computer.

Went into **Setup** and set it for zero redials – PHEW!.

When I returned from my planned trip to England I would backdate the computer time and date setting to match the calls forwarded by the computer and make real calls to the same numbers. Then I would delete the computer forwarded calls leaving the forged calls in their place. End up with my voice recorded by the computer, logged at the right time and date, to the right number, as confirmed by the phone company records. Made a final call from the mobile simulating the earlier call. It worked! Looked at the mobile, in fact, I could have been anywhere in the world on the end of any phone line with the computer locating me in Budapest.

From now on had to be more careful, no mastikes! József Lévai was about to go to England using his new passport, car, mobile phone and slight accent, all of them Hungarian. The Mercedes was a lumbering tank, an old man's car, but at least it was an older model, roomy enough to stretch my legs, unlike the accountant designed new models which had had the hearts and the leg room excised from their designs. Good enough for a long leisurely trip, but I much preferred the XJ. The Merc swallowed the miles and I arrived at Ramsgate before two, plenty of time to get to London by five forty-five. Had planned the route via Ramsgate because I had been a regular visitor via Dover on my British passport. No sense in attracting attention to myself with my new non mates in customs. If they spotted me, then my coming in on a Hungarian passport might be particularly memorable, especially with my English record. Had never been able to understand how real criminals could blend so well into their surroundings, had always felt I was a very tall poppy and even with my beard I couldn't imagine anybody who knew me not recognising me immediately. Mind you, even Zsofi had almost walked past me with my new beard, maybe I was being too self conscious. Remembered how the police used to stop me regularly on my motorbike, just because I wouldn't conform and wore a mod's parka instead of leathers. Looked down at my trademark high heeled Spanish boots, they would have to go. Felt like an amateur, but everybody had to learn, some time. This was shit or bust. And no quarter, so better learn faster and better than I had so far.

Drove straight past the customs personnel without batting an eye. Routine passport check, non EEC passport. Nem problema. Shit! The buggers insisted on stamping it. Presumably they stamped foreign passports as a matter of routine. Hadn't thought of that. Driving up the M2, another thought occurred. Couldn't afford to be seen by anyone that knew me, other than Zsofi. This trip, even though it was a practice run, was not taking place. Would have to buy some different clothes, maybe a hat. No, a hat was too unusual nowadays, too noticeable in its own right. A change of style, looked in the mirror. A very short haircut, perhaps, that would do. Called in at an East End hairdresser's near Brick Lane. "Sort of hit man look, nearly a crew cut, please. " Had once misjudged a hair trim with an electric beard trimmer and frightened myself for weeks until it re-grew. Everybody had said how different it made me look. The barber flashed his mirror. "Great, frightening, but great. " Gave him a good tip.

Zsofi put her hand to her mouth. "You look like a crim!"

"I am a crim. How are you?" She loved the flowers.

"Nice car, very snazzy number plate. "

Kicked my own ankle as I drove. "Yes, very snazzy. " Too bloody snazzy. Trust the Hungarians to have a full national flag in vivid red white and green, plus a bloody big 'H' for Horrendous Horror! You could see the plate a mile away and there weren't many of them about in London, or anywhere else for that matter. Why not get an advertising hoarding fixed to the car as well, do the job properly. Lucky this was a dry run, have to think again about the car. Kept a low profile throughout the next week and set off on the following Monday morning. Mind was racing round in circles all the way down the usually interminable autobahn and the sixteen hour drive just disappeared behind my exhaust until I hit Budapest.

Poured myself a Pálinka, realised that I had totally forgotten to ring the computer and it would have been a waste of time if I had because I'd left it switched off. What an amateur! Still, I consoled myself, I had tested the call forwarding and knew it worked, I didn't need to prove the point with a call from England. But, what else had I missed? Couldn't afford a single mistake, but I was making nothing but mistakes.

Thought of Lesley. Had always discussed everything with Lesley and she had often pointed out the flaws in my logic, but Lesley was gone. Was on my own, apart from the bottle. Finished the bottle and fell asleep on the sofa. Dreams of Lesley were so vivid that when I first woke up I called out to her, thinking she was asleep in the bedroom. Cried at the thought of Lesley no longer being alive and wanted her back. She seemed so real in my alcohol-sodden dreams that in the next few days I only went out for more Pálinka.

Zsu called round Friday evening. She was shocked by my appearance, suddenly, I looked a lot older. Had always looked young for my age. "Dad, are you all right?"

"No. Feeling sorry for myself. " We hugged and cried.

ZSu cooked a meal while I showered and changed. Apart from my criminal hair cut I looked a lot better after the shower. Felt a lot better, it was good to have company, especially Zsu. Zsu was a star and in spite of her own sadness over Lesley, which she hid for both our bene-fits, she cheered me up. Must get out more and certainly shouldn't drink for days on end, would kill myself. Zsu stayed the night and we went to Vienna for the weekend. Came back rejuvenated on Sunday night and dropped Zsu off at her flat. "Thanks, Zsu. I'll collect you Tuesday after work, we'll catch a film, check what's on. " We kissed and I returned to my own flat. Zsu had tidied up for me on Saturday morning, the only evidence of my lapse was the large number of bottles in the kitchen bin.

Checked my watch, ten thirty. Sat down at the computer and opened up a new file in Word. **Save As…Lesley. DOC**

Password to open…Bikaszár

Typed out a list of objectives, methods and various notes. Was about to save it when I remembered a newspaper article in which a criminal had been convicted using deleted computer files. When deleting a file from a hard disk the computer simply removed the first letter of the file name and the space on the disk would be available for re-use. If that space had not been re-used you could recover the file, assuming you knew how. I had read of criminals who had frantically deleted their hard discs with police at the door, thinking they were home and dry, only to find that the police recovered the evidence and gained convictions us-ing the recovered computer records as evidence.

Not with this Hungarian they wouldn't, too smart.

Deleted the file, emptied the recycle bin and defragged the disk.

Had an idea. A shelf full of photo albums behind me, picked out an early one and selected a photograph of Lesley, taken soon after we were married. Put it in the FAX machine and FAXed it to the computer. Then, using **Control Panel**, I selected the picture for my desktop background. Lesley's innocent, smiling face was now looking back at me from the computer screen. It was in black and white but it would do for now. When I had time I would get a colour scan made of the picture. Closed the computer down. "Thanks, Lesley. " I had just renamed the computer without realising it. In future, I could consult with Lesley anytime I wanted to. Liked the idea, I had loved Lesley and thought very highly of her opinions. It felt entirely appropriate that I should name my computer after her, not at all nerdy or weird?

Worked on an article until lunchtime and by then I had made a decision. Sell the Mercedes, snazzy number plates and all. Returned it to the same dealer who tried to sell me a different car but I wasn't even tempted, they all had Hungarian plates. Checked with the insurance broker to confirm I was covered for a foreign car I wanted to buy abroad and bring back to Hungary. They gave me documents confirming cover for any vehicle that had the honour of being owned by me.

Friday seven PM. Budapest airport for the Malev flight to Heathrow, a short trip to see Zsofi who was picking me up. Twenty-eight thousand Forints return, about a hundred and thirty pounds, a third of the petrol cost if I drove. Used my Hungarian passport, and collected a routine stamp at the airport. We enjoyed London over the weekend and then I searched for a suitable car after Zsofi went to work. Tracked down an F Reg Cavalier with a private owner advertising in the Exchange and Mart. Less than a thousand pounds. Promised I would take care of the transfer documents myself, all in good time. It had four months road tax and MOT left, ample. Kept the unfilled transfer documents in a folder in the dash. I was legally insured to use the car on the road in England and on the continent.

The two litre engine was quite pokey, it was a surprisingly quick car, more than quick enough. Have to be careful to drive within the limits, didn't want to attract attention. It was four by the time I had finished, take it for a proper spin tomorrow. Parked the car a few streets away from Zsofi's flat and started dinner. Off to the cinema later.

In the morning I collected the Cavalier and headed down the A13 for The Blackwall Tunnel. Budge's phone number was a Thanet number. Margate, Ramsgate, where all the Londoners used to holiday before they discovered continental holidays included the sun as standard. Two hours of easy driving, the Cavalier was fine, and I was in Margate. Parked near the station and went for a coffee in a seafront coffee bar. Margate was in a time warp. Coffee bars like this had expired in the sixties, but not here. The whole place looked to be past its sell by date, faded peeling facades that looked even worse set against the handful of new arcades and pretend casinos. Rusted railings overlooking the sands with a tidemark that promised genuine shit, judging by the seagulls swooping at the flotsam just a few yards out from the shore. The Victorian clock tower had clocked off some time ago, a big dollop of moss hung off the minute hand, and it told the right time only twice a day. The waitress lent me a phone book and I was pleased to find Ron Budge was in it. Thirty Crescent Road, Broadstairs. Broadstairs? It rang a bell, a ship's bell. Sad Old Sailor Ted Heath, the out of touch, missed his century, seventies Conservative leader had been brought up there. I had seen a documentary on Heath a few years back. Heath had come across as bitter, twisted and broken over his ousting by Thatcher. Twenty years had gone by and Heath still hadn't recovered. I had thought he was pathetic at the time but felt more sympathy for him now, now that I could understand the price Heath had paid for letting it gnaw his insides away. Had Heath done something about it, instead of just moaning and groaning, he would have been able to rebuild his life and get on with it. But Heath hadn't done anything about it, and it had fucked up his life. His choice, not mine.

Broadstairs was a lot better. Nice little harbour, blowing a real breeze with waves crashing clean over the fifteen foot harbour wall. It looked very cold out there so I stayed in the car and toured around the area. Dickens' Bleak House was the local landmark. Appropriate, with the rain sheeting in almost horizontally from the sea as the wind picked up and the sea front turned grey, melding with the sky.

Drove back to the harbour area and after a pub lunch at the Tartar Frigate, practically in the harbour, went for a walk. The wind had changed direction, blowing the sea away from the land. There were high cliffs at that end of the town, sheer drop all the way down to the walkway I was on, the sea below me. Quite scary, as I looked all the way up. Retraced my steps and called Budge from a call box.

"Ron Budge. " I nearly answered. It was interesting how people retained their work telephone answer style at home as well. Ron still sounded the same as he always had, "Ron Won't Budge", as Huszár had nicknamed him at the time. Monday afternoon and Budge was at home. He obviously wasn't clerking any works, he had retired, probably on peanuts so he wouldn't get out very much.

Got back in the car and easily found Budge's road. Pleasant quiet little road with two up two downs dating back to between the wars. Nice enough place to end your days if you didn't mind the quiet. I wondered if there was still a Mrs Budge. There used to be, but that was seven years ago. Anything could happen in seven years. Drove past the house, neat, overly patterned lace curtains. Well kept, but then Budge had been meticulous. He had meticulously forged over a hundred sheets of evidence in his laborious child like hand. I could picture him licking the tip of his pencil as he furrowed his brow and concentrated on joining up his writing. Ron was very dumb. If I ever had the opportunity I would like to discuss with Ron exactly why he had done it, presumably he was just obeying Elmore's instructions. It would be nice to know what Budge had thought he was achieving, apart from contributing to Huszár losing his wife. How would Budge feel if he lost his wife because of Huszár? I, fleetingly, had an idea, but no, that would not be at all fair. No, I wasn't going to be unfair.

Parked six car lengths down the street and huddled up in my scarf, pretending to be asleep. The windows soon steamed up and from the outside you could hardly see there was anyone in the car. It was getting dark. Stayed awake till after midnight when the upstairs light came on briefly and was then extinguished. Budge had gone to bed. I was stiff and cold from eight hours in the car. The seat was a very poor design, an osteopath's meal ticket, I couldn't keep this up for long. Rang Zsofi to say I was tied up and would be back tomorrow. Zsofi was beside herself, she had been trying my mobile and had been about to call the police.

"Sorry." I looked at the Panon phone in my hand. I'd forgotten to give Zsofi the number. "My phone's on the blink so I brought a Hungarian model. " Pressed a few buttons. "Stupid of me, I can't work out how to get the number. Try 1471. "

Zsofi tried 1471 and the machine told her the call was from a network that couldn't give out numbers. She thought dad was acting rather peculiarly lately but she couldn't put her finger on it.

Started up the car and headed back to Margate, knocking up the owner of a small sea front hotel who was drinking alone at his bar. We were both glad of the company. According to the owner, Margate had seen much better days, fifty years earlier, before his time. Bought each other drinks until two, when I cried off, leaving him to carry on for both of us.

I was back outside Budge's house by seven thirty. I had kept the heating and demister off for the fifteen minute trip from Margate. The car was still misted up as I parked, there was no one about. It was a filthy morning and I was feeling cold already, my day had only just started. Budge might not budge all day. I smiled at my inadvertent pun and gritted my teeth for the wait. I hated waiting, but then it was seven years since Budge had set the wheels in motion, had done his best to screw Huszár just to cover his, and a few other, bureaucratic arses at Oxford City Council.

Huszár would only have to wait just a little while longer.

There was a gas fire vent mounted on Budge's front wall that started releasing wisps of vapour. Budge must be up, he had put the heater on. I looked at the house and the ones either side. They had all met the same double glazing salesman who must have sold heaters as a side-line. "This heater will provide you with the very heat you wish to keep in, Sir. Would you prefer to pay up front or on monthly credit?"

"Errr…Monthly credit?"

"A very wise decision, Sir. " A wise salesman makes extra commission on credit sales, sometimes more than for the sale itself.

The three adjacent houses were identical, the same plastic framed, no need to paint, double glazed, large, featureless, panes that spoilt the look of the houses. The identical wall mounted gas heaters with their external vents were the last straw. They looked as bad as the externally mounted air conditioning units outside period office blocks in London. To me, it was like mounting a urinal on your front wall and pissing in it in public. As I watched the vapour rise, I saw that the hot fumes had melted the plastic cill just a few inches above, making a small section of the plastic sag and turn brown. I looked at Budge's damaged cill and remembered infinitesimal defects that Budge had condemned with a Clerk of Works flourish of satisfaction. "Not so fussy now, Budge! Not so fussy when it's your money at stake!" I looked at the three front doors – identical plastic doors, identical windows, identical heaters. These houses had something else in common, the owner, the local authority. It wasn't Budge's money, he didn't even own the house. Here at the boondocks end of Kent where property was cheap, Budge couldn't afford his own house.

I felt better – much much better.

Budge appeared at the door just before one and set off down the road, huddled up in his thin overcoat. He looked very different, he had aged a lot since I had known him. He looked like a tired old man as he shuffled down the street. I waited for two minutes and then followed in the car. Budge had gone round the corner into the teeth of the wind and didn't notice the car going past. I went back to the phone box I had used the day before and rang Budge's number, twice, to make sure I hadn't mis-dialled. No reply. No Mrs Budge, good, bloody good! Headed back to London, ringing Zsofi on the way to say I would collect her from work. We collected a Chinese and ate in. The evening shot past as we looked through Zsofi's albums and reminisced.

Got up at five and parked within sight of Elmore's house in his Cotswold village by quarter to eight. When I had known him Elmore used to be at his desk by eight thirty and would have had to leave around eight. A Rover four hundred was parked in front of the tiny cottage. Made a mental note of the number plate as Elmore drove past at twenty-five to nine, not as early as the old days. Elmore was obviously very familiar with the twists and turns in the road and I was soon losing ground, almost falling off the road at a hairpin bend where the camber was wrong. Slowed down, there was not much chance of losing Elmore between here and the A40, this was practically a one track road and I knew exactly where Elmore was headed after that. Oxford had been fighting, and winning, a car war for decades. The only place for Elmore to park all day was at the Westgate multi storey. Anyway, I had, Elmore's route to work, which had to be the same as his route home.

I memorised features of the route as I travelled to join the A40, narrow country lane all the way with only one T junction and one place to pull off at the entrance to a field. When I joined the A40 I could see Elmore's car just seven cars ahead and followed him all the way to Oxford. At the car park I headed on to a higher level as Elmore found a space on the second floor. Parked at a leisurely pace and strolled down to the lower level. There were surveillance cameras ostentatiously mounted everywhere. They were so obvious I wondered if they might not be fakes but I had to assume they were working. Walked slowly past the Rover, must be three or four years old and the tyres looked as if they were probably the originals. They looked OK but they were not over-endowed with tread. It was a sporty model in dark blue, all very wide low profile tyres, extra spotlights and go faster stripes. Called in at Tandy and bought a model remote control unit for cash – credit cards are as good as sat navs for tracing a route, especially a route you do not want traced.

The breakers at Berinsfield, on the A423, hadn't changed in twenty years. I cannibalised some electronic parts which I didn't actually need and bagged a boot lid spring in my toolkit, it had to be an English part. Made it back to London in time for lunch with Zsofi, scarcely giving the Leander Rowing Club a glance as I crossed the bridge at Henley – too busy with this life and Leander had been in a different lifetime, before I had met Lesley. After lunch I dropped the car off in an unrestricted parking area near the Portobello Road. Dicey area but I had to park it somewhere, nowhere is a hundred per cent safe, unless you are already dead.

I was due to catch the morning plane to Budapest so we ate out at a Mexican restaurant. Zsofi was very excited, she was short-listed for the BBC job, and there had been hundreds of applicants. Lucky she had moved to Notting Hill, White City was very close. We both took it as a good omen. A change of career would do her good, a chance to move on with her life, it was time for a change. "Good luck with the job, just tell them how it is, honesty shines through. " At least that was how I remembered it. It had always been much easier to be honest, perhaps I should try honesty again?

This was the first time I had ever flown to Hungary and it seemed very strange as the plane homed in from the North West. I could see the whole of the city centre area, with its Parliament building and other landmarks all clearly visible. It looked like a coloured relief map, more hilly than from the ground. Budapest was really a very small city with a huge dormitory area. The outer areas didn't even have metalled roads. I liked the hybrid style of old world city and third world fringe areas. I liked the home-made feel to Hungary.

It was bitterly cold as I came out of the airport, winter had arrived with a force only seen if you're far from the sea, unless it's the Arctic sea. Took a taxi to my flat and after making myself a coffee I called on one of my neighbours.

I wanted to garage the Jaguar and asked if they could help me find a lockup. The couple were very pleased to be of help, they had admired the car and had commented that it should not be left out in all weathers. After a few calls I had an address, just two blocks away. By six it was a done deal. The garage was more than big enough and it had electrical power available for a small extra consideration, it was the owner's electricity, electricity was expensive in a Third World country such as Hungary. I could use the owner's power tools as part of the small extra consideration. Less than ten pounds a month, all in, bring your own car.

Zsu was abroad for the week but one of the neighbours had invited me for dinner, so I was glad to accept. They partnered me with an attractive widow I had met on a previous occasion. Magda's husband had been killed in a road accident some four years earlier. He had been a teacher, very poorly paid under the Communist system but the family had money behind them so she and her husband had done quite well for themselves and they owned the flat next to me. The rampant inflation since the Russians had left in ninety-one was beginning to hurt her quite badly, her savings were losing value. She taught English at the university and was keen to improve her slight accent and colloquial English by talking with me. She seemed genuine enough and I found I was growing to quite like her, but I was wary. I had married Lesley when I was twenty one and she was the love of my life, I wasn't ready for a serious relationship, I couldn't imagine ever being ready. I told Magda about Lesley and about my grief for her. As we talked I realised that the first anniversary of Lesley's death had passed and neither I nor my girls had mentioned it. In fact, I had forgotten, blocked it out just as I had the anniversaries of my parents' deaths which I couldn't remember either, save for the time of year. I thought briefly about it, it wasn't an anniversary I wanted to remember, I didn't need to mark the day, every day of my life was marked by Lesley's absence. The girls would certainly have remembered but they probably hadn't raised it in deference to me. I thought about the girls, I'd been so wrapped up in losing Lesley I hadn't really thought of what they must be going through. I wondered how they dealt with Lesley's loss in their own quiet moments, on their own with nowhere to hide, their defences down in the dark of the night's smallest hours. Magda suddenly stood up and was making her excuses, I could see the hurt in her eyes. I stood up to leave with her and saw her to her door. "Magda, forgive me. I was lost in very sad memories, please understand. " I kissed her hand and she smiled hopefully at me as she closed the door behind her. I would have to make it up to her, I liked her and hadn't meant to be rude.

Spent the next two days working fruitlessly in the garage but my idea with the spring was not going to work. The spring tension had to be too powerful for it to work reliably with the small remote control mechanism, it jammed two times out of three. I also needed to find a system that would look innocuous if it was found, I might not have time to remove it. Have to think again.

Struggling for ideas, I went out the next day for a stroll round the city centre and its shops. Ideas just would not come to me, my mind was trapped in a cul de sac. At lunchtime I went out to Margit Island, floating in the middle of the Danube. It was bitterly cold but bright and very still. Some kids were out unsuccessfully trying to fly their kites but they were getting nowhere without the wind, just like me. One kid was flying a small model plane, powered by a tiny petrol engine that whined like a banshee, the wailing note changing as it came or went – Doppler was right. The plane was flying in a tight circle on a pair of control wires held by the kid, after a few minutes a miniature pilot dropped out of the bottom and floated to earth on a parachute. It was all very innocent and reminded me of my boyhood attempts with model planes. My planes were driven by elastic bands and I remembered vividly the sight of the balsa and rice paper frames buckling as I wound the elastic up with the propeller, weeks of painstaking assembly, crushed in seconds. I built a whole series of them but never did get one to actually fly, except fly apart.

I stood watching the kid go through the same routine with the plane, the little plastic pilot obliging him by jumping out right on cue at his deft command. Having seen enough I tracked down a model shop and pumped its owner. A genuine propeller head who knew everything about models. Looked through his stock and picked a plane that had been made in England, it would have been a mistake to get an Eastern European model. I was impressed that I had avoided the mistake, was learning fast?

I called in at a chemist, limping badly as I entered through the door. Anybody who had ever had a back problem would immediately have recognised my symptoms. A severe case of a trapped spinal nerve sending shooting pains down my buttocks, thigh and, in my case, as far as my toes. I had once trapped a nerve and had thought at the time that I might prefer to die, it had taken me more than year to fully recover. I easily drew on the memory of that pain now and looked convincing enough to fool the chemist.

The chemist was very sympathetic, yes a long coach journey would be nigh on impossible in my condition, but if it had to be Rohypnol, I would need a doctor's prescription. Yes, he understood that if I was to catch my coach I did not have any time to spare, I was welcome to have milder alternatives without a prescription. My face contorted with pain as I drew out my wallet and counted out five ten Dollar notes. For foreign currency, especially the much revered by the Hungarians, Dollar-rrr, because it was inflation-proofed against the drowning Forint, I

43

hoped that drugs regulations did not necessarily apply. Bought a small bottle, twenty tiny, purple, Roofie tablets. The chemist had in fact relented largely because, in my obvious physical state, there was no way I could utilise the drug for its other less acceptable use, that of date rape. And, from my cultured accent, I was old Hungary, family from the good old days of empire. He returned thirty of the dollars, in Forints. "Visontlátasra". I returned the old fashioned greeting, thanking him profusely and limped out of the shop, straightening up once I was round the corner. That year on my back had not been totally wasted, after all, nor were my father's old fashioned Hungarian mannerisms. That Eastern European charm worked a treat, especially on Eastern Europeans.

Magda met me in the communal inner courtyard balcony as I made my way to my flat. The lift was down, as usual, so I had climbed the one hundred and eighteen stairs. I had made a point of counting them before because I was surprised at how heavy my breathing was by the time I reached the top. Magda must have been looking out for me because she wasn't dressed for the cold, she was dressed to look good, pretending to tend her flower pots, all but emptied by the harsh winter. Would I like to come round for a meal that evening? She flashed a smile, very Hungarian with her colourful ethnic clothes and mannerisms. I was off to England the next day and this was to be a non trip. Better see her this evening and then she wouldn't be looking out for me for the next few days, less likely to notice my absence. "With the greatest of pleasure. I'll look forward to it with delight. " It occurred to me that the Hungarians might have a reputation for being brusque and very rude, I certainly had that reputation, but the language was exceptionally polite. Accepting a dinner invitation would practically be a proposal of marriage in any other language. As I carried on to my door, I remembered my disappointment when as a young alter boy I first heard the Catholic Mass recited in English instead of Latin. The Mass had lost all its romance, it sounded as stilted and forced as the Church of England services. I had never recovered from the blow and eventually concluded that the entire religion was stilted and forced.

Back in my flat I assembled and inspected the plane. A grown up child's toy, it represented the purest fun with no sinister overtones. Just good fun, especially the remote controlled bomb bay, my childhood planes had never had a working bomb bay. I thoroughly cleaned the plane and the equipment and carefully packed it in its box. Checked through Lesley. DOC . Satisfied, I deleted the file, emptied the recycle bin and defragged the hard disk. Ready.

Magda's flat was the mirror image of mine, each of our flats was on a corner of a nineteenth century block adjacent to Margit Hid, our balconies overlooking the Parliament building on the other side of the Danube. A brave man could probably jump across from one balcony to the other, if he wasn't worried about the eighty foot drop. Magda's inverted version of my flat was strangely disconcerting. Magda was a very good cook and even better company. My apology at the end of our previous meeting had opened the flood gates, I hardly got a word in all evening but I didn't mind. Found myself glued to every word. We both got slightly drunk on the Nagy Burgundy.

Nagy Burgundy?

BIG BURGUNDY!

Trust the Hungarians.

CHEW SLOWLY

I was lucky to get the last seat on the overnight coach for Victoria, couldn't risk pre-booking. Ninety per cent of the passengers were Hungarian and you could see why they had a reputation as the Gypsies of Europe. This was the poor man's method of travelling, less than ninety pounds return, Budapest to London and back. It was far and away the worst journey I had ever been on. There was an argument between the three drivers and Viennese customs over driving hours. The drivers had already come from London to Budapest, with just a half hour stop at Budapest. The Viennese officials insisted that the drivers rest for eight hours to satisfy the rules and proceeded to watch them for the whole of the eight hours whilst the drivers got even more tired, smoking and cursing the officials parked in front of the coach, in case they made a run for it. Rules is rules. Hitler had spent his formative years in Austria and even now Austria was riddled with ex-Nazis, playing a prominent part in their political system, regularly winkled out of the woodwork by zealous heroes such as Simon Wiesenthal. The war had taught them nothing, it could all happen again, probably start with a tired bunch of travellers throttling a few Austrian Border Admirals.

Dover customs. DOVER CUSTOMS! I had totally forgotten about my plan to avoid Dover when travelling on my Hungarian passport. I was herded through. Just another tired Hungarian on a nightmare coach trip. Saw my reflection in a shiny steel section of wall. Looked beat, just like a real gypsy.

Got off at Victoria after more than thirty-six hours on the coach, a dead man. Made my way to a bed and breakfast off the Portobello Road without bothering to check the car, I was in no state to do anything even if there was a problem with it. Check it tomorrow. Sleeping through till noon the next day I decided to have the day off, my return ticket was open ended and I was on standby anyway.

The Cavalier was exactly as I had left it, starting on the button. Rang Lesley using the code for Zsofi's MailBox, saying I would be away for the weekend. Easy ride down to Margate where I picked up a large bottle of Whisky and a couple of bottles of Newcastle Brown at an off licence. On to Broadstairs and I was parked round the corner from Budge's house by noon. I was counting on Budge still being a creature of habit. When he was Clerk of Works you could set your watch by Budge's visits. He used to turn up at three and hang about for half an hour because, by three thirty, there was no point in going back to the office, might as well go on home. Make up the time by coming in early the next morning. I could picture him repeating this line verbatim, twice a week. Budge never did make up the time in the morning, he always turned up late.

Budge passed the car at five to one, not noticing me apparently dozing . Adjusted the rear view mirror so I could see the pavement behind me and settled in to read the paper. I had lost the habit of reading the paper because my reading in Hungarian was still very patchy, the writing style in the Hungarian papers seemed to be very different, much more complicated than speaking. It was as if the writers were self conscious, putting on grammatical airs that nobody would dream of using in normal speech. Read The Times as if I was preparing for an examination, keeping an eye on the mirror. It was gone two before Budge returned, slightly more slowly than when he had been going, he was tired but the doctor insisted he should have his constitutional everyday, his circulation was poor.

Climbed out of the car, picking up the bag of drinks, and locked the door. Looked up at Budge, who was alongside the car on the other side, feigning surprise. "Ron Budge!" Budge looked at me, no sign of recognition in his eyes. "Ron Budge! It's me, Joe Huszár. " I smiled broadly at him.

Budge was beginning to remember and wasn't so sure he was pleased to see me. What did Huszár want? "What are you doing here in Broadstairs?"

"I'm on a day trip to the seaside. What are you doing here?"

Budge was defensive. "Just in the area. "

I clinked my bag. "I always felt bad about giving you a hard time. I know it was Elmore calling the shots, everybody had to go along with the bastard. He was in charge, he orchestrated it all.

Budge looked at the bag. On his pension a drink was a major luxury and it was days since he had treated himself to a half pint at the local. "Yeah, Elmore shifted the blame to everybody else, but you're right, he called all the shots. I did my best to keep out of it. "

All one hundred and eleven meticulous pages worth, not exactly keeping out of it. It was the sheer scale of the forgeries by Budge and Phillips that had scared off the arbitrator, there were practically more forgeries than real documents. The chicken shit arbitrator had taken the easy way out, if what Huszár was saying was true then this was too hot for him to handle, especially as his firm relied on the Council for their bread and butter work. So the arbitrator joined the queue and screwed Huszár instead. I clinked the bottles again, pleased I had thought to get enough to clink with, they sounded tempting. "I've got a bottle of Bells and Newcastle Browns, let's have a drink and make peace. "

This was too much for Budge to resist. He was salivating. "I live just round the corner. " I walked back with him, watching as he struggled to turn the key with his arthritic fingers. The man was totally shot away, hardly worth a bullet.

"Edie! I'm back, with a guest. "

EDIE!...EDIE!...Jesus Christ! I inhaled deeply before I spoke. "Edie your wife?"

"Yes. I am. " Edie had come out of the sitting room, she looked at Ron, eyebrows raised. She was a short dumpy woman, neatly present-ed and she spoke confidently, no sign of the laborious pauses that were a dominant part of Budge's speech. She could have done better than Budge, a good deal better.

"This is Joe. Knew him at Oxford. We're going to have a drink. " Edie didn't need to be asked twice, she went for some glasses from the kitchen as Budge ushered me into the sitting room. Virulent, light green and red, sculpted carpet, which clashed violently with large flow-er patterns on the three piece suite and the even larger flower patterns in the wall paper. Not a relaxing, soothing room, more of a full frontal assault on the senses. The suite was far too large for the room and I had to step over an arm to get into the corner chair. Budge and his wife both chose whisky, that was the most expensive. They didn't know that they had just failed a test. I had often noticed that most people ate and drank more expensively when it wasn't their round. Anal! After an hour we had all loosened up and Budge was into his stride. It was all the Tory Government's fault, especially that John Major. They didn't value the honest citizens' lifetime commitment to helping their country grow. All the way until three thirty in the afternoon I remem-bered. And what were the thanks they got? The government was cheese-paring their pensions because pensioners were no longer able to stand up for themselves, nobody cared for them. The youngsters weren't taught how to respect their elders, Budge was regularly pushed around by kids on the pavement and him a ratepayer, or was it poll tax? Edie did not bother to answer. She had heard this many times before and she wasn't paying attention. She had concluded a long time ago that her husband was a boring old fart. I had overheard conversations like this in pubs. I could picture the cogs squealing and grinding as the rusty secondhand sentences re-congealed into words writ in stone for the hundredth time in the fog behind the blank surly faces. I was nodding appropriately but my mind was elsewhere. Edie!

I had not planned on there being a live Edie.

Budge was droning on and on and on, repeating the same points, like a video multi replay of highlights, same head and hand movements, same laboured intonation. Budge's delivery reminded me of passing-through bit part actors in TV soaps. Maybe, I wondered, the bit part actors were in fact all Oliviers, all doing brilliant, Oscar worthy, renditions of the Budges in the world. Edie had stopped listening an hour earlier, she was concentrating on getting her share of the whisky, this was a rare treat and Ron could hardly hog the bottle when it wasn't him pouring.

The whisky was a very good malt and it was having its effect on both of them. I refilled their glasses and stood up, the bottle was almost finished. "Fancy a beer each to wash the whisky down?" I stepped over the settee and headed for the door with the beers still in the bag. "I'll get some more glasses. " In the kitchen, I poured three beers, hesitated and then dropped two Roofies each into two of the glasses, crushing them with a spoon. I would decide later, still thinking about it. The tablets were harmless enough, even in a beer, even alongside the whisky. They just made you very drunk and helpless, in about ten minutes. Pictured myself taking advantage of Edie, repulsive thought, I found her totally sexless. WD 40, Willy Droop at 40 metres. I brought the beers in, drinking from my glass as I came in. I had seen Danny Kaye in the Court Jester, the Vessel with the Pestle and the Chalice from the Palace scene. This was not a time to confuse glasses, or chalices. I was not about to drink from a poisoned chalice. Edie and Ron had both downed their whiskies whilst I had been out. They were competing for their share, both with each other and with me. Lifted the whisky, I poured the remains into their glasses, sharing it equally.

"Do have your share. "I thought of Zsofi's and Zsu's tearstained faces, as Lesley's coffin disappeared behind the curtain. Pictured Lesley's turning up for our first date in her cream coloured woollen mini dress with the bug-like pattern, her long red mane of hair, her amusement when I had said she was cheap to run when she asked for a half of cider, her friends laughing behind her flat door as I shook her hand at the end of the evening. There was no decision to make. It had been made over a year ago, Edie or no Edie, it made no fucking difference. "Here's to everybody having their share. " Within fifteen minutes they were both out for the count, she snoring louder than him. I collected the glasses and washed them in the kitchen. Returning them to the cupboard using a tea cloth. Bottles back in the carrier and I was almost ready to go. I pulled out a small plastic bag from my pocket and opened it. A handful of fibre glass insulation, enough to block the exit vent of the wall mounted gas heater. Stuffed it into the opening. These balanced flue fires could be draughty when they weren't lit and frugal people had been known to stuff this vent to prevent a draught from coming in. The flue was a safety requirement insisted on by the Gas Board, otherwise you could get a build up of carbon monoxide. Colourless, without taste or smell, carbon monoxide is lethal at concentrations above two hundred parts per million, just one measly little atom for each five thousand in the room was enough, so it wouldn't take very long. Blood cells latch onto carbon monoxide instead of oxygen, the symptoms are very bright red blood and you die for lack of oxygen.

Lit the fire, turning it full on, and after a final look around, shut the sitting room door using the plastic bag over my hand. Pushed the draught excluder from the front door tight against the living room door. Looked down at it and then kicked it back towards the front door. Nearly slipped up, it was impossible to fit that excluder to the door from the inside the room. The Budges were inside, warming up nicely. Stood motionless in the hall, anything else? Various film scenes flashed through my mind, punch lines, trip wires, booby traps. Looked into the under stairs cupboard to check the gas meter. It was happily whirring away and it wasn't a pre-pay meter so it couldn't stop short, miraculously saving the Budges for posterity.

Roger Waters had written a song about some poor woman who had tried to commit suicide using a gas cylinder. She survived because the gas cylinder had been too small and had run out. She couldn't afford the bigger one. She lived on, grateful for God's mercy in depriving her of the cash to kill herself. Now she was stuck forever in the sad song, on track twelve inside millions of shiny CDs, telling the world all about it. I wasn't giving God a look in, this was my show. Where the fuck was God when Lesley got hit by that truck - jerking off in the mirror?

Closed the front door behind me and looked through the window into the unlit room. Tiny little room with fully draught-proofed windows, guaranteed for life. I pictured the advertisement with the floating feather sailing straight down alongside just such a draught proof window. "If you want the best, fit Everest. " They had. "Ron 'Won't' Budge, ever again, thanks to draught-proof Everest. "

Strolled to my car and drove away, unnoticed by anyone. The sky was brightening up, it would be a nicer day tomorrow, even nicer than to-day.

Stopped for a coffee at the Penny Farthing service station on the M2. Dumped the bag of empty drinks bottles in a skip and, having filled the bottle of pills with water, flushed the Roofies down the toilet. The toilets were disgusting, how could people live like this, crap like this, animals? Washed my hands and watched them as I turned them under the blow dryer. Steady as a rock. Looked in the mirror, hair recovering from the escapade with the hair dresser, I was looking good, better every day. No trace of tiredness from the coach trip, I was on a high. The soup course had been great, gazpacho, with fresh rolls and butter.

Retraced the afternoon's events over a coffee which was the closest living relative to dish water, and was satisfied that I had missed nothing. Even if I had been seen entering or leaving the house there was nothing to link me with the fibre glass in the flue, no sign of foul play. The Roofie was virtually untraceable and would be dissipated by the time they finally expired from the carbon monoxide, probably in the early hours of tomorrow morning. It might be days or weeks before they were discovered. Anyway, Huszár was back in Hungary, he had never left. That reminded me, I rang Lesley using Zsu's code, asking her to ring me back when she had time. Pictured the computer forwarding the call to Zsu and smiled to myself. Drove straight through London, stopped at a service station.

Checked that the spare plastic petrol can was full and filled a new plastic can with diesel. The diesel was horrible smelly greasy stuff, good for dermatitis, getting it, not curing it. Petrol was much more pleasant and clean, you could almost get drunk on the fumes. Pocketed a handful of the thin plastic gloves provided by the garage and was on my way. Turned off the M40 towards Slough, needed a room for the night. Drove through the light industrial area looking for a neutral hotel equipped with rabbit hutches for bedrooms. A few miles, a few round-abouts, approach roads festooned with clapped out mini parades of shops huddling together for warmth against the icy blast from the out of town shopping centres. Keep it! They could keep Slough, Slough of Despond – not for me. Hadn't felt so good since before Lesley's accident, why spoil the mood. Drove on to Henley and stayed at the White Hart. I had stayed there once with Lesley, over twenty five years before, no chance they would place me? Went to bed pleased with the decision to come to Henley. From now on I would be more aware of doing things that made me feel good, less self pity, less despair. Slept soundly.

Drove past Elmore's house at eight the next morning just to check that his car was there. Drove on at random through the country lanes for over an hour and back from the opposite direction. The car was gone so Elmore must have gone to work as usual.

It wouldn't be dark until about four. Had time to kill, but nowhere to go. Bought a paper at a newsagents and a couple of cassettes. Had never in my life bought a pre-recorded cassette before, it was an inferior medium. Cherished my LP collection and subsequently my CDs. Pink Floyd and Lou Reed sounded remarkably good on the car stereo as I drove out to Cheltenham, killing time. Thought of calling in at Ray Finch's pottery at Winchcombe but rejected the idea. Couldn't take the risk, they might remember me. Thought of Lesley's love for Finch's home-made pottery stoneware. Tears came to my eyes as I drove past the end of the lane with the pottery kilns only forty metres away. It was the little unexpected things that caught you out, made it hard, I could barely see through the tears as I drove. It was the little things, they often turned out to be the most important. Thought of lots of things that reminded me of Lesley as I drove through the narrow Cotswold lanes.

Pulled off the road in a lay-by, sitting, staring straight ahead but seeing nothing with my eyes. Hurting inside. A passing truck brought me back, I had work to do. Got out and opened the boot. Putting on a pair of the plastic garage gloves I took out two large party balloons from a pack. Half filled a red one with diesel and a yellow one with petrol. Balloons appeared to be very unstable and wobbly, blew a little air into them before tying up the necks, fitting a stout paper clip in the knotted neck of the diesel-filled balloon. Stowed them in the boot with great care, cushioning them with the screwed up newspaper. Assembled the plane and put it on the back seat. Have to take it slowly, the balloons were important. Drove on, Wages of Fear, hands sweaty on the wheel as I tried, unsuccessfully, not to grip too hard.

Turned back towards Oxford just before three and arrived at the road leading to Elmore's at four. It was getting dark fast and there was a light drizzle. Parked in the field entrance on the far side of the road, eighty metres from the hairpin, out of sight of the road. Putting on a fresh pair of gloves I took the plane from the back seat and walked quickly down the road towards the bend, slipping into the roadside bushes when I was almost at the corner. Hid under a very attractive old yew which hung over the road, the lower branches neatly clipped into a flat overhang by the occasional truck passing underneath. Climbed easily into the tree and lodged the plane between two of the more substantial branches. The plane was above the road, looked at the angles, satisfied that it was just feasible for the plane to have flown there on its own. A car passed underneath but I wasn't noticed in my dark clothing. Climbed back down and collected the diesel filled balloon from the boot, checking that it was the red balloon, with the clip. The balloons were not interchangeable, it had to be the red one, filled with diesel. Re-climbed the tree and hooked the balloon to the bomb bay in the plane. From the road I looked back towards the hairpin, then up at the balloon. Satisfied, I paced out the distance to my car. Sixty metres from the car to the balloon. Climbed back in, placing the petrol balloon on the passenger seat, re-parking the car so that I could see down the road towards the hairpin and Elmore's village. Could see the cars passing on the other side. Five o'clock and it was all but pitch black, the drizzle had grown to a steady rain.

Looked at the seat beside me, everything was there. Opened the passenger window fully and started the engine, letting it idle. Fifty, maybe sixty miles an hour, about eighty feet per second, about twenty five metres per second. Not much more than two seconds between the car passing me and reaching the tree. About half a second to register the number plate as the car drove past, half a second to react, that left a second. Picked up the remote control and held my finger ready over the button, no time allowed for hesitation, lucky my reflexes were quick. A car passed, gingerly slowing down for the hairpin, it was raining heavily now, dripping in through the open window but I didn't notice.

Switched on the wipers, fast wipe, no milliseconds to spare between sweeps of the wipers.

Heard a car behind on the straight, it was in full rally mode, overhead camshaft screaming as the driver changed down to third just behind me. Registered Elmore's number plate, already knew it had to be Elmore, pressing the button as Elmore changed down to second, forty metres from the tree his large body and head silhouetted clearly against the rain drops reflecting his rally lights. Elmore was travelling very fast! Elmore didn't react when the dark red balloon plopped down ahead of his car, he thought it was just a falling leaf. His eyes were on the apex of the bend ahead as he was setting the car up to negotiate it, this bend was his favourite. He could take the hairpin ten miles an hour faster than anybody else in the neighbourhood, rain or shine.

The balloon landed with a mild plop, spreading out almost flat like an over large pancake, the downward momentum of the diesel fuel pushed it out to three times its normal diameter, it quivered like a jelly. Stretched so far, the tension in the balloon was now greater than the forces from the dropped diesel and the balloon started to contract as Elmore's car approached, less than ten metres away. The balloon was reshaping into a tear drop again, point aiming straight up at the sky as the thinly stretched rubber scraped back over a sharp piece of grit embedded in the asphalt. The balloon was below Elmore's line of vision when it finally split wide open, squirting the diesel in the path of the near side front tyre. The super wide, part worn tread filled with slimy, slippery diesel, just as he changed down to second and applied the brakes, heel and toeing the pedals. The car diesel planed towards the corner, spinning round as the near side tyres hit the muddy bank. It hit the tree travelling backwards at the apex of the bend. Elmore's changing gear and applying his brakes had locked the two outer wheels on the road whilst the inner wheels skidded forward without any grip. The car lurched forward after the impact as the front wheels momentarily bit again until the engine stalled. Elmore was blinded by my oncoming lights, he was badly winded and couldn't move, mouth open without gasping, diaphragm muscle locked, his internal organs still dancing from the impact.

I was already on the road, spinning my mud filled front wheels as the Rover came to a final stop. Within ten seconds I had pulled up, just past it, hazards flashing. Got out of the car, balloon and petrol can in my left hand and went back to Elmore's passenger door, opening it. Lucky it was a modern car with central locking. "You all right?" Elmore, badly shaken, was unhurt. The seat and headrest had absorbed the backward impact. He nodded, frozen face finally contorting as his diaphragm at last pulled some air in through his mouth. "It's tough, driving on diesel-filled treads, isn't it?" I was paraphrasing a snide crack Elmore had made to Huszár, eight years earlier. Elmore looked at my face, recognition just dawning as his view of my face suddenly changed to a bright yellow balloon coming towards him, the soft rubber enveloping his face and bursting as it scraped against the sharp frame of his glasses. His eyes were filled with petrol and he didn't see the spare plastic can land alongside him nor did he hear the distinctive sound of a match being struck, he did hear and feel the slamming of the passenger door. I was just past the end of the car when the petrol-air mixture ignited with a muffled explosion, leaving the windows still intact. As I engaged first gear the can blew up with a second more powerful explosion which blew out the windscreen. In my rear view mirror I could see Elmore's head and shoulders outlined by the fiercely burning flames. Elmore hadn't uttered a sound. Made a change, he used to be really full of himself, a real big mouth. Wondered about booking my space in Hell, might be full up?

The main course was great, perhaps the meat was a trifle over cooked, but the relish disguised it well.

Wondered briefly about going back for the model plane as I drove away but decided against it. The plane was clean and there was absolutely nothing to connect it with the diesel spilt on the road. It was raining heavily and by the time the police checked the crash there might not be any evidence of the diesel spill. The way Elmore drove, everybody would know he was on a mission behind the wheel. Nobody would be surprised that he had lost it on the bend in the rain. Less of the boy racer next time, except that there was no next time for Elmore. No way for him to alter this record with the benefit of hindsight.

Followed my nose north until I got to Banbury and joined the motorway there, heading north until I joined the M6 and then headed for London via the M1. It was a very wide detour but I was too frightened to take the direct route through the outskirts of Oxford. Oxford had been my old stomping ground and I couldn't afford to take any risks. Held my hand up, it was shaking. Every driver I passed seemed to stare, as if they knew. Arrived in London and settled for a small Inn in Edgware. Got drunk on Kronenberg and went to bed before midnight, shattered.

Elmore's ugly grinning face, melting in the heat of the flames, woke me throughout the night. By the third time I was getting accustomed to the dream and no longer found myself soaked in sweat. By the fourth time I was beginning to enjoy the dream and was disappointed when it ended. The Inn provided a massive full breakfast, sufficient to fully service a Sumo wrestler and the little boy employed to wipe his inaccessible arse. Barely picked at it but enjoyed the coffees. Nothing on the news. Remembered with a start that there was a second item of news to interest me. I had forgotten all about Budge, the Budges. Make that three items of news to interest me.

Paid the bill and sought out a back street car dealer who, having rung the previous owner of the car, was satisfied that it was mine to sell. Six hundred pounds in used notes, the dealer had been fair. Checked the boot and interior and found nothing to worry about. Left the new diesel can for the next owner to sort out. Nothing special about diesel, apart from the fact that it was a dirty fuel.

Caught a bus to Victoria and got a place on the afternoon coach to Budapest. Armed with a litre bottle of Vodka and plenty of tonic, it would help the time pass more quickly and more pleasantly. Rang Lesley again when the coach stopped off for an hour at Frankfurt, saying I was going to FAX later.

There were no unexpected hold ups and I was back after only thirty hours. Amazed at how relieved I was that it was only thirty hours. It was still a nightmare journey, but at least I had slept for six of the thirty hours. Took a taxi to the flat and crashed out on top of the bed with my coat on, it felt very familiar and comforting as I went out like a light. Awoke with a start, my neck and shoulders felt stiff and numb. There was a very bright light in my eyes and I was sitting naked on a stool, my arms behind me. My mind was racing, what was I doing here, where was I? Blinded by the near horizontal light, I couldn't see anything ahead of me, the floor underneath my chair was concrete and it felt cold on the balls of my feet. My feet were black with long encrusted dirt, crazed cracks in the joint areas showed up as marbled white lines. The only sound came from the high powered bulb element which was buzzing intermittently one metre from my face. Must be poor quality mains electricity, I thought, noticing that the light intensity seemed to vary every few seconds. My eyes hurt, my head hurt. Heard a heavy door slam in another room. Silence. Waited, helpless. The telephone rang just behind my head and I leapt up, falling off the edge of the bed. Looked down at the Casa Pupo cover Lesley had bought for our first proper double bed. I was in my own flat, I had been dreaming, sitting on the edge of the bed. Got up unsteadily, joints aching. The early morning sun was shining straight into the room, a plant on the balcony, waving in the breeze, creating a series of moving shadows. The communal central heating was clattering in the pipes, the system needed bleeding again. Turned to the phone which stopped ringing as I watched. Felt jaded and stale, hadn't bathed for days. Ran the bath and then made myself a full cafetière of coffee. Soaked for over an hour, sautéing my tired flesh. I had murdered three people. For what? What was I achieving? It dawned on me that I had in fact murdered four people, I had forgotten about Edie again because she didn't count, Edie was just a freebie. A two for the price of one offer. At least, I was assuming that the Budges were both dead, no doubts whatsoever about Bull and Elmore. Felt like a World War Two pilot, two kills, two probables, time to reload the ammo.

Pulled the plug on my thoughts, showered, half dried myself and put on my dressing gown. Lesley had made it for me because she had never been able to find one in the shops that was long enough in the arms and in the body. My arm span, at six foot eight, was six inches longer than my height and I also wanted the gown to reach my ankles. Normally human arm span and height measurements matched closely, I was a gorilla according to my girls. At least my knuckles didn't trail on the ground as I walked, thanks to my high heeled boots. Looked at the cuffs, they were beginning to show signs of wear. Lesley might be secretly making me a new one as she had on about four previous Christmases. Punched my palm with a clenched fist, Lesley was not making me a new dressing gown, not this Christmas nor any other Christmas. Poured myself a fourth coffee and filled a tumbler with Pálinka. Looked at the bottle. It was a litre bottle, one third full. Went to my desk for a marker pen and put a bold black line at the quarter full level, hesitated. What day was it? My mind was a blank. Lesley would know. Turned to the computer and tapped a key, the blank screen saver came to life after a few seconds. Double clicked with the mouse, it was Friday, Friday all day, guaranteed. Picked up the marker and wrote Lesley above the line on the bottle. I would allow myself to drink down to the line today, and no further.

Remembered a time when at eighteen I had come home rolling drunk and my mother had been embarrassed.

Not by my drinking but that I couldn't hold my drink like a man, a Hungarian man, a Huszár. Had got in a lot of practice since then but it still didn't take much to get me drunk.

"Cheers Lesley, I love you. "Toasted the image of Lesley's smiling face on the computer desk top. Opened up WinFax and checked the call logs. Incoming calls were matched by outgoing calls forwarded by the computer to the girls. Reset the date and time to match the first forwarded call and then made a call to Zsofi, she was out, but I left a thirty second message saying I would ring later. Went through the sequence twice more with calls to Zsu and then deleted the records for the incoming calls and the forwarded calls. Left the computer defragmenting the hard disk after I emptied the recycle bin and made myself a breakfast of Széged sausage and soft cheese. When in Budapest, do as you like, everybody else did. Finished the glass of Pálinka with my breakfast, returning the bottle to the shelf. Becoming an eccentric, it came with living on my own without the normal feedback of living and sharing my life with someone. I was probably talking to mydself by now, even if I wasn't, I soon would be. Unpacked my bag and checked my pockets. Segregated the foreign cash into the smaller bureau drawers I had set up for different currencies, smiling to myself at the drawer containing the English money – foreign Pounds. Opened my Hungarian passport and looked at the border stamps. If anybody thought to look, it would not be at all difficult to make the connection at the Hungarian Embassy between Huszár and Joe Lévai. If somebody were looking, he would find the dates matched with the Budges' and Elmore's deaths. The passport had simply been stamped at the borders, the borders had no record of their own. Walked over to the ceramic stove and placed the passport inside on top of the ready prepared kindling. Lit it and shut the door. Went back to the bureau, handful of pesetas, looked at them in my hand – no need, I'd been to Spain a few times for real, years ago. Looked at them again, yes there was, they were too new. Threw them into the Danube.

Rang the Embassy to report my lost passport and they referred me to the Passport Office. It would take a while, months not weeks.

Have to wait for the next course.

PEPPER AND SALT?

Detective Chief Inspector Mike Preston was pissed off, as usual. This wasn't police work, this was filing. Calling it Data Warehousing and Data Mining didn't disguise the fact that he was a glorified filing clerk. He looked out of his glass fronted office into the outer office. A couple of young detectives, Nixon and Miles, both graduates (both ballerinas as far as he was concerned), four computer operators and, lurking somewhere in the basement, the massive new mainframe computer that some smart arse had bought for the police force to kid Joe Public that the police had arrived in the twentieth century, but only just in time because the twenty first century was looming ever larger in the calendar. Somebody probably got a big backhander for ordering it. It had cost three million plus untold further millions to pay for the pensions of those who would be retired early, if it ever delivered anything that passed for useful. They'd be issuing ray guns next, who were they kidding?

Preston had been brought in to lend the new department credibility, his heavyweight presence showed that the Chief Constable meant business. The modern sophisticated criminal needed modern sophisticated methods to enable the police to catch him. The reality was that they were shovelling vast quantities of data into the computer but nobody really knew how to use the information, nobody knew what questions to ask the computer. Few knew what Data Warehousing and Data Mining even meant, least of all Preston, and he was supposed to be in charge of it. At forty three, Preston was a computer illiterate, his experience was limited to playing on his son's Sega games console. It struck him that it was a perverse coincidence that he had been sent here at forty three and that he was assigned to serve the forty three police forces in England and Wales. Presumably, he thought, the Scots still reverted to cudgels and Glasgow Kisses so they didn't need a computer. All Scotsmen were guilty anyway, you didn't need an expensive computer to tell you that.

To catch the enemy you needed to be fit and sharp, outplay and out smart him, just like the Sega games. Sitting on your slowly fattening arse in front of a console wasn't going to catch any criminals. A computer couldn't feel collars. He was day dreaming in front of his screen, eyes glazed over as only someone who is seriously pissed off can manage. A look that's impossible to simulate because you have to be seriously pissed off and totally unaware that you are doing it, to do it. It was a look he had been wearing more and more often.

Preston's door opened and Nixon tapped on the door glass as he walked straight to the chair in front of his desk, Miles followed, bringing his own chair. "Sir?" Preston nodded, a reflex reaction, his mind was still out to lunch. "We were wondering if we might get some new ideas for the database by pushing through a few trial runs. "

Preston looked up from his screen. Looked pointedly at the chair Miles had brought in for himself – pushy too, these ballerinas.

Keep the ballerinas dancing on the back foot. "And?"

"Well, Sir, for example, most murders are carried out by someone known to the victim so it follows that most suspects live nearby, or that they used to live nearby. Most crimes are, therefore, carried out by people with some connection to the area where the crime is committed. Chris and I feel that there should be a greater emphasis on possible regional connections between the crimes, the victims and the perpetrators. " Nixon examined Preston's face for a response. Preston's lack of enthusiasm for the project was affecting everybody's morale. Preston looked impassive, his mind was a blank. "We have a hypothetical example Sir and we've printed it out to illustrate the possibilities. " He passed a sheet over the desk. Preston looked at the sheet, his disdain thinly disguised. Bob Nixon and Chris Miles were always coming up with hair brained ideas on expanding the database instead of getting on with the job of entering in all the facts. Preston saw these as devices to relieve the tedium of getting on with the real work, which was stuffing the database, or, in office speak when out of Preston's earshot, "fucking the database". He summoned up some energy from his depleted resources and tried to look as if he was interested.

"Talk me through it, and try to do it in English, without the computer gobbledegook. Can you manage that?" He leaned back in his chair, arms crossed, mind closed.

 Miles pointed at the sheet with an extending pointer, proving to Preston once again that he was indeed a ballerina. "Take these fourteen attacks, most of them murders, Sir. At the time, everybody could see that they must be related, there were a lot of common factors, the hammer blows, the fact that they were prostitutes, or women on their own late at night, all in the same area. The police were all over it but still they didn't catch the guy until the fourteenth attack, and the reason it took so long, Sir, was they didn't have computers to collate all the information, so, even though they had the information they missed the connections, Sir. "

Preston raised his eyebrows, slowly, one after the other. These young swots couldn't see the wood for the trees. "Is this plane going to land at some time in our futures?" Preston had recently been on the receiving end of this phrase from a senior officer and he hadn't liked the way he had said it to him, especially in front of other officers. He'd been waiting for a chance to use it.

"Statistics show, Sir, that once someone has killed, they are forty times more likely to kill a second time than someone who has never killed before. So if someone has committed a murder then that same person is forty times more likely to be a real suspect for another murder than the average man on the street. Even if someone is only a suspect for a murder, then the chances of their being a suspect for another murder are also forty times greater. It's all down to statistical connections. "

Preston looked at the sheet, trying to recall some smart crack about lies and statistics but it just wouldn't come. The sheet was a bald list of events, with a brief description of each one, no dates, no names. But he recognised the case. What were the ballerinas trying to prove, trying to test him? Call their bluff. "So what does the Yorkshire Ripper case tell us that we don't already know? And, the Ripper didn't know any of his victims, what does that do to your theory. "

Miles was pleased that their plan had worked. Preston was glad to be able to show off his knowledge and they now had his full attention. "That list proves our point, Sir. You have a complete list of the all the events in front of you and you immediately see that it's the Ripper case. If we'd listed only half the cases, with some details missing, they could have been just an unrelated list. Chris and I think we should expand the database so that we can search for these statistical connections. It's up to us to tell the computer what to look for, otherwise it just sits on the facts, not telling us anything. "

Miles sat back, crossing his legs, Preston spotted his shoes. Looked like they were modelled on Cornish pasties, two shapeless pieces of light tan leather stitched together with cream string. "What exactly are you proposing? He looked pointedly at Miles' shoes again, how could you take a grown man wearing pixie shoes seriously? And, the twat had some sort of multi coloured picture on his kiddie socks!

"Well, Sir, the Yorkshire Ripper had been a strong suspect for the sixth murder because a five Pound note led the police to the trucking firm where he worked, but the police had missed other evidence.

The other evidence was buried in thousands of index cards spread across several police forces, so in spite of being interviewed on a number of occasions, Sutcliffe slipped through the net and wasn't caught until his fourteenth victim. Sutcliffe had gone on to kill seven more because the police hadn't been able to collate the evidence already in their system. What we're suggesting, Sir, is adding additional searchable fields to include, for example, possible suspects, regional connections. If they had had that in the Ripper case, then Sutcliffe's name would have kept popping up every time and they would have caught him earlier.

Preston thought about it. This was likely to be a huge extra workload in the end, it would send police running around everywhere following up dead end leads. But Preston was conscious of the fact that he himself was not much more than a figure head, with no real input of his own, he had been keen in his day, a long time ago, just like Nixon and Miles. The force needed keen people rather than tired old work horses like him. What if the price of their keenness did lead to some wasted computer resources and a few wild goose chases. If they were keen they would work longer, harder, better. And, he thought as he warmed to the idea, the ballerinas might even have a point. What wouldn't George Oldfield, the Assistant Chief Constable on the Ripper case, have given for a pair of ballerinas like Nixon and Miles to feed him with the links? He looked sternly at Nixon, "If you and Miles are prepared to do the extra work in your own time, then go ahead. How much work is involved?"

"To set it up Sir? A couple of weeks, tops. "

"Plus all the work putting in the extra information. "

"No Sir, not exactly Sir. All the information we have on each case all gets put in anyway, that's how we know the details on this hypothetical example. What we're suggesting Sir, is adding extra fields to the database so that we can search for statistical factors using the computer. At the moment this information is under a general heading so you can't search for it.

"What have the computer people got to say about this, they designed the database in the first place?"

"With every respect to them Sir, they're not detectives, they didn't think of it otherwise they would have included it in the first place. Chris and I can do this, please Sir? Nixon's eyes were pleading and he was shifting restlessly on his seat. He and Miles had been talking about this for weeks and it had taken ages to think up and then cobble the hypothetical case together in such a way that they would actually get Preston to think about it. They knew they had to come up with a specific example to have any hope of persuading Preston it was worth a try and Preston had swallowed the bait. Preston was a dead weight as far as they were concerned but they needed him along on the ride, even as a hitch hiker.

"Report back to me in a month and we'll see if we're getting anywhere. "

"Thank you very much, Sir. " Nixon headed for the door.

Preston's new found enthusiasm had already evaporated. "Be prepared for this to be dropped if it's not getting anywhere in a month. And if I decide no, that means no. No arguments.... OK? We have a budget and time targets to meet. And, another thing, what's with the kiddie socks?"

Miles looked down at his socks. "These? Present from my girlfriend, Sir. Bart Simpson. " He held his foot up. "Eat my shorts. " They shot out. Preston could see from behind that they were laughing at him but they stopped before they turned round. He was about to call out "Chair!", for Miles to come back for it, thought better of it. It was obvious that Miles had set him up for the joke. Present from the girlfriend? Preston looked again at the sheet, screwed it up and threw it at the bin. Missed! Losing his touch, he never used to miss.

He would probably go for retirement at forty five, if only he could think of something else he could do. He couldn't see himself as a night watchman or a shop security guard.

Three hours later Preston looked up, everybody had gone home. He switched his computer off, collected his coat from the rack as he made for the door. He looked back into his office, apart from the screwed up paper near the bin it was immaculate, clear desk, new filing cabinets. It didn't even look like a detective's office. He picked up the piece of paper, dropping it into the bin, only he missed! He took half a step back and kicked the heavy metal bin full force, sending it flying . He watched desultorily as it rebounded off the filing cabinet and into his door glass. It was empty, just like his job. As he walked out the door he saw the crack in the glass, running through his freshly painted name.

Fuck it! ......FUCK IT!

CLEAR YOUR PALETTE WITH THIS CHEEKY RED WINE

The four weeks leading up to Christmas flew by. Zsofi had got the job with the BBC and had her own office together with a new found power base. She was as happy as a pig in clover. Zsu was travelling to all sorts of unlikely Eastern European hideaways on behalf of Soros' foundation. I had been approached by two high tech firms who wanted me to deal with British, and in one case, American companies on their behalf. They hadn't known quite what to make of my fitted seventies suits. Hadn't needed to replace them since I hardly ever wore them and they did still fit, just. On my girls' advice I bowed to the inevitable and ordered replacements, still pin striped, but more restrained. It felt strange to be wearing them but they were more comfortable. I looked older than when I had bought my last suits twenty years earlier, about twenty years older. There was no going back in time, no second go, no trial run. Straightened my tie, Lesley had had a habit of straightening it for me whether it needed it or not. It hadn't needed straightening. I was adopting Lesley's little mannerisms incorporating them with my own. Zsu had commented that I ran my fingers through my hair as Lesley had done for me in the past. I had taken up crosswords in her place, she had been brilliant and I had never gotten the hang of it. Now I struggled with the easier Times crossword and was getting the hang of it.

Studied the two firms' products and visited their development facilities. They were in a related field for computer controlled micro engineering and seemed to have stolen a march on the competition. They were keen to cash in on their lead in the lucrative Western market. I was to be freelance with the companies meeting all my expenses and paying a handsome commission on any orders. I had insisted on the freelance aspect of their contract, I wasn't about to start answering to anybody for my time. I had done that for three years when I left college, that was enough. My degree from Oxford had been the main reason that the Hungarians contacted me, initially. To the Hungarians, a prestigious degree was what it was all about. Maybe? I took very little notice of these things but then, as Lesley had often said, I could afford to – I had an Oxford Degree. I had taken enough notice to put it on my letterhead, so who was I kidding? But I did at least stick to just BA Oxon and ignored the meaningless downgrade to MA.

Zsofi came for Christmas week and the new year. The three of us had come a long way since the previous Christmas, our first without Lesley, but this Christmas was harder to bear than the last one. Our losing Lesley seemed to hurt a great deal more than it had the year before.

Thought that we had still been in a state of shock the previous year and we were partially anaesthetised whereas now things were easier for us, the pain was a lot sharper without anaesthetic. We toasted Lesley's memory. The girls weren't so sure about the computer being called Lesley, somehow it felt sacrilegious but they didn't comment. They were both saddened to see my bachelor flat, my future looked sad, on my own without Lesley. If it made me happy to call my computer after their mother, fine, but they would not use the computer's name. I had always been a bit of a weirdo, they were used to it.

We delivered Zsofi to the airport and I dropped Zsu off at her flat. We had dinner and I left her doing her packing, she was off for ten days to Mongolia, another Soros deal. Have fun. I would be away on a trip to England when she came back so we would not see each other for about three weeks. It was good to be busy, best to be busy.

Asked Magda round for dinner for Saturday evening. She had been round for a drink with me and the girls over Christmas but had seemed to want to keep out of our way so I hadn't extended the invitation at the time. She had apparently spent Christmas on her own. I was relieved to find that she had seemed very pleased at the invitation to dinner and turned up on the dot of seven thirty armed with a very special bottle of vintage Tokaj. I recognised the significance of the antiquated label. Hungarians had fought, and lost, entire wars for bottles such as this. I was very pleased at what the bottle represented, Magda was beginning to be very special for me and this was a very special gesture on her part. The bottle was probably a family heirloom, much more valuable than if she had bought it.

I cooked Chinese and Magda had obviously enjoyed it. She had a healthy appetite. She had a daughter who lived in America but Magda had disapproved of her husband and they were more or less estranged, mainly more than less but she didn't want to admit to herself that it was over. She loved it when she found I didn't approve of Americans. A nation of Muppets. There are two kinds of Americans; loud mouthed Americans in America, and loud mouthed Americans in a venue very near you, no matter how far you travel.

I had already served coffees and Pálinka and I almost dropped my glass when Magda asked me, point blank, if I intended to remarry. I suddenly saw why people reacted as they did to my own directness. I wasn't used to it being applied to me and nor were my victims. "I don't know.

It's very soon, it's too soon. I'm not ready. " Hoped I wasn't hurting her.

She took it in her stride. "When you are ready.... Will you ask me?"

She had said it so naturally that I wondered if she was pulling my leg. . She looked totally composed and wasn't laughing. Raised my glass to her. "Magda, I promise that if ever I am ready I shall think of you first. "

She looked into my eyes, satisfied herself that I also was serious. "Thank you. " She smiled and raised her glass in turn. "If the right time comes, I have another bottle. Let me know when. "

Kissed her hand. "Magda, I don't want to mislead you. This is not a promise, but, I do like you very much. I need time to think. I have things to do before I am free to make any commitments, I have to close some doors on the past. "

"I understand. Imre died four years ago. If you had asked me two years ago it would have been too soon. Close your doors and talk to me when you are ready. And József, you will tell me even if your answer is no?"

"Maybe by the summer, I may be finished by then?"

"On the 20th August it will be St Stephen's day and this year is the one thousand one hundredth year. I will chill the wine for then and perhaps we will have more to celebrate than St Stephen's day. "

"You're very sweet, Magda. We can both decide on St Stephen's day."

She raised her glass. "To St Stephen. " We downed our drinks and she looked at her watch. "Time for me to say a goodnight and thank you. "

Saw Magda to her door and returned to the settee, pouring myself a large Pálinka. Raising my glass to the computer I said. "Hope you approve, Lesley, she may just be the one. " Lesley had always expected to be the first to die because both her parents had died young. She had insisted that I should make himself a new life without her when she was gone. It made me feel that Lesley had given her permission.

Looked into my own eyes in the mirror, without seeing myself. "I'll finish the job first, promise. " Have to see how it went, have to lock all the doors tight and make bloody sure I ended up on the right side of them. There was only Philips and Taylor left. Phillips had been the major force implementing Elmore's plans, he didn't deserve to be let off. Taylor, as arbitrator, had had the opportunity to put it all right and had decided to throw in his lot with the Council, probably in exchange for business with his practice. Whore! Neither of them deserved to be let off. If it had been Budge left till last I might have been tempted to leave it at that, Budge had just been a blunt tool used by Elmore and Phillips. It would be unfair on Budge to let the last two off and I wasn't about to be unfair. Everybody was entitled to their share and I would make sure that they got it. Poured another Pálinka, ruminating about finishing the job. Now that I had found Magda there was a new purpose to my life and I had more to lose, more was at risk. Thought of the girls, I was a selfish pig! Now, with Magda in the wings, I was thinking twice, but, the girls had always been there and I hadn't really given them a thought. Looked at the computer, no, nothing had changed, I owed it to Lesley to finish the job, thoughts of Magda were just softening me, mellowing me. . . . No Way! I would finish the bastards as I had promised Lesley.

It would take at least until March to get the replacement Hungarian passport which gave me plenty of time to plan things properly and finish in time for St Stephen's day. Then I would be free to get on with my life, probably with Magda if things worked out with her.

Went to bed realising that no matter how much I tried to kid myself, my resolve was weaker than it had been before Magda's question. Dreamt of Magda waiting and waiting for me and then finding out that I had been caught red handed trying to kill Taylor or Phillips. In my dream, Budge had survived and tipped off the police. Woke with the sweats again, feeling I hadn't slept all night.

Tomorrow I was flying to England on business. Had to travel north to discuss business with a couple of companies and I would also look in at the NEC later in the week. There was a high tech exhibition on and I might make some useful contacts. Would have to check what the press had made of the deaths of the Budges' and Elmore. If the police's suspicions had been aroused it might be too dangerous to carry on anyway. Spent the day alternately thinking of Magda and of how to check the state of play. Didn't have a good reason to travel to Broadstairs but thought a visit to Oxford would not arouse suspicions. How could I check on the Budges?

Collected my case at Heathrow and went through the customs check feeling very self conscious but nobody took any notice of my British passport. Must have been feeling paranoid at Dover when they checked me out, they couldn't keep track of all known criminals at customs.

As far as the police were concerned I wasn't really a criminal, least, not as far as they knew. The check at Dover was just a coincidence and I had been still smarting over my short stay at Ford. Organised a Jaguar as my hire car, the Hungarian firms wanted to create a good impression and had suggested it. It seemed strange to be driving on the left and the Heathrow edition of spaghetti junction caught me out, found I was heading south instead of north on the M25. Took this as a sign. Carried on down to Margate and went to the Isle of Thanet Gazette newspaper offices, it was four and they were shutting at five. Plenty of time. Chatted up the receptionist saying I had been away for a while and wanted to catch up on recent gossip.

The Budges had not been discovered for over a week. Nobody suspected foul play and the paper had followed up with a strong article about the dangers of blocking up gas flues. This was a known problem in the area because of the number of retired people in houses exposed directly to the winds from the surrounding seas. They were trying to save on heating bills. The local MP had joined the band wagon calling for heating subsidies for pensioners, chance to get his smooth, unworried brow in the paper again. Aitken? Didn't the family own the Express or the Mail, one of the mid range tabloids? It had been assumed that Ron Budge had blocked up the draughty vent in spite of the fact that as an ex clerk of works he should have known better. A case of a little knowledge being a dangerous thing. Budge had had his fifteen minutes of fame, thanks to me.

No charge, a gift, for old times' sake. And fuck you, Budge!

Left for London, mightily relieved. Free as a bird. Spent the night at Zsofi's flat and caught up with her news. She had a new beau and I would get to meet him at the weekend. Zsofi was glowing. Asked for his CV, in triplicate, plus fullest bank details. Pleased for her, everything was going well.

Turned off at junction nine on the M40 and headed down the A34 for Oxford. The old house looked even more nude and vulnerable than the last time I had seen it. Not a leaf in sight, the buggers had even cut down the fifty foot yew in the front garden.

Punched the horn in disgust. They had asphalted the gravel drive and replaced the original leaded windows with modern plastic units with simulated leading. Considered calling in to complain but thought better of it. It was none of my business, it was no longer my house. They had every right to bastardise it, and they were taking full advantage of that right.

Jude's was already filling up just after six when I turned up. Bought Michael a return pint. Tried to engineer the conversation towards Elmore's death but failed, could hardly ask if there had been any local people barbecued in cars lately. Check the local paper in the morning. Stayed till closing time and checked in at the Randolph, might as well do it in style. Pomposity was on the menu, the clientele more interested in being seen than in the food, which was not too special. Elmore's death had caused quite a stir in the local paper. The police had suspected foul play because Elmore had recently reported strange phone calls to the police, both at home and at work. The police had interviewed some dissatisfied contractors that Elmore had crossed swords with in the recent past but came up with nothing. They worried about the remnants of the spare petrol can in the front of the car, Elmore had another spare in the boot. They had found the tyre tracks in the field entrance, and near the burnt out car. In the end the police had found nothing that indicated outside interference and the coroner had recorded an open verdict. Nothing about the toy plane or the diesel on the road.

Huszár had a clean bill of health, Elmore's case was closed.

Rang Taylor's home number from a telephone box and recognised his wife's voice. Good.

 Phillips was not in his office but was due back at the end of the day.

Zsofi's boy friend was a nice kid and I liked him. He was as nervous as a cat with me at first but soon thawed out. According to Zsofi he was a rising star at the BBC and he liked his work. I approved and returned home to Budapest after the weekend. Realised as the plane was landing that this was my home, I would stay here and make a fresh start. Looking forward to a future.

READY FOR DESSERT?

March had come and gone. It had been a bitterly cold winter and it was too cold even for me. It was impossible to keep the flat properly warm when it was consistently below minus ten outside. I was paying the price for being on the top floor under an un-insulated roof space. Magda's flat suffered from the same deficiency but she was used to it, in Hungary, you expected to be cold in winter.

My replacement passport was stuck in someone's in tray and I had not had any luck tracking it down. I had worn out my welcome with the passport staff after only three follow up calls and was resigned to having to wait until it emerged under its own steam. I was beginning to see at first hand how thirty years of bureaucratic communism had knocked the initiative out of my countrymen. Having finished my third fruitless telephone call I could picture my file being slipped to the bottom of a massive stack of dusty applications, best to leave it alone. A part of me was pleased at the delay, wasn't looking forward to finishing the job.

At Easter I drove to lake Balaton with Magda. It seemed like the rest of Hungary had come to the same decision and we couldn't find a hotel anywhere. I looked at the map. Neither I nor Magda had ever been to Zagreb, only a hundred and thirty miles away and it was only five in the afternoon. Ten miles down the road when Magda mentioned the word, passport, we burst out laughing. Saw a sign for Pecs to the East, looked at Magda, she nodded her head.

As we turned up at the flats after a pleasant weekend away, I looked across at Magda and realised I had fallen in love. Resisted the temptation to lean across to her and take her in my arms and concentrated instead on parking in the garage. Clipped an adjacent Lada which was too close without even noticing. Our weekend had been very correct and platonic but I still felt I had betrayed Lesley. Magda and I hadn't discussed this but she seemed to understand and there hadn't been any awkward moments on the trip. She had been through the same experience after her husband had died. Saw her to her door and we thanked each other for a lovely time, kissing each other on the cheek.

Went to my own flat and switched the computer on. "Hi Lesley. " I toasted her image on the computer screen with a large Pálinka and looked at her face, expectantly. Watched the screen for over an hour and raising the third glass of Pálinka, I said. "I'll finish the job first and I'll ask the girls for permission. Then I'll decide. "

Spent the next hour checking the MailBoxes, this was no drill. I wasready, all I needed was my new Hungarian passport.

Rang the Passport Office in the morning and felt I was being told off again. It had been ready for collection for over a week and why had I been so tardy collecting it since it had been pushed through quickly at my request? Delighted, apologised freely for my incompetence. I was there within the hour. Looked noticeably older in the passport picture, checked in the car mirror, looked a good deal better now. Life was improving, thanks to Magda.

Spent the rest of the day touring the East side of Budapest and ended up in a small market town, Gödöllô. The dealer was intrigued that an obvious city type should be buying a cattle prod, especially the most powerful model available, since there was no way he was going to use it on cattle. I explained that I was wanting to develop an underwater stunner for sturgeon fishing and promised to send him some caviar when I made my millions. Typical hair brained Hungarian scheme to get rich quick, what impressed the dealer was that I made no attempt to haggle about the list price. He couldn't remember when he had last been paid list price by a local farmer. We shook hands and I left.

Back in the garage I opened up the casing and inspected the components inside the handle. Had no experience of what a cattle prod could do and I wasn't about to experiment on myself. Knew that prods were used by some police forces and that it was frowned upon by civil rights groups. Assumed that a full blown cattle prod was probably more powerful than the police prods but the more power the better. Checked the available space in the handle and went to the local electronics shop. A handful of smaller batteries and a selection of high voltage capacitors, the shop had everything I wanted. The shop reminded me of Henry's in the Edgware Road in the old days. Better than a wet dream. Redesigned the prod electronics so that, according to my simple calculations, it would deliver a much bigger belt than before but the battery would survive a smaller number of shots and would take longer to reload. The smaller battery allowed me to fit more capacitance, hence the bigger belt. Rigged up a light bulb with the terminals connected to the prod and gave it a shot. The two hundred and forty volt bulb blew instantly, the vaporised tungsten blackening the glass. Tried a few more bulbs.

Ready.

The coach system had joined the jet age at last it was no longer a thirty hour two night journey. It was only a twenty five hour one night journey. Looked at my reflection in the plate glass windows as I got off the coach. Nothing to distinguish me from the other passengers. Clothes and shoes, all bought in Budapest, looked the same as the other passengers. Cheap, poor quality with a sixties look about them which I attributed to the various grades of artificial material. Cotton and wool didn't come into it. They all looked tired. Shit, I was tired, never mind about looking tired. Patted my pockets, wallet containing the Hungarian passport and cash, Hungarian mobile. No credit cards– nothing to connect me to Joe Huszár.

Caught a tube and a bus and settled on a small bed and breakfast in Isleworth. Told the couple I was from East Anglia, looking for work. They weren't interested since I paid cash for three nights in advance. The greasy breakfast was still fighting an internecine war inside my stomach two hours later when I found what I was looking for. A boat chandlers that stocked small canisters of helium, as used by divers.

Called in at a pub for a mid morning pint of Kronenberg and a cheese and onion sandwich to sop up the indigestible breakfast. It took two pints and two sandwiches but it worked, at least it helped. Feeling better and now fully recovered from the coach trip and the breakfast I strolled around the less salubrious streets and found a house up for sale. A large detached late Victorian house, isolated on a corner plot. The windows were boarded up and a local agent's sign announced that it was due for auction in a few weeks time. It was probably a building society or bank repossession, it looked in reasonable condition and the plywood boards looked brand new, they hadn't weathered at all and the steel nails were still shiny. Private sellers didn't immediately board up their homes in order to sell them, it made for poor prices. Financial institutions weren't interested in getting good prices since by the time they repossessed they had written the debts off anyway, they played safe. What they wanted was an orderly sale as planned, without squatters delaying things. Anyway, it was the hapless owner's equity they were throwing away, as long as their debt was covered why should they worry and if their debt wasn't covered they could sue for the difference. Hence, price was not an issue, hence the boarded windows telling everyone this house was going for a song because the mortgagor was fucking the owner!

Walked openly into the front garden and looked up at the building. It was a rather nice house with its handmade red bricks and ornate stonework. Studied the substantial front door, also boarded up.

Strolled round the side and to the back. The first floor windows weren't boarded up but I was disappointed to find that the back was overlooked, no chance of climbing up without the risk of being seen. There were a pair of French windows, also boarded, and a back door fitted with a cheaper lock than the one at the front. It seemed to me that they had got it the wrong way round since it was easier to break in at the back which was less public than the front. Made a mental note of the lock and hasp design and returned to the front, making a show of noting down the agent's phone number. Checked my watch, just before three, time to make a phone call.

Strolled back to the Thames and picked an isolated telephone box in an open green where I would be able to see if anybody was approaching. Inside the box I put my holdall on the shelf and cracked open the valve on the helium cylinder so I could barely hear the hiss of the escaping gas. As I was waiting I thought back to a TV programme which had featured deep sea divers in a decompression chamber talking to the outside world with Donald Duck voices. Remembered the shock of hearing one of the divers voices when he emerged from the chamber, one of the deepest baritones I had ever heard. Helium was mixed with oxygen for deep dives because it helped to avoid gas bubbles forming in the blood as the diver decompressed. It worked because helium was about four times lighter than oxygen. Took deep breaths and filled my lungs with the part helium mixture in the phone kiosk. My voice box was now filled with an air helium mixture that was about three quarters as dense as usual, tested my voice. "Mr Phillips? My name is John Baynes. " I was amazed and involuntarily looked round. I was speaking but it was not my voice coming out! My normally deep brown voice was coming out a full octave higher than usual and I didn't recognise it as my own. Dialled Dave Phillips' office number in Hounslow and asked to be put through.

"Phillips. "

"Mr Phillips. My name is John Baynes. Bertrand's have a house coming up in Isleworth for auction and they recommended you. I'm in town for a few days and would like to meet up with you to survey the house together and appoint you as my buying agent. I shall be out of the country at the time of the auction. " I knew that in such cases the agent would be on a commission fee and Phillips would know he was in for the order of a thousand plus if he bid successfully for the house.

Phillips knew the score and checked his diary, it was very full that week. "It would have to be after six in the evening, how about tomorrow?"

"Suits me fine. I forget the number but it's on the corner of Silverall Road, you can't miss Bertrand's sign. I shall be there for six, come round to the back door. "

Dave Phillips put the phone down. He didn't know anybody at Bertrand's, somebody must have come across his tracks. Bertrand's were quite a substantial firm, this could be a useful new contact. He rubbed his hands in anticipation of an easy fee. Most of his work was fixed rate surveying for building societies and the price was cut to the bone. These building societies wanted a commission on everything nowadays, made a change to be earning a full, and in this case, fat, fee. He noted the appointment in his diary and wrote Silverall Rd/Bertrand's alongside it with a question mark.

Put the phone down and laughed. My normal very powerful laugh came out as a cackle. That was fun. Shut off the helium valve and picked up the hold all. Found an old fashioned iron mongers in the local shopping street and bought a new lock, bolt cutters and a torch, joking with the owner that I had lost a key and couldn't get into my own shed. The owner had heard it all before and didn't think twice about it, making a note to order more cutters as he only had one left in stock. Retired to a local pub and waited till after eight. It had been a bright day but the sky was reassuringly dark as I retraced my steps to the house. There was no sign of anybody about and I walked boldly to the back of the house as if I owned it, aware of the fact that my clothes were on the light side and pleased that I didn't actually look a likely burglar, whatever they looked like? The lock parted after three attempts with a surprisingly loud crack but I resisted looking around at the various lighted windows in the backs of the terrace twenty metres behind me. Took off the lock and walked in, shutting the door behind me, wiping it with my sleeve. Switching on the torch I looked around. I was in a rear lobby with three doors leading to rooms and what must be the front hall. The front hall was impressive with leaded glass doors leading into various rooms. The place was stripped of furniture but was otherwise intact. Returned to the hall and made for the under stairs cupboard, opening the full height door. Usual facilities, a modern fuse box, electricity meter, gas meter. Shone the torch on the meter, it was turning perceptibly. The mains switch was on and something was drawing current, perhaps a timer, something small. Pressed the trip and the meter stopped turning. The house still had mains electricity. The lever on the gas meter was in the off position.

Picked up a scrap of paper and using it to hold the lever turned it sharply on. There was a short surge of gas as the pipes filled and came up to pressure. Turned it off again. There was mains gas. Looked vainly in the holdall, knowing that I did not have a spanner. Looked at the bolt cutters, could work? Opened them as far as they could go and gripped the screw collar attaching the outgoing pipe to the gas meter. In spite of my considerable strength I just could not budge it. Within minutes I was steeped in sweat and getting nowhere. Leaned back on my haunches to think. Looked closely at the collar, it was obviously recent but had deep serrations round it where it had been tightened by a Neanderthal fitter with the mother of all self grip spanners. Looked around and then took the gas lever off its square shaft, placing one end against the end of a flat on the collar. Hit it with the heavy end of the cutter, no joy. Hit it again with all my strength, still no joy. Sat back to consider the options, looking at the incoming pipe with its shut off valve, the pressure regulator which looked to be quite a delicate instrument, the meter with its incoming and outgoing pipes and the pipe disappearing into the wall. There was a proprietary connection to the regulator valve which must have been factory fitted rather than by the Neanderthal. Tried gripping it with the cutter handles, smooth as silk. Loosened the collar about half a turn and turned on the gas with the lever, there was a satisfying shhhh as the gas escaped. Turned it off again and turned to the incoming electricity cable coming up through the wooden floor. The heavy sheathed cable fed into a twin large casing which contained the hundred amp electricity board cartridge fuses, each about the size of a bumper sausage. These fuses were locked in with wires crimped and lead sealed by the board. Punters were not allowed to touch these fuses. Snipped through the restraint wires and pulled out the fuses, using a piece of paper. Placing them loose on the floor I backed up to the door. Fuse box and fuses on the far left, gas meter and fittings on the far right. Satisfied I shut the door and exited the house as I had come. Fitted the new lock and pocketed the key.

Hopped on a bus and finished the evening at an Indian restaurant in Soho. Didn't want to establish a presence in Isleworth and Soho was about as cosmopolitan as you could get.

Woke at seven am sharp. Last night's Vindaloo was still gurgling high up in my throat and it felt good. Declined the offer of breakfast and settled for toast and extra coffee instead. Explained to the land lady that I had a job interview and , if successful, might not come back but she was to keep the money anyway but to hold the room for me, just in case.

Packed my bags and left them in a locker at Paddington, keeping the hold all with the prod and tools inside. No need to check for Oxford coaches, they ran every time you blinked. The M40 was filled with London to Oxford coaches, nose to tail, they must look like a special road line from the traffic helicopters.

Looked at my watch, eleven thirty, time for a phone call. Rang Taylor's home number in Woodstock. No reply. Rang his office number, trying to disguise my voice but not bothering with the helium. Taylor had retired and they only saw him very occasionally at the office, had I tried his home number? "Yes thanks, no message. " Hung up. Would try again later. Looked at my watch again, this was beginning to be a reflex action. Eleven forty, it was going to be a very long day, Huszár had never learnt to wait, hated waiting. Consulted an A to Z. Kew Gardens, I had never been to Kew. Lesley had occasionally suggested that Kew might make an interesting day but we had never got round to it.

I had always had a blind spot about the London Underground system in spite of the very simple and logical colour coded route maps. The back of the A to Z made it simple. Catch the district line at Paddington and jump off one stop after Gunnersbury. In a world of my own, marvelling at how full the carriages were at this time of day, hanging onto the strap, making sure not to catch the eye of any of the harder looking passengers. The stations slipped smoothly past and I was reminded of my very poor feel for the London areas, it was all arse about face from under ground. Parson's Green, Putney Bridge, East Putney. "East Putney! No way Jose!" My geography wasn't that bad, got off at East Putney and turned back, changing at Earl's Court. What was the point of a beautiful colour coded idiot proof system if you buggered it up by putting random branches onto it? Looked around as the other passengers moved effortlessly on and off the train whilst I pored over the mystifying spaghetti printed above every window and on the A to Z. With some relief, I eventually got off at Kew and headed for the gardens. Must be the pressure, called in for a couple of pints to calm my nerves. No Kronenberg, just Holsten Export or Carling Black Piss. Holsten would do. Drank three. Wandering round the gardens became acutely aware of Lesley's absence. This would have been ten times more interesting with her, she knew all about plants and would have been trying to steal shoots to plant in the garden. I took a few samples in her memory and put them in my bag. Sat on a bench and cried silently, oblivious to the stares from passers by. Eventually, red eyed but feeling better for having let my feelings go, I checked my watch. Four, at last. Time to make my way over to the house and make a call on the way. After three quarters of an hour I was at the same phone box as before at the river side. Rang Taylor's home number, after two attempts a sleepy young man's voice answered the phone. Talking through my hand I asked for Taylor. Taylor was away at his cottage and would be back at the end of next week. The cottage was in Wales and wasn't on the phone. Said I would leave a message at Taylor's office and hung up. Shit! Hadn't counted on Taylor's being away. Nobody went away at this time of year, unless, of course, they were retired and had their own cottage in the wilds. Rang back, the kid took ages to answer the phone and was surly. He grudgingly gave me the address so I could write to him to call back. Could hear a female voice giggling in the background, that explained his tardiness in answering the phone. Young Mr Taylor was entertaining illicit guests, and his father so prim proper and correct. Called a MailBox, leaving a message for Zsu.

Got to the house at five twenty and let myself in the back door, carefully pocketing the lock and key, leaving the door ajar. Inside I put cotton gloves on and assembled the two halves of the cattle prod and felt its weight, it had a good swing to it which might turn out to be useful. Put the bolt cutters in my pocket as an extra precaution and placed the bag inside the room across the hallway, out of sight. Placing the lit torch on the floor in the under stairs cupboard I pushed the door almost shut and walked back to the doorway leading to the back hall. The boarded windows made it quite dark and the outline of the under stairs door was clearly illuminated by the light of the torch behind it. Closed the door leading to the back hall and paced over to the door opposite the under stairs, opening it fully and standing hidden in the totally dark room. He would have his back to me as he looked inside, expecting to see Baynes.

Held the prod and fingered the bolt cutters in my pocket. Both felt reassuringly heavy, I had never hit a man in anger in my life. Hadn't hit anybody in anger since I was thirteen. Remembered back to an incident at the school gym. By pure luck I had caught the kid on the tip of the jaw, laying him out. The kid had not been hurt but my reputation, along with my subsequent fifteen centimetre increase in height had meant I had never had to get physical again. Thought back, remembering Phillips. Seven years ago Phillips had looked lean and wiry, shorter than me by some ten centimetres and lighter by about fifteen kilos. On one occasion Phillips had turned up when we were about to unload a steel girder and had joined in just to show off. We had almost dropped the girder because Huszár and his two men had assumed Phillips would make a useful contribution to the lift. Phillips was not as wiry as he looked. Phillips was not a strong man, I was a very strong man. At College they had had to juggle the crew in my eight to counteract my enormous pulling power. I still had that strength, but I no longer had the staying power to pull my lungs forcibly up out of my throat and spit them out into the bottom of the boat, which is what rowing in a College eight felt like when you were in danger of being bumped by the crew behind. I thought of my three years rowing, must have been mad. Flexed my arm, leg and torso muscles, limbering up gently. This was not the time to pull a muscle.

Waited, continuing my exercises to keep my mind off what was to come. In the dark I could not see my watch but it was an academic point. Phillips would turn up in his own sweet time. Recalled the occasions when I used to wait endlessly for Phillips to turn up for valuations, always late with a deliberately transparent excuse, just taking the piss. Phillips had been on a permanent power trip and had loved every second of it but Huszár never gave him the satisfaction of showing any sign that he was annoyed by the delays. He always had work to get on with and Phillips would always have to attract his attention when he turned up. Never, ever, show an enemy that they are getting to you, it de-motivates them if you don't notice that they're trying to get at you. Immersed in my exercises and my thoughts when I heard a car pull up at the front of the house. Now the boot was on the other foot, Phillips had turned up early, keen to make himself some money. Waited, Phillips was about to get paid off, without a P45.

Phillips closed the car door and walked round to the back of the house. Too dark for a proper inspection from the outside but the house looked to be sound, subsidence was not a problem in this road. No sign of lights, maybe the client hadn't turned up yet, he was five minutes early. Coming round to the back he saw the rear door ajar, good, Baynes was here after all. He walked through the doorway, noting the good heavy quality of the door and saw the darker outline of the through door. He felt in his pocket for his torch and made for the door and opened it. Seeing the glow around the under stairs door he strode forward. "Hello. Any luck with the lights? I have a torch. " He pulled the door open and leaned forward to look inside.

I took a step forward out of the room. "I'm here. "

Surprised, Phillips straightened up with a start and turned round, arm outstretched, ready to shake hands. "Dave Phillips. "I slowly raised the cattle prod as if to point and feeling the tip connect with Phillips hand I fired it, saying. "József Huszár. Eat this, mother fucker!" In the dark conditions I saw a faint blue glow at the end of the prod as Phillips' body convulsed with the shock and flew backwards into the cupboard, falling in a seated position, back resting against the wall. Came forward and Phillips looked up at me thinking I was very familiar but the light from the torch on the floor made my features look distorted and very different. Could see the confusion in Phillips eyes and said. "I told you I always finished the job didn't I Dave? Time to sign the completion certificate, no forgeries this time, this one is permanent. " Saw with satisfaction the horror of recognition and fear in Phillips eyes as I pushed the prod inside the collar of his jacket and fired again. Phillips body convulsed with the shock and straightened with a power that slid his head up the wall and his feet forwards, knocking my feet from under me. Phillips head slid down the wall, his body still rigid, with me on top of him scrambling to get up. Got up on my knees and pulled myself up using the door frame, shaken and breathless with excitement. Phillips was out cold and looked strange, it took a few seconds before I realised what it was. Phillips toupee had fallen off as his head had scraped the wall. He was practically bald as a coot! My shoulders sagged with relief, it had worked. Pulled Phillips body upright into a sitting position. Grabbing him by his arms, I pushed his knees up to his chest and manhandled him over to the far corner of the cupboard, facing the electricity meter and fuses. Picking up the prod, I gave him another belt in the hand, the shock sent Phillips body convulsing backwards into the gas meter with his legs shooting forward and kicking the wall in front. Looked at the scene, perfect. Leant behind Phillips, hearing his faint breathing before I opened the gas cock wide. Stepping back, I picked up one of the fuses and his toupee dropping them in between Phillips' legs.

It looked as if Phillips had made a mistake trying to replace the fuse.

"Time toupee, arsehole!" I laughed to myself as I shone the torch around the cupboard, no obvious signs of the struggle anywhere on the floor or the walls. Pushed the door almost shut and put the two halves of the prod into the holdall, taking a good look around both halls and the room. It looked good. Returned to the cupboard and pushed the door slightly ajar. Taking a deep breath I looked inside, Phillips hadn't moved and the gas was belting out. Phillips eyes were wide open but from my position in the doorway I couldn't see his pupils, couldn't be sure. Pushed the door almost shut again and waited for what seemed like ages. Checked my watch, twenty five past six. A final look inside and I was satisfied.

Pushed the back door shut with my elbow and walked to the front of the house. Heard Phillips car phone ringing as I went past. This is no longer a working number, I hummed to myself as I walked away, please redial your call. Your party doesn't live here any more. He's dead! Delicious pudding, better than creme brulé.

Shattered, but elated, as I walked the four miles to Kew underground. Not taking any chances and the walk calmed me down, could feel my pulse slowing back to normal as I walked. As the tube turned up and I saw the sparks from the track I wondered if Phillips body might get blown up in a gas explosion, hadn't considered that. No chance, no electrical power in the house, no possible source of a spark and anybody turning up at the house would smell the gas. Pictured Phillips slumped in the corner, head back and eyes open, mouth agape. Liked the image, loved the image.

Got off at Oxford Street and raided Milletts for a complete set of top clothes. Cheap trainers, socks, jeans, jacket, shirt and then made my way back to Paddington on foot. The next coach for Hungary was at ten in the morning and I had time to kill. Collected my bags and changed in the toilets. The beggar at the front of the station didn't seem very grateful for the bag of clothes, maybe the Milletts bag was too down market for his taste? Further on, down Praed Street, binned the hold all in an almost empty skip. Barring an impossibly miraculous bit of forensics there was nothing now to link me physically with the unfortunate accident at the Silverall Street house. Anyway, I rang Zsofi's MailBox, I was back in Budapest around the time of Phillips' accident – if you don't believe me check my phone records.

Checked in at a small hotel and ate at a local Chinese. Ordering the third Tiger lager it dawned on me that I had dropped the idea of calling on Taylor at his Welsh cottage. Excused myself on the grounds that without a car I would be too conspicuous in a remote country area but at the same time I was aware that my hunger for revenge was perhaps, at last, sated? Pleased with the way Phillips had got his, pleased that I had had the pleasure of seeing the terror in Phillips' eyes as he recognised me, pleased that the bugger had lost his hair, his life.

Perhaps I had had enough of this eat it cold, revenge shit?

Finished the evening at a pub with four more pints and slept soundly. The coach trip to Budapest passed quickly enough, I was getting used to it, you can get used to anything, so they say.

Dozing in bed, it was gone ten. Had woken at seven as usual but I was tired and enjoying a rare lie in, was used to lie ins after my eat it cold trips. It had become part of the ritual, it had been part of the ritual. The phone rang, it was Magda. She had heard me arrive in the small hours and thought I might be tired after my trip. Did I fancy lunch in her flat or at a local restaurant? Left the choice to her and she opted for her flat.

Bathed and dressed and drank three coffees as I checked in with Lesley. Finally, I had finished deleting the Mail Boxes and left the computer defragging the hard disk after I emptied the recycle bin. Looked through my new Hungarian passport with its French and German border stamps confirming the trip. Seemed a shame to go through all that hassle again, perhaps there was no need to burn it? The computer had finished defragging and I sat down to look at Lesley's image on the screen. "Think I'll leave it at that, Lesley, Taylor's retired and probably shot away anyway. I'm tired of wiping out these clapped out nobody's. No point in taking any more risks, Taylor's just not worth it. With your permission, I'll call it a day and if the girls approve I'll make a new start with Magda. Vot u tink, Lesley?"

Stared at the screen until Magda rang to say lunch was ready.

Lesley said "OK. "

Opened the drawer and taking the passport out put it in a folded newspaper, loaded it into the stove. Magda was waiting for me and lunch would be getting cold. Had a belly full of cold dishes and Magda's hot soups were exceptional.

COFFEE WITH PALINKA?

Detective Rick Stevenson came in for his Monday morning shift an hour early. He always liked to get a flying start on a Monday, it set the tone for the week. He had been promoted less than two months and he was keen and he was proud to have earned the nickname "Mustard". He leant over the counter at the desk sergeant seated behind it. "Just give me the facts Sam, just the facts. "

It had been a long night and Sam was not in the mood. "I thought they paid you to find the facts, don't ask me for them, I've got my own job to get on with. "Stevenson looked over at the sheet Sam was filling out. "Missing person, eh? Lovely jubbly, good way to start the week. " He watched as Sam finished the sheet and waited expectantly for Sam to pass it over for him to read. Sam took out another sheet and laying it on top of the pile started to fill it out. It was his time sheet, he was due for three days leave. He started to fill it out and when it became obvious that Stevenson wasn't going to bite he pulled out the lower sheet and handed it over. No joy in needling someone that refused to react.

Stevenson read through the sheet, summarising the facts in his mind. Surveyor called Dave Phillips, not seen since Thursday afternoon. His wife was climbing up the wall about it and was in danger of fusing the switchboard with her calls. Phillips wasn't answering his car phone. Wife had been away till yesterday with relatives. "That's the trouble with car phones, the bugger could be the other side of the world for all you know, no way of telling where he could be. " Stevenson straightened up, tapping the sheet with his forefinger. "Hang on a minute. Hang on just a minute, number one son. Can I borrow this?" He was off to his office before Sam could answer. Stevenson shared an office with two other young detectives but they would not be in for the best part of an hour. He rifled through their in trays until he found a technical sheet. They never read anything so it was still there. *Mobile phones –tracing locations*. He scanned through the memorandum. The newer digital mobile phones sent out a homing signal every half hour so that the system would know roughly where to send the signal to. Otherwise any signal sent to a mobile set up for roaming the globe would have to be sent all over the globe every time and the system would be permanently saturated.

The service providers had thought about it. He looked at the mobile number on the sheet. 0860—a Cellnet number, good, not one of these Mickey Mouse chicken shit Orange numbers that restricted you to your own back garden, not much better than a tin can and a piece of string. He checked a number and rang Cellnet. "Detective Stevenson, Hounslow police. We have a missing person with a car phone that's switched on. Any chance of locating their position?

The girl was efficient. "Putting you through to engineering Sir, they will help you out. "

Engineering were equally efficient and rang back within half an hour. Stevenson looked up at the clock. "Not even eight yet, that's what I call a flying start. "

"Flying what Sir? Your missing person's phone is about a mile away from where you are Sir. The Ordnance Survey Grid Reference is TQ 156 758. "

Stevenson was impressed. "Good work, how do you do it?"

"Easy, Sir. We have receivers/transmitters all over the place and we just triangulate the phone's position by checking the received signal. The computer does this automatically to save resources. "

"Yeah, I read about that, that's why I thought of ringing you. Thanks, thanks a lot for your help. " Stevenson checked the car number and description as he walked back to the desk. Dropping the sheet back on Sam's pile just in time for him to pick it up as he packed away. Sam was finished for the day. "Start of my shift Sam. I'm off to solve my first case for the day. Back for morning coffee. "

"Smart arse! Mind your head in the traffic. " The worst thing is, thought Sam, the bugger probably had a point.

Stevenson found the car blocking the entrance to the house. All the doors were locked, no sign of anything untoward. He rang in. The Sergeant gave him Mrs Phillips number. "Mrs Phillips? Detective Stevenson, I've found your husband's car here at Isleworth. No sign of your husband, any idea what he might be doing here?"

Mrs Phillips was beside herself. "Is he all right?"

"No sign of him Mrs Phillips. The car is fine, no sign of trouble. It's parked here in Silverall Road. Any friends or relatives of your husband's round here?" Or girl friends, he thought, boy friends even?

"Not that I know of. He's a surveyor, his office might know more. I'll give them a ring. " She hung up as Stevenson was protesting that she should give him the number but he was talking to an empty line. He waited for two minutes and then rang the line until it was free and she answered. "What did your husband's office say, Mrs Phillips?"

"There is a diary note for six last Thursday evening marked Silverall Road with the name Bertrand's. "

Stevenson looked out of his window at the Bertrand's sign. The appointment was three and a half days ago and Phillips' car was still parked here. He tried to make it sound routine but he was too inexperienced. "Thank you Mrs Phillips. I'll get back to you later. "

She detected the attempt to lighten his tone, the change was obvious, even over the phone. "Silverall Road, wasn't it? I'll catch a taxi. "

"No! Please Mrs.... " He was talking to an empty line again. Shit, this could turn out to be very painful for her, not exactly a beach party for him. He couldn't handle it when civilians got emotional. He got out of the car and went up to the front door. No way that anybody got in that way. Trotting round the side and the back he looked at the upper windows, all shut. There was a padlock hasp on the back door and no pad lock. He turned the handle and it turned easily in his hand at the same time he recognised that what he had been smelling was gas. A strong belt of gas came out of the open door. This was bloody dangerous. He paused in the doorway. The rules said he should call the gas people and they would shut the gas off outside the house and allow time for it all to escape. Maybe even evacuate the area? What if the gas had only been on a short while and Phillips was still alive? He looked inside, the smell wasn't quite so bad now but the house would be full of it. He hesitated, looked down at his shoes and took them off. They had steel tips, might cause a spark. He took a deep breath and walked quickly through the two halls, stopping by the under stairs door way. He could hear the gas escaping. He opened the door and looked in. In the white painted under stairs he could just make out the outline of Phillips body slumped back against the wall. He felt his neck, stone cold. Nothing he could do here. He calmly walked back out of the house leaving the door open and putting his shoes on, returned to his car.

He asked the desk to get the gas board out here, pronto and hung up as Pat Phillips' taxi drew up. He leapt out and held the taxi door tight shut. "Mrs Phillips, you can't come out, it's dangerous. The house is full of gas and might blow up at any moment. " He turned to the driver. "Deliver her to Hounslow Police Station driver, that's a police order. " He showed his badge, dropping it as Phillips' wife managed to push the door open. He pushed back with both hands. "Please Mrs Phillips. "

"He's dead, isn't he?"

Stevenson couldn't bring himself to speak but his face said it all, in full Dolby Stereo with gut wrenching sound effects which turned her guts.

He heard her muffled screams as the taxi shot off up the road, her face framed by the rear window as she pounded on it. Forensic turned up and Stevenson was handed Phillips' wallet and car keys. Back at the station Jane and Pat Phillips were in one of the interview rooms and Pat knew from Stevenson's face exactly what he was about to say. He sat down opposite her and drew out the wallet and keys, placing them silently on the table. "Your husband wear a. . ?"

"Toupee. " She finished his sentence with a very quite voice and sat there looking at her husband's wallet, hands in her lap, motionless.

His voice was breaking as he said. "I'm so sorry. Can we call any one for you?" She just sat there mute and Jane caught his eye. He stood up without a word and left the room. Nothing he could say or do would make one iota of difference so it was best left to Jane. Lucky Jane was on shift, she was the best they had, by a mile. "Super Jane. "

Forensic were almost finished by the time he got back. Phillips body was already at the mortuary and with the lights back on it was only the faintest whiff of gas that indicated anything might be amiss. He walked into the cupboard, no sign. No sign at all. He came out and collared Nobby Clark. "What have we got, Nob?

Nob had seen it all before. Twenty one years in forensics and nothing surprised him. "On the face of it, poor bugger came to look the house over, surveyor, main fuses were out so he tried to put them back in. Got a shock, fell back into the gas meter and popped a joint. Temporary shock from the electricity supply and gassed while he was out cold. "

"How do you know?"

"Carbon monoxide in the gas turns the blood very bright red. You could see the colour of his open mouth. Post mortem will confirm that. "

"But you're not convinced?"

"Maybe, maybe not. " He looked up to marshal his thoughts. "No padlock or key on him. Torch in his pocket, no use to him there. Look. " He turned off the under stairs light. "See those big black things, near the bottom, fuses? Would you climb in and put those in, keeping your torch in your pocket? I bloody wouldn't, I can tell you that. "

Stevenson looked in, imagining having to replace the fuses. Electricity didn't worry him but he wouldn't go for it in the dark without a torch, no way. "Maybe the torch was duff and he was in a hurry for some reason. "

Nob looked to the ceiling, this time for divine help. "The torch worked fine. Don't you think I checked it?"

Stevenson patted him on the shoulder. "Sorry Nob. Just thinking out loud, that's all. " Stevenson had worked with Nob several times already and he was good, as good as they come. "Fingerprints?"

"All over but not necessarily useful. By the looks of it this house was only boarded up a short while ago, we've probably got the owner's prints. Should know by the morning. "

"I'll check with the agents. Any other ideas?"

"Not yet. " Stevenson walked around the entire house to get the feel for it and then checked the garden. He wasn't excited about the pad lock, could have been removed earlier by thieves who, finding nothing to interest them, went off quietly to another job where there was something to interest them. The torch? Probably didn't mean anything. Experienced surveyor, confident he knew what he was at, torch in his hand would just get in the way. He went back under the stairs to check the gas leak. It looked fine until he turned the lever and heard the escaping gas. He partially shut it and felt for the leak, gland nut by the regulator. He pictured Phillips body, flung back by the shock, falling back against the meter and regulator and disturbing the joint. He made a mental note to check his own system when he got home. He turned the gas off, switched off the lights and left forensic to seal the place up. Another week started, one already in the bag, literally.

Stevenson's in tray had nothing that couldn't wait till morning so he went home to check his gas meter. The joints on his own regulator were much less tight than the other joints. He couldn't even shift the other joints with his made of butter Woolworths spanner. He'd like to see the guy that tightened those main joints up, he must have forearms like a gorilla, maybe he wouldn't like to see him, unless their were bars in between. He pushed firmly against his gas meter and watched the incoming flexible pipe easily take up the movement. He pictured the meter at the house but couldn't remember if that had a flexible pipe or not. He pushed against the flexible pipe, Phillips must have disturbed the joint by hitting the flexible pipe.

By the time Stevenson sat down for his evening meal he was satisfied that there was nothing fishy about Phillips' death. Just an unfortunate accident. He thought of Mrs Phillips anguished face as she had held her husband's wallet in her hand. He wondered what she was doing at that precise moment. He put a forkful of food into his mouth and smiled at his wife. "Tastes good. "

"Good day today?"

"Cleared up an accidental death. Just got the paperwork and background to check tomorrow. We found the body by tracking his mobile phone, didn't know you could do that. Anything good on tele?"

Stevenson was at his desk for seven the next morning, checking yesterday's in tray. Just routine. He started to fill out reports on Phillips' death. Phillips' office didn't answer the phone until nine twenty. This seemed to be a growing trend nowadays, he should be used to it by now but it wound him up. He had work to do. The receptionist read out the entry for six pm last Thursday. Silverall Rd/Bertrand's ? "Bertrand's, who are they?"

"Don't know Sir. I can ask around in the office for you. "

"Please. "

By the time she came back to the phone he had recalled the sign outside the house. "Could be Bertrand's the local Estate agents Sir. I can give you their number if you like. "

"Yes please, and could I make an appointment with a senior partner at your office? I need a background check.

"One moment..... . Two this afternoon, Mr Knowles?" She gave him Bertrand's number.

"Fine, thank you. "

Stevenson rang Bertrand's. They had no record of any connection with Mr Phillips and Silverall Road. The property was handled by Jonathan Milton and he was adamant that his records and memory were perfect. Milton had last shown the property on Wednesday and the locks were intact at ten thirty in the morning when he left. No point in boarding a place up and not locking up properly. Stevenson found him almost surly, but OK. So the lock had been removed some time after Wednesday morning. By whom? He made a note in his book.

Knowles was shell shocked about Phillips death. Phillips had joined the firm about seven years earlier and had progressed to junior partner. He had his file on the desk. They had been slightly concerned about taking him on because there was a query about his reasons for leaving Oxford but his references had been exceptionally strong. There had been a court case and he had subsequently had to take two weeks leave to attend the hearing. Knowles remembered that there were a few funny calls left for Phillips around that time and that Phillips had been visibly rattled over a period of months, particularly over the phone calls.

Knowles had told him off about a number of telephone calls to Oxford which weren't on the firm's business. Phillips had paid towards the cost and that had been the end of it, six years ago. No unusual problems since then, Phillips had proved to be a good steady worker, reliable. No known enemies. "Do you suspect foul play?"

"No Sir. Just routine. A sad accident. May I borrow the file?"

"I would rather give you copies. "

"If it's all right with you Sir, we prefer the originals, keeps forensic happy. You could take a copy for your own records. "

Knowles looked at the file. "No need, just as long as we get it back. "

As Stevenson drove back to the station he went through the points in his mind. Everything seemed kosher except for Phillips being at the house in the first place, and of course, the fact that he was dead. He checked his note book for Bertrand's address, see if Milton could shed any more light on it.

Milton was a very unhappy man. "Detective Stevenson. This property is coming up for auction in less than three weeks. Have you any idea of the effect a murder has on a property's value?" Bertrand's were on commission and this could cost them if word got out. Stevenson looked at him. Every inch the chinless estate agent. Expensive double breasted suit, Veltshoen shoes, obligatory floppy haircut, late twenties, crapped out at the expensive school daddy had paid for. Statutory affected accent and clipped voice...not Stevenson's cup of tea, not by a country mile. He was doing his best not to wince every time Milton opened his mouth. Pound to a piece of dog shit the family claimed a connection with the original Milton.

"Nobody is calling it a murder Sir. Looks like an unfortunate accident but we always check everything, just for our records. "

"What I want to know is how did he get in? What was a professional surveyor doing in the property without contacting us first?"

"That's precisely why I am here Sir. His diary entry mentions Silverdale Road and Bertrand's. How do you account for that. "

This jumped up Oik was beginning to annoy Milton. "I don't account for it, detective. That's your job isn't it?"

Stevenson was used to this. He was one of the new breed of graduates in the force and Joe Public, especially Toffee Nosed Joe Public generally assumed he was a Constable Plod, just like in the novels. "Yes Sir. The sooner I deal with all these loose ends the sooner we can release the property and let you get on with your business, but first, I have to finish my business. Would you rather I called back in a week or a month or two or could we deal with this now, since I'm here?" Stevenson looked him straight in the eye.

Milton pretended to look in his diary, he was in fact free for the rest of the day. "I prefer to get this over with as quickly as possible. "

"Even though you are the one handling this property is it not possible that someone else took a call from Mr Phillips and arranged a viewing in your absence. "

"No. "

"Have you checked?"

"No need, I know that to be a fact. "

"With respect Sir, anything is possible. Would you please check? Now might be a good time. " Stevenson opened the file on Phillips and proceeded to read it.

Milton's veins were standing out in his forehead but he was beginning to realise that this Oik Stevenson was not about to let the matter drop and he could easily keep the property sealed for months. "Very well, I shall ask my secretary. Janet, could you please check if anybody fielded any calls for the Silverdale Road property and arranged a viewing?…. Yes I know. Just do as I ask, will you. Detective, some of our staff will obviously be out, perhaps we can contact you?"

Stevenson had been thinking, no way Milton was going to be reliable. "Certainly. Perhaps you could send a memo to all members of staff at this office and get them to confirm in writing, that way we can be sure we haven't missed anybody. Would that be all right? I can collect the copies when they are completed. "

Milton had had enough, there was only one way forward. "I'll ring your office in a day or so, soon as it's done. "

"Take just as long as you like, Mr Milton. I'm a very patient man. " Milton knew he was being put down but couldn't think of a winning reply, so he let it pass. Round one to Stevenson, not that he had been looking for a fight but he was used to prejudice both from inside and outside the force and he knew how to deal with it. If Milton wanted to get smart he had come to the right place, he was the one in a hurry to get the police out of the house. Even so he thought, the point needed to be clarified. "I'll call in at the end of the day tomorrow if I haven't heard from you beforehand. "Milton waited until he had gone and asked Janet to see everybody personally and get their signature. Best to nip this one in the bud before the local grapevine got hold of it and they ended up with an un-saleable white elephant on their books. Ghosts were not a marketable period feature unless you were selling a castle.

Back at his office Stevenson cleared his in tray. He re-read the reference from Phillips' previous employers at Oxford City Council.

This was too good to be true. If Phillips was that good why hadn't they promoted him to chief honcho and tripled his salary? He rang the number. "Extension 311 please. "

"311"

Stevenson was irritated. He was ringing a person, not a bloody number. "Mr Elmore please. "

"He's no longer with the council. "

"Do you have a forwarding number?"

"Fraid not but it wouldn't do you any good anyway, he died last year. "

"I'm sorry to hear that. Do you mind telling me what he died of. "

"Yes I do. Who are you anyway?"

"Detective Rick Stevenson, Hounslow police. And you are?"

"John Thomas and I don't know exactly how he died, road accident, I think. Not long before Christmas. "

John Thomas, no wonder he was like a dick with a sore head. "Well thanks, anyway, John Thomas. "He put the phone down and rang Oxford CID, eventually tracking down DI James Reed who had investigated Elmore's accident. Reed had other things on his mind. "Yeah, we had a good nose around because there had been a few breather calls to the deceased before he died but no sign of any outside interference. He was a heavy smoker, must have been smoking at the time of the accident. Stupid to carry a petrol can in the front of the car, we thought he might have found it or something because his normal can was in the boot. It's all in the file. I can send you a set or it might be quicker if you check the new Database in London. That's supposed to speed all these things up. "

Stevenson had heard the horror stories about accessing the new database. "Be handy if you sent me a copy of the file, just in case. I heard Central are struggling a bit and they're a bit touchy right now. "

"Sure, on its way. What's your interest, by the way?"

"Guy called Phillips, used to work for Elmore six seven years ago. Managed to electrocute and gas himself all at the same time. Just filling in the gaps, somebody has to feed the Database. "

Reed was beginning to get interested. "Phillips receiving threats?"

"No. At least, not recently as far as I know. Got some hassle calls shortly after he left Oxford, years ago, but I don't have any details. "

"Mind sending me a copy of your files on Phillips?"

Stevenson had noticed the change in pace at the other end of the line. He was spotting more and more every day, he loved the job. "Sure, you got something on this?"

Reed was searching his memory. "Bells are ringing somewhere but I can't make the connection yet. There was a connection between Elmore and Phillips.... there was a complaint about them. " Stevenson could hear him drumming his fingers on the phone. "Rick, where do you stand on influence?" His tone was tentative.

Stevenson knew what he meant. "I don't belong to any clubs, they never helped to catch any body, except for innocent punters who got screwed by the members. "

It was all coming back to Reed. He had interviewed Elmore, Phillips and a couple of others back in ninety not long after he was made up to detective. A local contractor had accused them of forging records. Reed had found that three of them had practically made a career of it and was all set to follow it up, he even went to the council with a warrant to impound the evidence, then, his boss had ordered him off the case. It got buried by the department and he knew enough not to make waves, bad for your career, bad career move to buck The Club. He never did find out what had happened but it had left a bad taste in his mouth. "I was on a case not long after Phillips left the area, he'd done a bit of file doctoring but I was told I was too busy on other cases, never got to finish the job. In fact, the job never did get finished as far as I know. I remember Elmore and Phillips getting phone calls but didn't want to pursue a complaint, wanted it dropped. Sound familiar to you?"

"Sounds very interesting. I'll ring you again and compare notes if you like. Influence still a problem at your end?"

"No. The influence retired, early, too much of a good thing. " Having finished the call, Reed sat back in his chair. Six years was a very long time, people didn't wait that long to make their point. Anyway, Elmore had died in an accident because he thought he was Mark Thatcher and crapped out just like Thatcher did. Might be interesting to find out what the contractor had done about the forgeries, though, he hadn't struck him as the type to let go easily. He made some notes and checking the time, left for home. Another day down, late for dinner, again. The next morning Stevenson was called out at four in the morning to cover an armed warehouse robbery and he didn't even get to his office for two days. It was a coolly executed professional job, not much hope of finding anything but he had to try, always worth a try.

Friday morning Stevenson called in on Nobby Clark to collect his report on Phillips. "What do you think, Nob?"

"Fits like a glove. Phillips had received an electric shock in his right hand, his fingers were still locked tight, just like a frog's leg. Must have been trying to refit the fuse and caught the gas piping when he recoiled backwards from the shock. He actually died of gas poisoning. Post mortem didn't find much carbon monoxide in his blood so he must have been nearly finished by the shock in the first place, his heart had taken a severe beating. Quite likely that he was touching an earthed pipe when he got the shock, that would account for the severity. They estimate that he was breathing gas for only a couple of minutes before he died. It's all in here. " He handed over the report. "Satisfied with the answer?"

"I think so. Accidental death then. I'll write it up and send it on to Central, give them something to do. Thanks Nob. Anything on the warehouse job?"

"Think we might have some prints from an abandoned van. "

Super Jane had left a report on his desk. Mrs Phillips had no information on anybody who might have had a gripe against her husband, she couldn't think of anybody worth naming. Milton had had the signed sheets delivered to the station, nobody at Bertrand's knew anything. He looked at Milton's cover note, at least he was being honest when he said nobody at his office knew anything. If they were all like Milton then Stevenson had no problem believing it. He read through Elmore's file and the note from Reed. Reed had been very thorough and the file looked convincing, just another car statistic. Couple of guys who had once worked together killed in unrelated accidents a few months apart, seven years later. No big deal. He filled out his reports and completed the paper work for Central. He dropped the files in his out tray with a satisfying thump and rang Milton. "Mr Milton, you can have the house back but please avoid the under stairs cupboard until after the inquest, just in case. " Milton was grateful and thanked him effusively.

Stevenson stretched his arms up above his head, pleased with his week's work and was looking forward to a weekend off.

Reed was wrapping up for the week and he was glad to see the back of it. The file on the Council forgeries by Phillips and Elmore had gone missing and he was pissed off about it. He remembered where the contractor had lived, funny road Squtchey Lane, and was going to call in on his way home. He would then check his notes from the time, they weren't missing because he kept all his own notes filed at home.

Reed called at the house and spoke to the new owners. Joe Huszár had sold up and moved out of the area, they had no idea where he could be contacted. Huszár hadn't left a forwarding address and they had returned all his mail. Nothing personal for Huszár for over a year. If he'd moved right out of the area that probably ruled him out anyway. Reed read his notes over the weekend and reread the file on Phillips' accident on Monday. Looked like a dead end, it certainly was a dead end for Elmore and Phillips.

From his old notes Reed was reminded that he had worked with another young detective at the time who had since moved to Kidlington. He rang him on Monday morning. "Jake, James Reed, how you doing?"

Jake had liked Reed. "Good, thanks, I'm doing well over here. "

Jake had been sharp and useful. "Glad to hear it. Jake, do you remember that foreign contractor, Joe Huszár, big guy with a weird sense of humour?"

"Do I? I arrested him a year or two back for VAT and Tax fraud. He got banged up for a few months at one of the holiday camps, got the wrong judge on the day. I heard he lost his wife and buggered off back to Hungary, or was it Poland. Why?"

"Remember that case of his with all those Council forgeries? Couple of the forgers died recently in accidents, I'm just turning over a few rocks. "

"I saw about Elmore, who else died?"

"Phillips, household accident in London week or two back. "

"You can't seriously suspect Huszár? He wouldn't be that stupid. Anyway, six seven years later, no way. "

"How'd he lose his wife?"

"Car accident while he was banged up. Didn't help the appeal judge to be lenient.... . No sign that he blamed anybody if that's what you're thinking. He was very cut up about it but philosophical, didn't even get excited about the truck driver who caused the accident. It was partly the truck driver's fault, but there was no hassle from Huszár about the driver being put away even after the driver got off with only a fine. Now if the driver had a funny accident, then I'd be looking for Huszár.

"So his wife dies, it's somebody else's fault and he didn't get excited? You met him Jake, if I had just told you what you just told me, would you be surprised?"

Jake had seen and accepted Huszár's response at the time, it had seemed perfectly genuine. You knew where you stood with someone like Huszár, he delivered straight between the eyes, both barrels. "I saw him react at the time. No reaction against the driver whatsoever, no sign that he blamed someone else, just took it very hard and sorted it out with himself. "

"What happened over that case of his against the council after we got warned off?"

"He got shafted by the Club. He took the case to the high court, spraying bombs and bullets at the forgers and the arbitrator. Get this, he even had the arbitrator bang to rights for cooking his answers and hiding evidence but he eventually ran out of steam because of the costs. His solicitors were warned off by the Club and dropped him like a hot potato. "

" I heard the Club even fucked up one of his contracts for nine months just to slow him down, trumped up story over a listed building, it was in the papers. ""Word was he had a lot of the local gang members sweating cods and they were all very relieved when his company went down. He never got a chance to get his act together after we were pulled off so they got away with it in the end because he ran out of time and money. "

"How do you mean ran out of time. "

"Time barred by the high court, he had six years to follow it up. The Club were celebrating when he got banged up because he wasn't due out until after the case got time barred. "

"So the shafting wasn't complete until early last year? Until last year he might still have got justice over the forgeries? Fuck me, Jake, fuck me!"

"You're a lovely fellah James, but no thanks, you're not my type. "

"Jake, you got any notes, diaries, anything about Huszár or his cases? Anything at all?"

"Probably, I'll have a look. You really think he might be on the war-path against those forging bastards?"

"I wouldn't blame him. "

Jake cast his mind back. "If it had been up to me they're the ones that would have been shafted, not Huszár. I couldn't believe how the arbitrator let those guys off the hook until the Club choked us off as well and we joined their team like a couple of lambs. I still feel bad about that. "

"Nothing we could do to stand up against orders, was there?"

"We could have blown the whistle, but yeah, we would have been squashed and it wouldn't have helped Huszár anyway, I suppose. "

"Do you remember how cool he was when we had to tell him we were pulling off? Didn't bat an eye, didn't whinge or complain, just carried on to the High Court without our help. I wouldn't be surprised if he followed it up once he ran out of firepower through the courts, classic vigilante type. If I had crossed him like that, I wouldn't sleep easily. "

"There's one flaw, Elmore died in an accident because he drove too fast, that's what the coroner said. "

Reed doodled on a sheet. "Yeah. I looked closely at it myself at the time, it's just Phillips' dying brought up the connection. Maybe there is a God after all and he's sorting them all out for Huszár?"

"Yeah, who's going to volunteer to nurse maid the arbitrator, not me. "

"Send me what you've got anyway, will you Jake?"

Jake made a note in his diary. "Sure, you still at the Oxford shop?"

"Yeah, and thanks. Meet up for a beer soon?"

Jake liked the idea of a beer with Reed, he might learn something, Reed was definitely going places. "Give me a ring, any time. Make it soon. "

Reed carried on doodling on his pad. Elmore and Phillips dying shortly after Huszár's case expired was well worth noting. Some people never gave up and Huszár was one of those people, but murders? He filled out a request form for the Council forgeries file, might turn up. The main filing system was shit, they were always losing files. He tapped a memorandum into his computer to remind him to follow it up.

Mike Preston had been away on a computer course. Waste of his time. The training centre had been a stylish Country House but even that had become a bore. Most of the men treated the course simply as a chance for foreplay with the women on the course but Preston wasn't into that. His office seemed a great deal more interesting, he didn't feel he had learnt anything significant but at least he was two weeks further down the line. He strolled into the main office and looked over Bob Nixon's shoulder as he deftly keyed into the computer. "Miss Me?"

Nixon hadn't heard him come up and was startled but didn't miss a stroke as he carried on. "Of course Sir. " He finished the page and turned round. "We've caught up with the new area data fields, watch this. "" He punched keys until with a final flourish, he hit Enter. The computer scrolled through hundreds of names, isolated in clusters of varying size, as they shot past his eyes at what seemed like lightning speed. Nixon looked back at him. "All these clusters are connected by area, the area fields really throw up a huge amount of data. "

Preston watched the screen. Name like that, must be guilty of something, if only of murdering the English language.

"At this rate, we'll need another database to analyse the connections. How do you propose to check all those out? You're swamped with information already. " He had his training hat on. "The secret of good detective work is to sift out the important facts from the unimportant ones and put them together coherently to form a picture. Any fool can see all of the information if it's there, piecing the right bits together and coming up with the answer is what it's all about. " He turned and walked, talking over his shoulder as he went. "What you need is to have the computer pick out the juicy bits for you and clear away the dross. This looks like the same old dross, you've just got it in a different order, a different mix-up. " He thought he saw an image of Nixon's hand come up to his forehead in his door glass as he pushed it open. Dick head? He'd show them dick head. "Get onto services about my name on the door and tell them the glass is loose. "

Nixon's hand had shot back down and he caught Miles' eye across the desk. Miles had seen Preston's head respond to Nixon's image in the glass and he was keeping his nose clean, he looked pointedly back down at his key board and carried on. Nixon had already progressed the sign writer when he first came in, knowing that Preston would complain about it. "Already rung them this morning, Sir. " Nixon was not going to volunteer that services had said they would be round at the end of the week. He looked at the computer clock. Nine thirty and Preston had already pissed him off, it was going to be a long week. The last two weeks had flown by and he and Miles had made a lot of progress with the database. They had added more fields and improved the search facilities and they knew they were onto a winner, he didn't need to waste his time proving the point to dinosaurs like Preston. One of his friends had been on the course with Preston and he had said Preston was just a tourist, hadn't asked a single question. Closed mind.

Preston sat at his desk and switched on his computer. His in tray was empty, so was his out tray. "Nixon!"

Nixon came to his door. "Sir?"

"I thought I told you to do an extra copy of all my output so I could see what had been dealt with while I was away. "

"Yes, Sir. We did Sir. " Nixon was going to enjoy this and he tried to look as neutral as he could, almost succeeding but Preston was far too experienced to miss the signs.

Preston had spotted Nixon's muscles relax as he stood back onto his heels and off the balls of his feet. He had deduced that there hadn't been any output on his behalf because there hadn't been any input and Nixon was dying to tell him just that. His in tray had remained unused for the two weeks he had been away. He looked right through Nixon. "Carry on. "Nixon delayed for just enough milli-seconds to make his point and turned for the door without replying. Fuck him! Nixon would get on with the job in spite of him.

Preston sat back, pretending to study the screen. He had heard about cases like his on the sour grape vine. Sideways promotion to a non job with no work. Empty in-trays watched by good men emptied by the system, sucked bone dry by it. He cracked his knuckles in a familiar gesture. Not for him, he wasn't dead yet and he wasn't about to take this lying down. He picked up his phone and rang an internal number. "Sally? Mike Preston. Any chance of a half hour meet with the boss?"

Sally worked for Chief Inspector Cole, she checked his diary. "Thursday morning is possible if he finishes the staff assessments in time. I know he's very busy with those. Can I ring you back and confirm?"

"Sure. " Preston had forgotten it was assessment time. "Actually, Sally, it'll keep for now. I'll catch him later when he's less busy. " Not a good time to rock the boat, wait till after the annual rises.

Reed switched on his computer and waited for it to boot up. He hadn't been at his desk for almost a week. Half a dozen reminder flags popped up, including his request for the Council forgeries file. He worked through his in tray for the rest of the morning and then sat back with a sigh, knees pressed against his desk. Records had responded to his request by confirming that the file he wanted was definitely lost from the system. "Definitely lost?" He said it out loud. No such bloody thing! Records never said something was definitely lost. How could something be definitely lost unless you had seen it getting definitely lost? Reed thought about the logic of that point and was sure that his logic was irrefutable. There was no such thing as definitely lost at Records, they weren't sufficiently well organised to have definitely lost anything, apart from their arses. He tapped away with his pen, having made a decision, stood up abruptly. "Anybody wants me, I'm at records and I'll be gone until I come back. " The girls in the office knew what he meant. Anybody desperate enough to go searching at records was best advised to take supplies for at least a week. No such thing as a quick visit to records because you only went there if you had a problem with records.

"Send us a post card. " You could rely on June for a snappy reply.

The records clerk was new and didn't recognise him. "DI James Reed, Oxford. Want to check a case I dealt with back in eighty nine and ninety. " He signed in and the clerk took him to a desk.

"I think it was me who tried to look for you Sir. Funny file name, some foreigner, all ss's and zz's and a local council?"

"Huszár?"

"That's the one, couldn't find it anywhere Sir. Sent you a memo saying I would keep trying but it looked to be a lost one. "

Reed pulled out the memo. "This your memo?"

The clerk studied it carefully and handed it back. "No Sir. That's not the memo I sent. Looks like somebody picked up my memo and decided to send their own, but... . . they used my initials. "

Reed was not a detective for nothing, he smelt a rat, or was it a Club member? He had noticed the clerk's careful scrutiny. "You recognised the writing. " It wasn't a question, Reed could tell that he had recognised the writing. Good clerks were good at that.

The clerk looked surprised. Having nothing to hide he answered immediately "That form was filled in by the Deputy Chief Constable. "

"Not much point in looking for the missing file then. If the deputy chief says it's definitely lost it's definitely lost. "

"I should say so Sir. Definitely lost. " He looked embarrassed.

"Would you prefer it if this conversation had never happened?"

"I would rather, if you don't mind Sir?"

Reed looked at the clerk's identity tag. "I don't mind at all, John. Just as long as you're sure it was the Deputy Chief?"

"As you say, Sir, you don't mind at all. "

Reed understood. "One more thing, is it possible that my attendance slip could also be definitely lost?"

The clerk led the way back to his desk and picked out the slip Reed had filled in earlier, handing it over. "I never lose anything Sir, it's my job to keep track of things. " He smiled as Reed pocketed the slip and made for the door. "Anytime I can be of help, don't bother with the paperwork, just give me a ring. "

Mike Taylor turned up for the meeting feeling he was something of a stranger. He had only become a Mason because it had been made clear to him as a junior at the practice that all partners were expected to join The Club, it was good for business. When he had been put forward for membership he had realised that this would mean promotion and, sure enough, he was made up to partner shortly after he was inducted. he hadn't been to a meeting since his retirement. Peter Witts had rung him out of the blue asking him to attend this meeting. Witts had made Deputy Chief constable years ago and was stuck behind the main man, who was younger than him, and rumour had it, a lot better at his job. Taylor looked around him at the familiar but distant faces. Self serving faces, no longer interested in his face because, having retired, he was out of the game as far as they were concerned. He saw a less uninterested face approach from almost behind him. "Hello Peter. How are you?"

Witts was in a rut and was coasting to retirement. He didn't like trouble and was hoping to nip this one in the bud. "I'm fine. Just a little mutual problem that I thought I should warn you about. We'll talk after dinner, there's someone I want you to meet. He's very useful. "

Taylor didn't like mysteries and he certainly didn't like mutual problems. When somebody referred to a mutual problem what he usually meant was he was going to dump one into your lap and that it wasn't a mutual problem at all, it was all yours, they would make sure of that. He picked at his meal. These people cheese pared for a living and applied the same principle uniformly to everything they did. Having retired early, Taylor had been looking back at his life and wondered if he might have been happier doing something else. His father had bullied him into choosing a profession when he hadn't made it to university.

He had even been bullied into joining the Masons. Even as a senior partner at the practice he had been bullied into doing things against his will.

He thought back to the only time he had had serious dealings with Witts. Surely this didn't concern that Joe What's His Name and the arbitration. That was the only thing he had had in common with Witts, apart from both being Club members.

Witts had rung Taylor in just this way, back in eighty nine. Taylor had been squashed by his partners over an arbitration case against the council and he had been persuaded to ignore all the evidence of forgery and leave it for Huszár to follow it up with the police. No sense in the practice soiling its own door step when the police would set the matter right anyway. There was a lot of business on the line, the Council were one of the biggest local spenders after all, lots of business all round. Taylor had been caught napping when Huszár had issued new summonses against him and the council. He could still remember the bad taste in his mouth when Huszár, had turned up and delivered the summons in person. He remembered his panic and the panic stricken partners' meeting afterwards. Then, the partners appeared to blame him for the mess. The publicity was bad for business and under the circumstances the council could hardly give them work with the megawatt spotlight shining on all of them. He was struck dumb at the meeting and felt unable to point out that this had all resulted from the pressure they had put him under to let the council off in the first place. He had been betrayed but knew that if he raised the point they would simply pretend that the double speak conversations used to arrange such matters had either never taken place or that he had misunderstood. He was the scape goat by a unanimous vote taken in his absence. When Huszár had approached his association with his complaint Taylor had almost felt like coming clean about the whole affair but his wife had persuaded him that they would all gang up against him and he would be hung out to dry. At the time he had been relieved to find an ally in Witts. Witts had told him an anecdote after the club dinner about how the police had lost vital evidence in some court case or other and that the case had foundered. Taylor took the hint and 'lost two letters'. The missing letters gave the police the excuse they needed not to pursue the case against the council forgers. Taylor had always been particular and pedantic. Taylor knew they were forgeries, it leapt out at you from the pages. So, eventually, Taylor had been able to discount this mistake as not of his own making but he still felt bad about it every now and again. He wondered if he had his time again whether he would have the courage to stand by what he had seen and heard at the arbitration. He was honest with himself and decided he probably would have done the same, it wasn't in his nature to stick his chin out. Taylor was, after all, a surveyor and not a doer.

The meal was still repeating in Taylor's throat when Witts finally approached him with a younger man in tow.

"Mike Taylor, Dick Jacey. Dick's at the Kidlington shop. "

Taylor looked at Jacey and took an instant dislike to him. Too flash for a policeman, too cocksure. A barrow boy in a suit. Taylor looked at him expectantly. There was a silence, finally broken by Witts, who was beginning to feel uncomfortable. "Dick has his ear to the ground, Mike. Remember a problem I had a few years ago when records lost a file?" He looked at Taylor for confirmation that they were on the same wavelength. He could see from the way Taylor's jaw was ticking that they were, they had never been comfortable bed fellows. "We lost another file only a year or so ago, after a certain period had expired and, suddenly, one of our Inspectors is showing definite signs of interest. "

"Who?" Taylor could feel a cold clammy hand on his heart, familiar from the last time he was involved with this case.

"Same man who was on the case at the time. You will have seen him. "

Taylor remembered Reed turning up at his office with a warrant for his files and the subsequent disbelief in his face when he returned for the missing letters and Taylor claimed he had returned them at the time of the hearing. He could tell that the young detective knew exactly what had happened and was relieved that he didn't drag him away in a fit of anger. "I remember him. "

"Well it's him. He's looking for the file. I intercepted the paperwork and told him the file was definitely lost. "

"Definitely lost?" Taylor looked at him in surprise. "Isn't that an unusual reply?" Taylor could see why Witts' career had stalled.

Witts looked at the incredulity on Taylor's face and then at Jacey. Jacey had no problem with 'definitely lost' and his face showed it. He was definitely confused. "Well words to that effect, telling him that there was no point looking further because they were lost. " Witts was beginning to falter. He might have waved a red rag at Reed and actually attracted his attention instead of putting him off. "Anyway, thought I'd tip you off just in case he contacts you. He's got nothing to go on so need to give way on anything. "

What he means, thought Taylor, is "I know you were never happy about this, keep your mouth shut, no need for alarm" but Taylor was alarmed. "Why would he contact me?"

"Reed's a bit of a terrier, once he gets his teeth in he chews the whole bone. If he does contact you, what we would like to know is why he's interested after all this time. I understand he's very busy, so why is he spending time on this. He must have a very good reason. "

Jacey spoke for the first time. Taylor liked him even less, he had a smarmy supercilious tone to his voice. "I'll be doing a little digging myself, see what I can find out. I'm checking on some of his recent cases, give me an excuse to contact him with a query about something . "

Taylor was no detective but he had an ordered mind. Jacey was coming in half cocked and could make things worse, just as Witts had done with his ill judged memo. "Might be best just to wait rather than arouse his suspicions. He might be wondering already, any follow up would stick out like a sore thumb. "

Jacey had his thumbs in his trouser belt, no sore thumbs there. "He will never know I even asked a question. "

Taylor had heard enough. He could see why the Masons were often referred to as the Black Hand Gang. He could see how this had escalated under Witts's hand six years earlier. The man was actually stupid, how on earth did he get so high up in the force. As he walked away he had his answer, Witts strolled over to a group of influential members, he was in his element. Taylor left, disgusted with himself for ever having been part of it, vowing this was the last time he would ever come here.

Reed picked up his ringing phone. "Do you want a beer or a poke in the eye with a sharp stick?"

"If it's a beer with you Jake, I'll go for the stick. Seven tonight? Make it the Turf. " The Turf was a student pub buried in a wall behind the colleges. It was practically police proof and they had met there in the past. Jake had something important for him.

Reed spotted Jake as he came in the doorway, ducking his head under the low beams. He had already ordered two beers and took them to a corner. "Thought you should know, James, people have been asking about you. A brown nose called Dick Jacey. "

"What does he want?"

"He wants to pretend he's not asking anything but he's useless at it. His nose is all the way up the Deputy's arse and I think he's doing his leg work. What are you up to that makes him so interested?"

It crossed Reed's mind that Jake was asking the very questions that this Jacey was wanting answered but he trusted Jake and didn't hesitate. "The Deputy doctored a memo to me about the file on the Huszár case. Wrote that it was definitely lost and used the records clerk's initials. "

Jake rolled his eyes to the ceiling. Based at Kidlington, he was hearing more and more stories about Witts' incompetence. "Man's a dildo, and, his batteries have run down so far they're leaking acid. Everybody thinks he's booked for an early bath, they just need an excuse. So you think it's the Huszár case that is winding them up?"

"Could be?"

"Who was it that called us off at the time, you never did say?"

"I never knew myself. Tom just called me in one day but he was just the messenger and he didn't like it any more than I did. It came from higher up. Could have been our current deputy, maybe that's why he's still interested. "

Jake raised his nose in the air. "Fe fi fo fum, I smell the brown noses of The Club. I heard Jacey recently made it to The Club and if I remember correctly that arbitrator guy was definitely in the same gang. " He put on an imaginary glove and held up his hand. "Fits, you can't even see the join. "

They had another beer and parted company, they both had families to enjoy. Reed spent the rest of the evening at home but his mind was churning over. He would wait to see what crawled out of the woodwork.

Reed was not at all surprised a few days later to get a message from his boss asking for an activity report. For the last year or so he had simply waited for Reed's reports when he chose to present them, now he was asking. He looked in on the Chief Inspector. His name was Andrew Gosling but everybody knew him as Ducky, some joke from the past.

"Ducky, got your note. I'm burning the oil at the moment, can't it wait?"

Ducky had been given the nod to find out what Reed was up to. He didn't like the way it was done but he knew Reed was fire proof so he had decided to just ride the punch. "James, It's not me who wants to know, I'm sure you know that. Use your own judgement and produce whatever you want and whenever it suits you. Someone has a reason for asking, do you have a reason not to tell?"

"I'm watching worm holes, Ducky, I'd rather not frighten any of them into staying put. I think I know who's asking and I think I know what he's looking for. I could do a current report and still leave him guessing because the source of his problem is not one of my cases. "

"Fine, James. I don't need to know any more, do I? Let me know if you need any help. " He turned back to the file he was studying.

Reed produced his report and dropped it onto Ducky's desk on his way out to lunch. He had made no mention of Stevenson's query over Phillips and the Elmore case or of his request for the Huszár file. That should get them crawling out on all eight legs at once. He pictured a swarm of pink slimy bugs appearing from dark holes, this was beginning to be interesting.

"Inspector Reed. Detective Jacey, Kidlington. "

Reed smiled broadly to himself. It had taken a week and here was the first worm on the other end of the phone line. "Yes, detective?"

"We're trying to tighten up all our systems. I've been assigned to polish up records and I see you were let down recently over a file that's gone missing. "

Reed was not about to give anything away. "Happens all the time. They usually turn up later, if it's a problem then I follow it up. "

Jacey was looking at the follow up reminders from Reed. "Any outstanding files that are causing you problems?"

"None that I can think of, off hand. You can chalk me up as reasonably satisfied. "

Jacey was getting frustrated and couldn't contain himself any longer. "There's this file you asked for...Hussy.... Hustler? That ever turn up?"

"Now you mention it, no. I'd forgotten I asked for it, why?"

"Any particular reason why you wanted it?"

"I worked on the case at the time. " Reed thought fast. "I had made notes about some forgery techniques, wanted to freshen my memory about the techniques. Wasn't important. "

"So you're no longer looking for the file?"

"No, just a bit of homework for another case. "

Jacey didn't know when to drop it. "What sort of point were you wanting to check?"

Jesus, thought Reed. This guy is a detective? "There was a contractor involved in that case, Joe Huszár. His name cropped up recently and it reminded me of the case. There were some obvious forgeries involved and I wanted to make some comparisons with another case. Now detective, I'm a very busy man. ?"

Jacey knew he'd over-cooked it. "Sorry. Just trying to see if you wanted us to keep looking for the file or whether you were happy for us to leave it. "

"Be nice to find it but don't go to any special trouble. The case is dead, I just wanted to check some details, that's all. "

"OK, if we do find it we'll let you know. "

Reed drew a pig with wings on his pad. Witts must be very worried and Jacey knew why he was worried. He rang Jake. "Jake, James. Your mate Jacey has just been trying to pump me about that missing file. Any chance of your pumping him as to why? He's thick as a plank, he wouldn't even notice a smooth operator like you milking him dry. "

"I'll try but don't hold your breath. I think the man's an arsehole and I can't see how I could engineer a chat. I'll keep a look out for a chance."

Jake didn't have to engineer a meet because Jacey appeared at his own local a few days later. Jake saw him come in and knew straightaway it was him, he concentrated on his pint. Jacey's theatrical recognition would have done the local theatre club proud. He all but put his hands to his mouth with excitement. "Remember me? We met at the shop the other day. Pint of best and another of those, please. "

Jake wanted to pump Jacey so he wasn't playing hard to get. "Yeah. You're going places, according to those who know. Very high places."

Jacey preened himself. "Nice to hear that. Nobody tells me, just doing what needs to be done. "

"Word is you're looking for bad business, that true?"

Bad business was a euphemism for bent coppers. Jacey saw no harm in people thinking he had power. "Just doing what needs to be done. "

"Catch anybody lately?"

"Not a question of catching anybody, just steering things in a straight line. Keeping the wheels oiled. "

Jake opted for the full frontal approach, Jacey was so busy trying to ingratiate himself he might just cough. "Reed from the Oxford shop. Heard he might be in trouble? He always did stick his nose in where it wasn't wanted. "

Jacey had an ally. "Not trouble, exactly. Maybe he's poking his nose in too far, raking up old coals that are best left alone. "

"Reed and I used to be mates, want me to give him a tip? The force is too important to have one man making unnecessary waves. Job's tough enough as it is. "

"We... I was just wondering why he was into a particular case, that's all. One best left alone. " He tried to look knowing and simply looked as if he had something in his eye.

"I could do some fishing for you, if you like. What's the case?"

"Some Hungarian, Joe something or other, had quite a big barney with a local council a few years back. "

"If I can help, do I get browny points? Who would be grateful?"

This was more to Jacey's taste, he liked Jake. "The Deputy himself, and, there was a local arbitrator on the case. His trousers are pretty brown, I can tell you. They would be eternally grateful. "

"I'll get back to you, got to get home. "

Jacey reported back to Witts. "I've got a friend of Reed's who is going to nose around. It appears that Reed heard recently about a Hungarian contractor ...a Joe Huszár. That's why he wanted to look up the file but he doesn't seem too bothered about it now. "

Witts consulted the file "Reed makes no mention of seeing this Huszár in his report. " He looked up across his half moon glasses at Jacey. "Why is he lying about this? See what you can find out and report back, soon as you can. " Jacey hadn't spotted that Witts had misinterpreted "heard" and turned it into "see".

Witts rang Taylor. "Meet Pint at lunchtime, usual pub. " Taylor recognised the urgency in his voice and turned up early. He didn't normally drink much but was on his third gin. "You're late. "

Witts ordered a pint and made for a discreet table in a corner. "Our mutual friend has been making a good impression on the detective who was on the case at the time. The detective seems to have picked up the cudgel for him and is searching for the file and it looks like he's planning to be difficult. He's going to some lengths to hide the fact that he's delving into the case and that's a very bad sign for you... us...both of us. He's very good, apparently, so this could be a bit of a problem. " He looked into his glass and drained it. "For you and for me. " He stood up picking Taylor's glass up as he went to the bar. "Same again. " Taylor looked as if he needed it and Witts knew he needed it.

Taylor measured his words carefully when Witts had rejoined him.

"You've probably guessed that I feel a measure of sympathy for this contractor and that I am uncomfortable about the whole affair. "Witts nodded. "I really do not want this hanging over my head any longer and would like the matter closed. "Taylor stared at Witts. "Once and for all. My view is that it was the council cover up that led to all this and I lay the blame entirely at their and at your door, it was your combined actions that precipitated the problem. "

" If this continues to be a problem then, if asked, I am minded to clear the decks properly and salve my conscience by openly declaring what happened. It is entirely up to you what action you take but I consider this to be your problem and your friends' problem. As of this moment, I wash my hands of it. " He stood up. "I have already had too much to drink, thank you. Good bye. " Taylor went for the door.

Witts ordered another drink. "Jesus Christ! What a bloody mess!" Taylor's new found conscience was going to be an insurmountable obstacle. He knew Taylor was profoundly religious and he had obviously made up his mind, or, in effect, Taylor's God had made up his mind for him. The success rate for getting between a religious man and his God was not very high, especially when the religious man knew you were lying through your teeth. Taylor was at the end of his tether and Witts could see no way out, he would have to eliminate this problem at source.

The next day Ducky called Reed into his office. Reed could see that Ducky, unusually for him, was wound up like a tempered spring. "James, the Deputy has just finished bashing my ears about you over this Huszár case. He wants you to drop all enquiries that are in any way connected with Huszár. " He looked out the window and then at Reed. "Sir, Council employees forged a lot of paperwork and Huszár provided us with the evidence. The arbitrator connived with the cover up. We had them all bang to rights but we were warned off the case...by The Club. The Deputy interfered with the files and forged a memorandum to cover it up. There are a couple of recent accidental deaths that might even be related to this case. It's a real crock of shit, Sir. "

Ducky didn't like the Club and his career had suffered for it. He had been passed over more than once, losing out to inadequates like Witts. "Carry on, James. But be careful, or they'll nail us instead. "

"Thank you, Sir. " No question but that they were on the same side and he rated Ducky highly, was beginning to understand why Ducky hadn't made it – he'd been shafted for refusing to join the Club.

Ducky immediately rang Witts. "Peter. I've had a word with Reed and he tells me that he has evidence that your department has interfered with files. He also tells me that he is investigating the possibility that a couple of recent, so called, accidental deaths may be connected to this case. " There was silence at the other end of the line. "Peter, your wanting Reed to drop this, is that an order?"

"Murder? Eh, no, obviously not, under the circumstances. "Witts slammed the phone down. "Shit! Shit! Shit!" He called Jacey. "If there's any chance of pinning anything on Huszár, do it!

Jacey called in on Reed who was on the phone. From his arrogant manner and the timing, Reed guessed this must be Jacey. He cradled the phone and looked directly at Jacey, raising an eyebrow.

"I'm Dick Jacey. The Deputy has asked me to look into the Huszár case. " Reed just continued to stare at him. "So...would you mind if I had a look at what you've got?"

"Check with records, they're the ones that lost the file. "

"It was the accidental deaths that the Deputy was interested in. "

"Doubt if you will get anywhere, it was accidental deaths involving council personnel named in the Huszár case. The only connection was that they used to work for the council. Been cleared by the coroner. "

"I want to see the files. "

"Sure. If you wait I'll get copies made right away. " Reed pulled out the Elmore and Phillips files and took them out to June to copy. "Quick as you can, June. I want the prat out of my office. "

"Reed, this missing file thing. Might be wise to forget it. "

June came in with the copies. Reed's eyes moved towards Jacey and June handed them over. Jacey looked at her, at Reed and at the files in his hand. "If that's how you want it?" Jacey walked out.

Reed looked at June. "Makes you proud to be in the force, doesn't it?"

"Just you watch your behind with these people. "

"June, I'd much rather watch yours. Why don't you ditch your husband and run away with me?"

"Because you're already married and Sue is my best friend. "

"Excuses. "

CLEAR THE TABLE

Jacey returned to his office. Bloody queer name József K Huszár. Shouldn't be at all difficult to find. He spent the morning on the computer and came up with only one Huszár in the whole of England. Zsofi Huszár, a London number. According to his police records, this must be one of his daughters. He rang and left a message on the answer phone for Zsofi to contact him.

"Hi crim! The police are after you again. What have you done this time?"

I was used to being called a crim by my girls, it was a compliment. "Tell them I was abroad at the time. "

"No, really. A detective left a message for you to ring an Oxford number...Richard Jacey. Sounded like a pleb. "

"Well, all coppers are. " My mind was racing. "Any indication as to what he wanted?"

"No, that was it. He wasn't very comfortable talking to the machine, all umms and ahhs. Took him two goes to leave the message. "

"I'll give him a ring. Might be coming up soon Zsof. How do you feel about meeting Magda?

Zsofi hesitated for a second. "Whatever is good for you is good for us dad. " She had discussed Magda with Zsu. "Just...it's upsetting..."

"Promise me you'll say. You and Zsu are the most important people in the world for me, ahead of Magda. "

"It's serious, isn't it?"

"Depends on you and Zsu. Zsu's coming round to meet her this weekend. She's promised to tell me what she really thinks. "

"I know, dad. So will I. Don't be put out if I'm upset though. I miss mum. "

"So do I Zsof. Pencil me in for the weekend after next. Lub you. "

I booted up the computer and added Jacey to the phonebook. "Detective Jacey!"

"Yes?"

"Joe Huszár. You left a message with my daughter. "

Jacey had expected to have to speak to Zsofi first. He wasn't ready for this powerful cultured English voice. Thought the bugger was supposed to be Hungarian. What was it with the accent? "Eh, yeah. You're Huszár then. "

"All my life. What can I do for you?"

"Just routine inquiries. I would like to meet up with you, go over a few points. "

Time to take the initiative, make the pleb spill what he knew, wouldn't take long. "You realise I live in Budapest?"

"What! Budapest, in Hungary?"

"Let me just check out the window. Yeah, I can see the Danube, so must be Budapest, in Hungary. What's this about?"

Jacey hadn't intended to let on, keep the suspect under pressure, but he'd lost the initiative. "Concerns your case against the Council. "

"Really? Time ran out on that case and I dropped it. What exactly did you want to know, perhaps I can deal with this by phone and FAX?"

"Well. I'd rather we met up. Can you come to Oxford?"

"You kidding? I'd need a bloody good reason to come all the way from Budapest to Oxford to talk about a case that is out of time and dropped. Give me the full story and I'll think about it, but I still can't see why we can't deal with this at long range. " I just did not believe that this call was about the Council case. The stutterings and fartings from Jacey confirmed that. Jacey had a hidden agenda and I had a good idea as to what it was. Jacey was fishing, someone had made a connection between Elmore, Phillips and Budge and someone capable of making those connections was more than capable of connecting them to me. Fuck! Fuck! Fuck!Held my hand out in front of my face, surprised at how steady it was.

Jacey's brain had stalled. "Well, actually, it concerns two accidental deaths. Elmore and Phillips, you accused them of forging a few years back. Just a few details before we close the files. "

"Elmore and Phillips, dead. Fucking great, serves the buggers right. How did they die?" So they hadn't connected Budge with the other two. I relaxed, but only a little, Elmore and Phillips was bad enough.

"Car accident and…. electrocution and gassing. "

"Sounds good to me, my compliments to the chef. They were a pair of arseholes. Put that in your files, that's "arseholes", one word and

111

there's an r in it. People often misspell it by making it into two words or they miss the r out. " I measured a four second pause. "Why are you ringing me about this?"

"Well, you had cause to bear a grudge against both of them. "

"Not according to the cops, I didn't. They dropped the case, told me at the time that I was paranoid. Now you're telling me I did have cause to bear a grudge. Why, exactly, what's changed your mind?"

"Your daughter lives in London, you must have visited her. "

"Of course. "

"When?"

"When did B…. Elmore and Phillips die?" I had nearly said Budge

Jacey was concentrating on not giving anything away and missed the slip. "Can you prove when you were in Hungary and when you were in Britain?

"What you mean is can I prove I was not in Britain when those bastards died. "

"I suppose so. "

"When did they die?" I was guilty then I would know when they died, if I was innocent then Jacey's trying to pin me down was a waste of time. Either way, there was no point in Jacey holding out on the dates.

"I'm asking you when were you in England?"

Jacey was a dummy. "How far back are we talking about, hours, days, weeks, months, years, millennia?

Jacey was getting very frustrated, suspects were supposed to be respectful to the police, especially detectives. "Months. Where were you over the last four months, say. "

"I was in Budapest most of the time but I probably made a couple of trips to England…. I don't keep track… I don't keep a diary, I live on my own and I go when and where I please. I don't have a clue exactly when, where or how I made trips to England and I don't have the time or the inclination to trawl through scrappy bits of paper to find out. How could I prove I wasn't in England at the time those bastards died any way? For all I know, maybe I was. Jacey couldn't tell if I was just being arrogant, or evasive. "It is in your interest to co-operate, it can only go against you if you don't. "

The moment had come for me to hand back the hot potato. "Tell you what, Jacey, I work from home and I make regular phone calls. Check my phone calls with the phone company and get back to me if I'm not covered for the dates you're interested in. I'll FAX the details. And Jacey, we'll both save a lot of time if you just tell it to me straight. All this pussy footing around doesn't impress me and I can hear your brain grinding away even on this long distance line. Now make my day, tell me exactly how Elmore and Phillips died. Was it excruciatingly painful?"

I opened a file, deadbastards. doc and typed in all the details Jacey had given me covering Elmore and Phillips. The cops obviously didn't have anything concrete to go on otherwise they would have come armed with a warrant, assuming they had jurisdiction in Hungary? From Jacey's phrasing someone had made the grudge connection with the council case because I had accused the two of them of forging. Dead right, but they had nothing else to go on. Even if they had evidence of foul play they couldn't pin it on me. At the very worst they might have a weak circumstantial case. My phone records should pour cold water on their desires. One thing, Jacey was certainly a dummy and he sounded very green and inexperienced, the police couldn't be taking it too seriously otherwise they would put a heavyweight onto it. It was only possible murders they were looking at, after all, nothing concrete.

Witts was apoplectic and Jacey was visibly cowering in front of his desk. "So, there is a possibility that this Huszár character is going round killing council employees that upset him a few years ago and you just ring him up and tell him he's a suspect?"

"Actually Sir, he rang me, Sir. "

"He rang you? Why?"

"I left a message for him to ring me, Sir. "

Witts smacked his forehead with his palm. Jacey was a serious mistake, and he was now a full Club member, on his recommendation. He gave him a withering look. "So, has he been killing these people?"

"I'm trying to find out, Sir. I've FAXed the phone people in Hungary for his phone records. He claims he lives in Hungary most of the time now, just visits England when it suits him. "

"What about these two deaths? Are they murders?"

"Both coroners passed them as accidents, Sir. No suspicious circumstances but, this Huszár guy Sir, he fancies himself as a real smart cookie. Got all the chat, didn't seem at all put out when I told him he was a suspect. "

"Maybe that's because he knows he's innocent, Jacey, have you thought of that? What else are you doing, what else are you screwing up?" Jesus, thought Witts, you tell Jacey to stitch someone up and the next minute the klutz believes they are guilty.

"He has a mobile phone line with Vodaphone, Sir. They can track his phone when it's switched on and he's definitely in Hungary right now. Vodaphone have instructions to let us know if he makes a move, especially if he comes close to England. "

Witts hadn't realised this was possible, he was impressed. "OK, keep me informed. We'll see about his phone records when they turn up. "Witts skimmed through the report sheet Jacey had given him and the FAX from Huszár. This Huszár was a smart arse, he had headed the FAX Dick Tracey, Detective Expectorate.

Almost funny. He toyed with the pages for some minutes and picked up his phone to ring Taylor. "Mike, I have some positive news. Our mutual problem now lives abroad and I've got men pressurising him as a suspect for the murder of Elmore and Phillips. "

Taylor couldn't believe his ears. "What did you say?"

Witts could tell from Taylor's voice that this call was a mistake, he had wanted to reassure Taylor, not upset him. "I have men pressurising our friend about the deaths of two of those council people. That should send him back into his box, he'll be too scared to co-operate with Reed and Reed will run out of steam. End of problem. "

"Are you saying he could have murdered two people connected with the case? What about me? What if he decides to come for me? I can't feel safe with people like Jacey (and Witts, he thought to himself) handling this case. I'm a sitting duck. "

This was getting out of hand. "We don't have any evidence that he did anything, we're checking out his alibi right now. I'm just saying that this should frighten him off and Reed will drop it. "

Taylor was shaking with fear. "I am not prepared to take this sort of risk. If there's any chance at all that he murdered anybody I want him dealt with and out of harm's way. In fact, even if he hasn't murdered anybody, what's to stop him starting, with me? Your actions must have brought all this to the forefront of his mind. You might well have awakened a sleeping monster with your crass actions. "

Witts was getting annoyed. Who the hell was Taylor to tell him he was crass. "Calm down Mike, we know what we are doing. We can trace his whereabouts at all times and if he comes within a hundred miles of here we'll let you know. You can go holiday in that cottage of yours that you're so proud about. "

Taylor was sceptical. "How can you possibly track him?"

"His mobile phone, the service provider can tell us exactly where he is at all times. " Witts sounded sure of his facts.

It didn't occur to either of them that Huszár might travel without his phone, rendering the tracking facility useless. Nobody travelled without their mobile nowadays, unless they had another one to play with?

Taylor put the phone down, pleased that he was ex-directory and that he had moved a few miles from his old address just before he had retired. He had forgotten that his number was still the same as at his last house and that he had only gone ex-directory after he moved.

I was in a very good mood. Zsu had approved of Magda, Magda had approved of Zsu, I approved of both of them. Magda was sitting beside me in the Jag as we approached Calais, she was nervous in spite of the fact that things had gone so well with number two daughter. Number one daughters were famous for never letting their mothers go, this was a much more daunting hurdle and Magda was clasping and unclasping her hands as I was trying to ring Zsofi on his mobile. The signal was marginal, I had never been able to phone as reliably on the digital handset as he had on his original analogue one in spite of the in car booster he had fitted. Still, the analogue phone would not have worked on the continent at all. After five abortive attempts he got through to Zsofi at the BBC. "Hi, prawn, we're running a little late probably get to your flat about eightish. Eat for ninish, fancy a takeaway?"

"I'll let them know dad. Dad..... I'm nervous. "

"Join the club prawn. You spoke to Zsu, she's happy. "

"That makes it worse, all the responsibility is on me. What if we don't get on, then it's all my fault. "

"Prawn, I trust your judgement. If you have a problem then I would want to know about it. I want a third opinion and you get the job. Just be yourself, you're nothing like as nervous as Magda, she's chewed a hole in the dash just while we've been talking. "

"She can hear you?"

"Of course, no secrets here. I'll ring again when we hit the road at Folkestone, fix the time for dinner. How's Andrew? I bet he's nervous as well. "

"That's the other thing, what if you and Andrew don't get on?"

"Then Andrew can run off with Magda. " I laughed loudly at my bad joke. "Tell Andrew to wear brown trousers, just in case. "

Magda had followed most of the conversation from my half of it. "Zsofi is nervous as me?"

"Yes, nervous as you, Magda. " I touched her hand to reassure her. We both knew we loved each other but neither of us had actually said so because of the girls. Magda had readily understood that if she was to join my family it had to include the girls, even though they had their own lives. . "Zsofi will probably be upset over Lesley's memory so be prepared for that, it won't mean she doesn't like you. If you are not sure of what she thinks, ask her point blank. "

"Point blank?

"Ask her anything you like and she will give you a straight answer. Point blank means straight between the eyes. "

"Straight between the eyes?" She laughed. I had been relieved to find that Magda had a good sense of humour, most of the Hungarians I had met were a dour lot. The only jokes they understood were childish anti communist jokes rooted in junior playground humour. A sense of humour had always been one of Lesley's tests with new acquaintances. No humour, no progress on the friendship front. I looked sideways at Magda and thought what a lucky bastard I am. Two good women in one lifetime, I am a very lucky bastard. Magda caught my look and blushed like a seventeen year old.

We sailed through customs with my English passport and they hardly glanced at Magda's. Rang Zsofi as I got onto the M20. "We'll easily make eight, see you then. "

The huge engine was purring along at less than three thousand revs, maybe seventy five miles an hour when I saw a police car do a frantic start on an over head bridge, billows of smoke from the tyres. I pointed it out to Magda. "They've had a call and they're after someone. " About four minutes later they were practically in my boot, lights flashing, siren blaring. They were after me!

"Do you mind closing the door and waiting in the car Sir?" I had pulled over and had made to get out the car. The other cop was talking on the radio, looking pointedly at my car. They both came over to my side of the car. "Step out of the car. József Huszár, you're under arrest. "

"What for?"

"You'll be informed at the station, Sir. " I looked at Magda in the car. If you come with me to the squad car, Sir, my partner can drive your car if your…wife wishes. "

I looked at Magda, she nodded. "She wishes. May I use my phone?"

"All in good time at the station, Sir. It's only fifteen minutes away.

I rang Zsofi from Ashford police station and waited with Magda in an interview room. We were given tea but no explanation, the cops appeared to be waiting for someone. We had waited less than an hour when there was a flurry of activity outside the door. Dick Jacey came sweeping in, loving every second. "Detective Jacey. . József Huszár? He'd been practising all the way in the car. Jacey had been informed the day before by Vodaphone that Huszár was on the move and had stopped at Frankfurt for the night. They had tracked Huszár across France and then it was just a question of ferry or Chunnel. Jacey had set off from Oxford as soon as he knew it was Chunnel and here he was.

I looked at my watch. "You were quick, all the way from Oxford?"

Jacey was prepared and he wasn't about to give his secret away. "Your fancy car was spotted at Calais, I wanted to speak to you. "

"You need only have asked. I assumed you were satisfied by my phone records. So I'm not actually under arrest, am I?"

"Arrest, no. What made you think that?"

"The policeman said I was under arrest. "

"Misunderstanding. Difficult over the radio. They were just looking out for your car. "

"On your instructions?"

Jacey realised he was losing control. This tall Hungarian bastard had an authority and a bearing about him that he found daunting, even though Huszár was sitting down. "Nobody instructed that you should be arrested. I just wanted to arrange an appointment in Oxford, seeing as you're in the country. "

"Thursday, ten thirty at the Oxford police station. " I stood up and taking Magda's arm walked to the door. I stopped and turned back. "Who's your boss?"

"I answer to The deputy Chief Constable, Peter Witts. "

"Where can I contact him?"

"Kidlington, same number as mine. Make it the Kidlington station on Thursday, that's where I'm based. "

"I'll speak to him early next week. No doubt he'll inform you if there's any change in our appointment. " Sonny! I thought, and strode away to my car.

Magda had hardly batted an eye. The Hungarian police were far less polite than the English police. I explained that I had sued the council in an old case and there was a bit of muck raking going on because some of the forgers were worried. I wasn't sure why but they were trying to discourage me even though I had dropped everything more than a year ago. I wondered, if they were so worried, maybe they were vulnerable. I still had a score to settle with Taylor. Nailing Taylor would be sweet, very sweet. The pompous self opinionated prat! Lucky I had kept the files in store with my furniture. I was going to sort that out this trip, Zsofi could have whichever pieces she wanted and I would send the rest to Hungary, if things were going to work out with Magda. I turned and smiled at Magda, it looked like a very small if. She smiled back, encouraged by my good mood.

We turned up at Zsofi's and she had the takeaway warming in the oven. Andrew was very pleasant, obviously besotted with her. I liked him and was optimistic it would work out for them. Andrew couldn't take his eyes off Zsofi.

After a stilted start because they were both so nervous, Zsofi and Magda were getting on like a house on fire. The Pálinka had helped to loosen everybody up.

After a couple of hours Andrew and Magda were swapping jokes. We were a family, it was as if we had all known each other for years. There was a slight hitch, Zsofi had assumed that Magda and I would be sleeping together and she was embarrassed because she and Andrew were. I got the couch. I hadn't thought about it but I was pleased that Zsofi would feel more able to express any reservations since my relationship with Magda had obviously not been consummated. We all slept soundly.

I woke first and delivered coffees in bed. Magda was radiant, she liked Zsofi and she liked Andrew. Zsofi leapt out of bed and joined me in the kitchen, talking ten to the dozen about breakfast. "Zsofi. " Her head snapped round. "He's terrific, we both like him. "

She hugged me. "We both like Magda, dad…. and I'm not so upset over mum. She would be pleased for you. " Tears welled in her eyes and my eyes filled just as fast as we hugged each other.

"Thanks, prawn. I love you, and I will always love mum. "

"I know. "

Took my coffee in to Magda and sat down on the bed. She burst into tears as I took her in my arms and told her I loved her.

"I loved you from the first minute I saw you. " She kissed me wetly on the lips and we held each other until Zsofi called out breakfast!.

Breakfast was even merrier than the previous evening and we celebrated with a Pálinka toast, or three. Andrew was a car and Hi Fi and computer freak, perfect, the son I had never had. Just perfect!

Monday. Zsofi and Andrew had gone off to work and I was going to show Magda bits of London, but first, I rang Deputy Chief Constable Witts.

"Constable Witts, I have a complaint to make about your trainee detective Jacey. "

Witts felt intimidated by Huszár's booming delivery but he was not going to rise to the bait. Constable? Trainee detective? Who the fuck did this foreign bastard think he was talking to? Witts had learnt that in these situations the less you said the more you learnt.

"Yes?"

"Jacey organised my arrest on a pretext when I came back into the country and then claimed it was all a misunderstanding. I believe it was police harassment and I would like an explanation. What exactly is your department's interest in me and why is Jacey wanting to hound me?"

"I am sure, Mr…. . Huszár that detective Jacey is not wanting to hound you. He is a very good detective and is simply carrying out routine investigations. My advice to you is to answer his questions as best you can and there will be no further misunderstandings. "

"What case is he on, and, am I a suspect?"

"I leave those sort of details for my men to sort out. Detective Jacey is tying up some loose ends over a couple of accidental deaths, I suggest you go through these points with him. "

"Jacey's a bit green to take on this sort of responsibility, isn't he? He's traffic cop material. "

Witts was stung by my remark. He was beginning to get regular feed-back about Jacey's lack of finesse and inexperience and was feeling defensive about it because everybody saw Jacey as his protege. "Detective Inspector Reed is also on the case. "

Huszár recognised Reed's name from the forgeries case and guessed that it could be the same man. "So should I be seeing Jacey or the Organ Grinder when I come up to Oxford on Thursday?"

Witts knew Huszár must be getting at Jacey but he didn't understand the joke. "No need whatsoever to see Detective Inspector Reed. "

I detected the tightening in Witts' voice and the "whatsoever" had a strained note to it. Witts didn't want Huszár seeing Reed. "OK. I'll see Jacey and if I find him unreasonable you'll hear all about it. " I cut the connection and redialled the Kidlington number. "Detective Inspector Reed, please. '"DI Reed. "

"József Huszár, we may have met some seven years ago?"

"We did. I remember your case. In fact I was trying to check the file only a short while ago. "

"Trying?"

"It's been mis-filed and hasn't turned up yet. "

"Anything I can help with? I still have the all original paperwork

Reed was trying to keep it low key. "Wouldn't do any harm if it's convenient for you, where are your files?"

"I'm coming to Oxford on Thursday to see Jacey, I'll drop off a set of copies for you. Where's your office?"

"I'm still at the Oxford station, near the courts. "

"I'll drop them in Thursday afternoon. Are you likely to be in?"

Reed looked at his desk diary. "Try and make it after four. I'll get a message to you if I can't make it. "

"Ring my mobile, it's 0836 473 473. I'll look forward to seeing you

Reed made a note in his diary. Thursday 4 pm. JH. This time he would not be pulled off the job and he wasn't going to give anything away to the enemy until he was full and ready. There was too much at stake. He trusted Ducky but even Ducky would be on a need to know basis. He would sort this out with Jake just like they should have done seven years ago, never too late.

Reed rang Huszár on his mobile. "DI Reed. Would save me a lot of work if you could let me have two sets of the paperwork. Can you manage that?"

I was surprised at the request, didn't the cops have copiers? "Sure, I'll bring two sets on Thursday and I'll hand them to you personally. " I had guessed that Reed's request involved internal politics otherwise he would run off the extra set in house.

Reed rang Jake. "Jake, any chance of a meet in my office next Thursday after four?"

Reed's economy of words told Jake he didn't want to enlarge on it. "Sure. Deal me in. "

It was forty years since I had first seen London as a kid and I had lived there and been there many times since. Now my home was abroad and with Magda's fresh eyes it all seemed fresh and new again. I had forgotten what a wonderful capital it was, in the same league as Budapest.

I turned up Thursday morning, on time to see Jacey and was kept waiting for forty minutes. Pathetic ploy, used by inadequates. My self confidence grew with every passing minute and Jacey's position drained away with every passing minute. Jacey's delaying tactics showed he had nothing in his hand, he was bluffing and, probably trying to get his own back for the last time we met. Eventually, a young policewoman came to collect me and delivered me to Jacey's office. Jacey made a big show of being fully occupied at his desk. "Ah, yes, Mr Huszár. "

"I take it constable Witts had a word with you about my call?"

"Deputy Chief Constable. We have spoken to each other, of course. " Jacey pointed to the office across the hall.

Next door, all the more handy to clean his boots, thought Huszár. "Fire away then, Jacey, I assume you have a list of questions?"

Jacey looked at his prompt list on his desk. "Well, yes, I have. You know that Colin Elmore and Dave Phillips both died recently? Apparently you crossed with them some years ago over some contract with the local council. " He tried to look menacing as he looked up from his paperwork and stared at Huszár. "Do you bear them a grudge?"

"Since they're dead, bore a grudge would be grammatically more appropriate than bear a grudge. And, yes, I did bear a grudge. "Fifteen love. "I don't give a shit about those guys, alive or dead. I was pretty mad at the time. If they had been caught in my headlights I wouldn't have swerved to miss them, but I wouldn't have aimed to hit them.

They're nothing to me now, just dried dog shit on my shoe, ex dog shit now. "

"It's just that there were a few unanswered questions about their deaths. " Jacey was fishing, hoping for a slip or at the very least he wanted to scare Huszár off. "

"Such as?"

Jacey read from his notes. "Phillips was a metick…meticulous surveyor. He died trying to replace a mains fuse in a house he was surveying. "

I smiled, the jerk-off definitely had an empty hand and he was low on chips as well. "I bet ninety per cent of deaths from electrical shock are qualified electricians. It's like the argument that most accidents occur in the home so homes are dangerous. If everybody spent less time at home, then less accidents would occur in the home. So Phillips died whilst he was working as a surveyor. The fucker was a surveyor. Very suspicious Watson, don't you think?" Thirty love.

"Elmore died in a car accident and was burnt alive in his car seat. He had an extra petrol can in the front   as well as one in the boot. Questions were asked. "

"And?"

"There is no satisfactory explanation for the extra can. "

"And?"

"The question is, did a third party place it there?"

"And?"

"We don't know. "

"Snap! Neither do I. "

Jacey had been studying Huszár's response and he seemed to be taking this as a joke, no signs at all that he was getting rattled. "I have your MATAV telephone records, they turned up two days ago. "

"Do they confirm that I was at home at the times of the accidents, or not?"

Jacey passed the sheets across the desk. There were two periods of several days highlighted with a fluorescent pen. "See for yourself. "

I looked at the sheets and recognised the numbers in the marked sections as the calls made by the computer MailBox. "I take it the highlighted sections cover the periods when the bozos died?.... So can I take it you're not about to cuff me and slap me around?"

"They would seem to, yes. Assuming that the calls were made by you and not by someone else in your flat. " Jacey was trying to sound matter of fact as he delivered what he thought could be a bomb shell. I was ready for this one. "I make most of my calls via my computer. If my computer records confirm that the calls were made by me, would that help?"Forty love and match point.

"Are you saying that you have computer records that match these logged calls and that they prove that you made the call?"

"I'm saying that most of my calls are logged by my computer and if I made the call via the computer it will have a record of the time, date and a recording of the call. If these marked calls are logged and my computer confirms the time and date then the voice recording will confirm that it was me making the call. I was leapt over the net, throwing my racket in the air. Game set and the championship, to Huszár!

"I suppose if your computer proves these calls were made by you then you can't have been in England at the same time. "

"I'll eMail my WinFax computer records to you next week, on one condition…. . . . . . that you give me your eMail address. " I stood up.

"Eh, one or two more questions, if you don't mind. "

I sat down. Jacey was using some very old movie tricks. What did he think I had to hide now, illicit duty frees?

"Shoot. " But not until you see the whites of their thighs.

"You're seeing my colleagues at Oxford today?" Jacey was still fishing.

"DI Reed. It's about the case concerning Elmore and Phillips. "

Jacey had been told about Reed's "JH" diary entry and he had guessed right. "What exactly does Reed want from you?"

"Don't know, you'll have to ask him yourself. " Jacey obviously had a problem asking Reed direct and I was more than happy to have Jacey sweat, no freebies, everything had to be paid for with cash, up front. I glanced through the list of calls and spotted the lone call to Spain. Shit! "Can I take these? The Hungarians don't provide them for customers yet. To save time you could copy the two sheets you're interested in. " I handed over the two sheets. "Or, you can copy all…ten odd sheets if you like. " I held them up trying to make them seem voluminous.

Jacey took the two sheets, he'd had enough. "I'll keep these two sheets, evidence. " He placed them back in the file and closed it, feeling that at least he had won on that point. "If your computer bears them out as your calls then you can have them, later. "

"Fine. Are we done?"

Jacey was feigning busy with another file on his desk. "Yes. My secretary will show you out. "

As soon as Huszár had left Jacey wnet to see Witts. "Reed is definitely up to something with Huszár. They're meeting up this afternoon about that case with Taylor. "

Witts had put his glasses down. "Find out what they're up to. Without the file, Reed can't get very far. Find out if Huszár is feeding him anything useful. " He pulled out a cloth and started polishing the lenses. Taylor would go bananas, best to keep it quiet for now. "Taylor doesn't need to know about this, yet. "

"Sir. " Jacey liked being in Witts confidence. This was important work. He rang June at Reed's office and asked her to keep an eye on things that afternoon.

I had been in two minds about the Oxford visit with Magda but I had decided that it would be ridiculous to avoid taking her to see what was effectively my family's home town, in spite of the memories. Magda was family now. We had stopped briefly outside the house and it hadn't been as painful as I had expected. It still looked denuded and vulnerable to my eyes but this had turned out to be a help, it was no longer my house and the garden proved it. Just a house. It was the girls and Magda that counted, and Lesley's memory. We lunched at Brown's. I had made a point of never having been to Brown's in the almost twenty years it had been established in Oxford. Brown's was amazingly popular and it was the norm to see queues going round the corner in all weathers. I had often passed the queues on my way to the Indian in Walton Street and shouted out to the queues that the food was crap and not worth queuing for. The food was fine but I still couldn't see what all the fuss was about. Another poseurs paradise. Been there, done that, pissed on it. I stopped off for a pee before we left. I could add Brown's to my CV in the section, "So What"?

We walked around a few colleges until four and turned up at the police station and asked for Reed. Jake came down to see us and usher us in. "DI Jake Heal. We've met before. "

I remembered him as one of the officers that had arrested me over the VAT fraud. "You came to arrest me. "

Jake looked troubled. "I was sorry to hear about your wife. "

"Thanks. So was I. This is Magda Pesti, a very good friend. "

Jake showed Huszár up to Reed's office and explained that Reed would be a little late. "What is this about?"

"It's about a forgery case from a while back. " "You were the other detective with Reed at the time, weren't you?"

Jake had wondered if Huszár had recognised him at the time of his arrest. He stroked his prematurely thinning hair. "Long time ago, but I remember it very well. We were sorry to drop it at the time. James and I were looking forward to issuing a few more warrants. "

"I suspected the Black Hand Gang. "

Jake grinned. "The Club. " He winked. "The Club is a little out of favour nowadays." Jake realised his enthusiasm was getting out of hand. "Best if James fills you in, I'm just here for the ride. "

They waited for Reed who finally turned up, breathless, after five. "Sorry to keep you waiting. Jake filled you in?" No sign of any files?

Huszár saw the question in his face. "Two sets of files in the boot of my car. Didn't fancy carting ten box files around Oxford, people might mistake me for an academic. "

Reed was relieved, for a moment he thought Huszár might have been pushed into reneging. "We can collect them later. "

Intrigued and also needed to clear some points in my mind. "What livened this up, it's practically history?"

Reed had been wondering how much to tell Huszár and since bull at a gate Jacey was involved there seemed not much point in holding anything back. Huszár probably had most of it pieced together. He told Huszár about Rick Stevenson's query and the connection between the two deaths and Huszár and the case, watching for a reaction. He got none that he could see.

"Jacey has checked my phone records in Budapest with the times of the deaths and they prove that I was in Hungary at the time of the deaths. I'll be sending him my computer records which should satisfy him that I actually made the calls. I can send you a copy of my computer records direct, if you like?"

"No need. " Reed was an experienced detective. He could tell when somebody had something on their conscience and Huszár's conscience was clear. He wasn't to know that when it came to avenging Lesley, Huszár had found his own God. "Well, since you're in the clear, what we really want is to follow up the forgeries. The file Jake and I set up has gone AWOL so your files will be invaluable. This may be what we need to weed out a few people who shouldn't be where they are in the force. "

"Half Witts?"

Reed and Jake couldn't help laughing. . "And one or two of his friends."

I couldn't believe my ears. "His friends. You mean Fucking Taylor?"

"I believe it's Mike Taylor. Is that a Hungarian pronunciation?"

"Last time I saw you guys I was still working on the case, piecing it together. I think I can show he also forged stuff and cooked his figures deliberately. "It came back to me in vivid Technicolor. "Forty nine out of forty nine errors, all in the council's favour. All cooked by Taylor. " I was getting excited as June came into the office.

June had a sheet of paper in her hand. "Sorry to interrupt James. Possible meeting tomorrow afternoon, you free?" She looked down pointedly at the diary on his desk.

Reed looked at the empty page for the next day. "Yes. " His face clouded slightly as he turned back to me and he hesitated until June had left the room, leaving the door ajar.

I had seen the signs so I said, loudly. "I had the file all set out ready for the case but then I was so pissed off when time ran out that I trashed the lot. "

Reed looked down at his diary at the appointment for today. That was why he had wondered about June. She looked after his diary and knew it better than he did. He had just come in and she would have checked his diary already that day. She had no need to ask him what was in it, she could have told him. He thought further, maybe not, he might have made arrangements during the day. But, she had looked down at his diary, knowing that the diary at least, thought he was free for tomorrow. Jacey knew of his appointment with Huszár. How? Apart from the diary entry he hadn't mentioned it to anybody other than Jake.

Jake had been reading the scene like a book. "Haven't spoken to Jacey since last week, James. "

Huszár leant over and whispered. "Jacey knew of our meeting and was trying to pump me. I have the complete set of paperwork tying it all together. I was going to hit them with it in the High Court, you can finish the job for me. "

Reed nodded and spoke quietly. "Jake, we get a set of files each. Now you know why. "

Huszár was impressed at the obvious rapport between the two detectives. Lucky they were on my side. "I'll keep the master set safe, in case anymore sets go AWOL. My car's parked outside Oxford University Press in Jericho, one of you should come with a car and collect the goodies. White XJ, a Mark 1, you can't miss it. "

"Thank you, Mr Huszár. I'll be in touch. "

"It's Huszár, or Joe. My mobile number is in the file. "

Magda had followed the conversation and as an outsider had seen most of the undercurrents. "Is this work dangerous for their futures?"

I was amused at her literal translation of the Hungarian phrasing. "Yes, dangerous, but not physically. The English are very polite about these things, nobody does anything serious but treachery and back stabbing is allowed. One of the big chiefs has obviously passed his sell by date. "

"Sell by date?"

"He's no longer useful, maybe because he's gone too far up the ladder for his competence level. It's the Peter Principle. " I looked at her. She knew that these in phrases were my idea of a harmless joke at her expense but it was her turn to tease me. "Even in Hungary, we have heard of the Peter Principle, smart man."

"What does it mean?"

She poked me hard in the ribs. "I do not knaw." I had guessed, I was getting to know her better and better each day.

We waited in the car until Jake turned up and took the ten boxes of evidence away in his car. I was very excited at the prospect of finishing the case after all. I looked at my watch, it was after seven, may as well spend the night in Oxford. "Let's stay in Oxford for the night. We'll have an Indian and get drunk, I feel like celebrating. "

"Maybe, maybe no. "Magda's smile said YES!

I had eMailed my computer records to Jacey, knowing that they would leave Jacey with no option but to drop the enquiry. Magda had effectively moved in with me and I showed her how to attach files to eMails.

I had asked if she minded Lesley's picture on the computer desktop and she had very firmly said that I should keep Lesley's picture and brought in a photograph of her husband the next day for the mantelpiece to endorse the point.

WHO SPLIT THE WINE?

Spending more and more of my time working with the computer and I was aware that all the times and dates in the computer records were in fact very easy to forge. You just told the computer whatever time and date you fancied, recorded or logged your actions and then reset the time and date, the computer believed you. The computer then had a faithful record of your actions, back dated, back timed, untraceable, as long as you didn't miss anything. Soon, the integrity of computer records would not be worth the paper they weren't printed on.

True to his word, Jacey posted copies of the retained MATAV telephone records almost by return of post. He had discussed this with Witts and they had decided it better to let sleeping Hungarians lie. The more you prodded Huszár the harder he pushed back. Maybe if they stopped prodding he would go back to sleep and the whole thing would blow over.

Witts rang Taylor. "We've decided to let it drop with our mutual friend. He's got a new girl friend back in Hungary, he'll soon forget all about this little matter. "

"Is this why DI Reed has been trying to contact me?" Reed had left a message with Taylor's son.

"Reed? He's contacting you? What for?"

Taylor was unhappy, again. "You tell me. He's the one who had his teeth into this at the time, isn't he?"

No point in lying, thought Witts. "Yes, he is..... I'll get back to you. Leave this with me and don't answer Reed's calls. By the way, Huszár destroyed his files so you're in the clear with Reed. He has nothing to work on. "

"I'll wait till I hear from you. " Taylor put the phone down. This was getting out of hand. Taylor had done some checking of his own, Reed had a powerful reputation and Taylor's records at the office were still intact. Now they were the only surviving records. He hadn't dared interfere with them whilst he was there because the case was still lodged at the court. It was still with the court when he retired.

Taylor rang his old office and spoke to his one time secretary. "Sandy, Mike Taylor. I'm missing some records that should still be in the computer or in the files. I'd like to come in and get copies. "

"Certainly, Mr Taylor. Come in anytime. Every desk has a computer now so we have spare stations even if everybody is in. "Computer access used to be a nightmare in Taylor's time. Computer time had taken on the mantle of a key to the executive washroom, there had been a rigid pecking order that wasn't based on merit or need. "Maybe later today?"

Taylor sat down at his desk and turned his computer on. There were no problem files in his home computer, he just wanted to practice what he was going to do, his computer experience was limited to basic word processing and he relied on his son to sort out any glitches on his home computer. He had never been at ease with the more complicated programmes or the file systems. The only file that really meant anything to him was one you could hold in your hand and put in a filing cabinet. He tried, half heartedly, to find his way round the computer file system. He was going to need a little help from Sandy, but, Sandy was straight as dye and had shown signs of being suspicious back in eighty nine. She had never said anything but he knew she was not happy.

Sandy didn't look over the moon when he turned up. Nothing he could put his finger on, theirs had always been a relatively formal relationship, maybe he was being paranoid. She set him up at a desk with a screen and what seemed to him to be a minuscule computer. He looked around, they were all the same. She smiled. "These are all just work stations on the network. The actual computer and all the real works are in the old copy room. All of the firms records are centralised in there. Here let me open up your file system. " She deftly struck a few keys across his left shoulder and opened up a directory. "All the files you were ever concerned with should be here, in alphabetical order. " She looked at him for a response in case he wanted help to find a specific file. "Any files more than four years old are copied into the computer and the papers destroyed, we're going paperless, eventually. Some of the later files may be part in the computer and part in filing. "

"Thank you, Sandy. I think I can manage." He hadn't intended it to come out like that but from the look she gave him she felt she had just been dismissed. He cursed silently to himself and tried to smile, making it even worse. He wasn't very good at this, the pressure was beginning to make him sweat. It was a while since he had been so aware of sweating under pressure as he used to in the days before he retired.

Taylor struggled at random for half an hour and eventually got a feel for the system, finding the file he wanted and opening it. There were all the records that he had so painstakingly cooked at the time. He had never expected to have them challenged, Huszár was just a builder after all, his fancy degree not-with-standing. Taylor had been caught out by Huszár's facility for figures and by his tenacity. Huszár was like one of those south American animals that locked its jaws, once locked it didn't let go, even when it was dead. He had no answer to his allegations, because he hadn't allowed for any questions. You weren't supposed to challenge an arbitrator. Taylor was getting angry at the thought that this upstart should have challenged his decision and caused him such difficulties.

All forty nine errors Taylor had made had been in the council's favour. He looked at the damning letter from Huszár. The odds against forty nine honest consecutive errors, all of them in one of only two possible directions, were a billion billion to one (Taylor tried to do a mental calculation but it was beyond him, was it really that much? Forty nine consecutive heads on the toss of a coin—a billion billion to one?) Or, according to Huszár, the odds could be accounted for if Taylor was a crooked arbitrator. He was acutely aware that he was sweating more freely as he read the exchange of letters. It looked far worse than he had remembered it to be. It looked irrefutable, he could tell, he was an experienced arbitrator. How had he ever convinced himself that this pathetic attempt would work. He remembered the conversation with Witts at the club. "Just do it Mike. Nobody will ever check into it. This will finish him and he'll be too busy fighting off creditors and summonses to look into it. He's only a builder, what are you scared of? Don't forget the rail station contract is coming up. "

It was the rail station contract that had motivated Taylor's partners who had also joined in the argument. Later, Huszár had created such a fuss that the council hadn't dared to give them the contract after all. It had all been for nothing. Satisfied that this was the file he closed it and selected it for deletion in File Manager. He couldn't believe his eyes,

This is an Archive File. .

Password to delete…………. .

Taylor was sweating rivers and could feel his shirt getting sodden all over. Password? He hadn't thought of that. He stared, unseeing, for several minutes. Sandy had keyed in a password when she had opened up the computer. Sandy was the most senior secretary there, maybe her password would be good enough, maybe it wouldn't? He switched the work station off, letting out a groan as he did so for Sandy to hear. He switched it back on and waited till the screen demanded the password, Sandy was on the phone he could hear her talking. He stood up and walked over to her desk. Sandy excused herself and covered the phone, Taylor still had the irritating habit of assuming that his time was more important than anyone else's. Sandy was making a private call and felt guilty about it even though it was none of his business. "Sandy. I'm afraid I've been a silly ass and switched off by mistake, I don't want to interrupt your call. " He paused long enough to let her know he knew it was a private call. "I need the password. " He tried to say the last sentence with just the right balance of apology and authority.

Sandy looked at him. Nobody really took this password thing seriously anyway. It was more trouble than it was worth. "Ydnas. "

Taylor looked bemused. "Sandy backwards?" He nodded his thanks and returned to the desk. He breathed a deep sigh when the computer accepted the password as authority to delete the file. He pretended to carry on at the computer until the end of the afternoon and then left it for Sandy to shut down the work station.

Sandy waited till he had gone and went to the computer. She searched for amended files in his directory. No amendments that day and he hadn't copied anything to disk, she had been watching. And yet, he had looked visibly relieved shortly after he had the password. She opened the Recycle Bin, there it was. She took a floppy disk out of a drawer and, checking that the file was small enough to fit onto the disk, she tried to copy it onto the floppy. The programme would only allow her to cut the file out of the Recycle Bin, which would mean losing the confirmation that it had been deleted that day. She thought for a moment and decided to leave it where it was. The system backup tapes would have the file anyway so Taylor's visit had been a serious mistake, he'd shown his hand and all he had achieved was to attract attention to himself and leave evidence that he was interfering with evidence. She had known he must be up to something. She had never liked Taylor, he was too full of his self importance, especially after he had become an arbitrator. He had thought it was confirmation that he was, after all, very bright. One of the elite he had failed to join when he flunked out at school. "Not bright enough to know how a computer manages its files, Sweaty!" She said out loud as she pushed the drawer home with a flourish. "Not as bright as you think. "

She waltzed down the stairs. Today had been a good day, Sweaty was in trouble again and this time he wasn't going to get away with it.

Reed had been trying to catch Taylor for over a week without success. Ducky had fielded a query from Jacey about what he was up to and Reed was stalling on his reply. He'd like to keep Taylor under as much pressure as he could. He remembered back to Taylor's breaking out in that god awful sweat when he and Jake had seen him in his office. It had been embarrassing. Apart from the smell of fear emanating so strongly from him he had made such a meal of mopping himself with all those tissues and missing the bin as he threw them away. Reed had been particularly disappointed that he was called off before he could call back again and nail him. Taylor had pretended he had to attend a meeting with his partners and fobbed him off. He pictured Taylor exiting his office and sidling into an adjacent office.

"Office! Taylor's office records!" Reed looked at his watch, not yet four. "See you tomorrow June. " He was at Sandy's desk by ten past.

"DI Reed...Sandy?" He was looking at her name board.

She remembered him from the last time he was there, six years earlier. She remembered the look on his face as Taylor had ducked into the next office. "Yes. How can I help you?"

He saw the recognition in her eyes, he had quite fancied her when he had last called. Had wondered about asking her out. "You may recall I was here on a case six years ago, it involved an ex partner. Any chance of checking some of his files, please?"

She motioned him over to her side of the desk and opened the Recycle Bin in the computer. The file that Taylor had thought was gone forever was still there. She pointed at the screen under the section, date deleted. "Mr Taylor called here that day and asked for my password. " She turned round to face him. "You need the password to delete files. "

Reed smiled broadly, he had missed a chance when he hadn't asked her out all those years ago. Sandy was a star. He looked at the wedding ring on her finger and fingered the ring on his own finger. "You know, Sandy, I rather fancied you last time I was here. Missed my chance, somebody beat me to it. "

She positively glowed as she retrieved a floppy disk from her drawer and went to copy the file to it. "Consolation prize, detective. Take the file on this disk, and yes, I can confirm the details of Mr Taylor's visit. "

Reed caught her wrist before she could confirm the copy. "Wait a minute. I've tried this before. Copy it and you lose the deletion evidence. Any chance of getting a print out of the screen first?"

"Easy. She pressed **Print Screen** and then opened up a new Word document. A picture of the screen had been pasted into the document. She saved the document to the floppy and then copied the deleted file to the floppy. She saved the new file under a password in her own directory.

Reed was impressed, he hadn't known you could do that. "Thanks a lot, Sandy. " He looked around, nobody appeared to have been aware of his visit. "Don't get into trouble over it, but if possible, I haven't been here. "

She winked. "Anything is possible detective. I never volunteer anything and nobody will think of asking. " She remembered Huszár's regular calls at the office and Taylor's agitated state at the time. "Is this good news for that tall Hungarian man, the angry one, I felt sorry for him. "

"He might just crack a smile when he hears about this. "

"Good. "

Reed could hardly contain his excitement. Taylor couldn't have picked a worse thing to do. And for nothing! The silly sod would be sick when he realised that he hadn't succeeded in losing the evidence and that Reed had it. He patted the disk in his pocket, he would check it this evening at home and file a spare copy with the files Huszár had given him. Reed called in on Ducky first thing in the morning, shutting the door behind him. Ducky looked up, knowing the significance of the shut door. "Spill it. "

"I've got Taylor interfering with evidence at his practice, in the last week. I have a witness and I have computer records confirming what he tried to do. The evidence he tried to lose looks pretty good for us, very bad for him. "Ducky gave a low whistle. "Any direct connection yet with any other Club members?"

"Not yet. "

"It would be nice if you could get it. Any ideas?"

"Not really. You?"

Ducky had an idea but it was too early. "We'll see. I take it Taylor doesn't know about this yet?"

"No. "

"About time you told him. I'd like him rattled sufficiently to give our friend upstairs a hard time. Hard enough for our friend to ring me and perhaps let a few things slip out. "

Reed made for the door. Ducky had another idea. "I think I'll go see Witts right away. He's been avoiding me for over a week. "

Reed loaded up the disk into his computer and printed out three copies of some pages, working from a list he had made the night before. He collected the pages, three sets of eleven. He weighed them in his hand, but worth their weight in Semtex. He formed a picture in his mind, these eleven pages plus Huszár's originals, plus Huszár as a witness…Witts and his cronies looked dejected in the corner of his picture. "That'll do nicely, SIR. " He wasn't thinking of American Express.

Reed dropped off a set of pages for Jake, leaving them in his desk and then drove on to Taylor's house. He parked a few houses away, out of sight of Taylor's windows and walked up to the front door. He was surprised. He had expected it to have some style, Taylor had done quite well for himself, but it was just a large characterless box on a characterless estate. Suits you Sir. The door was answered by Mrs Taylor. "Michael, a Detective Inspector Reed to see you. " She had practically bawled it out to somewhere at the back of the house. Taylor appeared over a minute later.

Reed watched him as he came along the hall. He looked like shit! The years had not been kind since Reed had last seen him and he looked as if he hadn't slept. Pressure getting to him. Bloody good. "Mr Taylor. You haven't returned my calls. "

Taylor didn't want his wife to witness any of this. "This way please, Detective Inspector." He led him to his study and shut the door. "Please sit down. "

Reed sat in the chair and looked around him. Plasticy desk and shelves, looked like MFI. Not in the same class as the furniture at Taylor's old practice. Taylor was tight, Reed wouldn't give fifty quid for the contents of the entire room, even the computer was an old 386 war horse, obviously salvaged for free from his office. The screen was tiny and the red gun had failed, giving it a green tint to match Taylor's face. The wall behind Taylor's head had a graduation photograph of his son and a pair of certificates, he was a fellow of a couple of self serving associations. No certificate for the Club on his wall, no silly apron or trowel. Taylor spotted him looking so Reed turned away to pick up his briefcase, noting the threadbare carpet. Even tighter than he first thought. The car on the drive had a recent plate and it was a big Rover, albeit with the smallest available engine. Everybody could see the car but not the tacky carpet in his tacky office. Taylor was a red hat and no knickers man. Reed recalled the natty suit Taylor used to wear at his office and compared it to the shapeless cardigan, baggy trousers and two day old shirt Taylor had on. "I'm sort of picking up where I left off, Mr Taylor. I've had some difficulty because the police file appears to....... be definitely lost. " He looked for a response.

Taylor remembered Witts' crass note only too well and was already starting to sweat in earnest. Reed's measured pause had made it very clear that he knew what was going on. How much did he know?

"What do you want with me?" He had been unable to disguise the irritation he felt at being pursued by this upstart.

Reed pulled the printout of the computer screen "This sheet mean anything to you, Mr Taylor?"

Taylor looked at the print out. Recycle Bin

Name   HussOxfd. Doc   Date Deleted   14. 8. 96 4. 15pm

"I don't recognise the nomenclature. Is it some sort of computer coding?"

Reed was going to enjoy this. "That's the date when you called into your old offices. " He pointed at the date on the sheet. "That's the file you deleted and that's the time you deleted it. "

Taylor reached for a tissue and mopped his brow. "No, I did no such thing. I was looking for some of my files on the computer and I inadvertently switched it off. This must have been one of my files and it got lost when the computer crashed. "

"Mr Taylor. There is only one way this particular file could possibly have appeared in this Recycle Bin on the fourteenth of this month at four fifteen in the afternoon. It required a password to be entered and a fixed sequence of keyboard strokes and mouse actions to put it there. You were at the keyboard at that precise moment and you had the password needed to make the deletion. "

Taylor was recovering his composure. The file was gone and Reed wasn't going to get anywhere without any hard evidence. Witts was right, he was in the clear if he kept his head. "If my actions inadvertently led to a file being deleted, then I am sorry. I am not very familiar with computers, let alone the new system at my old office. Was the file important?"

Reed pulled out the rest of the pages he had printed from the file earlier and put them on the desk. "Have you seen these papers before, Mr Taylor?"

Taylor took the sheets and leafed through them. He recognised them as coming from his file. Some of the sheets contained unique notes of his that had never been published. He leafed through them again. None of them contained his signature or his initials, no direct evidence to link him with the sheets. "It's so long ago, I really can't be sure. These are just figures, they don't seem familiar." He pushed the papers back.

Reed ignored the papers. "Take another look, something might come back to you. "Taylor could feel Reed's eyes boring into the top of his head as he went through the pretence of studying the pages, the pages that had been burned into his brain for years, the pages that had been responsible for ruining his peace of mind. He raised his head and started to shake it as Reed pointed to the print out of the computer screen across the desk. "As you say, Mr Taylor, you are not very familiar with computers. That screen print out and a witness proves you tried to delete the file that contained these sheets. " He paused while Taylor registered that he had said 'tried', seeing his neck muscles tighten another notch and the colour of his green sweaty face gradually blanche. Taylor didn't dare raise his eyes in case the fear in them showed. "The file has been recovered and its full contents are damning evidence that you interfered with documents and perverted the course of justice. I shall shortly be submitting a report asking that you be indicted for these offences. I shall also be obtaining a statement from Joe Huszár to corroborate all of this. Do you have anything you wish to say?"

Taylor kept his eyes on the sheets and said, almost inaudibly. "I never wanted this. "

Reed waited for him to say more and after a long wait. "Do you have anything else you wish to say, Mr Taylor?"

Taylor pulled himself together and pushing the sheets back at Reed, said, "You are trying to catch me out on matters that occurred six years ago and I tell you that I do not remember any of the details you have referred to. The files and records at my old office have been available for any number of people to tamper with in the eighteen months since I retired. Their credibility as evidence of what I may or may not have done at the time of the Huszár case is nil. "Taylor stood up. "This interview is ended. Please see yourself out and if you wish to see me in the future you must make a formal appointment and I shall arrange for my legal representative to attend. "

Reed left the papers on the desk and closing his case made for the door. "I take it you will be available at all times."

He left without waiting for a reply that he knew would not be forthcoming. Reed was disappointed, he had hoped Taylor would give more away. He was right about the evidence in the computer. Without more evidence the second generation computer images probably would not be enough. Lucky he had Huszár and his original files, but, Reed was not as supremely confident as he had been earlier. If Taylor stuck to his guns he might get away with it.

Taylor picked up the phone and rang Witts as soon as he heard his front door shut. Witts was out but his secretary gave him his mobile number. "Peter! That man Reed has been round unannounced and he has my file with everything in it. You said you would deal with this. "

Witts was in a car with three of his men, they were off to an inter regional meeting which, from recent experience, was not going to be pleasant for them. The young Turks from adjoining regions were impatient with the lack of progress in inter department communications, particularly via the new computer database. The Chief had put Witts in charge of this and his hand picked team were almost as incompetent as he was. He turned to Jacey and mouthed, Taylor. "We're on our way to a conference and it is difficult to talk right now. Could we meet up tonight at the Club, around nine?"

"You'd better have some positive proposals for me, Peter!"

"I'll bring Jacey and we'll put the matter in hand straight away. " Witts turned to Jacey. "You heard that? Nine at the club. " Jacey nodded. Another top notch high powered meeting with the people that mattered, and, he was in a position to help them out. They would be suitably grateful and his career would benefit. Bad news for Taylor and Witts was good news for Dick Jacey.

Taylor turned up at the club in a taxi. He had finished the gin at his house and needed more, so he was over an hour early. There were a few new faces that were unfamiliar but it was mostly the same old faces. It seemed to be a very busy night. He ordered a double gin and sat at his old table. By the time Witts turned up with Jacey, his speech, had he had anybody to speak to, would have been slurred. He didn't have any body to speak to because everybody seemed to him to be studiously avoiding his gaze. It was as if they had decided that he was no longer one of them, he felt like a leper.

Witts had had a very embarrassing day. His lack of feel for the project and his staff's lack of motivation about it had shown them up badly. A number of the areas were already effectively cutting them out of the project because they were holding them up. It would get worse before it got better. Witts was going to have to replace at least two of his team and one of them should be Jacey but he couldn't afford to do that. He would replace one man but recruit two new members, inject some fresh blood and momentum. He would keep Jacey busy with other, more serious, problems. Taylor, the leaking balloon. He was getting tired of having to pump him up all the time. "What's yours Mike?"

"Large gin and tonic. " Taylor looked very tired and very emotional. Witts sent Jacey to the bar to fetch the drinks on his tab. "Mike, you shouldn't let this get to you. It will run out of steam soon enough, we just have to sit tight until it blows over. Reed hasn't got enough to make anything stick. You mark my words, we'll be celebrating by Christmas. "

"Just like we did when we thought Huszár had dropped it?"

Taylor's voice had been too loud and Witts looked around, nobody was paying any attention. "Mike, no names. Mutual friends might hear you. "

Taylor was getting into his stride and carried on at ninety decibels. "Our mutual friend, both our mutual friends, have got their hands on my files and are working in cahoots with each other to make a very good case. I'm warning you, Peter, I will not carry this can alone. "

People were beginning to turn their heads and this was getting uncomfortable. "Mike, lets go talk in the car. " Taylor picked up the drink Jacey had brought and followed them to their car. Witts motioned Jacey to the front and sat sideways in the back, looking pityingly at Taylor. "What exactly have they got, Mike?"

"Reed has my file from the office. I tried to destroy the computer file but he managed to recover it in some way and he has evidence that I tried to destroy it. " Taylor grasped Witts arm. "He can even prove exactly what time and what day I did it. " His voice had risen an octave and he was close to tears.

Jesus H Christ, thought Witts. He extricated his arm from Taylor's grip and tried to sound reassuring. "One six year old computer file, two years after you retired, what's that worth? Nothing! Just keep yourself together man and face them out of it. "

Taylor was anything but reassured, Witts didn't sound as if he was convinced. "I'll be struck off by the association, both associations. "

Witts couldn't get excited about Taylor being struck off by any one, the fool was retired anyway. "Nobody is going to get struck off, just keep your mouth shut and deny everything. You can't remember a thing!"

"I'll take you down with me, Peter Witts, Deputy Chief Constable. You were the one who ordered me to do this and you'll pay for it. "

Witts did see. He caught Jacey's eyes in the rear view mirror, could see the whites rolling. He was going to get nowhere talking to Taylor in this state. "Drive us to Mike's house Dick. We're dropping you off home Mike. You can collect your car tomorrow when you're sober. "

Witts discussed their problems with Jacey until the small hours and then Jacey dropped him off. They would continue in the morning. Witts would have to get hold of Ducky and sort this out once and for all.

Ducky was in his office and June put Witts' call through. Ducky was ready, he watched the tape start to roll. "Morning, Peter. "

"Andrew, I owe you an apology. " Ducky was not going to make this easy and just waited. "This Huszár case that Reed is working on. There are some important people who think it would be much better if this wasn't pursued. "

Ducky paused, he had rehearsed his answer. "I'd like to help Peter, but, it's a little too personal for Reed. You see he was the one called off this at the time and he didn't like it then and would like it even less now. In fact he probably won't wear it a second time. He has some very powerful evidence that the arbitrator connived at some very serious forgeries at the time and has interfered with evidence as recently as last week. I know Reed, push him too hard this time and he is quite capable of taking this above all our heads. He's the best man I have and he's not the green rookie he was six years ago, he just doesn't take no for an answer. That's why he's such a good detective. "

"Can't you bring him round? Offer him promotion?"

"Not sure you could buy him off so easily. He knows he's good, everybody knows he's good. He knows he'll get there on merit without help from your Club.... Peter, why are you so concerned about this one? The main target has retired and is nothing to do with the force. I know he's a friend of yours but do you really want to stick your neck out so far for him. Why not let him go down after all, since he's already retired there's not much on the line for him, or anybody else for that matter?"

"Andrew, if you can help, in any way, I shall personally be very grateful.... . If the man gets into trouble over this, any trouble at all, he'll try to take everybody down with him. He blames me, Andrew. "

"Can he make it serious for you, Peter?"

"Mud sticks. He was doing us a favour at the time and I was the one who persuaded him to do it. He was pushed into it at the time and has got cold feet since. In his mind I forced him to go ahead. "

"Is he saying that he trashed Huszár on your instructions?"

"Effectively, yes. "

"Was it on your instructions?"

"I wouldn't use the word instructions. I simply said people would be grateful if the forgeries aspect of the case wasn't made out. "

"You know that Reed is satisfied that the forgeries are made out and that Taylor was a party to it?"

Witts hadn't appreciated that it was so cut and dried. "What, he's got proof that the arbitrator forged evidence in a case he was handling?"

"Powerful evidence together with Huszár's testimony, yes. Huszár makes a very convincing witness. With Huszár's files and his statement together with the arbitrator's interfering with evidence, it would be very difficult for any one to stop this, you must see that. "

Witts had had June's feedback that Huszár had destroyed his files. "Huszár still has files?"

"Of course Huszár has files, he'll be bringing them with him. "

Witts was trying to piece all this together. "So Reed needs Huszár and his files to be sure of finishing the case. "

"Huszár and his files are central to the case. From what Reed tells me Huszár is on a mission to prove all this and even if we could persuade Reed it would be impossible to turn Huszár. This is really Huszár's baby and Reed has joined him because he has his own axe to grind. "

"Reed doesn't like The Club and neither do I, Peter. "

LEFTOVERS

Mike Preston was reading through the minutes of the regional meeting. Information 2000. It was 1996, who was responsible for such a corny title? Some wet behind the ears whizz kid? Preston had been at the meeting and the minutes had it about right. This was a very half hearted exercise and most of the regions were going through the motions. Only two of them were even properly on line with the new database and even those two had only made a handful of enquiries. Preston had a database stuffed full of goodies, according to Nixon and Miles, and nobody gave a toss. He dropped the minutes into his out tray. Cole had asked to see him, he was obviously not impressed with progress. He called out through his closed door. "Come in, both of you. "

They exchanged glances as they got up from their desks and went into his office. Preston sounded like he was even less happy than usual. "Sir?" Preston waved his arm, they sat down.

"Seen the minutes?" They nodded. "I'm seeing the boss this afternoon and he is going to want to know why nobody is taking advantage of our wonderful multi million pound system. " He looked at Nixon. "I don't need another chewing over like last time, give me some good ideas, give me good news so I can keep him off my back. "

"Sir. It's obvious, people don't know what the system is capable of. The publicity in the police rag and the memos to the heads of departments.... nobody takes any notice. I've spoken to a quite a few detectives, clearing up points on their case memos. They see us as extra work, extra forms to fill and they don't realise we can give them back a lot more than they put in. Most of them don't even know that they can access us from their own computer stations. They think we're some special facility that they have to contact separately. They just don't know we're on line and running. It's sickening, Sir. " Nixon was getting angry. It really pissed him off at how reactionary the detectives out in the field were.

Preston had had the same impression at the meeting. "We need ideas on how to get this across, suggestions? Give me something positive. "

Nixon and Miles had been discussing this very point. Miles spoke up. "Sir, we have to take it to them. We have to get leads out of the database and hand it over on a silver plate to the detectives on the job. "

Preston scratched his chin. "Might do more harm than good. You know what a bunch of prima donnas these detectives are, nobody tells them how to do their job…. And, a handful of duff leads could kill our reputation overnight. "

Miles could see he had a point. "Could still work, Sir. We dig out a lead and ring the detective on the case. Chat him up and point him at the lead, let him think he found it for himself…he tailed off…something on those lines, Sir. " Suddenly it didn't sound so easy.

Preston was warming to the idea. He liked the personal touch, that's how the best detective work was done. That's how he liked to work, eye ball to eye ball so you could smell their sweat in your nostrils, see the damp patch spread under their armpits as you cracked them wide open, just like an egg. A bloody computer was no good at interviewing a suspect or digging up evidence, or scaring the crap out of an inter-viewee, it didn't know when to shout at him. "So, detective on a case sends in his case memo to us. We find a new line and ring him up, spoon feed it to him, very gently so he doesn't gag on it? Well? What are you waiting for? Get on with it then." They scurried out of his of-fice. Preston had his proposal for the Chief inspector, and he liked the idea. Preston could even see this working, at least it would buy him some peace. He'd had enough hassle for one career and he didn't get a buzz out of it like he used to in the old days when he liked being has-sled, liked the surge of adrenaline coursing through his heart. Truth was, he'd had enough,

PERI-BLOODY-OD!

Martin Cole was, in turn, having to answer to his boss and he didn't want to get it in the neck either. Three million was a lot of money. "Think you might have something there, Mike. We just haven't sold the service. We need a good high profile case, solved with the comput-er, put us right on the map where those provincial plods can't miss it. Find that case and milk it for all it's worth. Get us a two pager in the Gazette. " Martin Cole would also live to fight, or at least sit at his desk, for another day.

Witts had been briefed by Jacey and had worked through Reed's Huszár file for himself. "Your opinion, Dick?"

"Taylor's file is a bit light weight on its own, Sir. Huszár could stone-wall it if he kept his act together. All depends on what Huszár has in the form of hard evidence and how good a witness he would make. Trouble is…will Taylor stand up to him? He's giving a pretty good impression of someone who's lost it. I think he's about to bottle out.

Given half a chance he would have told the whole Club about it the other night. " Jacey's mouth distorted in disgust at Taylor, he was the enemy. No longer worth his place at The Club.

"I'm afraid you're right. We can no longer rely on Mike to hold his end up. " All we can do is try and stop Huszár and his files. " He passed the file back to Jacey. "This isn't strong enough on its own, we could block this as long as Reed doesn't come up with any more material. " Jacey looked at him questioningly. "Huszár is due to come back into the country to make his statement, find out when. Hungary has developed some Western problems since the Russians left, organised crime, prostitution, drugs.... It would be most unfortunate if Huszár was arrested for bringing drugs in, he wouldn't be much use to Reed with a drugs charge hanging over him. " He wrote a name and number on a sheet of paper and gave it to Jacey. "Use my name. "

Jacey thought it was Christmas. He was in, big time! "My pleasure, Sir. "

St Stephen's day. I had tracked down an antique ring at a local dealers, a semi-precious stone in a beautiful intricate setting. I had surreptitiously borrowed one of Magda's rings and a jeweller had adjusted the size to match. I knew Lesley would have liked the ring and hoped Magda would like it too. I took it out of its box for the thirtieth time that day. It was a brilliant ring and Magda would like it.... but that wasn't the issue.

Since we declared our love for each other in London our relationship had remained platonic. I wasn't ready. Even though the girls had both approved without any apparent reservations it was still too soon. It felt like I was closing a door on Lesley and no matter how I looked at it, it felt like a betrayal. Magda had taken her cue from me and the matter had not been discussed since, although I knew that she was more than a little hurt, I could see it in her eyes. Magda had reminded me on Sunday that Tuesday was St Stephen's day and that we had a dinner date planned. I had been plucking up the courage to broach the subject myself and was wrong footed, my momentary hesitation had not passed Magda by. She looked at me questioningly but tried to disguise it. I had kissed her on the cheek saying that I had not forgotten and was looking forward to it. She was cooking for a meal at eight. I had been away till late the day before so I had not seen her since then. It was three. I stalled for more time and opened the ring box for the thirty first time, placing the opened box alongside the computer key board. I needed approval.

I rang Zsofi at work and explained the pre arranged dinner date and my dilemma. What did she think? Zsofi told me to stop messing about and go ahead. She and Zsu both liked Magda and wanted us to be happy together. Zsu said the same thing, in her own way, when I rang her. They had both been wondering at the delay and had discussed it. Having decided not to raise the subject directly with me they had been waiting anxiously for my call.

I touched the key board and the computer woke up from its sleep. Poured myself a stiff Pálinka and sat watching the screen until six. Picked up a picture of Magda with her husband and a photograph album from the shelves. I removed the picture and scanned it with my latest toy, a colour scanner. Leafing through the album I picked out photographs of Lesley with the girls, a recent picture of me with Magda and scanned them into the computer. By seven I had finished my new desk top, it included images of all of us pasted into a single picture. Magda was not replacing Lesley, Magda and her husband were joining my family. When the time came I would add the girls' husbands to the picture. Raised my glass to the screen. "Hi family. I love you all. I shall always love you, Lesley. "

Knocked almost tentatively on Magda's door at seven thirty. I had bathed and changed and felt as if I was sixteen again, calling on my first serious girl friend. Magda came to the door and opened it after seven pounding beats of my heart. My heart beats were echoing round the entire landing as I realised that I had forgotten the ring, it was still by the computer. "Pardon me, I've forgotten something. " Went back to my flat and took the ring from its box. Magda was still waiting patiently in the doorway. Pecked her on the lips. "Sorry. I haven't been so nervous since before I was married. "

Her smile lit up her face and, to my eyes, the entire hallway. "Neither have I. " She kissed me back and we clung to each other. "Shall I get the Tokaj?" Overcome and, unable to trust my voice, I nodded. She brought the vintage bottle to me together with delicate antique glasses I hadn't noticed before. Taking her hands in mine I asked her to marry me. With tears in both our eyes she said yes and put on the ring I had brought. We toasted our future and went to bed.

In the morning I woke late. I couldn't remember when I had last slept so soundly. Magda was awake next to me but had her eyes closed. I took a deep breath, God she was beautiful! I cupped her face in my hands and kissed her on both cheeks. "I love you. " She opened her eyes and kissed me full on the lips.

We mooned around the city for the next two weeks like star struck lovers. It really was a wonderful city. I suggested selling the flats and buying a house, I fancied the extra privacy and freedom of not having to worry about disturbing neighbours. Magda wasn't sure so we agreed to hang onto her flat as a base in the centre and buy a house in the Buda hills, overlooking the Danube. Best of both worlds. I had yet to grow accustomed to the fact that, in Hungary, my bit of capital made me a wealthy man. Not wealthy enough to stop work, though, and I was brought back down to earth when I checked for messages on my computer after a ten day absence at Magda's flat. DI Reed from Oxford wanted to see me and several clients were expecting me to work on their behalf on my next trip to England, preferably yesterday! Time to go to England. Magda was coming as well so we drove, stopping off in Paris for a pre wedding honeymoon. I had often been to Paris with Lesley and we easily found a small private hotel on the left bank, not one I had been to before. Magda had never been and it was a thrill to show her the sites.

Jacey knocked on Witts door. "Huszár has been in Paris, Sir. Vodaphone picked up his mobile there over the weekend. He's headed north on the French N1, looks like he's headed for the ferries. "

"Or the Chunnel, Sir. The best route is via Calais so he could take either but he'll be spotted there and we'll know which one he's on. It'll be either the Chunnel, Dover or Ramsgate and we can cover them all. No problem. If he comes on the Chunnel we'll have to nab him on the motorway. If he comes by ferry, customs will get him. "

"Good. Keep me posted, day or night. "

I rang Reed. "We're running a day late, you free tomorrow morning?"

Reed had been expecting me that afternoon and was put out. He had already had to juggle his diary. But, he needed Huszár's input and Hungary was a long way away. "Early as you can. Seven?"

"Sure. Sorry to mess you about. "

Reed was pleasantly surprised. Few people would have agreed to seven in the morning, Huszár hadn't batted an eye. "Seven then. By the way, your friend Jacey has been sniffing around like a dog in heat. Watch out for him and don't give him any excuses to hold you up. "

"I'll keep my eyes peeled. You got a mobile number in case I need your help?"

"The number is on my Faxes to you. "

"I have those. See you tomorrow. "

I bought Zsofi a superb Pentax SLR camera at the duty free shop. She had asked me for advice about buying one and this was one step better. About time she had a serious camera.

The Chunnel was routine, no fires, no hijackers, no signal failures. We were on the M20 and it was like an action replay. The squad car on the bridge caught up with us more quickly this time because I had been driving at sixty nine and a half miles an hour and not seventy five. These guys were so ham fisted I would have been alerted even without Reed's warning. At least it was a different copper this time, on his own. I rang Reed as the squad car turned on its blue flashing lights behind him. "We're pulling over, just past junction ten on the M20. " I looked at the map Magda was holding up for me. "The next junction is junction nine, basically, we're at Ashford. Presumably we'll end up at the same station as last time. "

"Keep your phone on, I'll get back to you. Don't let them search your car, they might plant something. "

"How can I refuse?"

"Insist on an independent witness before they touch it. Don't let it out of your sight, whatever you do. "

"Thanks for the tip. "

The policeman came over to the car. "Mr József Huszár? Would you mind getting out of the car and opening the boot, Sir?"

"Yes, I would. " I climbed out of the car with Zsofi's new camera. It didn't have a film in it but who was to know? "Officer!. " I lifted the camera and pressed the shutter. "You're welcome to search my car but I want an independent witness, just in case you plan to plant anything. Perhaps you could call in for assistance now? I say that bulge in your pocket is a plant. " I photographed the copper's jacket pocket.

This was new territory for the copper. He wasn't used to being photo-graphed by people he stopped and since he did have a packet of heroin in his jacket pocket he suddenly felt very vulnerable as Huszár contin-ued to photograph his epaulette number and his car before returning the camera through the window to Magda.

"There was a complaint concerning this car. Sir. I'll call in and get it checked, right now. " He returned to his car and went through the mo-tions of calling in on the handset. "Right. Right. OK. " He turned to Huszár. "Computer glitch, Sir. Unpaid parking, but, not this car. Safe journey. " With that he got back in the car and made a real call to Jacey. "Dick. No go. The bastard was prepared for me. Insisted on an independent observer and accused me of planning a plant, took my photo. I've sent him on his way, OK?"

"No its not OK. You were supposed to nail him. Witts won't like this, he won't like this one jot. " Jacey had been doing some reading.

"Can't be helped. He wouldn't open the boot and the woman with him had a camera ready. I would have needed help and I couldn't ask for it, could I?"

Jacey was thinking but he couldn't see any way out. He couldn't risk bringing anybody else in on this, couldn't risk it with the heroin. "OK. Drop it. Where are they headed?"

"North on the M20 at Ashford. "

"Tail them up the road. I want to know if they're headed for London or up the M25. "

I rang Reed. "I frightened him out of it and he's let us go. He had a suspicious bulge in his pocket and shit himself when I accused him of trying to plant something in the car. His epaulette number is 369, presumably based at Ashford or nearby. " "We've passed Ashford and he's still behind us, dragging his feet. I think he's tailing us. "

Reed was pondering the problem. Witts was going to exceptional lengths over Huszár. Might be best to keep him away from the station. "We should meet away from the station. Too many interested parties. "

I looked across at Magda. This was a special trip, after all. "We'll stay at the Quatre Saisons at Milton. Come for breakfast at seven. "

"That the French chef's place?"

"Yes. I'll keep my mobile on in case you need to ring, and, thanks for the tip. I think you were right, they were planning to stitch me up. "

"I'm about to ring Ashford to tip them off about this 369 man of yours. "

"Not my man, your man. You're the copper, I'm just an innocent bystander. "

Twenty miles further and the copper was still half a dozen vehicles behind us, I had eased off to sixty miles an hour and was hemmed in by trucks and geriatrics. I turned to Magda who still wasn't batting any eyes over my being harassed. "We'll drive straight through London and double back through Aylesbury, keep the buggers guessing. "

We were lucky at Le Manoir. They had only one suite left and the meal was exquisite, all three fork fulls, and they weren't big forks. Topped up with drinks at the bar and retired to our room with a bottle of champagne. We were enjoying our pre honeymoon.

I had ordered three full English breakfasts in our room and they were being delivered as Reed turned up. We tucked in as we discussed the case, Reed had to get on with his day. With the statement signed and witnessed by all three of us Reed summarised the position for Huszár's benefit. "Witts is very rattled by this and I don't know why because this is very bad news for Taylor, not Witts. I assume he was involved and Taylor will drop him in it if he gets into trouble. Taylor is nervous as a cat about this. Jacey is hand in glove with Witts and is doing his dirty work for him. They know that without you and your files Taylor has a fair chance of bluffing his way out of trouble, that's why I thought they might be gunning for you. The case really hinges on you and your files. "

"Just like it always did. I'm the one they shafted. Do you really think they're desperate enough to make a serious play for me?"

"Who knows? Don't forget these Club members are used to fixing everything and once they're caught up in it up to their necks then everything is on the line as far as they are concerned. You know what they say about a cornered rat. Dangerous. Taylor is behaving like a cornered rat and Witts is panicking. "He lowered his voice. "Witts is past his sell by date and even his Club connections are beginning to wonder about him. He's not far off retirement and his pension could end up on the line. Take him very seriously, he has a great deal to lose. "

"The files are safe. So all they can do is try to scare me off…or frame me?"

"Yes. They were very upset that your phone records gave you an alibi. They really thought they could make something out of that. "

"Best to finish the job then. How long before you get some serious action on this?"

Reed held up the statement. "This statement and my files are going forward to the CPS by the end of the day. My boss is backing me to the hilt…. A few months, hopefully. In time to spoil their Christmas. " Reed stood up. "How long you over here for?"

"Couple of weeks but I can stay on if you need me. "

Reed was on his way out of the door. "See you. Thanks for breakfast. "

"That copper, 369. What happened?"

"I rang his station but I didn't get very far. I didn't have enough to accuse him of anything so I just asked them to keep an eye on him for attempting to harass you. Might help later if you have more trouble with him, it's on the record. Could establish a pattern. "

"Thanks. "

Jacey stormed into Witts' office. "The bastard is at Milton just down the road. He stayed the night there, the mobile hasn't moved since yesterday evening. "

"Get a car out and track him down so we know where he is. "

Jacey was beginning to wonder about Witts. "Sir, we know where he is, at least within a couple of hundred yards. We could always ring him and ask him to come in. "

"Of course, it's a mobile phone, isn't it?"

"Yes, Sir. Why do we want him in, he'll ask?"

Witts racked his brain. "We don't have a reason, just push him. I want him to feel surrounded, I want him to feel it's all too much trouble. "

"He's not the type, Sir. The harder you push him the harder he pushes back. Pushing is no good. You have to hit a man like him, knock him down so hard he can't get up. Finish him!

"Are you saying we have no chance of scaring him off?"

"In my opinion, Sir, no. When the word got around about his claim against the Council the local grapewine labeled him a Bulldozer. "

"Every man has his limit. Every man has his Achilles heel. Find Huszár's and stop him. "

Nixon and Miles were both working late. They were getting an encouraging response to their friendly calls offering hints to detectives on the job and they were cross checking each other's work. Nixon sat back in his chair and stretched as he looked at his watch. Ten again! His wife would divorce him. "Chris, you know that example we looked at a few weeks ago, the accidental gassings?"

Miles leaned back in his chair, stretching his arms out. "Budge and the other guy with the Oxford connection?"

"Yeah, Budge and Phillips. The computer has thrown up a third connection with Oxford, same department as before. " Miles was tired but he sat up straight, also checking his watch. "A surveyor called Elmore, blown up in his car with an extra spare petrol can. He was Budge and Phillips' boss in Oxford in the late eighties. "

"Coroner?"

"Accidental death. No suspicious circumstances. Worth a ring?"

Miles had had enough for the day. "The other two…both got a clean bill of health from the coroner?"

"Yeah. "

"Do we know any of the detectives on the job?

Nixon scrolled through the three cases. "Ovenden down in Broadstairs, Stevenson at Isleworth and Reed at Oxford. "

"Try Stevenson, don't bother with the hicks from the sticks, they think a com…puter is some kind of communist drinking mug. "

Rick Stevenson was flustered. He had come in two hours early, at six, to try and catch up with his paperwork and after four hours his in tray was higher than when he had started. There was an army of people on roller skates feeding his in tray. He picked up the latest bundle which was two fingers thick and examined it, mostly with indigestible trash destined ultimately for the great shredder in the sky. Most of the up-stairs crew never read anything, they just measured the thickness of the files and then stashed them away. The phone rang. "STEVENSON!"

Bob Nixon held the receiver away from his ear and winced across the desk at Chris Miles. "DI Rick Stevenson, this is Bob Nixon, Central Records. This a bad time to call?"

Stevenson was slightly mollified. It was rare to have someone aware that they were interrupting. "Best time is three in the morning, when I'm home in bed. Leave a message…But, since you're on, what can I do for you, somebody stolen your computer?"

Nixon raised a laugh, if he had a Pound for every time he had heard that one? "If only. Recent case of yours has come up on the computer. Dave Phillips, accidental death. He was a surveyor, used to work at Oxford. You comfortable with the Coroner's verdict?"

Stevenson cast his mind back. "Yeah. We wondered about it but it all checked out, forensics had a good hard look at it and were satisfied. Why, what you got?"

Nixon had found that he got a better response if he explained what they were up to. "Well, the computer is rigged to throw up common factors and we have some connections that might be worth a look. "

"You talking about the other accidental death in Oxford. Somebody who had worked with Phillips a while back?"

"Yeah, Elmore. How did you connect the two?"

"Elmore gave Phillips a funny reference when he left Oxford. Too good to be true. That's the connection. "

Nixon was even more impressed. This detective was good. "There's a third connection. Another accidental death, someone from the same department and from the same period. "

Stevenson reached for his pad. "Tell me about it."

"A retired Clerk of Works, worked with Elmore and Phillips at Oxford. Died in a domestic accident a few months ago. He and Phillips both left Oxford at the same time back in eighty nine. Individually, all three deaths were just a little out of the ordinary but, put the three together.... maybe there's something going on?"

Stevenson was doodling on his pad, thinking. "These three all in the computer and accessible from the station network?"

"You interested?...I'll FAX you the file references."

"Just read them out for me."

"I'd rather FAX so there's a record. We're trying to get a name for the department, boss thinks nobody out there is aware of what we can do. "

Stevenson knew exactly what it was like to be unappreciated. "Give me the numbers now and FAX me anyway. If this comes to anything you'll get the credit for the call. "

Stevenson made his way to the computer room and printed out the three files. This was much more interesting than pushing trays of paperwork round his desk. He would read the files tonight in front of the TV, it was a crap night on the box He returned to his paperwork with a second wind. Maybe Central would come up with even more connections.

In the morning, Stevenson could hardly wait. He rang DI Ovenden at Broadstairs. "DI Rick Stevenson, Isleworth. You covered an accidental death in Broadstairs a while back. Mr and Mrs Budge, domestic accident. Anything funny about it?"

Ovenden was flattered to get a call from a London detective. That's where all the action was, not in a sleepy holiday town like Broadstairs which was in hibernation for half the year and moved at walking pace the other half. "Don't recall any problems. Couple got gassed in their own sitting room because they had blocked up a gas flue. Broadstairs is a draughty place in the winter. "

Stevenson scanned down the page. "Both pretty drunk, judging by the alcohol levels. Did you consider suicide?"

Ovenden hadn't. There had been no evidence of drinking at the house, he had been surprised at the autopsy report, both of them with over a hundred milligrams of alcohol in their blood. "The house was clean at the time. No sign of alcohol. No bottles, no glasses. They were just dead in their chairs, fallen asleep in front of the fire. "

"They must have downed at least a bottle of spirits between them. Must have been to the pub then?"

Stevenson was stacking Elmore's and Phillips' files onto Budge's, chasing shadows, again. He looked more closely at Elmore's top sheet and back at Budge's. "SHITSTICKS!"

"What?"

"Elmore died within a day after the Budges…Mind if I come down and nose around on this one? There are a couple of other deaths that might just be connected. "

"Sure, let me know when you're coming. "

Stevenson did a sum. "You going to be in around noon?"

"I'll get the file out and check through it again. " Great some action, maybe? Ovenden went to his filing cabinet and pulled out a slim file.

Ovenden was ready when Stevenson turned up. "Let's go, thought you might want to see the house. The keys are with the estate agents. " Ovenden rattled on as he drove. "House has been on the market ever since they died. Their kids live up in the north somewhere. Agents say the house hasn't even been cleared out, the furniture is up for grabs with the house. " They pulled up outside the house. At first sight you couldn't tell it was empty, it didn't even have a for sale board up. Stevenson looked questioningly at Ovenden. "For sale?"

"Half the street is up for sale, half of Broadstairs is up for sale. The agents only put up a few sample boards on rotation to fool the out of towners looking for a retirement home. "

"Obviously doesn't work if half the place is up for sale. How much does a bungalow like this go for?"

"Thirty five thousand, if you're lucky. "

"I'll take a dozen. That's cheap. "

"It's not selling. " He let them in. The house was dry and airless. Absolutely no ventilation, no wonder they got gassed by the fumes. Ovenden had done his homework. "Budge had bunged up that gas vent, part of the flue arrangement. People often do that because of the draft. Thing was, Budge was a Clerk of Works and used to spend his time making sure people put vents and flues in. The Gas Board insist on them. Saving tuppence on their heating bill cost them their lives. "

Stevenson surveyed the room. "Assuming he did it. Clerks of Works are famous for being nit pickers. They're the highest ranking admirals in the car park. Most of them would rather die before they used their initiative, friend of mine's a builder you should ask him. He says Clerk's of Works get a tax allowance towards the cost of laundering their brains every Monday morning before they start work. How old was he?"

Ovenden had the file ready. "Sixty seven.... Clerk of works for fifteen years before he retired...used to be a plumber before that. "

Stevenson had discussed this with his builder friend, it was a tough trade for all concerned. "So, got tired of working on his hands and knees as a plumber and retired to a local council job as a Clerk of Works. "

"Everybody hates a Clerk of Works but he stuck it out till retirement. " He looked around the room. "Not much money, waiting for his God to call his turn. I still smell suicide or an outside hand. He paused at a photograph on the mantelpiece. "This the Budge's?"

"That's them. "

Stevenson looked at the picture which must have been about twenty years old. The two of them outside St Paul's. There was a set to Budge's face, a blank look that contrasted heavily with his wife's open smiling face. Not a flexible man, standing rigidly to attention with his furled umbrella beneath a bright blue sky. Out for the whole day in London so he wore his suit and took his umbrella, everybody else in the background was in shirts and shirts. He looked at the gas heater, built into the front wall under the window. "Budge took that grill off and stuffed the vent with...?"

"Fibre glass. "

"And then lit the fire? I don't think so, not unless it was suicide. " He went into the kitchen. "This how it was?" Ovenden gave him a photograph from the file. "This was how it was. Where did they get the booze if there were no bottles in the house?"

They walked around the area and found Budge's regular pub. "Strictly half a pint a session, two or three times a week. Never seen him in here with his wife, never drank shorts. Too expensive. " The landlord gestured around the small bar. "We only keep the spirits for the holiday makers. The locals don't run to that sort of money. "

Ovenden organised copies of the photographs and scene of accident notes just in case they showed up something that was missed in the computer and Stevenson left for London. He could hardly wait to get back as he looked out the car window at the flat featureless countryside. It was a wonder that Julius Caesar hadn't said, "I came, I saw, I buggered off back to Italy. "

Stevenson went through the details of Phillips' death as he drove up the motorway. Phillips was a very experienced surveyor and an important part of his work was to assess the safety of houses, particularly electrical and gas installations. Both known killers. So Phillips tools up to the house, keeps his torch in his pocket and handles an electricity board main fuse with his bare hands whilst touching an earthed gas pipe, he recalled the bright green and yellow cabling snaking round the under stairs cupboard like an out of control creeper. "I don't think so, and this was not a possible suicide. " A passing driver looked hard at him, he was talking to himself. He looked at his car clock. By the time he reached the office it would be too late to ring Reed, might as well head straight home. Surprise his wife and get in a take away as a treat. This was a good day.

Reed was busy for the next couple of days so Stevenson turned up at Oxford at eight on Friday morning. Reed had reread the files and had studied Budge's file. He was driving. Stevenson was very attentive as he went through the history of the Huszár case. "James, you know this guy Huszár, reckon he could have murdered all three?"

Reed had given it a lot of thought. "Anybody can do anything if they really put their minds to it. He was in building and probably knew more about these things than these surveyors. I remember a crack he made once when he was wanting us to push ahead with the forgeries, "These guys are surveyors, I'm a doer". Struck me as a pretty fair remark at the time. These three had all gotten together and made a real stab at forging over a hundred documents. If they had applied only a small part of this energy into the job in the first place they wouldn't have had to bother with the cover up. If…these deaths were organised by one man then, yes, Huszár could certainly have been capable of doing it. There is a snag, he was in Hungary at the time. His phone company records apparently give him a good alibi. "

"Phone company? They can prove he actually made the calls?

"They confirm the calls. His computer telephone records back him up, the calls are recorded by the computer. We had it checked. "

"Computers are supposed to be dumb, maybe he's found a way of fooling the computer records. "

"A full blown programmer might be able to do it but he would have to know all about computer codes, even our specialists couldn't doctor the data files without it showing. They confirmed that these calls were genuinely recorded by the computer and hadn't been doctored. "

"Theoretically though, it could be done?"

"Somebody must be able to do it. We're here. "Reed had pulled over into the field entrance where Huszár had waited for Elmore, almost nine months earlier. He pointed at the ground, "There were fresh signs of a car having parked just here and heavy track marks as it pulled out spinning its front wheels. This is a known spot for lovers after a bit of nooky out of sight of the road. Local constable didn't see anything special in the tracks but we have pictures. " He held out a picture from the file he was carrying.

"Bit of a greasy spot on the road about here, spilt diesel, might have caused the start of the skid. " He was under the yew tree and held out another photograph. "Skid started here and the car ended up hitting that tree, backwards. You can still see the scars on the bark. " He handed him a photograph of the burnt out wreck with Elmore's charred carcass still at the wheel. With no windscreen in the way to obscure the view it looked very gruesome, a blackened skull with very large teeth bared in a silent scream, some shreds of burnt flesh still stuck to it. His hands were still on the wheel, just as if he was still driving. Stevenson pulled a face. "So the only query is what was he doing with an extra spare can in the front of the car? Hhow could anybody possibly plan this accident as a murder? Must be a thousand to one shot. "

"The coroner bought it as an accident. Elmore was a known rally enthusiast and bragged in the local how he could take this corner faster than anybody else. It was raining and he lost it, possibly on a patch of diesel. He had tanked the car up on a credit card only five miles up the road, could have found the can at the garage and just stuck it in the front. Landlord at his local said he was not noted for buying his share of rounds, landlords notice these things. A free plastic can of petrol with the lid still loose because the real owner forgot it, a dropped cigarette and BANG! He was a very heavy smoker. "

Stevenson looked again at the photograph. Elmore's bulk dwarfed the car, he had been a very big man. "Yeah, very heavy smoker. "

Reed was walking back ahead of Stevenson who stayed to picture the car backed into the tree. "Difficult to see how anybody could have engineered this, too many variables. " He stopped to wait for Stevenson who had now finished and was pacing the distance to the start of the skid. "He was going too fast and poof, straight up to heaven. "He looked up into the yew tree. "What's that?"

Stevenson followed his gaze. "That's a model aeroplane...looks in good nick. My kid would fancy that, OK with you?"

Reed nodded his head and continued to stare at the plane and then at the ground at his feet. He took out a photograph of the start of the skid and squinted at it. He compared the road edge details in the photograph with the verge and looked again at the plane as Stevenson was extricating it from the branches. "That plane fly up there or was it planted?"

Stevenson hesitated as he pulled the plane clear. "Could have flown, just. Could have been planted. " He brought the plane down. "No sign of any damage as it hit the branches. Could have been planted. "

Reed lifted a wing tip to raise it so he could see underneath. "This a remote operated bomb bay? He held up the photograph of the road and pointed at a shiny metal clip on the end of a shredded balloon. "This a diesel bomb?"

Stevenson whistled through his teeth. "Forensic keep that balloon?"

"I don't remember it coming up. No mention of it in their report. Lets get back and blow this picture up. Better keep your hands off that plane, fingerprints. " Nine months in a tree, doubt it, he thought. Anyway, Huszár wouldn't have left any prints, he was too smart for that.

Stevenson drummed his fingers. "You reckon this one was murder?"

"If that plane was planted there and it dropped a balloon full of diesel by remote control, yes. The murderer could have waited in the field for the car to pass, knowing that Elmore drove fast, hoping it would catch him. The extra can could have been thrown into the car, plus a match. "

"If we could place Huszár in England instead of Hungary at the time of the murder then...

Reed cut across him. "There was another ruckus involving Huszár not so long ago. A local developer went down owing him a whole lot of money. The developer died in a boating accident in Spain, last year. "

Stevenson laughed. "Just copy the whole of the coroner's lists straight into Huszár's file. Save everybody a lot of work. "

Reed smiled. "Yeah, he probably did for Lord Lucan as well. " They chewed over the case at lunch. The plane was with forensics and they would have a report and blown up pictures in a couple of days. They both mulled over the case that evening, wondering if they had missed any clues connecting the three deaths to a man who had already proved that he was in Hungary at the time. In the morning Reed rang Jacey. "Jacey? It's Reed. I'm tying up some loose ends here, I understand you have copies of Huszár's phone records from Hungary. Mind letting me have a set?"

Jacey wasn't in the mood to be civil with Reed, or helpful. "They cleared him so I let him have them back. You'll have to organise your own set if you want one. I'm busy right now. " He put the phone down.

Reed took it in his stride, what did you expect from someone like Jacey. He went to the outer office. "Jane, can you get hold of Jacey's secretary for details on how we can get a copy of Huszár's phone records from Hungary, please. They had a set but lost it. Get a set for us, would you?" Jane nodded from above her screen, she understood the politics.

Taylor had taken to drinking at the Club two or three times a week. He was drinking heavily and his wife was constantly nagging him about it. She could only come to the club on wives' nights so he was safe here. He was on his third double when Jacey came in through the door. Jacey thought quickly, he could hardly ignore him and, maybe, he could do his boss some good. He brought a treble for Taylor from the bar. "Gin?"

"Yes, thanks. "

Jacey was feeling self conscious. He didn't like Taylor, he was the enemy, trouble. "Peter's doing what he can to get the report buried at the CPS. " This was a mistake. Taylor hadn't known it had gone that far, it was obvious from his expression. Jacey tried to back track. "That is, of course, assuming it goes forward to them in the first place."

Taylor hadn't missed the slip. This bloody great Damocles sword was not just hanging over him, he could hear the rush of air as it was coming down. "Tell Peter not to trouble on my account. I have had enough. I shall draft my report and send it to the CPS. Peter had better concentrate on getting that one buried, he's going to be the star turn. " He picked up the glass Jacey had brought and downed it in one. "Cheers. "

Jacey was gob smacked. Best to keep Taylor talking and get Witts on the phone. He downed his drink and stood up. "I'll get you another. " He made it another triple for Taylor and just a tonic for himself, got to keep a clear head. He eyed Taylor warily from the bar, he mustn't let him go. He sat down again, Witts wasn't answering his mobile. "Peter's pulling all the stops out, this one won't get anywhere. You can depend on that, I promise you. Peter and I are both onto this. "

That's what worried Taylor. This pair of buffoons couldn't even think without moving their lips.

"No. I've thought about this a lot lately and my mind is made up. I want this off my conscience, once and for all. I'm retired and I want a peaceful retirement, free of all this. What have I got to lose?" He got up to go, unsteady on his feet. "Thank you for the drinks, goodnight. "

Jacey jumped up and took his arm. "Have another drink before you go, I'll drop you off in my car. "

Taylor was too drunk to use his discretion, he liked gin and his wife would tell him off anyway. He sat down. "All right. " Jacey got him another triple. Jacey finished his drink quickly and stood up, looking at his watch. "I'll meet you outside at the car, I need to phone my wife to tell her I'm dropping you off and I'll be a little late. " Taylor just nodded. His eyes were getting heavy.

Jacey waited in the car until Taylor appeared and flashed his lights. He had been unable to get through to Witts. Taylor shuffled his way over to the car and climbed in. "This is very good of you. Tell Peter I'm sorry but I did give him fair warning. He's let me down badly and I've reached my limit. " His head dropped momentarily to his chest. Jacey came to the Oxford ring road and turned left instead of straight across towards Woodstock. From the corner of his eye he could see that Taylor's eyes were shut, he was out. A mile along the A40 he turned right into a muddy contractors entrance. The gravel pit had been started only two or three years earlier and consisted of no more than three large lakes with excavating equipment on the banks. He drove in the massive ruts left by the heavy lorries and turned off his lights. He parked by the edge of the largest lake and waited till his eyes were used to the gloom. Cars and lorries were screaming past on the main road less than fifty metres away from him. It was a three lane section of road, notable for the frequency of fatal accidents between oncoming cars in the middle lane. Everybody thought they had squatters' rights for the middle lane, some paid a high price for it, especially if they hit a truck.

He got out of the car and opened Taylor's door. Taylor's head came up. "We here already? She's gone to bed, the lights are out. " He fumbled for his keys as Jacey helped him out of the car. His hand was still in his pocket as Jacey summoned all his strength and using Taylor's outstretched arm as a sling swung him through the air and into the gravel pit. Taylor struck the water full length with a dull splash as his body skimmed along the surface for almost three metres before it came to rest. Jacey watched as Taylor, floating on the surface with his face down, buoyed up by the air in his heavy overcoat, tried in vain to get his face out of the water, weakly flailing his arms. His water sodden sleeves were so heavy that he barely got his elbows out of the water. After six or seven attempts, he lay still in the water. Jacey sat in the car and waited for ten minutes as Taylor's body slowly sank further into the water until all he could make out was a small part of the back of his head and part of his coat. He started the car and made for the exit, putting his lights on as he rejoined the road. No cars in sight in either direction.

He looked at himself in the mirror as he drove away. His face looked normal. Plenty of browny points for this one.

Reed picked up the report on his way to his desk. Forensics had worked late the evening before to finish it. He collected a coffee and sat down to read it. No fingerprints on the plane apart from Stevenson's, nine months in the open, could be something? The plane's fuel tank was empty, and, there was no trace that it had ever had any fuel in it. The engine had never been run, gasket cements used in its assembly had not been heat hardened. NO WAY! The plane was manufactured by a British firm and this particular model had been out of production for more than six years. The remote controlled bomb bay mechanism was fully functional. He studied the blow up of the photograph, amazing detail from the high definition negatives the police used.

Elmore had been murdered, by a diesel bomb made of a rubber balloon and a paper clip? Reed would testify to that.

Cruising back from Edinburgh and Scotland's silicon valley. Felt strange to be watching the speedo so carefully, seemed painfully slow, sixty nine and a half miles per hour. I patted the steering wheel, "Sorry

Jag, I'm as embarrassed as you are, have to wait till we get to the continent. No wonder the Americans were so manic, stuck with a speed
limit of fifty five. The phone rang, jolting me out of my reverie. It was
Reed, preparing evidence for a strong letter from Reed's boss to the
CPS about Taylor. They were going for Taylor hammer and tongs.
Magda and I had been in England for eleven days and we were headed
back to Budapest. "Do you need me to actually call in at the Oxford
shop, or can we sort this from London, I'm there this weekend?"

Reed sounded apologetic. "Fraid I need you here, new evidence for
you to look at. That OK?"

"OK. Monday, eight in the morning suit you?"

"Fine. "

I switched the phone off. Reed must be having a tough day, his voice
seemed edgy, not as laid back as he usually was.

It was almost lunchtime, Witts called through his office door for Jacey.
"Sir. " Jacey knew what was coming.

"I've just had Mrs Taylor on the phone. Seems her darling husband
didn't get back last night. He was last seen at the Club with you,
around ten last night. He left shortly after you did. " He looked up
from his notebook.

"I bought him a few drinks, Sir. He was moaning about the case, said
he wanted to speak to you about it today. I told him you'd be pleased
to speak to him and left him to it. He was pretty far gone, probably just
fell asleep somewhere. He got any mates in Oxford?"

"Taylor's not the matey type. Make a few calls, see if he checked in at
a hotel or something. Mrs Taylor was whingeing about his drinking too
much, if he'd had a skinfull then he might have been well advised to
steer clear until he was sober. Try the North Oxford hotels and give her
a ring anyway, reassure her. We want to keepthem happy. "

Jacey went through the motions of ringing a few hotels and then rang
Mrs Taylor. "He was fine when I left him at the club, but, he'd had a
few drinks. He's probably sleeping it off at a friends house. Have you
tried his friends?"

Mrs Taylor felt they were patronising her. "Of course I have! Do you
take me for an idiot?

"I'm sure he'll turn up soon, Mrs Taylor. Please let us know when he
does so we can stop looking for him. Meantime, we're on the look out
for him. Oxford is a small place, he can't be lost. "

Jacey smiled to himself, wait till she finds out, then she'll blow a gasket.

Jacey rang the Oxford station and spoke to the desk sergeant. "Unofficially can you ask the men to keep their eyes peeled for a Mike Taylor. Early sixties, lives in Woodstock. Didn't come home last night. "

The Sergeant was up to his eyebrows. "You'll have to wait till it's official. We've got our hands full down here. Some geezer drowned in a gravel pit just up the road. Everybody has shot up there for a look. "

"Forget it then, till I ring you back. Maybe Taylor will turn up in the meantime. " He rang Vodaphone. Huszár was almost in Leeds, still on the move. He drove the three miles to the gravel pit and turned up in time to see Taylor's body being zipped into a body bag. He spotted Reed talking to someone from forensics who was making casts of prints in the ground. "Suicide?"

Reed turned round quickly, recognising Jacey's voice. "Could be, body is unmarked, far as we can see. Recent car tracks near where he went in and some extra footprints, we're casting them now. Jim thinks he could have been pushed, reckons the foot prints tell a story. "

Jacey looked around the area. "I was with him last night at the Club. If there's no car, how did he get here?"

"It's a half hour walk…. He was with you at the Club?"

"Yes. He was well away. Drunk enough to fall in and not notice. " Jacey spoke with authority but Reed didn't notice anything strange in his delivery. He never took much notice of also rans like Jacey. He was full of shit.

Dud from forensics looked up from his work. "Watch where you put those plates of meat, unless you want me to take casts of your prints. "

Jacey leaped back. "Sorry, Dud, wasn't thinking. " Dud sighed. Some of these dick heads couldn't detect themselves out of a car park. Now he would have to get a cast of Jacey's footprints for elimination purposes. He looked angrily at him. "Said I was sorry! I'm off, got to report this to his wife. She was asking about him earlier. " He was off in a shower of gravel.

Dud gestured towards the car as it left the site. "Jumped up little prick!"

Jacey checked back in at his office, no sign of Witts. He was dying to tell him the good news, but, how to put it? How could he get full credit without the risk of Witts turning on him and without the risk of getting into trouble? He sat and put his elbows on the desk, head in his hands. If this went wrong he could be in serious trouble…. he'd killed Taylor. For the first time the enormity of what he had done struck him, full force, in the belly. It had seemed a good solution at the time and he had imagined Witts would be very pleased with him for solving the problem, but who was he kidding. Witts would bang him up so fast his feet wouldn't touch the ground. Witts hadn't meant him to do anything this serious to anybody. Witts was gutless and all he wanted was an easy life with no hassle. Killing Taylor was hassle, hassle in spades, hearts clubs and diamonds. Jacey had solved one problem and created a bigger one. Worse, it was a much, much bigger problem, and it was all his.

Vodaphone rang back at half past two. Huszár was near Leicester, on the motorway. Jacey pictured the route from the M1 back to Oxford. Hour and a half, maybe two hours away. Easy hour and a half on a Thursday night with no traffic. Nice fit. He rang the Leicestershire police and put the phone down just as it was answered. Take it easy, take it easy. Nothing to say Taylor's death wasn't suicide or an accident. He was probably heading back to his daughter's flat in London, he was a strong family type. A foreigner.

Jacey doodled on his desk pad. What he needed was something to connect Huszár with the gravel pit, just in case. He was interrupted by Witts appearing out of nowhere by his side. "My office. " He waited for Witts to check his in tray and then sat when he was motioned to do so. "Taylor is dead. "

"Yes, Sir. I saw his body at the pit. "

"What happened?"

This could be Jacey's chance for claiming the credit without any risk to himself. He thought fast. "Looks like it was suicide, Sir. I had a few drinks with him at the Club last night, he was desperate about the forgery case and was wanting you to bale him out. I told him he was the one that did it and there was no way he could spread the blame to you. . "

Witts was disconcerted that Jacey should have taken such a risk. He had ordered him to mollify Taylor, keep him sweet, not inflame him. "How did he react?"

Jacey was getting into his stride. "He was well away even before I saw him, Sir. I quickly realised that he was desperate and when he started talking about your protecting him or finishing himself off I judged that the best thing to do was show him he was on his own and push him to solve the problem for himself. Looks like he decided to solve the problem himself. " Jacey tried to sound matter of fact. "I wasn't to know that he actually meant it. I was trying to gee him out of it. "

Something jarred with Witts, Jacey was not noted for his understanding of human nature. He brushed the query aside, his problem with Taylor was solved for good. "So, when he thought he would be put through the wringer he just drove over to the gravel pits and jumped in?"

"Didn't have a car, must have walked. It's only a couple of miles. "

Witts pictured the site from the road. He had often driven past. "These pits are the ones off the A40. No entrance gate or security or anything?"

"No Sir, just a short gravel drive straight to the water and you can drive.... or walk in anytime you like. He must have seen the pits from his car in the past and just headed for them last night when he knew he was on his own. Sir, I haven't told Mrs Taylor. "

"Leave it to the officers on the case. The less we have to do with this, the better. " He looked at Jacey's face, he seemed relaxed enough. "Looks like you did me a favour, putting Taylor off. He had been talking of taking me down with him. Well done. "

Jacey tried to look casual. "No problem, Sir. Shame poor old Taylor couldn't take the pressure over what he had done. Shame for Mrs Taylor. "

"Exactly. A sad loss. "

Jacey was having to consciously not rub his hands together as he headed back to his desk. Witts was pleased, and grateful. It had turned out all right, in fact, it had turned out great! He basked in the glow of the glory that was now his. He had been instrumental in helping the Deputy Chief out of a serious hole, that was the way to progress at the Club, help out the senior members. Vodaphone rang. Huszár was in Notting Hill. He checked his records, his daughter lived in Camden, must be shopping or something.

Reed drove to Taylor's house and this time, parked in front of the drive. He'd had to do this a few times in his career but it wasn't one of the chores anybody ever got used to. He geared himself mentally for Mrs Taylor's reaction. She answered the door quite breezily. "You've found him then. Drunk, as I understand it. "

He took her arm and led her into the front room. "Please take a seat, Mrs Taylor.... . I have very bad news...your husband was found drowned in a local gravel pit. " She looked at him, her uncomprehending face looking very white in the light from the window. "I'm afraid we need you to come and identify him, please make an appointment, somebody can come and collect you. "

The expression returned to her face and in a low measured voice she said. "Let's go now. Get it over with. " Reed hid his surprise and followed her to the hall where she put on her coat and led the way to his car. "You were the one that came here before, you met him...So it is definitely my husband?"

"I'm afraid so. I'm so very sorry. " She hid her face behind her hands and wept silently, tears flowing down her chin from behind her hands and dripping onto her coat. Reed drove the car gently on a circuitous route to give her time to get used to the idea that her husband was dead and she was now on her own for the rest of her life. She couldn't be more than late fifties. He felt sorry for her. Still, he consoled himself, she didn't have to go through his being banged up for the forgeries. THE CASE! The case had completely slipped his mind. With Budge, Elmore Phillips and now Taylor, all dead, none of the forgers were around to answer for the forgeries. There was no case, not any more.

He took Mrs Taylor in to identify Taylor's body. She nodded when they pulled back the cover. Taylor looked peaceful in repose. On their way back in the car he asked if he could check his office in case he had left a note or any indication that he might be contemplating suicide. "He had been very sullen since before you came to see him, something was on his mind but he wouldn't say what it was. If anything he seemed a little less tense than usual yesterday before he went off to the Club. He's been drinking very heavily and took to going to the Club because I was nagging him about it. No, I don't think he was planning suicide. "

Reed found a draft letter in Taylor's computer, spilling the beans on Witts' involvement in the Huszár case. It was a rambling incoherent account that would not stand up in court without Taylor there to back it up under oath because it would be treated as hearsay evidence without him. Witts exerting his influence had been restricted to private conversations at the Club, no witnesses. Witts would simply deny it, and, get away with it. He copied the file to disk. There was nothing else of interest. He asked Mrs Taylor to keep the room undisturbed just in case. She had made tea and he stayed to drink it out of sympathy and politeness. Back at Reed's office there was a message to contact Jacey, urgently. Five thirty on a Friday and Reed was ready to go home, enough was enough. Maybe Jacey had something, he rang and Jacey picked it up immediately, he had been waiting anxiously for the call. "Ah, Reed. Your mate, Huszár, I'd like to have another chat with him. I can't get a reply from his daughter's flat, know where I can contact him?"

Reed could tell from Jacey's hesitant tone that he was up to something. Why was he asking about the daughter's flat, why didn't he just ring him on his mobile? "Tried his mobile?"

It dawned on Jacey that he had missed something obvious. What he really wanted was to catch Huszár off guard and he had in fact found that his daughter had moved out.

No forwarding address because the good old Post Office redirected automatically. He wanted the address of Huszár's daughter's new flat.

"Eh, yeah. It's switched off. Got the flat number, maybe I have it down wrong?"

So that was it. Jacey didn't have the number or address of the new flat. Reed checked the file and read out the old flat number, he wasn't about to help that turd Jacey. "That's the number I've got. Have to keep trying then. "

Monday morning and Reed was bang on time for our appointment. So was I. I pulled up alongside him in the car park, Magda was with me. Reed organised coffees and we sat down in his office. Reed was slightly uncomfortable, he hadn't been honest with Huszár. He had worked out what he was going to say over the weekend. "It hasn't been released yet so you won't know that Taylor was drowned on Thursday night. "

"Taylor's dead?

"He drowned in the gravel pits just up the A40. Where were you on Thursday night?"

"We dined in at the hotel around nine. Arthur's View Hotel, Edinburgh. We drank at the bar till about half eleven. The barman took us through a guided tour of single Malt whiskies. It's obviously his party piece, he won't have forgotten us. We stayed the night and left after breakfast. " Huszár smiled. "I won't deny that I'm pleased to hear that that conniving little shit Taylor has met his comeuppance but I don't have the satisfaction of having killed him. Does our hotel cover the crucial times?"

Reed had already checked that Huszár's mobile was near Edinburgh when he had answered his call on the Friday morning. It was at least a five hour drive so if he was there after seven in the evening he couldn't have been in Oxford round midnight when Taylor drowned. "Taylor drowned around midnight so if the hotel confirms you were there, then yes, you are in the clear over Taylor's death. "

I spotted the careful wording Reed used and Reed's discomfort. "In the clear over Taylor's death – but not someone else's death. " He hadn't finished the sentence. They must have made the connection with Budge. Budge, Elmore, Phillips and now Taylor...full house! No wonder Reed was uncomfortable. Huszár was a prime candidate once you connected the first three deaths, assuming of course, that they were murders and not accidents. I needed time, Taylor's death was a total shock, especially as I had actually planned to kill him before Reed came back on the case and I could get justice through the courts. Pulled out my wallet. "I paid by credit card at the hotel and the bill included the evening meal. " I leafed through various invoices. "Here it is. One night with breakfast included, evening meal and a very healthy bar bill. Healthy for the hotel that is, not healthy for our livers. The bar chits have my signature. "

Reed was satisfied that Huszár's alibi covered him over Taylor. He took the receipts and chits and placed them on his desk. He looked straight at Huszár to gauge his response when he dropped the next bombshell. "Elmore was murdered, it wasn't an accident. "

The plane, I thought, they found the plane. Best method of defence is attack, here goes. "So, Budge, Elmore, Phillips and now Taylor, all dead. The four forgers that got away with screwing me six years ago. Are you just fishing or am I a serious suspect?"

Reed was still casting his line. "Budge, a Clerk of Works, died because his gas flue was blocked up. Phillips, an experienced surveyor, died replacing a complicated fuse in the dark with a working torch in his pocket. Taylor drowned in a gravel pit and it looks like he was delivered there by car. " I noted that Elmore's death was out of sequence, his death was the problem death. Reed was about to play his ace. "Elmore was murdered with a balloon full of diesel dropped from a model plane. "

I had had time to prepare myself and, of course. I balanced carefully on the tightrope Reed had prepared for me. I looked Reed straight in the eye. "I can see why you are interested in me and I don't blame you. I had good reasons for bearing a grudge against all four of these men.

A knowledge of building is a common factor in the first three deaths and my experience embraces these.... Had I put my mind to it I'm sure I probably could have organised their deaths. But, to paraphrase Margaret Thatcher, I was on holiday in Hungary at the time. Jacey checked out my phone records in Hungary and was satisfied that I made calls in Budapest when Phillips and Elmore died. My stay in Edinburgh covers me for Taylor and that just leaves Budge unaccounted for. Hopefully my phone records will cover me for Budge as well. When did he die?"

"Within a couple of days either side of Elmore, he had been dead for some days before he was found so they couldn't fix the exact day. " He studied Huszár. "Mrs Budge died with him. " No sign of guilt or remorse from Huszár. Don't you think it's strange that Budge and Phillips both died in circumstances which they knew enough to avoid?"

"Tiger keepers are killed by tigers. I knew both these prats and they both thought they were smart, smart enough to forge over a hundred sheets of evidence. Smart enough to backdate letters on new letterheads that didn't fit the originals. " The only death that seems strange to me is Elmore's. How was he killed with a diesel bomb?"

"Remote controlled model plane dropped a balloon full of diesel in his path as he headed for a hairpin bend. He crashed and a spare can in the front burst into flames. "

"So the fat bastard got fried in a car. " I openly savoured the moment. "Phillips got fried by electricity and Budge got gassed. Couldn't have happened to a nicer trio. " I looked upwards. "Maybe there is a God after all.... Taylor's death presumably stops the forgery case?"

Reed stood up. "Yes, the forgery case is dead since all the accused are dead but, we're still looking for a possible killer over Taylor. "

"Would you mind checking me out with the hotel, now? I'd like to think that there's nothing hanging over me and that I'm in the clear. "

"I can't do that properly over the phone, but in any case, if we turn up any forensic evidence linking you to any of the other three deaths we would want to look more closely into your telephone alibi. So if anything does turn up you're not in the clear. As I understand it your alibi relies on computer records to prove you were in Hungary. "

This was not a time to be hesitant, Reed obviously knew that the integrity of computer records was flawed. "I don't remember the dates involved but it would seem impossible for me to prove conclusively that I was minding my own business in Hungary at the time, who remembers specific dates?. My phone and computer records are all I have, best I can do, officer. For the record, nothing was too good for those four bastards and it gives me some satisfaction that they all died early. My wife died early and I blamed them. "

Reed had one card left, now was the time to play it. "And John Bull, did you blame John Bull?"

I had not expected this and my head snapped round at Reed. "Yes, and John FUCKING Bull. I heard about his boating accident and I even went to the local rag's offices to read about it. I blamed all five of the bastards. "

Reed was done. If Huszár had had a hand in any of these deaths there was no evidence to link him to any of them. "I was sorry to hear about your wife. I can see how you might feel gratified that these people are all dead, but as a policeman, I don't share your sentiments. "

"If Saddam Hussein died would you be pleased?"

"That is not the same. "

"Far as I'm concerned these guys were all Saddam's. They fucked up other people's lives to serve their own ends" Huszár stood up, looking at his watch. "Now if you have finished with me, I'd like to go catch a chunnel. "

"I'm sorry but I have to ask you to stay in the country until we have checked with the Edinburgh hotel. Would you mind leaving your passport, it should only take a few hours. I will ring you on your mobile as soon as I can. "

This seemed a cheap price to pay, considering that Reed had a pretty good idea that Huszár might be behind all this. I asked Magda for my passport and handed it over. "You can use the picture and FAX it to Edinburgh so they can identify me. If it takes all day we'll be staying at the Randolph. I appreciate what you tried to do over the forgeries. "

"Least I could do since it was me that let it go in the first place. I'll ring as soon as I can.... Jacey been in touch with you? He was wanting to contact you?"

"Haven't heard from him. "

"Might be a good idea to contact him and clear up any loose ends before you leave the country. You wouldn't want to get held up on your way out...home. "

"Ring him and tell him I'm here. "

Jacey was looking at Budge's file as the phone rang. He had been tipped off by June that Reed had obtained a copy, it made very interesting reading. "Reed! I was just going to ring you. There's a third case linked to Phillips and Elmore. "

"I know, Budge. I have Mr Huszár with me right now. I had the impression you were wanting to contact him. "

"You're damn right I want to contact him. Put him on…. Mr Huszár, I have some questions that need answering. Mind coming over to my office, now?"

I was in no mood to be conciliatory with a little shit like Jacey. "I'm not exactly over the moon about it Jacey but presumably I don't really have a choice, so OK. About twenty minutes. " I handed the phone back to Reed. "Time for a reprise?"

"Detective Jacey fancies his chances. He's picked up Budge's file. Try not to annoy him, he does have influence at high levels. "

"The Deputy Constable? I'm not impressed. I'll look forward to your call. " I took Magda's arm and we left for Kidlington. I tried not to look relieved in front of Magda. Was surprised at how cool I had been as Reed unveiled his suspicions. I recounted the story of the forgers and Taylor's cover up as we drove to Kidlington. Jacey was waiting in his office, a small stack of files on his desk, pretending to be too engrossed to notice us come in. I knew how to play the game. Pulled up a chair for Magda and continued with my story as to why Reed had been wondering about me.

Jacey knew he had been outflanked again and interrupted abruptly, his irritation showing in his voice and his stilted delivery. "You think you're very clever, don't you Mr Huszár?"

I turned to Jacey and looked meaningfully at his Club tie, no brains needed. "What you mean is you think I'm very clever. You've seen my file, I am very clever. You haven't asked me here to compliment me?"

"Jacey tapped the files on his desk. I'm not as easy to fool as DI Reed, his heart is bleeding for you because he feels he let you down over that Council case…. I know you killed these men and I'm going to prove it. "

"Which men exactly, Budge, Elmore, Phillips and Taylor. You crediting me with all of them?"

"Yes. I have applied for a search warrant, it should be here any minute, so we shall soon be searching your car. "

I looked at Magda, she didn't look too concerned. These English police were all talk as far as she was concerned. "I don't trust you Jacey, I know it was one of your merry Club members that tried to plant something in my car on the motorway. I want a solicitor to witness the search, just in case you have any fancy ideas about fabricating evidence. My Oxford solicitor is Julian Hatton, I want him called right away. " Jacey left us in his office and we waited for almost an hour, there was no sign of him in the outer offices when I searched for him.

Good old Julian turned up before the warrant had come through. He was impressive and had managed to take some of the wind out of Jacey's sails. He came to see me. "Jacey's flying on a wing and a prayer, he doesn't have anything concrete. You crossed with him before? He seems to want it to be you, almost as if it's personal for him. "

I thought back to my previous experience with Jacey. "You know me, Julian, I've always had the unfortunate ability to make inadequates feel inadequate. At first I had the distinct impression that Jacey was trying to cover up over the forgery case because of the Black Hand Gang's involvement through Taylor but that no longer applies. Maybe he genuinely believes what he is saying. He'll soon find he's up the creek when Reed finishes checking me out and that should put an end to it.... . He appears to have a problem with Reed, got a point to prove with him as well. He would love it if he could prove me guilty after Reed had missed out on the evidence. Maybe he's more interested in proving he's better than Reed, maybe I'm just caught in the cross-fire?"

Julian considered the point. "No, it's you he's after, I'm sure of that. The issue with Reed is a side show. Is there anything in any of this that we should be worried about?"

"You mean apart from the fact that he's accusing me of murdering four people, no. Nothing at all to worry about. What are the rules on this, am I under arrest?"

"No. You're helping them with their enquiries. Look upon it as helping them to eliminate you from their enquiries and it will do you good. No sense in getting their backs up unnecessarily, just play along with it and smile. Don't try to be too clever. "

"Reed warned me that they might try planting evidence on me to slow me down over the forgeries case, that's why I insisted on having you here. The forgeries case is a dead issue but who knows what he might try, he might even want to frame me for these deaths just to further his career. "

Julian thought Huszár was way over the top. "I hardly think so, he may not be the world's brightest but you must admit that if these people were murdered you would be an obvious candidate for the starring role."

"You howled loud enough to wake the dead at the time and history shows that when it comes to avenging their loved ones almost anybody is capable of rationalising murder as being an appropriate punishment. All that's missing is the voices from above. " He suddenly looked thoughtful. "Don't take this the wrong way Joe, but it just struck me that you are the ideal candidate. "

"I know that, that's why you're here Julian. I've got some corroborative evidence that I was in Hungary at the time of some of the deaths but it's not set in stone. "

"What sort of evidence?"

"Phone company records of outgoing calls from my flat backed up by my computer file records which confirm it's my voice on the line. "

"I see what you mean. Too many smart computer frauds nowadays, judges tend to be sceptical about computer evidence, even banks have been caught doctoring them. But, there's nothing linking you to the actual deaths anyway, is there. "

"Not that I know of and you're here to make sure they don't fabricate any."

Jacey came in. "The warrant seems to be taking a long time. You could save yourself some of your own time if you give us permission to search the car anyway. You and Mr Hatton can witness the search. "

Julian nodded at Huszár, Huszár nodded back. "OK, let's go. " Huszár tossed his keys at Jacey, aiming to make him miss but Jacey had a remarkably quick reaction time and caught them behind his right ear with his left hand. Jacey headed for the door, smug at having won his first ever point with this arrogant bastard.

We watched while two detectives carried out what seemed a fairly perfunctory search of the car and declared they had found nothing interesting. Jacey commented that the insurance documents and road tax were British and yet I lived in Budapest. "I'm sentimental about the number plate and the insurance is cheap through the Jaguar Driver's Club."

Shit thought I, contrary to my personal code I was in fact the member of a club that was prepared to have me as a member. Groucho Marx would turn in his grave if he ever heard about it.

Jacey joined in. "And from next year the road tax will be free, it will be more than twenty five years old. "

Having lived abroad I hadn't heard about the budget change. "Really? I hadn't heard about that. " It was the first time Jacey had shown an ability to string one idea along with another. "Am I free to go?"

"Yes, have a good journey home. " Jacey strolled off purposefully towards his car. "I have to go. "

Julian and I shook hands. "I'd better give you my address so you can bill me.

"This one's on the house. Call in when you're in the area again. " Julian shook Magda's hand but she insisted on kissing his cheek as thanks for his help. "Joe, good luck. "

"I'll FAX you when I get back. You're welcome to come and stay with us, any time. . Hungary is a beautiful country, worth a visit. "

"Thanks, I'd like that. " Julian had seen police searches often in the past and this hadn't been a police search, not by a long chalk. He didn't believe that Jacey had applied for a warrant and he didn't believe that Jacey was interested in searching Joe's car. It didn't fit.

I rang Reed from the car. "Edinburgh rang earlier Mr Huszár and I'm expecting their FAX any minute. By the time you get here I may be able to hand you your passport back. "I took the scenic route round the west Oxford bypass and pulled up onto a bridge to show Magda the dreaming spires that Oxford was famous for. If you filtered out the electricity pylons and some of the crass modern carbuncles from the view, it really was a pretty city, I had been happy here. Cleared my throat, I probably would not be back, I was starting again with Magda in an equally pretty city, as yet, unspoilt.

Reed wished us well as he handed over my passport. Magda shook Reed's hand, he didn't qualify for one of her kisses.

Jacey pulled up on the A40 near the gravel pit entrance and opposite the spot where Taylor had drowned. There was nobody at the site. He took out some tissue wrapped keys from his pocket, and threw them into the sealed area marked off by the police tape.

YOUR BILL SIR

We were packing my things when there was a single loud imperious thump that spoke volumes. I was moving in with Magda and my flat was going on the market, we hadn't found a house yet. My arms were full so Magda answered the door, two uniformed policemen with guns on their hips walked straight past her. " József Huszár?

"Egen. "

"Rendorseg. Yutunk ki kutotni a lakasodat. " They had come to search the flat

I looked at them and then at Magda. Magda shook her head, you didn't mess with these Hungarian rendor, and taking my hand she pulled me back to a neutral wall, she could see I was about to challenge them about a warrant. "Tesek. " She gestured with open arms and the rendor went ahead, they didn't need a second bidding and they didn't need to show any authorisation for the search. After two hours all my packing was undone but without any apparent breakages. The rendor checked under the carpets, checked the floorboards, checked the lavatory flush units, they were very good at it. I didn't bat an eye as one of them opened the stove and drew out a folded newspaper and shook it. I didn't bat an eye as a small booklet fell to the floor. I had totally forgotten that I had placed it there months earlier in the spring and winter hadn't arrived yet so I hadn't ;it it. It was Magda who put her hand to her mouth as she recognised the Hungarian passport floating as if in slow motion down to the carpet and she realised the significance of such a valuable item being wrapped in newspaper in a stove, ready to be burnt. There was no honest reason for burning a passport. I watched as the rendor bent over with his long arms to pick it up and open it.

"Lévai József?

"En vagok. " I explained about the lack of paperwork on my father's side leading to a Hungarian passport in my mother's maiden name. Explained that Zsu was also living and working in Budapest for George Soros and that her passport was also in my mother's family name of Lévai. The rendor was surprised at my polished Hungarian. He had been told I had been raised in England and he had expected, at best, the usual pigeon Hungarian that even Hungarians brought up in Hungary usually came back with after a few years in the West. They had really only come for the computer.

The English rendor had wanted to obtain it without giving Huszár a chance to doctor it first. This Huszár was a real Hungarian with a Hungarian passport and from his accent was obviously from an educated family. He closed the passport and folded the newspaper over it. Looking around the room at the packing cases he turned to me and handed me the passport inside the paper. "Szerencsére találtam ezt, hogy elfelejtette. Veszélyes, hogy elrejtsük egy tűzhelyben, de hibásan felégethetted. Óvatosabbnak kell lenned vele. "

The rendor was right, dangerous to have forgotten the passport and I might have burnt it by mistake.

The rendor left with the computer and as the door closed I realised that I had no proof that they had been. No receipt for the computer, no nothing. I made for the door but Magda held me back. "Leave it Joe. Leave it. They're not like the British police, you have to be careful here. " She took the passport from my hand and opened it, leafing through the pages until she got to the border stamps. "You went to England with this passport instead of your British passport. " It wasn't a question. "Without these stamps is there any proof that you went?" I shook my head. She ripped the pages out and returned them to the stove with the rest of the passport and the newspaper. Lighting a match from a box at its base she held it near the newspaper and looked for my assent. I nodded and she lit the paper, closing the stove door after she had seen the stamped pages destroyed by the flames. "Let's finish packing tomorrow, now, we both need a Pálinka. "For once in my life I was at a loss for words as I followed her to the door and she locked it behind me. It was a relief to be back in the civilised order of her flat with huge Pálinkas in our hands. "Yo serenchet. "

"Good luck. Thank you Magda. I did kill them, you already know why. " I looked at her questioningly.

She leant over and kissed my lips. "Would you kill for me?"

"Yes. Did you have anybody in mind?"

"No. I just wondering if you loved me enough. "

"Do you want me to tell you any more about it. "

"Only if you want to. They are on your conscience?"

"No. I'm comfortable about it, as long as the police don't find out. In fact I get a lot of satisfaction from knowing that those bastards got theirs. "

"Got theirs?"

"Got what they deserved. Got what was coming to them. "

She drained her glass and then pointed her finger at me. "You know that you are now under my control. Refill my glass!"

"Yes, MADAME. "

We drank together and basked in the warmth of our love and mutual trust. I didn't even need to ask her how she felt about my being a multiple murderer. She trusted my judgement and I trusted hers. After all, we loved each other. I really would kill for her if the need arose. I was surprised at the relief of her finding out. Hadn't felt that she was suspicious or snooping it was just good not to have any secrets from her. I had never had any secrets from Lesley and life was much easier that way. I felt even closer to Magda now that this barrier was gone, I looked forward to spending the rest of my life with her. We slept in each other's arms.

The next day we finished the packing and having cleaned out the stove left the flat empty for the agents to sell. We went house hunting for the day. The police were waiting for us when we returned to park the Jag in the garage, it was the same pair. Not as aggressive as the day before. Could I please allow them to take impressions of my car keys, the English police wanted to eliminate me from their enquiries in a case. Easy, they could have my spare set from the glove compartment. It was almost impossible to get replacement ignition keys so I kept the spare keys there. The door keys were standard FS keys that you could get anywhere, I had been stranded once and had had to dismantle the steering lock to get back from Cornwall. I turned the car inside out but could find no sign of the spare set. The policemen took an impression with the kit they had brought and thanked me for my help. Magda was impressed with their new found deference. When they had gone I searched the car again. Magda had never ever opened the glove compartment which was kept locked. I thought back to when I first got back into the car to get the keys, the The compartment had not been locked. Somebody had taken my keys but presumably hadn't been able to defeat my anti theft circuitry so they had simply left the car, taking my keys with them. Cunning these Hungarians. I eyed my only remaining ignition key, better see if I could get one cut, two would be even better. I didn't wonder why the English police were interested in my keys, I was relieved that my favourite toy hadn't been stolen.

Witts looked up as Jacey came in. "Sir. Those keys found at the scene of Taylor's drowning. I played a hunch and it's paid off. It's a very unusual key dating from early Jaguar XJ's...it's a match for Huszár's car keys. Fancy ignition key and different model door key, both match. We've got him bang to rights Sir, right at the scene of the crime. Chances of another pair of keys matching up like that must be millions to one. "

"Get a warrant and go get him. And Dick, cuff the arrogant shit.... well done!" Witts hadn't felt so good in a long time. The shadow of Taylor's implicating him was gone and here was a chance to show up Ducky and his crew for what they were, a bunch of conniving amateurs. Reed had given Huszár a clean bill of health and had been relying on Huszár's help to smear the Deputy Chief Constable! He would show them who was trying to use influence. Witts day had come, the Chief Constable was working up to early retirement on the grounds of his wife's bad health and he, Witts, was ready to fill the breach. He locked his desk drawers with a flourish and set off for The Club. This called for a celebration.

Jacey braced himself in his seat but tried not to show it to the junior detective accompanying him. This was his first ever flight and he was scared. The horror stories about eastern European flights, particularly the Russian's Aeroflot, were making his stomach churn and constricting his breathing. This was the first available flight and it was Malev, the Hungarian state airline. He should have waited for the BA flight a few hours later but he had been so excited he hadn't thought. The air hostesses were yammering away in some God forsaken tongue that was totally alien to him. He made a good job of filling the sick bag as the plane lifted off the ground. Jesus, he hadn't realised his stomach could hold so much. He was retching bile within minutes and his teeth felt like they were dissolving fast. John Spinks was doing his best not to notice and downed both of the strange sausage and cheese based meals provided. He hadn't had a chance to eat and was hungry. Spinks looked sideways at Jacey. Spinks had only recently joined the section and this was his first close encounter with Brown Nose Jacey. The only person that appeared to like him was the Deputy Chief and that was rumoured to be because they were both Club members. Jacey usually ignored Spinks and had ignored Spinks protestations when he had ordered him to drop everything and fly with him to Hungary. Jacey's face, now a lurid shade of green contrasting heavily with his red neck, went a long way to make up for having to make this trip. Served the little turd right, wait till the gang hear about this.

 Spinks concentrated on the food in case his pleasure at Jacey's discomfort showed, Jacey had a reputation for being vindictive. On second thoughts, he would have to be very careful who he told, might backfire on him.

They were met at the airport by the Hungarian police and had to wait while Jacey bought a shirt and changed. By the time they arrived at Huszár's flat it was gone midnight but the police showed no restraint in pounding on the door when they found they weren't getting a response.

After about five minutes I appeared at Magda's door, woken by the noise at my own flat. Still half asleep I nevertheless recognised Jacey immediately and knew this was serious trouble. I stood watching Jacey, my brain warming up slowly, wondering what Jacey had uncovered. What had I missed? Spinks spotted me and touched Jacey's arm, Jacey turned and followed his gaze. In spite of his delicate stomach he crossed the five metres separating us in what appeared to be one bound and taking my fore arm delivered his pre rehearsed line. "József Huszár, I arrest you for the murder of Michael Taylor... Cuff him Spinks. "I was too surprised to react until Spinks had me cuffed. "DI Reed cleared me of suspicion and checked my alibi. "

"DI Reed isn't handling this case. We have evidence placing you at the murder scene. Where are your car keys?" I indicated towards the hall chest behind him, my key ring was in a bowl. Magda had come out of the bedroom and watched with her hand to her mouth as Jacey picked up the keys and compared them with Huszár's spare set from his pocket. He turned triumphantly, waving Huszár's spare set of keys. "These are your spare keys and they were found at the spot where you murdered Michael Taylor. "

I remembered the cosmetic search Jacey's men had carried out on my car. It had been a perfunctory search because Jacey had already broken into the car and taken the keys while I and Magda had been waiting in his office, the search was just a cover. "Jacey, we both know you took those keys from my car and planted them, you won't get away with this. "

Jacey smirked and turned towards Spinks. "Read him his rights, Detective, before he says anything else he might regret. "

Spinks read me my rights and I was uncuffed whilst I got dressed and Magda packed me a bag. I spoke quietly to Magda in Hungarian, reassuring her that the murder he was being arrested for was not one of the three I had committed. I phrased it carefully so the Hungarian police would not be able to read anything into it. Magda understood that I was being framed, but there was still a beaten look in her eyes. Innocence was not a reliable defence in Hungary. She would follow on by plane in the morning and she would tell the girls. We kissed and I was taken away.

After a sleepless night in a Hungarian police cell we caught the morning BA flight, it was public money so Jacey didn't think twice about giving up the return tickets on MALEV, he wanted to get back fast. By two in the afternoon Jacey was interrogating Huszár at the Oxford police station. Jacey had been on a high on the return flight, no air sickness. Julian Hatton was due in less than an hour but Huszár was eager to find out what he was up against so Huszár didn't demur when Jacey consulted the file and started the interrogation. "On the night of Taylor's murder you were last seen by the barman at…eleven twenty five and you weren't seen again until nine fifteen in the morning when you settled your bill. Breakfast was served in your bedroom and the waiter only saw your wife. "

"Magda is not my wife and I was in the shower when the waiter turned up at eight. "

Jacey read through the waiter's statement. "The waiter confirms that he did not see you in the room. Even if he confirms the shower was on, that could have been a subtre. . subter   a cover up by your lady friend. You drive a Jaguar, an XJ12?"

"Yes. " I knew what was coming.

"It is perfectly possible in your car to drive the round trip from Edinburgh and Oxford between the hours of eleven thirty at night and nine fifteen in the morning. " He consulted a single sheet with figures and distances. "A round trip of exactly seven hundred and thirty two miles giving an average speed of seventy five miles per hour."

"Assuming I didn't stop to kill Taylor at this end. "

Jacey hesitated and started flailing at the keys of a calculator. I wanted to get on with it. "Make it eighty miles an hour average that would give me half an hour to kill at this end. "

Jacey was too busy with the calculator to notice the inadvertent pun.

"Right, so you could have been in Oxford by…"

"Four am. "

"By four am. " Jacey looked at the coroners report. "The body was examined at three fifteen in the afternoon and was estimated to have been dead for between twelve and sixteen hours. " His face looked pained as he tried to translate the figures into times.

"Eleven thirty the night before to three fifteen in the morning. Edinburgh at eleven thirty to Oxford by three fifteen…. that's an average of over ninety five miles per hour for the trip." I was encouraged. An average of ninety five miles an hour was impossible over that route. I jotted some figures down. "You ever driven that route, Jacey? The stretch just from Edinburgh to the M1 takes well over an hour. It's less than fifty miles but goes through every village and croft in Scotland, all fully decorated with thirty limits and traffic lights. That would need an average of about a hundred and ten miles an hour for the rest of the trip. Have you any idea what it takes to average a hundred and ten miles an hour? No way, Jose. I couldn't have got their in time, the coroner's report rules me out. Anyway, Magda can testify that I spent the night at the hotel .

No problem, thought Jacey. "Well she would, wouldn't she? The coroner's estimate of the time of death is a rough estimate. It depends on all sorts of factors. You admit you could have been at the murder site by four in the morning. Your car keys prove that you were at the site so Taylor must have died after four in the morning, after you turned up. "

"What was Taylor doing at a gravel pit at four in the morning and how the hell would I have known he was there? Your story just doesn't hang together Jacey. Have another go. "

Jacey had this one sewn up, ready. "You had arranged a meet because you were blackmailing him and he was waiting for you. I was with him earlier in the evening and he mentioned that he would be meeting up with you. He was drunk by then and I took no notice because he was rambling on about that forgery case of yours and how he wanted it stopped. Afterwards, I recalled his mentioning that he had an appointment with you to sort things out, I had no idea that he meant later that night. Obviously that's why he was getting tanked up, he was under pressure. " He leant over the desk, his face centimetres away from Huszár's "So you met up with him as arranged, lost your temper and threw him into the lake. It wasn't difficult, him being so drunk and with your strength. You just yanked his arm and threw him in. " Jacey simulated yanking Huszár by his left arm.

Faint bells rang in Huszár's brain. Leaning across the desk Jacey's voice had taken on an extra measure of authority, an extra level of credibility, he was convincing. That part of the story was obviously true, only it was Jacey who had thrown Taylor in the pit. That's why he had gone to the trouble of planting the keys, that's why he had stuck his neck out so far. Jacey had been trying his damnedest to put Huszár off the forgery case because his boss the Deputy would be implicated. Reed was getting too close to Huszár and when Jacey saw his boss was getting hemmed in he saw a chance of solving the problem at source and took it, probably on the spur of the moment.

"Where did you see him earlier that evening, at the Black Hand Club?"

"I ask the questions, you answer. " There was a knock on the door. It was Julian. "Joe! Detective, I take it my client has been formally charged with murder. "

"Yes, and his rights were properly read to him. "

Julian looked at the twin tape recorder, red recording light glowing. "Then you know better than to interrogate him without his being represented. That tape is inadmissible evidence. "

I nodded my head. "I'm happy with the tape Julian, I agreed to it, as long as we get a copy it's fine. "

Julian eyed me, eyebrows raised. "I can still have it ruled out. "

"No it's fine, really. I'd like the copy now and we can go through it again for your benefit. " I tried to inject the correct tone into my voice so that Julian would realise I was actually pleased with the tape and Julian was not to rock the boat. I didn't know if Jacey had the option to veto the tape.

Jacey was thinking hard. He had never before had a suspect push to keep a tape, they were always glad to have any excuse to trash tapes. "We'll cancel these and start again then, anything to make solicitors happy. " He turned to Julian. "Don't want to give you an excuse to shout foul later, do I?"

Julian went to the machine and deftly extracted one of the tapes. "If my client is happy with the tape then I certainly have no objection to it being on the record. " He sat down with the tape in front of him on the desk. "Let's start again shall we?"

Jacey took out the remaining tape and loaded a fresh set into the machine, wondering what he might have missed. He set the machine running and they went through it again but this time Jacey didn't volunteer his explanation as to how the murder had been committed by I in spite of several prompts. Jacey was learning and Julian's presence made him vary, Julian had a good reputation.

Afterwards Julian was closeted with me in private. "This looks bad Joe. What's your side of the story? If you're pleading not guilty then I don't want to hear anything that might show you did it. "

"Julian, relax, I didn't do it. I was in Edinburgh that night with Magda. She can testify to that and maybe something will come up that proves I was there, although, since we simply spent the night in the room alone I can't think what. Anyway, I was there through the night and maybe I'll be able to prove it. I assume Magda's testimony won't be worth very much?"

"Her testimony will count for very little. How do you account for your keys being at the murder site?"

"Remember when we waited for you to turn up at Kidlington to monitor Jacey's men searching my car? I wanted you there so they couldn't plant anything. What was your impression of their search?"

Julian cast his mind back to the previous week. He pictured the two men searching and Jacey standing watching. "It wasn't really a search, they went through the motions.... And, considering the lengths he had gone to, Jacey wasn't at all interested in what was going on. He seemed very casual and laid back about it. I've witnessed many searches before and usually the detective involved is running round like a puppy with two tails, waiting for bones to pop out all over the place. "

"Precisely. We had been waiting and you came in with him. "

"He met me at the car park as I turned up, I thought he had been waiting for me. "

"Or, he had already been to my car. The spare keys were locked in the dash. The door key and the dash key are the same type, remember those antiquated little FS keys, the ones that are no better than a bit of twisted wire. Thieves don't even notice they are there they open so easily. When I went to get the keys the dash had been left unlocked, I never leave it unlocked. "

Julian was making notes. "So you believe he took your keys to plant them at the gravel pit. "Because he in fact killed Taylor in order to bury the forgery case and protect his boss the Deputy Chief Constable. He was with Taylor at the Club earlier in the evening, Taylor was drunk. The coroner estimated the median time of death as around one in the morning but quoted eleven fifteen to three fifteen. That would fit with Taylor's leaving the club. " I pointed at the first interview tape. "Listen to that tape when you get a chance and tell me what you read into it, I shan't prejudice your view by commenting on it now. Note my calculations about getting to Oxford in time to carry out the murder. I think we have a strong argument to say that I couldn't have made it in time. "

"Do you favour any particular barrister to represent you?"

"Well, I'm glad to say my experience of criminal barristers, assuming they're not all criminals by definition, is nil. What do you think of my handling it myself?"

"Dangerous, but it can work in your favour with a jury. They're often put off by slick barristers and you could gain the benefit of the doubt if you handled it yourself. What experience do you have?"

"I have been to the cinema, and, I have handled some significant civil cases. I have no trouble making the opposing legal eagles get sweaty, always affects their judgement. Lets see how the evidence stacks up and take it from there. You happy with the responsibility of you and me trying it in the meantime?"

"If you're happy then it's no difficulty for me. I've often fancied playing a bigger role in some cases but the barrister normally takes over leaving me with the drudge work. We need to see all their expert evidence, see what they have other than the keys. You realise it's only circumstantial evidence unless they have something to link you directly with the body. "

"Tip DI Reed off about this. He looked into this and decided I was in the clear. Listen to the tape and tell him what you think, maybe even get him a copy of the tape. Hey, what are the chances of my getting bail?"

"The police will oppose it, of course, but with a witness swearing you were hundreds of miles away and since the evidence is circumstantial, you should be OK. They'll want your passport since you live abroad. "

"I'm used to that. It's on an elastic band I've given it up so often. "

"I'll look in tomorrow and drop off whatever I can get hold of. Want any books?"

"All the relevant legal books you've got, I have homework to get on with. Where will they keep me tonight?"

"The Old Goal, it's not too bad. "

"Magda may need your help. I'll leave your number with my daughter in London. Actually, you'd better have her number, I forgot to bring my mobile. " I gave him both of Zsofi's numbers.

Jacey came in, gloating. "Time for beddy bies. We're taking you to the nick. " I saw no purpose in talking to him without a recording, might make him wary and clam up if he pumped me too obviously. I offered my wrists up for handcuffs and kept silent.

I spent the night in a remand cell on his own and was grateful to find that I was exhausted and fell asleep almost straight away. Woke at four thirty, unsure initially where I was. Then it came flooding back. My mind numbed I made rough notes in my Filofax. I had found some years earlier that if I went to sleep on a problem I often woke with solutions to my problems. Looked around the cramped cell as I wrote, it would need a bloody big solution to get me out of this one.

Breakfast and lunchtime both dragged past before Julian turned up after three. He looked agitated, thrown off his usual imperturbable perch. "Bad news, Joe. They're charging you with a whole series of murders...Mr and Mrs Budge, Colin Elmore, Michael Taylor, David Phillips and John Bull. "

I sank back onto the bed. They'd even rounded up John Bull's death. "Fuck me, Julian! Jacey's lost touch with reality!"

Julian looked at the list. "Maybe so, but this snookers any chance of your getting bail. What's the connection between all these people, what makes the police think you killed them all?"

"Bull was the prat with the hotel, remember? I asked for your advice at the time when his companies went down owing me four hundred thousand. He died in a boating accident in Spain. The other four were all connected with that forgery case at the council. They all died in not so funny accidents, you already know about Taylor. Reed and Jacey checked this out a short while ago and were satisfied that I was in Hungary at the time. Have they come up with new evidence that they should raise these again?"

"I don't have any details, just that they are charging you with all six murders. I've already taken the initiative and rung a barrister, he'll be here tomorrow for the arraignment. The police are very confident about opposing bail, count on staying in jail. "

"Magda? Will I be able to see her?"

"She and your daughter are coming to Oxford tonight and will see you tomorrow morning. The arraignment is at two thirty. I have some books for you but nothing else. Should have more tomorrow when the barrister gets here at eleven. "

"I take it that's it for today?"

"I'm afraid so. We're in limbo until we get to see what the police have got. "

"What about Reed?"

"I've left him a message to contact me urgently, he's away on a case but should be back tomorrow. That's all for now, I must get on. See you tomorrow with the barrister. "

"Thanks, Julian. "

When Julian had gone I sat for an hour collecting my thoughts and then reread my notes from earlier in the day. Made some amendments and additions and then picked up the smallest of the three books Julian had left. EVIDENCE IN CRIMINAL CASES. Occasionally I placed strips of paper to mark pages I wanted to refer back to, finally putting the book down after midnight. Needed to be fighting fit the next day and managed to fall asleep by concentrating on the exact definition of hearsay evidence.

Magda and Zsofi turned up shortly after nine, doing their best to hold back their tears. I did my best to reassure them that the whole case was a half baked attempt by one rogue detective to make the accidents fit his concocted story but Magda, of course, knew better. There wasn't much I could do to make her feel optimistic about my chances. Nevertheless, Magda did a good job of bolstering Zsofi and she left a little less unhappy than when she had come. Magda had an appointment with Julian and was going to swear that she and I had been in each other's pockets for over eighteen months and she would have known if I had been abroad for more than the two business trips that she recalled my going on during that period. I was impressed with the ease with which Magda repeated this in front of Zsofi with no sign at all that she was making it up. Felt a lot better having seen them, needed their support and Magda would make a good liar in the witness box.

 Needed all the help I could get.

The barrister was not only a devils advocate he was the devil! Whilst he denied it vehemently he was obviously convinced by the prosecution evidence and believed I was guilty.

"Mr Huszár, whilst you are perfectly correct in saying that all the evidence against you is circumstantial, the sheer weight of evidence and the balance of probabilities forms a very powerful argument. I would not be discharging my duty if I did not tell you to expect a custodial sentence for first degree murder. The chances of an acquittal are minimal. " Leigh Hurst, a senior counsel from prestigious chambers in the

Temple had delivered a long and detailed monologue summarising the case against me and had refused to allow me to interrupt him. I looked at my watch. Just under two hours to go before the arraignment, have to see what I could salvage. "With respect, Mr Hurst, I know it's trite to say so but for the record, yes I had cause to bear a grudge against all these men and, yes I'm perfectly happy for them to have died. So bloody what! The fact that, unlike you English stuffed shirts, I freely express and admit my feelings doesn't then mean that I killed these bastards. The people to watch are the ones that bear grudges and bottle them up. That's the type of character that festers and then does something extreme. I always freely admitted that these people had cheated me and I was mad with them, but, the line I used was that whilst I would not aim at them if they were in front of my car I would not take avoiding action either. In other words, if they kept out of my way I have a life to get on with which does not include them. " I could see from Hurst's expression that I wasn't going to get through this man's prejudice but it might prove valuable experience for the hearing, a chance to deal with the weaknesses in my defence with somebody that was as good as on the other side and who believed I was guilty.

Studied the half dozen pages that Hurst had prepared. "Advice Crown V I and signed Leigh Hurst BA. " Hurst had prepared this hand written missive that morning, whilst studying the Crown's evidence which stood ten centimetres deep on the desk. Poncey, flowery, indecipherable signature. If you didn't know the name you had no chance of reading the signature. I laid the Advice on the desk, tapped the pile of paperwork provided by the prosecution with my finger and having looked at Julian I turned to Hurst and looked carefully at him. Late forties, over weight with a florid complexion. Missed his chance to get his silk and had been to a red brick university. Within his sphere of work at the Inns of Court he was definitely a B Team player. "I take it you picked this bundle up this morning and your advice flows from, what, three hours spent working on this?"

Hurst looked uncomfortable. "Perhaps a little less than that. "

"I've always been impressed with the facility the legal profession have to assimilate a complex file from scratch and get straight to the core, but, are you confident that your opinion is sound? Are you confident that you haven't been swayed by what looks like a full and complete argument? Are you confident that in less than three hours you have a balanced view of their case against me?"

Hurst was livid. The red was rising slowly from his jowly neck and up along his chins and cheeks. His hands shook as, looking at Julian, he said. "As your barrister I am warning you that the crown have a very strong, albeit circumstantial case, the sheer weight of circumstantial evidence is likely to see you convicted. "Great I thought, from a standing start and in only two sentences, I've got him wanting me proven guilty just to confirm his half arsed opinion is right. "Consider John Bull's death. The man's headless body is found in the Mediterranean, his boat swans in to the harbour under the power of its own, ENGINE DRIVEN PROPELLER, they have nothing actually linking me to his death, other than hope. The Spanish coroner decided it was a boating accident and I was in Hungary, six hundred miles away at the time. There is no evidence that I was ever there or that it wasn't an accident. Are you telling me that's an answerable case for first degree murder or is there something I have missed?"

"Put alongside the other, similar cases, yes. It adds considerable weight to the police case. "

"Well in that case, FUCK OFF, YOU'RE FIRED!" Hurst just sat there open mouthed. "OK. OK. Please be so kind as to fuck off, I have work to do. " Hurst picked up his obligatory barrister's brief case and stalked out muttering about my being foul mouthed and uncouth. Julian grimaced. "I appreciate that these circumstances are very difficult for you Joe but that didn't help your case, did it?"

"Getting rid of Hurst helps my case enormously. "

"I haven't seen the files but the way you summarised the Bull case I'm at a loss to account for his thinking there is a case to answer on that one. I'm sorry you didn't find him helpful, he stood in at short notice for the man we wanted. "

"It's always a problem, the best men are always busy. I suggest we put our two best men onto this, clock's running and it's our move. Julian, please read the police files and I will run through my defences. "

Julian sat back in his chair. "All they really have is your keys at the site of Taylor's drowning. The rest simply challenges your alibi in Hungary but they have nothing to actually put you at the scenes of the other alleged crimes. They have a ton of motive but very little proof that you are involved at all. I must say I think we are much better placed to argue for bail today than Hurst would have had us believe. "

"Did you go through the first interrogation tape with Jacey?"

"Yes. I've formed an opinion, what is your theory?"

"Jacey got me to his office on a pretext and broke into my car to steal my keys in order to plant them because he in fact killed Taylor. Did you notice the change in his tone, the confidence in his delivery as he told me that I grabbed Taylor's arm and threw him in?"

"Yes, I did. You're going to say the change in tone was because at that point he was describing the event as it had actually taken place, because he actually did it. "

"Precisely. I saw the same happen at the forgery hearing. I remember that when these forgers were being cross examined they mumbled and farted most of the time, hiding their mouths in their hands and looking away, giving very short answers that had to be dragged out of them. When they got prompted onto an easy bit that they had rehearsed, they were totally transformed. Suddenly they sat up bolt upright and we got eloquent unprompted speeches. The contrast from one minute to the next was absolutely amazing, like turning a light switch. It wasn't so obvious with Jacey but if you had been there it wasn't just his voice and delivery that changed, it was his whole demeanour. It was as if he had grown in stature and confidence in a split second. "

"I was of course looking for it because you prompted me but it did come through clearly on the tape, even without the visible feedback. That's good because Jacey is the one we need to discredit, we need to break his story in the witness box. According to the file he was the one that went back to the site with another detective and they found your keys together. Your theory fits quite well. "

"Jacey is a dummy, if he broke into my car and took those keys there may be fingerprints. It would have been a bit obvious for him to hover round my car with gloves on and the dash compartment catch is awkward. It's shiny varnish and you have to push the door in before it then releases and drops down. There's a definite knack to it, none of my family could actually get it to open without a struggle. We need to get the car tested for his prints and I want to be there so there are no cock ups. "

"Time to see the judge. I'll speak and you prompt me whenever and as often as you like. This is no time to be shy and polite, we need all our firepower. "

My knees gave a slight twitch as I stood to go. Immersed in our discussions it was easy to forget the possible consequences. Felt a lot better about it than two hours earlier, thank God I'd blown Hurst away. I had seen Julian in action and he was good under live pressure. "Let's go kick arse. "

It felt strange to be escorted by a policeman and I felt self conscious as I came up into the well of the court. Zsofi and Magda were there, smiling and waving discreetly but looking tense. The circuit judge came in and everybody stood, just like the films, I thought. Jacey was with a solicitor and barrister in the front benches alongside me and Julian. The enemy barrister stood up and recounted the charges. Six charges of first degree murder.

Julian stood up. "My Lord. The police evidence is purely circumstantial and there are no witnesses to any of these alleged murders. The accused's home is more than one thousand miles away from each and every one of the scenes of these unfortunate accidents and there is hard evidence that he was at home at the times when these accidents occurred. We also have a sworn witness statement from his partner confirming that he was indeed more than one thousand miles away on all six...excuse me, five occasions. The only tangible evidence the police have is the accused's car keys which were found at one of the accident sites. I myself, My Lord, will testify that the Detective presenting the evidence for the police had the opportunity and the means to take these keys from my client's car. My client will allege that this Detective has fabricated evidence by placing these keys at the scene. It was this very Detective, who allegedly found the keys" Julian looked across at a poe-faced Jacey..."Some days after the site had been thoroughly searched by the police's own forensic department. "

I was impressed, we had talked around all these points earlier but the way Julian presented the facts, the way he delivered the points was certainly better and more clearly put than my version would have been. "Since there are very serious doubts as to the authenticity of the police evidence and since there are no witnesses, it is essential My Lord, if justice is to be done, that my client be given every opportunity to refute the somewhat hopeful, and indeed, doubtful case put forward by the police. My Lord, I ask that my client not only be allowed bail on his own recognisance but that he be allowed to travel freely to his home in Hungary in order to obtain the evidence that will show this case up in its true light, an amateur concoction tailored to fit my client simply because he knew the victims of this series of unconnected accidents. The accidents took place in two continents, and the events connecting my client to the dead people took place more than six years ago. " Bloody hell, thought Huszár. For the first time in his life he appreciated what true advocacy really meant. Julian's performance was breathtaking!

The opposing barrister leapt to his feet. He had seen Hurst earlier in the day and had had a hand in demoralising him over Huszár's chances.

When Julian stood up he had expected an easy ride, what could a small time Oxford solicitor do against a man of his might. "My Lord, the police most strenuously oppose bail. The accused has already murdered six people as part of a planned campaign for revenge. Releasing him will put other lives at risk. Given that the accused is a foreign national whose home is abroad it would be most unwise to allow bail. "

I was writing notes furiously as he spoke. Julian stood up and read my notes as I continued to write. "My Lord. My client has dual nationality and freely opted to become naturalised whilst studying at this very university. He has lived here in England almost all of his life and has had a temporary home abroad for less than two years. His Budapest home is actually on the market and he plans to return to England. His two grown up daughters both live in England and they comprise his entire known family. It was the untimely death of my client's wife that led directly to his temporary domicile in his home country, a period of recovery, as it were. All of my client's substantial assets are held in his English bank account and it would be a simple matter for the court to control his access to these funds. The defendant has important evidence with which to refute these false allegations amongst his property back in Hungary. It is essential that he be allowed to properly present the best possible evidence in his defence. It is the very seriousness of the charges that makes it imperative that he be given every facility to prepare his defence. "

" If he is not allowed to properly defend himself then no doubt it will form the grounds for a successful appeal, in the unlikely event that the police's somewhat shadowy case persuades a jury of his guilt. Further, the defendant..." I had written " I love you. " on the pad and Julian, into his stride, had continued presenting his points as I wrote. "The defendant.... is considering his position on the matter of a counter charge of wrongful arrest and thus it would be very much in the police interest to suppress any evidence he may have to support this charge. "The judge looked at the police barrister. "In the absence of any witnesses to these alleged murders, I am minded to grant bail on the defendant's own recognisance and subject to a garnishee order on his bank accounts. Do you have any further arguments...Mr Jeacock?"

"My Lord, whatever evidence the accused has, no matter whether it is in England or abroad, surely it is for the police to collect the evidence. That is their function. "

The judged looked over his pince nez, as judges are supposed to. "Under the circumstances, when the defence are alleging that the police have already tampered with evidence I have no doubt that Mr Hatton will object to the prospect of those self same police garnering the defendant's evidence, in his absence, from another continent. In anticipation of that objection, I accept it as valid. No, the defence are perfectly correct in pointing out that should I impede their ability to put up the fullest possible defence against these very serious charges then I would expose myself to the charge that I had promoted a miscarriage of justice and an appeal would most certainly succeed. I see no purpose in wasting court resources on a trial doomed to fail either on its own merits or as a result of such obvious and foreseeable grounds for an appeal. In the interests of justice I have no alternative but to grant bail and allow the defendant leave to travel abroad. If the prosecution feel that there is a serious risk of the defendant absconding abroad then, with the defendant's co-operation they might perhaps accompany him on his trip, but, in a passive role. Subject to the garnishee order being confirmed, the defendant is released until the trial date which I set at the first available date after fifty six days have elapsed. " The judge stood up and left the court.

I looked across at Jacey and prodded Julian. "Check Jacey. "

Jacey was standing up and looking uncomfortable as he listened to whatever Jeacock was saying to him under his breath. Julian nodded. Jeacock's discomfiture was more than losing the argument about bail. The man was having difficulty even looking his own barrister in the eye and from Jeacock's rigid stance it was not lost on him. Julian knew Jeacock and he was a pro, he presented his case and accepted the consequences. "I'll go discuss things with Jeacock. Fancy a chaperone. ?"

"Sure, but not from Jacey's section. Ask for someone from DI Reed's section or tell them I may prove a little elusive when abroad. Can I tag along?" I looked back at the gallery and smiled at Magda's and Zsofi, their relief plainly visible on their faces. I was in the thick of it and it was much easier for me than for them, I was too busy fighting to have time to worry. It was always much harder to be a helpless onlooker. I mouthed that they should wait at the hotel.

Jeacock and Jacey joined us in a private room. "Well done, Hatton. You did rather well. "

"You mean for a solicitor, do you Jeacock?

"No, rather well and much better than I was expecting from your barrister. " Jeacock raised his eyebrows.

191

I raised mine. "I read Hurst's opinion and fired him. This police escort, not one of Jacey's Black Hand Gang. I trust DI Reed and will co-operate with him about an escort but I will not co-operate with any of Jacey's lot or the Deputy Constable's. "

Jeacock looked meaningfully at Jacey and back at me. "I take it those are euphemisms for the Masons and for Detective Jacey's superior officer, the Deputy Chief Constable?"

"Euphemisms is right, I could have said arseholes and crooks I shall be proving that the Masons are a major factor in Taylor's murder and that Jacey and the Deputy Chief Constable are involved. "

Jeacock pulled a face. "You would do well to consider your words when making such serious allegations, Mr Huszár. "

"I have, those words are apt and correct. Do I have permission to approach DI Reed about an escort?"

Jacey pondered the point. No way he wanted Reed involved, helping me get my act together. "No need for an escort. "Jeacock turned to Julian. "Hatton, you do propose to have a barrister?"

Julian looked at me. "Yes. "

"When you do appoint one perhaps you would let me know. These charges may benefit from a little pruning, subject to a preliminary discussion. "

Julian was beginning to enjoy this. "We're here now. I take it you're thinking of dropping the charge concerning Bull?

"Yes, subject to Detective Jacey's approval. Detective?"

"Drop Bull, but we go forward with the others. "

I couldn't resist. "Drop the Bull it is then. "

Julian had urgent work to get on with and we arranged a meeting for two days time. I was hanging on to the file, need to do more homework.

The garnishee order wasn't confirmed at the bank until ten the next morning and I walked free at ten thirty, the box of files under my arm. It occurred to me that I didn't know where Magda and Zsofi were staying but they were there waiting for me as I came out. Julian had rung them. "Hi family. Where we staying?"

We hugged. Magda couldn't bring herself to speak. "The Randolph. " Zsofi answered. We were at Jude the Obscure, on our third round of drinks. Zsofi had been shaping up to ask me and I was prepared when she said. "Dad…"

"Yes, I did. But not Taylor, I think Jacey did that. "

Zsofi's face fell. "Aren't you scared?"

"Course I am, but the only evidence they have is over Taylor and I didn't do that one. I just have to prove Jacey did it, or actually, the police have to prove I did do it. The keys don't prove anything, they just indicate that I might have been there.

It might even be enough to show that Jacey might have planted them…. Are you shocked?"

"Why did you do it. "

"I blame them for mum's death. I was at Ford because of the VAT fiddle and I fiddled that because all of those bastards screwed me over money and I needed the cash flow. I promised mum that I would get them for her. "

Zsofi could see my logic and looked at me with new eyes. "Do you feel any different?"

"No. " I was surprised at how easily it came. "I haven't had a single sleepless night over it, not even in jail. " Raised my glass in a toast. "Fuck em. " Zsofi and Magda joined in the toast.

"This OK with you, Zsof?"

"As long as you don't get caught – you crim. You seemed so calm and normal at the times when you came to stay. "

"Different trips, you didn't know about them, they were off the record. I came by bus on a Hun passport. Don't ever discuss this with Zsu on the phone and please don't tell anybody, not even Andrew. "

"Don't worry, I wouldn't dare. Andrew wouldn't be able to cope. "

"You're a brick, Zsof. I'm glad you know and we don't have any secrets from each other. "

"Just remind me not to upset you, you're dangerous. "

"I'm Hungarian. "

"That's what I said. "

THEY'VE LOADED MY BILL!

Julian was exuberant. We were in his Dickensian office over looking Oxford High Street. All it lacked was a roaring log fire in the grate and Silas Marner's ghost. "I FAXed a summary of the shenanigans at court to Patrick Eccles and he can't wait. He apologises for Hurst, says he was the only one available at the time. " He consulted a hand written FAX. "He says Hurst is not unaccustomed to rejection. "

I could sense Magda's spirits lifting over Patrick's mood, she was trying hard to keep cheerful on my account but it was proving to be a heavy burden. I squeezed her hand. "So, Patrick Eccles is keen?"

"Very keen. He wants to study the file properly before he provides his opinion but is satisfied from my summary that your chances are certainly hugely better than Hurst would have had us believe. The judge's decision alone tells him that. He recommends getting our own forensic and computer experts in to refute theirs. He's also wondering how best to handle the break in to your car. If Jacey did break in and there is forensic evidence to prove it then he says an English court won't take evidence from a Third.... " He hesitated.

"World?"

Julian smiled. "I wasn't sure if you might be sensitive about it. Third world forensic expert's opinion as seriously as an expert accredited by the Law Society. "

I laughed and Magda just smiled. "I'd wondered about that. Not the Third World bit but the credibility of a forensic test carried out in Hungary on a car unavailable to the other side. What if I drive the evidence back here, intact. Then it can be done under proper supervision?"

"Good idea but aren't you risking destroying the evidence?"

"The most likely area is the dash board and I can seal that and protect it. We both drove back in the front of the car so I can't imagine that there's anything on the front seats or the steering wheel worth recovering. "Shall I organise the experts? Provide a selection?"

"Is it reasonable to meet up with an expert candidate before making the decision to appoint him?

"Of course. "

"OK. Do it. We'll fly back to Hungary this evening if there are seats available and we should be back in three or four days. You can catch me on my mobile anytime day or night after I get back. Could you organise a full set of copies of the police evidence, please. For when I get back?"

"They're already being copied by my secretary, we all get a set. "

I stood up, taking Magda's hand as she followed suit. "Oh, and Julian, you very impressive in court, thank you. I liked the way you extrapolated and decided I was selling up to move back to England because I love it so much. "

"I would also like to thank you, you vere wery wery good. " Magda smiled at Julian and meant it

"My pleasure, I was enjoying myself. I enjoy a bit of colourful embroidery and it did work rather well, didn't it?"

The secretary came in with a complete set of the copied files. Julian's office may have had a Dickensian setting but their photocopier was state of the art, it almost opened your briefcase for you.

I sat back in the plane seat thinking there were disadvantages to being taller than average, lucky it was only a two hour flight. Took Magda's hand and she squeezed hard on my fingers. Leant across and kissed her. "I'm sorry this is so hard for you Magda but it should be over in a couple of months. "

"Yes, but it is dangerous, isn't it?"

"Yes, it is dangerous but you saw for yourself, they're very short on evidence. " Magda had insisted on reading the files the previous day, even though her reading was nowhere near as good as her spoken English.

"Yes, but I vorry. "

"Remember when you first asked me what I felt about you? This was the thing I had to do before I could close the door on the past. I had promised Lesley. "

"I finished early because of you, that's why I wasn't interested in Taylor. I knew by then that I loved you and I had done enough. I'm not going to jail for the murder of a man I saved. I had decided to let him off because I had a new life with you. "

Mgda kissed me back. "Can we drink to celebral…celebrate?"

I ordered a bottle of champagne, I wasn't superstitious. "

We slept in the next morning. I planned to work with the computer, forgetting that the police had it. Felt naked without my computer. The police were challenging my computer alibi. They had an expert who said that with the computer facilities available it would have been a simple matter to programme it to forward my calls from anywhere in the world. Meaning that the computer records did not prove that I made the calls from the flat. They were right, of course, that was exactly what I had done. Worked through the sequences in my mind, trying to see if there was a flaw in my method. Couldn't see a flaw but it was difficult to be sure without the computer. It was difficult enough to see flaws with the computer. Would have to get a lap top and work with it. Collected all the CD ROMs I would need to set up a new computer and put them in a bag. Get a lap top in London when I got back. Hungary was a couple of years behind with its computer stocks, two or even three generations in computer terms.

I sat at my desk to reread the police files, there was an important point that bugged me but I could not recall it. Found it after half an hour. I had been tracked via my mobile which confirmed I was on the M1 near Edinburgh, I had assumed that was when I spoke to Reed. What had stuck in the back of my mind was that Vodaphone had confirmed to the police that I ended up in Notting Hill. I hadn't used my phone after the M1 calls and nobody had rung me, so how could Vodaphone have known if I didn't transmit a signal by being called or by using the phone? Pulled out my telephone accounts file and rang Martin Dawes in Warrington, they provided my Vodaphone service. "I have a Roamer facility on my phone and I'm now living abroad. I was wondering if when somebody rings me in England, does the signal get sent all over the world until it finds me?"

The engineer was highly amused. "No way! Can you imagine what that would do to our call capacity? No Sir, when your mobile is switched on it sends a homing signal out every half hour. Our computer system registers where it is and beams any calls to the region where it last called in from. We need this facility just to cover England, let alone the whole world. That's why we're so keen for clients to swop over to the digital GSM system, the old analogue system doesn't have this facility and it's getting clogged up fast. " He chuckled at the thought of every single call clogging up the world system.

"Thanks. Very clever system. My compliments to Mr Dawes. "

"It's Vodaphone's system, we just rent it out. "

"Thank Mr Dawes anyway. " I looked at the pair of mobiles nestling in their charging cradles. Lucky I had thought of not being tracked by using the phone, lucky I had left it at home when I made my off the record trips and taken my Hungarian phone instead. From now on I would have the Vodaphone switched off and travel with my Panon phone.

Later, I checked the car and strolled into the centre for a leisurely lunch with Magda. It was good to be back, shame Zsu was out of the country again, dealing with the third world for Big S. Walked back along the Danube bank and past the amazing parliament building. It was a bright sunny day and the city looked beautiful. Carried on to the next bridge and onto Margit Island, which sat in the middle of the Danube between the Margit and Arpad bridges. Sat on a bench and admired the views. I had grown to love the city, I looked sideways at Magda, I had grown to love Magda. All this was on the line and I didn't want to lose it. Magda read my thoughts.

"What if you don't go back to England?"

"I was wondering about that. Then I couldn't stay here either. They've arrested me here once already. "

"We could go somewhere else. "

"Where?"

"I don't knaw. " She relapsed into silence again and we both looked wistfully around our city.

Eventually I stood up and, taking Magda's hand, we walked the one kilometre length of the island and turned left at Arpad Bridge and along the Buda side of the river. After five kilometres we came to the last of the six bridges that comprise the centre of Budapest, the centre of our world, and crossed back to the Pest side. Passed Rosey O'grady's Irish pub and I looked back at the reassuringly familiar façade. "Let's get very drunk, starting with this pub. "

I woke at nine to the smell of Magda frying eggs for breakfast. If I didn't know better I would have thought I had a hang-over. Sat up and leant back against the headrest. Struggled through half the breakfast and lay back in bed. "Think we'd better postpone the trip till tomorrow, Magda, I'm not up to the drive. "

Magda looked disapprovingly at my self pitying expression. "I will drive, this is not a problem. I will make more coffee. " She was right, of course, I had work to do. Magda did all the packing and by eleven we were loading the car. I had planned to seal up the fascia on the passenger side to protect any fingerprints but opted instead to leave it untouched. I would lie in the back and when I felt able to drive Magda would sit in the back, leaving the front safe.

Magda drove throughout the day and with a brief stop for lunch we pulled off the autobahn at Wurzburg just after six. Booked into a hotel and by the time we had found a restaurant at seven thirty I had recovered my appetite for food and even a couple of beers. Toasted Magda. "You done good, Magda. You're a star. "

"Film star?"

"No. It's an American expression. Means you're great, fantastic, terrific, wonderful. " She had put her finger over my mouth, people at adjacent tables were looking and she was embarrassed at being complimented so effusively in public. I looked at the people at the other tables and pointed at Magda. "She's a star. " I raised my glass and two of the men reciprocated whilst Magda kicked me gently on the ankle. Winked at her. "Does it embarrass you that I think you're so wonderful?" Magda blushed like a teenage girl.

Shared the driving next day and reached Zsofi's flat in time for a leisurely meal, cooked by young Andrew. It was his turn. Our appointment with Julian in the Barrister's chambers next day wasn't till the afternoon so we were free until then. Talked till the small hours about everything except the case, getting to know each other better. Zsofi and I exchanged looks, we were both pleased with the other's choice of partner.

The barrister was like a breath of fresh air. Patrick Eccles was in his late thirties, had yet to lose his enthusiasm for his work and was very bright. To him this was just a game but a game he had no intention of losing. He was good to have on Huszár's side. He had a pair of experts, ready to be appointed, one in computers and the other a forensic expert. The forensic expert would carry out the tests on the car and would also do his own report on the police evidence. Since they were both London based I could meet up with them the next day to decide on appointing them. I looked down at my brand new lap top computer in its case, I had bought it on the way to the barrister's chambers at Tottenham Court Road. "Can we fix the appointments for tomorrow afternoon, I have preparatory work I have to do first so that I know what to look for with the computer nerd?"

I spent the evening loading WinFax and experimenting with MailBoxes to see what the police might have found in my computer. Nothing. Couldn't see a flaw in my system. There was no way that the police could prove I had used a MailBox and then substituted time and date adjusted files to replace the real records. It was impossible to doctor the time and date on an existing file and I was hoping this would throw them off the scent, my scent. MY SCENT!

Zsofi woke us with a coffee at eight, she was off to work. I had slept badly. "You OK, dad?"

"Probably. I had dreams about computer records popping up all over the place. I'm not used to having a guilty conscience. "

She kissed me, her face showing her worries. "Good luck, dad. "

"Thanks. " I had another session with the computer and left to drop the car off with the forensic expert.

The forensic expert was expecting me and he had a police expert with him. They took my and Magda's prints for elimination purposes and I left them to it. They were going to dust the entire car and would take the rest of the day. I examined his card. Alan Cooper, mid forties and a whole alphabet of qualifications after his name. Should look good to the jury. I hoped he would find something worth looking good about.

The computer expert lived in a huge sprawling Hampstead house. He looked about twenty six going on twenty one. I admired the house and Nick Hopkins explained that his father was rather rich which enabled him to play with computers all day, every day. He was twenty three. We discussed the case and I offered him the WinFax CD Rom. "No need, I have it on the computer already. " He led me to one of four computers in his living room and booted it up. "So, you made phone calls that were logged by your computer and the police say that this doesn't prove you were there to make the calls at the time. "

"That about sums it up. "

"They're right. It would be easy to set up. Have you ever used the MailBox?"

"No, but I saw references to it in the handbook. "

Nick dialled the computer using a hand phone and then waited. A minute later the Fax machine responded to a call and spewed out a message in what seemed, to me, four foot high letters. "You have received one message. " it said, through a purple haze.

I tried to sound casual as I read the Fax. "But my computer has a recording of my call, not a Faxed confirmation. "

"No problem. " Nick proceeded to forge a recorded Wav file exactly as I had done. "The only limitations are that the original call logged with the phone company would be around twenty to thirty seconds and, of course, your normal punter would never work this out in the first place. How long were the contested calls?"

"I don't know, if I caught the girls' answer machines, quite short. If I caught the girls themselves then anything up to an hour or more. "

I knew the alibi calls were short, I had made sure the girls were out when I made the phantom calls for that reason. My alibi calls fitted the requirements for the forged calls exactly because they were forged.

"Well Joe, the bottom line is that computers are too easy to fool. There's virtually nothing my computer records could prove beyond a shadow of a doubt because I know how to manipulate them. The police are right that the records aren't conclusive, but, by the same token they can't necessarily prove you didn't make the calls. "

"The records you just doctored, can you tell they have been doctored?"

"Yes. "I tried not to sound too interested, "Even if the recycle bin has been emptied and the drive has been defragged?"

"Yes. I need an image copy of your computer hard disk and I'll do a report for you on what could and could not have been done. I'm afraid it won't say that you were definitely there to make the calls but it probably won't say you weren't there either. I'll see what I come up with but you realise that for my evidence to be worth anything I have to be impartial?"

I tried not to breath too deeply – so defragging did not work! But, the police had to prove I actually did it, not that I might or could have done it. I smiled and nodded my head. "Of course. My solicitor will arrange for the police to send you my hard disk. You satisfied with that?""It will be an image copy because in these cases they always hang on to the original, for obvious reasons. "

"Yeah too easy to doctor…. . What's to stop the police doctoring my hard disk?"

"They have a central computer imaging facility at West Mercia run by a guy called Roger Barker. They make very special copies of all disks and keep the original as a master. If the police can't prove it went to Roger with full security then the disk is useless as evidence and will be thrown out by the court. He and his assistant Sue Roberts are a pair of Rottweilers, you cross their system at your peril. Let's see what I find, you're jumping the gun a little. "

Must be over anxious, here was a kid telling me to calm down. Where was Huszár's legendary ability to take it all in his stride? "Sorry. The police have already planted evidence and I don't trust them. "

"Leave it to me, nothing will get past me, I promise. I'll communicate via your solicitor, looks better that way for the court. "

Went back for the car. There were useful fingerprints on the dash but they hadn't had time to eliminate Magda's and my prints and match them to anybody else's. That would take a few days. They wanted to keep the car.

Brain was reeling as we returned to Zsofi's flat and we all went out for an Indian after a few morbid drinks at the flat. Everybody was flat enough to slide under the door.

Jacey picked up the phone, it was Vodaphone. "Detective Jacey? This mobile you wanted tracked, you still interested? Only it's back in the country, it's been at the same spot at Hackney over night. If you want the grid reference it's TQ 352 844?"

"Thank you. Let me know if it moves. " Jacey had known about the forensic test taking place and he was waiting for the results. Wasting your time, Huszár! He took a tissue from a box in his drawer and wiped his desk surface clean. "You won't find my prints anywhere in that car. " He tossed the tissue into the bin. Julian rang on the following Monday. "Joe, both reports are ready. I've authorised the experts to release them to you so you can collect copies for yourself. Looks bad, Joe. The computer expert has found concrete evidence that you didn't actually make the calls and they couldn't find Jacey's prints anywhere on the car. "

"BASTARDS! Did the expert mention the possibility that the police could have forged the evidence?" I was beginning to sound paranoid since I believed that Jacey had forged evidence with my car keys.

"No. You'd better sort this out with him, Joe, it's all above my head I'm afraid. He has to play it straight Joe, don't treat him like the enemy whatever you do. "

"Don't worry, I know he's not the enemy. No fingerprints?"

"None of Jacey's. "

"That's a blow. Any sign of the dash being wiped clean?"

"He made no mention of it. Get back to me when you have had time to think Joe, we'll need to have another conference with counsel. "

"Thanks, Julian. " Thanks for nothing I thought, Julian had me down as guilty, or at the very least, successfully framed. There was no doubt from Julian's voice that he thought I had lost.

The fingerprint expert was convincing. No sign that fingerprints had been wiped off anywhere, the car was covered in prints, especially the dash board which had yielded good quality prints. There was no evidence Jacey had ever laid a finger on the car, literally. It had been worth a try. I had hoped that Jacey's planting the keys would fuck their case and the hard drive evidence would be discredited. Jacey's prints on the car would have been sweet revenge for Jacey's trying to frame me but Jacey had been too clever to leave prints, or rather, not stupid enough to leave prints. He was, after all, a bloody detective. I had been kidding myself. I had hoped to have a mitigating clause to help me over the hard drive evidence, if the cops forged the key evidence then they forged the hard drive evidence – melud! SHIT!

Nick Hopkins was unequivocal. He had found deleted, but recoverable files on the hard disk that indicated that I had replaced them in exactly the way he had shown me it could be done. He showed me the files on his computer. "On this evidence the police can prove that you doctored the records and deleted the replaced files. "

Tried to look calm. Had known this was coming. I had done exactly that and I now knew that defragging didn't work. "Could you tell if these damning deleted files were planted by the police?"

"Maybe? It's possible, of course, but the hard disk was sourced from West Mercia so they would have had to have intercepted it before it got to them. If they did forge these files then it was slightly more difficult for them to successfully reproduce them because of the way they had to actually produce false files. Your way, if you pardon the expression, was easier because all the files you were working with were genuine. It was just the times and dates that would have been doctored, the files themselves will have been genuine records of genuine events. "

"What was to stop them forging the files by ringing my daughter's numbers? They could have done it from a private phone line. "

"That way it would be just as easy as your way. " Nick deftly moved between files, using the mouse. "Yes, if they had access to a phone whose records would never be available to us then they could have done it. Either side could have forged these records in exactly the same way, assuming they had access to it. If they have been forged, there is no way of telling who did it…. you or the police?"

"You are prepared to give evidence that it could just as easily have been the police that doctored these records, and not me?"

"As I said before, anything is possible with computer records. You'll need to check if Roger's compliance procedures were adhered to. If he's satisfied, then the evidence on the disk will stand. "

"What's to stop you checking this point now?"

"Nothing. " Nick was already dialling. "Roger Barker, please. It's Nick Hopkins…. "Roger, Nick. Your reference OX 769 HUS, I've got the disk in front of me. Mind checking it out for me?…. Thanks. " "He'll FAX confirmation of the security details so that I can check this disk came from him and also that the disk was secure when it got to him. "

. "Could you link up your computer to mine and copy the whole of the disk onto my hard disk?"

"I can't copy the part deleted files across because, of course, the computer can't see them properly until they've been recovered. I can give you copies of the files in recovered form and print out the details of the deleted files. "

"I take it the police facility can copy deleted files across. "

"Yes, they image it. Even I don't have the facility to do that. "

The FAX started buzzing away. Nick read it. "Joe, if you genuinely made those calls they've done a pretty good job of undermining your evidence. I'll have to say in court that I'm satisfied that the disk that arrived at West Mercia could not have been tampered with by the English police. Your computer was sealed with Roger's system in Hungary and arrived intact.

Roger has a very stringent tamper proof in house system to prevent anybody at his end tampering with the evidence. From my position I see no evidence to prove which party is telling the truth but one thing is for sure, either you or the police doctored the computer. "

" I can see the police could have done it. Those part deleted files and their replacements mean somebody who knew what they were doing made a deliberate attempt to falsify the evidence. The point to remember is that the jury won't know much about computers and the police will point at the part deleted files and give their version of events. The part deleted files look very bad for you, even though a professional will know that it is just as easy for the police to have planted them. It will look very convincing from the juror's point of view. If it's a stitch up then unfortunately it does look to be an exceptionally good fit. I'll do my best to get this remote possibility across, a lot depends on how good your barrister is. This case may well hinge on how good your barrister is at making it clear for the jury. "

"He seems very good to me, let's hope he knows what he's doing. Will you be able to coach him beforehand?"

"Against the rules for me to coach him but I'll make the point and you can say anything you like to him at any time. You can prompt him as he interrogates me in the witness stand. I'll emphasise all this in my written report. If the jury miss it it won't be because we didn't try. "

"Could you get onto your mate Roger and organise an image disk for me to work with. I'm Intrigued as to how these guys managed to forge the files. " I realized suddenly that I was was beginning to believe my own cover story.

"I'll get it sent direct to your address, take a few days. "

I was pensive as we drove back to Zsofi's flat. The deleted files looked bad because they were bad. If they were a police plant they would of course fit the case. Add my keys actually at the site of Taylor's death and it did rather feel as if I was pushing liquid manure uphill with one of those old fashioned pitch forks. It looked damning because it was damning. I had actually killed five of the six people I was accused of murdering. I was finding it harder and harder to put that point into the background, I was, after all, guilty as hell.

Too wound up to work with the computer that evening so Magda and I went to the pub after dinner. Zsofi and Andrew were having their first big row. It was a bad day and I got very drunk, nothing Magda was able to say made me feel any better.

In the following weeks I spent well over a hundred hours poring over the computer but just as I hadn't been able to find a flaw in my own doctoring I couldn't find a flaw in Jacey's counter evidence.

Three conferences with Julian and Patrick and the best they could come up with was a negative defence. I had to hope that the police case didn't hold together well enough in the juror's minds for them to believe it beyond a shadow of a doubt.

"We'll have to see how the case runs and maybe not put you in the stand at all. "

"If I refuse to go into the stand won't the average layman think that's suspicious, that I have something to hide?

"Not refuse, decline to go into the witness stand. Since under English law they have to prove that you're guilty then you are perfectly entitled to leave it all up to them and keep your mouth shut. The judge would have to direct the jury very clearly on that point otherwise you would have instant grounds for a successful appeal. "

"And get it quashed?"

"No, a retrial. "

"I don't even want the first trial. Let alone a retrial. Patrick, I am Hungarian and the Hungarian in me tells me that my refusing to testify is an admission of guilt. I will testify! I would feel guilty if I didn't"

Patrick showed his irritation. "You're missing the point I'm making, Joe. We would not be aiming for a retrial, I'm emphasising that the judge would make it very clear that your not taking the stand should not in any way be construed as an admission of guilt or that it implied you had something to hide. It is a valid and often, the best, method of defence. "

"You're the one missing my point Patrick. Where I come from refusing to testify is an admission of guilt. I won't do it!. "

"Joe, there is a good case for you to consider not taking the stand. If you are guilty as charged then you would have to be very good with computers and very clever. I have got to know you very well at these meetings and if I were the opposing barrister I would have no difficulty prodding you into making your glib and smart replies. I could make you come across to the jury as a smart Alec who would be more than capable of fixing the computer and, what's more important, more than capable of planning these deaths and making them look like accidents. I could also draw you out to show the jury that if you did bear these people a grudge and if you chose to do so, you would be more than capable of carrying these murders out, not just technically but physically and mentally. I would show that with your exceptional self confidence, your relevant experience in building and your self taught skills with the computer you could easily have committed all these murders without batting an eye. I do not believe that you did kill all these people but I do believe that had you chosen to you could most certainly have done so. Now do you understand why you should consider not taking the stand. "

"You forget, I'm Hungarian and a Bastard to boot. I can show the jury that I am too smart and clever not to have covered my tracks. "

Patrick was not in the least bit amused. "Under these circumstances, whilst the opposition certainly would not use those words, they would indeed get it across that you were a foreigner, an outsider. That would not help with some jurors and in that scenario your impeccable English would only serve to show them how adept you are at presenting a false front. Believe me, that could very easily be done in subtle ways that you would not even recognise. "

I had never thought of my Oxford English as being false because to me it wasn't, I couldn't help the way I spoke, but I could see Patrick's point. Suddenly, I felt a complete amateur and the thought of representing myself or even of Julian representing me looked stupid. "I take your point. I apologise, but, it's not just a question of sitting back and saying they can't prove it. They have actually gone to the trouble of planting evidence and doctoring my computer records. Since I didn't do it I would be comfortable with the idea of leaving it to them to try and prove it, if it wasn't for their fabricated evidence. The fabrications frighten the crap out of me, I have no way of gauging how effective the fabrications are in front of a jury. The stakes are too high, a minimum of fifteen years, probably more if they peg me as a serial killer.... they might as well shoot me. " I simulated a gun to my head and pulled the trigger.

"We don't need to make the decision until after we have heard their case in full. If it's a weak circumstantial case we can even move for dismissal saying there is no case to answer. "

"You're not expecting us to be in that strong a position?"

"Probably not. It depends on how well we can undermine their evidence and particularly on how well Detective Jacey comes across in the witness box. If as you say, he actually killed Taylor and planted your keys I may be able to break him. You have dealt with him, what is he like?"

"He's around thirty, not very bright but not exactly stupid either, fly, is how I would describe him. He's on the make. He's a Mason and wants to impress the Deputy Chief Constable who is also a Mason. He's brown nosing his boss and I think he killed Taylor to help cover his boss's tracks. I could see you getting him to sweat in the box if you managed to get to him and rattle him. "

"That's precisely what I shall attempt to do but we will be up against the fact that he is a policeman and no doubt will get a glowing reference from the Deputy Chief Constable. The jury will find it very hard to believe that they will have had a hand in anything like this. The extreme nature of your accusations may actually back fire on you even if they are true. The harder I attack them the more it could look as if we're trying to shift the guilt because we have nothing to lose. "

"But it is all based on circumstantial evidence. All the five.... six deaths could have been accidents and there is no evidence that they were anything else, is there?"

"I shall argue that strongly. They have, however, built up a a framework of circumstantial evidence that shows that it is theoretically possible that you did murder them all. They will claim you had a motive, that you had the skills, they will claim that a confident purposeful person like you decided to carry out these murders and succeeded. So you see how your history and your character can go against you. It is easy for an outsider to see somebody like you, who came over as a child refugee shortly after the war, who went to Oxford against all the conventional odds, as capable of doing almost anything you set your mind to. "

I was rocked. This was exactly how I saw himself. "Sounds like I should develop a stutter and start scratching my head before I answer any questions, how about losing a few inches in height?"

"You would certainly be well advised to leave those high heeled boots of yours at home, the less imposing you look the better. In fact you might consider looking a little more conventional, it might help. "

"I'll think about it. I would hate to make the mistake of throwing McEnroe out with the bath water. "

"What?"

"McEnroe, out with the bath water. When John McEnroe curtailed his histrionics to mollify his critics he lost his motivation and started to lose matches. . . . I'll think about it and I'll finalise my decision when we've heard the police evidence in court but my instinct is to come out of my corner spitting blood, gore and guts. Their blood gore and guts, not mine. Don't lose sight of the fact that Jacey knows he's guilty and that he framed me. He'll be scared as hell and I'm not. They picked on the wrong fucking Hungarian!" At that moment I decided I would fight the case all the way in full regalia, tallest boots, University tie and my loudest and most confident voice. "Fuck them!"I would do it my way!

PAY UP!

They were all assembled at number three court at the Old Bailey. The stress of waiting had cost me four or five kilos. I hadn't lost my appetite and I couldn't account for the weight loss in physical terms, nevertheless, I had lost the weight and felt fitter for it. Zsofi, Zsu and Magda had been a great source of strength during the interminable waiting, I hated waiting, always had. Zsu had arranged leave and had been over for almost two weeks. At Magda's suggestion, I had rented a flat nearby. Zsofi's flat was too small for all of us and we could all do with some privacy, occasionally.

I had been to a few hearings at the Old Bailey in the last fortnight just to get a feel of the place. It had been very sobering watching criminal cases, with suspects found guilty and sent down for years. It all seemed so very easy, so very casual. Guilty! Seven years! You watched the poor bastard disappear into the well of the court knowing that he would surface years later, broken. I looked back at my family as the judge came in and everybody stood up. I half remembered a poem I had memorised at school. "Half a league, half a league, half a league onward

Into the valley of death rode the six hundred.

Cannons to the right of them, cannons to the left of them….. "

That couldn't be right. I couldn't remember who had written it but hadn't the cannon all been in front of them? What was the poet thinking of? Should have done his homework.

So should I!

"Not guilty on all the charges, My Lord. "The prosecution kicked off with Jacey. He was their main man and he was in the box for two days just going through the evidence with prosecuting counsel. Counsel was still Jeacock and he had done his homework. It all sounded only too plausible and convincing   Patrick had his go at the start of the third day. He stood up leaving his notes on the desk. "Detective Jacey, we have heard your evidence with interest over the last two days and I should like to clarify some points with you and perhaps introduce some new ones. " He seemed to be trying to put Jacey at his ease, presumably planning to shoot him down when his guard was down. "In the case of the Mr Budge's and his wife's deaths, detective Jacey, would you please tell the court what evidence there is, if any, actually linking the accused to their deaths?"

"Well, Mr Budge forged paperwork and cost the accused a lot of money. That was his motive, revenge. Mr Huszár is an experienced builder and he would have known the importance of the fire flue being blocked up, he would have known they would die from the fumes. "

"Yes?"

"On its own, this one case may not seem enough, but, put it alongside the other cases and it all adds up. "

"Adds up to what, Detective Jacey?"

"A planned campaign for revenge, that's what it all adds up to. "

"What evidence do the police have that Mr Huszár was ever at Mr Budge's home?"

"They died, didn't they?"

The crowd laughed but Patrick ignored this, no advantage in drawing attention to such a crass remark. "What evidence is there that they were murdered and that it wasn't just an accident brought on by Mr Budge's blocking up the vent to stop draughts and save money? The Budges were, after all, living on a subsistence pension. "

"It could have been an accident if you looked at it on its own but the second murder took place within a day or two of this one. The second victim, Elmore, had also forged paperwork at the same time with Budge. That's why the accused had a motive to kill them both. "

"Answer my Question, please Detective. What evidence is there putting the accused at the scene of either of these deaths?"

"Well, it is indirect evidence but, the accused's false computer alibi is very strong circumstantial evidence that he had a good reason to pretend he was abroad at the time of the deaths. If he had nothing to hide why would he have gone to all that trouble with such a complicated alibi?"

"Apart from the last death, Mr Taylor's, when the accused was indeed in England, you have no direct evidence that he was here in England, no correct that, Scotland, at the times of the deaths?"

"No. But the dates of the forged computer records coincide exactly with the deaths indicating two visits from abroad by Mr Huszár to come here and kill the victims. One visit to kill the Budges and Elmore. Another visit to kill Phillips. Each visit is covered exactly by the forged records. These matches are too good for this to be a coincidence. "

"Apart from Taylor's death, what evidence do the police have actually placing my client here in England at the times of the other deaths, let alone committing the murders. "

"None. "

"Apart from the keys found at the site of Mr Taylor's death, what direct evidence do the police have that my client was ever at the scene of any of these murders?"

"None. "

"So apart from this so called revenge motive because of some minor forgeries carried out by the victims more than seven years ago, you have no evidence whatsoever placing my client at the scenes of the deaths of the Budges, Phillips or Elmore?"

"It is strong circumstantial evidence. Mr Huszár had a motive, the opportunity and there is the evidence that he forged his alibi to coincide with the times and dates of the deaths. "

"Nevertheless, you do not have any actual evidence that he was even in England or that he harmed the first four victims in any way. "

"No, I suppose not. "

"You suppose not?"

"No, there is no direct evidence linking the accused to the first four murders. "

"Alleged murders. "

"Alleged murders?" Jacey looked at the jury, putting on a pained and harassed expression, asking for their sympathy.

"Is it correct that you told the accused that you had a warrant?"

"I asked the accused if I could search his car and he wanted his solicitor present so we waited. "

"I put it to you that you told him that a warrant to search his car was on its way. "

Jacey was squirming. "I may have said words that gave him that impression. "

"Was there a warrant on its way?"

"No, but I could have obtained one easily enough if he had refused. "

"So you lied to the accused when you said there was a warrant on its way. "

"I did give him that impression, I wanted to save time. Anyway, he agreed to the search. "

"Do you often lie to save time, Detective Jacey?"

"I wasn't lying, I just gave him the impression that I had already arranged a warrant that I could arrange any time I liked. "

"You were the one that found the accused's car keys at the scene of Mr Taylor's drowning, is that correct?"

"That is correct. "

"Were you alone, or was there someone with you?"

"Detective Appleton was with me. "

"When was this?"

"Two or three days after the murder. "

"The alleged murder. So you found the keys two or three days after the death of Mr Taylor. After the forensic department had finished a thorough search of the area and had failed to find these keys. "

"Wasn't thorough enough, otherwise they would have found the keys. They obviously missed them. "

"Describe the exact circumstances in which you found the keys, Detective Jacey. "

"I drove up with Detective Appleton in the car. We just wanted to get a better feel for the scene of the murder. We found the keys lying in the gravel inside the area taped off by forensics. "

"So the keys were visible to the naked eye and yet the forensic department, using sophisticated equipment did not find them. How do you account for that?"

"I don't know. Maybe an animal or bird disturbed the sand and exposed the keys. Detective Appleton will confirm that the keys were there when we turned up. I spotted them and pointed to where they were, he picked them up. "

"How far were from the keys when you spotted them?"

"About fifteen yards. "

"When Mr Huszár was waiting in your office for his solicitor to turn up, where were you?"

"I was around the offices. I probably checked with the typing pool about some of my letters. I don't actually remember. "

"Do you often leave suspects alone in your office while you go off somewhere else?"

"Not often. We had to wait while his solicitor turned up so I made myself useful, I didn't want to waste time. I'm very busy. "

"How long were you out of the office?"

"I don't know, exactly. Twenty minutes, maybe a little longer. "

"And when Mr Huszár's solicitor turned up, where were you?"

"I had just gone out to the car park to see if he had arrived. "

"Just gone out. And Mr Huszár's car, how far was it from where you were?"

"Don't know, I hadn't spotted it. I was looking for his solicitor. "

"Mr Huszár's car is a very unusual 1973 Jaguar, painted white. You have seen Mr Huszár in the car and yet you didn't notice it less than fifteen metres from where you were standing when his solicitor turned up, a large white Jaguar with distinctive lines. "

"I told you, I was looking for the solicitor, not the car. "

"The very car that you were wanting to search a few minutes later. A 1973 white Jaguar. A car more than one metre high, more than one and a half metres wide and five metres long. When you did see it would you say it was very obvious in the car park, alongside the other cars, more modern cars?"

"Once I spotted it, yes. But I hadn't spotted it. "

"But you did spot a set of keys half buried in gravel from some fifteen metres away?"

"Yes. "

"And you are a Detective, trained to be observant?"

"Yes. "

"And you have been on a training course on picking locks?"

Jacey visibly blanched but kept his cool. "Yes. "

"Are you familiar with the design of Mr Huszár's car?"

"No. I've never been in a Jag that was that old. It's a very early model. "

"Are you familiar with Jaguars that are somewhat newer?"

"Can't say I am. "

"When you left the accused in your office for some twenty to twenty five minutes, would you say that would have been enough time for you to go to his car, pick the lock and remove the keys from his dash compartment?

"It's possible. It would depend on how difficult his locks were to pick. Lock picking is a bit hit and miss, sometimes it takes me seconds, sometimes ages, sometimes, never. If you pick the same lock twice there is no guarantee it will take the same length of time to pick both times. "

"You said it depends on how difficult his locks were to pick. Surely it only needs one lock to be picked to get into the car?"

Jacey wanted to make it sound difficult. He didn't want there to be enough time for him to have taken the keys. "There was a lock on the dash compartment. "

"You say there was a lock on the dash compartment and it needed to be picked to gain access to the keys?"

Jacey knew he had made a mistake. "You said the keys were in the dash compartment. I assumed that it would be locked since the keys were obviously important. It would be stupid to keep spare car keys just loose in the car. That's why I assumed they would have been locked. " Jacey glanced at the jury, none of them seemed to be excited at his slip, maybe he had got away with it.

"Do you accept that, with luck, you could have had time to pick the door lock and the dash compartment lock, take the keys, all in the time you left Mr Huszár in your office and his solicitor first saw you, not fifteen metres from the Jaguar?" Patrick delivered this as one sentence to make it sound like a single act.

"It's possible. But I didn't touch the car, not even when it was searched later by two of my men. "

"If you had taken the keys, is it possible that it was you that put them at the site on a previous visit after the forensic department had finished their work and you then took Detective Appleton to find them?"

"I suppose someone could have done that, but I certainly did not. "

"You were with Mr Taylor on the night he died, isn't that so?"

"Yes. He was there at the club and I bought him a drink. "

"A drink?"

"Several drinks. "

"Were they singles, doubles, trebles?"

"I can't remember. One might have been a double. "

"I put it to you, detective Jacey, that you bought Mr Taylor three treble gins, within the space of about forty minutes, whilst you yourself drank a single beer and then changed to tonics. "

"I can't remember. "

"Mr Taylor didn't buy any drinks while you were with him?"

"I think he bought one round. "

"Detective Jacey, the steward at the club will testify that you bought all the drinks and that he remembers this precisely because you drank only one beer and switched to tonics whilst buying treble gins for Mr Taylor. The steward joked, to one of his colleagues, that you must be planning to rape Mr Taylor. He will also testify that it was most unusual for you not to be drinking your usual…. four pints of beer. "

"I didn't feel too good that night, I didn't feel like drinking. "

"And yet you went to the bar, where all they do is serve drinks. You left minutes before Mr Taylor and didn't speak to anyone else. Why did you go there in the first place if you didn't want a drink?"

"I told you, I wasn't feeling too good so I went out hoping to meet someone at the club. There was nobody else there that I knew well so I went home. "

"Leaving Mr Taylor to finish his drink? And you didn't see him again?"

"Next time I saw him he was dead, beside the gravel pit. "

"Who else was there when you saw him dead?"

"DI Reed and Dudley Jenkins from forensics. "

"And you entered the roped off area where the key was found. "

Jacey could see where this was leading. "That was some days before I saw the accused and his car was searched. "

"Before you had a chance to take his keys you mean?"

"I never took his keys. You accused me of taking his keys from the car park so I was pointing out that when I saw Taylor's body it was before I could have taken the keys to plant them so I couldn't have planted them then. "

"So you planted them on a later occasion?"

"I said I never took his keys and so I could never have planted them. " Jacey was looking uncomfortable but it just looked like he was being hounded by Patrick, not that he was guilty.

"Apart from circumstantial evidence do you have any hard evidence to show that Mr Huszár actually harmed anybody?"

"No. "

"Are there any witnesses who can say they saw Mr Huszár in England at the time of these alleged murders?"

"No. "

"So you agree that the police case is entirely circumstantial?"

"I suppose so. "

"Are there any witnesses that saw you killing Mr Taylor?"

"No. I mean, NO, because I didn't kill Mr Taylor. "

"Thank you detective, no more questions. "

Jeacock stood up. "In your professional opinion, detective Jacey, do you believe that the accused is guilty of these murders?"

"Yes. "

Patrick leapt up. "Objection, My Lord. The detective's opinion is not admissible as evidence. "

"Objection sustained. The jury will disregard the witness's last answer. " The judge glared at Jeacock. "Approach the bench please... Mr Jeacock, you know better than to test my patience with such a flagrant abuse of court rules. "

"I beg your pardon, your Honour. I was carried away. " "You may stand down, detective, I have no more questions. "

The judge looked at his watch. "This is a good point at which to adjourn. The court will reconvene at ten am tomorrow morning. "

The team adjourned to a private room. Patrick glanced quickly through his notes and looked up at Huszár's pensive face. "Could have been worse. I wasn't able to rattle him but he had to concede that they didn't have any hard evidence. "

"Apart from the keys at Taylor's drowning and the deleted computer files. " My voice sounded accusatory, I had expected Jacey's evidence to be more effectively undermined and I was disappointed with the day's results.

"We haven't done our bit yet. Lets hear out their experts and then shoot them down with ours. We have as much circumstantial evidence to throw at them as they have to throw at us. Anything further to add?" I shook my head. "Be here for nine in the morning and we'll discuss tomorrow's tactics. We'll be hearing from their experts. It's the expert evidence, or rather lack of it, that we will be relying on. " Patrick looked at me, noting that with the loss of a few kilos my face looked drawn. "Take the evening off and try and get a good night's rest, treat yourself to an extra toddy of rum. "

"Pálinka. I'll do that, thanks. " I took counsel's advice and we all went out to the cinema followed by a very routine Mexican meal in Leicester Square. It reminded us all of "Ding curries" we had occasionally eaten. The chef was obviously a keen microwave fan. We waved the place goodbye, for good.

I woke early and read through the forensic evidence, trying to see it through the eyes of the jurors. They were a motley crew and Patrick had advised me very strongly not to stare at them. Three of them were women, they seemed very intense. The men were comprised of a vet, an accountant and various employees of a diverse range of companies. Only one of them ran his own business.

A good steady jury according to Patrick who was happy with the mix. I made a mental note to try and gauge their reactions more closely as the evidence was heard. I had been concentrating entirely on Jacey in the box and couldn't tell how he had gone down with the jury.

Martin Davies took the stand as the police forensic expert. He was very short, hardly more than five foot, his head almost out of the judge's line of sight. He delivered his evidence very effectively, he was used to being a witness and knew his stuff. In this case there wasn't much stuff to know and Jeacock had finished with him by lunchtime.

Patrick stood up after the lunch interval. "Mr Davies, in your professional opinion as an expert on forensic evidence.... is there any evidence that any outsider was directly involved with any of these unfortunate deaths? For example, the Budges?"

"There is no evidence of any other party being involved in the Budges' deaths. "

"Phillips death?"

"There is no evidence of any other party at the scene. "

"Elmore?"

"The model aeroplane which was planted in the tree. "

"Correct me if I am mistaken, Mr Davies, but there is no evidence linking the aeroplane in any way with the actual accident. Even if the plane had been fitted with a diesel filled balloon, as is so fancifully proposed by the prosecution, there is no evidence that the aeroplane and the alleged balloon had anything whatsoever to do with the accident. Am I not right?"

"There was no evidence that the car skidded as a result of a balloon being dropped by the model plane, no. It is simply a possibility that the balloon was a factor in the accident. "

"So you concede that there is no forensic evidence linking the accused to any of the first four deaths, nor is there any forensic evidence to say that any of these deaths were in fact murders?"

"I do. "

"The only evidence linking the accused to any of these deaths, is therefore, the set of keys found at the scene some days afterwards. Some days after you yourself had investigated the scene. "

"Yes. "

"And even the keys only link the accused to an accidental death, not a murder?"

"Murder has not been ruled out as a possibility. "

"Did you use metal detectors in order to find evidence, such as keys?"

"I personally did not. The initial site tests were carried out by a colleague who was taken ill after the first day and I took the case over from him. "

Patrick looked at the report on his desk and leafed through the pages. "There is no mention of anybody other than you being involved in this investigation. Who was the expert you replaced?"

"Dudley Jenkins. He didn't turn up the next day because he had some virus, Meningitis, I think it was. I was allocated the job at short notice and finished off his work at the site. "

"How were you able to carry on from where he left off?"

"I worked from his site notes which were on his desk at work. "

"So it was Mr Jenkins notes that told you that he had searched the area with a metal detector?"

"Yes. "

"So is it possible that the keys were missed?"

"It's possible, of course, but Dud was very thorough with his work. Since he had searched with a metal detector there was no reason for me to repeat the search. All he had found were footprint and tyre tracks. near the bank where the body was found and I eliminated them from our enquiry because they matched up with those of the investigating officers. "

"What, exactly, did you do at the scene of the accident?"

"Dud's notes said that he needed to make more footprint casts. "

"And what did you find?"

"Apart from Dud's footprints I found only footprints belonging to Detectives Jacey and Reed. I also found that the tyre tracks were made by Detective Jacey's car, just like Dud's notes indicated I would. "

Patrick looked at his copy of the forensic report. "None of this appears in your report. Do you still have Mr Jenkins site notes?"

"No. I just checked his notes and carried on from where he left off. His notes made it clear that Detective Jacey had visited the site and left tyre tracks and footprints which he would have to eliminate. It's just the same as eliminating a householder's prints from the fingerprints at a burglary at his house. You then look at the remaining evidence to pin down the culprits. "

"And in this case all the footprints and tyre tracks came from detective Jacey when he visited the site, as witnessed by Mr Jenkins?"

"Exactly. The result was that apart from Dud Jenkins and Detective Jacey.... and of course the victim, I found no forensic evidence that anybody else had been at the scene. "

"You are aware that on a subsequent visit Detective Jacey found the keys.... within the area marked off for forensic testing?"

"Yes. "

"And your and Mr Jenkins' work involved you in casting a number of foot and tyre prints in the same area and you did not see the keys?"

"No, I did not see the keys. "

"You cannot, then, confirm that the keys were there when you visited the site? Nor can you confirm that they weren't planted there after you had finished your work?"

"That is correct. "

"Neither you nor Mr Jenkins discovered these keys which were found a few days later lying on top of the gravel?"

"That is correct. "

"And neither you nor Mr Jenkins found any evidence at all that links the accused to the scene?"

"No, we did not. "

"But you did find evidence linking Detective Jacey to the scene?"

"Yes, but Dud Jenkins witnessed detective Jacey parking his car at the scene, so that rules him out. "

"That does not rule detective Jacey out from having visited the site to plant the defendant's car keys on an earlier occasion. You have confirmed forensic evidence linking Detective Jacey to the scene but there is no evidence linking the accused to the scene apart from the keys which were not there when Mr Jenkins and then you looked but they were there later when detective Jacey looked. That is correct, isn't it?"

"The keys could have been there all along. "

"But, are you not surprised that if they were there that Mr Jenkins did not find them, since he looked for them with a detector or, indeed, that you yourself did not see them since Detective Jacey saw them fifteen yards away?"

"I would have expected Dud Jenkins or I to find them, yes. Maybe he was already feeling off colour, he was rushed off to hospital that evening. He didn't even finish off the casts in one go, I finished for him. "

"You weren't off colour and yet you didn't see the keys?"

"No. I just found footprints and tyre tracks, that's all?"

"None of which link the accused with the scene, correct. "

"Correct. "

"Thank you, no more questions. "

The judge adjourned till the morning.

Patrick was pleased with his day's work and we went our separate ways. The next day it was the turn of the police computer specialist and I knew that the deleetd files were Jacey's best shot. There was no honest explanation for the files being there, either they were genuine and damned Huszár or the police had planted them, but, Nick Hopkins was satisfied that they could not have tampered with the disk before it got to West Mercia. I had a bad night. The following day was Friday, so I would have a chance to work through the evidence so far.

The police computer expert was Richard Sergeant, an independent consultant, Nick Hopkins knew him and rated him highly. He had been given the hard disk to assess by Jacey and his remit had been to check out the authenticity of the phone logs which were Huszár's alibi. Jeacock was out of his depth with computers and he made heavy weather of the examination, which lasted all day.

Jeacock summarised the day's evidence. "In your expert opinion then, Mr Sergeant, the deleted files you found and recovered on the hard disk prove conclusively that these phone logs are not genuine?"

Sergeant had had a tough day trying to get his evidence across to Jeacock. "Yes. The deleted files show that, up to 12th July, the computer had the facility to be called up from a remote telephone and the computer would then forward the call to the predesignated numbers. The deleted logs of calls received by the computer tally exactly with the calls then made by the computer. The accused could have been anywhere in the world at the time the deleted calls were made. "

"So, in your expert opinion the computer records prove that the accused made the calls from somewhere else and could not have been in Hungary at the time?"

"No. The computer records show that the accused could have been anywhere in the world on the end of a telephone, he could have been in the next road, or even the same room on another line. "

"He could have made the calls from England?"

"Yes. "

Jeacock turned to the Judge. "No more questions. "

"The court will adjourn till Monday morning. "

Patrick's face was set as we entered the private room. He looked at Nick. Nick looked apologetic. "I can't see any weakness in Dick Sergeant's evidence. I believe him. "

I had seen this unfold all day and I also believed Sergeant's evidence. "If Sergeant is telling the truth then he was given a doctored disk. "

"There's no way we can unsettle Barker's confirmation that the disk was genuine when he received it. I think you have to take the computer evidence on the chin, the police have got you on that point. "

Patrick had formed his opinion. "Consider your position over the weekend. Consider it very seriously, this computer evidence is far more damning than the keys. We may have undermined the police evidence on the keys but computer evidence is very strong. "

I worked hard to disguise my disappointment. "Nick, I couldn't get the hard disk to work with my laptop, any chance of borrowing one of your computers for the weekend? I really want to work on this at first hand. I have the advantage of knowing that those files were planted, maybe I can find something?"

"Sure. I'll lend you one of my old 486's. "

I came out of the court and joined my family. They could all see from my face that it had been a bad day. They had all seen in the court that it was a bad day. I collected the car from National Car Parks and Nick squeezed in with the four of us. We drove in silence to Nick's house and Nick booted up an old computer. "No point in giving you a duff computer. By the way, I'm away this weekend, ring my mobile if you need me. "

I set up the computer as soon as I got back to the flat. Magda did her best to make light conversation as she prepared the meal and I installed the hard disk in the computer. No matter what I tried the computer would not see the disk.

"József, you must eat, now. "

I had already postponed the meal by an hour and a half and Magda would not start without me. Stood up, stretched, and went over to Magda, encircling her trim waist with my arms as she took the cue and started to serve the meal onto the plates. "You're a brick, Magda. I love you. "

Magda spoke without turning round as she ladled sauce onto the plates. "A brick? I am a wall?"

Kissed her neck. "You're my wall and I want to hide behind you. "Chewed thoughtfully as Magda asked about the case. "Today, was it wery bad for us?"

Nodded. "Our barrister obviously thinks I did it and I can't blame him. There is no honest explanation for the computer files, apart from the fact that they were planted by the police but I have a problem proving that. " Gestured hopelessly at the computer. "I can't get the disk to work in this computer either, it just can't see the disk. " Doodled on my empty plate with my fork and suddenly stood up and went over to the computer, punching a few keys. Shoulders sagged visibly as I turned back and took the empty plates to the kitchen. "My computer has the latest Windows 95 and it has a different disk file system. Nick's computer has the earlier version of Windows. " Came back from the kitchen and back to the computer. "It doesn't have a CD ROM so I can't even load the new version of Windows 95 into it. Have to wait till Nick gets back on Sunday night. " Switched the computer off, thinking to myself that I was chasing rainbows anyway.

The planted files were good enough to convince Nick and Sergeant and they obviously knew a lot more than I did. What chance did I have of digging up the planted files? "Nothing useful I can do till Monday. Let's go to the pub, we need a drink. "

Woke from a sound sleep at five on Monday morning. Had consciously blocked out the case for the weekend and I felt refreshed. Looked across at Magda's face, she looked like a little girl when in repose. Magda opened an eye. I kissed her cheek, realising that she had not slept well. Her loving support overwhelmed me and she saw the tear coursing down my cheek before I wiped it away. "Crying not because of the case, but because you love me and I love you. " Took her in my arms and held her close, her body was very warm. "You're like a hot water bottle. "

"I am hot stuff?"

"Very hot stuff. "

Patrick was half an hour late for the pre-court discussion. Losing his motivation? He looked uncomfortable under my gaze as he opened his case. I opened the conversation. "I took your advice this weekend and I have considered my position and it is this. I know that the computer evidence is damning and I accept there is nothing we can do to discredit it. I also know that the police planted evidence. Jacey also knows that I didn't kill Taylor and I think he probably did, unless it really was an accident. I assume neither Sergeant nor Roger Barker had anything to do with it so we won't achieve anything by trying to discredit them, they're giving honest opinions. " I looked at Nick and Patrick for a response. They were both nodding. "So, where do we go from here? In answer to the question you haven't asked, Patrick, I will not change my plea. "

Patrick looked relieved for a split second, he had been working up to asking that very question. "We need to undermine the finding of your keys at the site. The more people we have saying they didn't see the keys, the better. I'm going to ask for Dudley Jenkins to be called to the stand. If we can cement the suspicion in the jurors minds that the keys were planted then we may, by inference, do the same over the computer evidence. " There was a new found confidence in his voice that had not been there on Friday.

"Patrick, you just made a decision, what was it?"

Patrick looked surprised and paused before he spoke. "With the computer evidence on Friday I thought that you must have doctored your computer and the only reason for you to do that would be if you had something to hide. This morning, your reaction convinces me otherwise. I believe you when you say that the computer evidence is false but you're right that there's nothing we can do about it.

" In fact, without something concrete to back it up it might even backfire. " He turned to Nick Hopkins. "I'll finish with Sergeant by the end of the day and then it's your turn, Nick. You know what we need, just answer my questions, don't make it look as if you are eager to volunteer points in our favour but if I miss anything then get it in, somehow. "

He looked at his watch. "We're on. By the way, Joe, I think you might do well in the stand after all. I want you on, you're very convincing. "

I was immensely relieved as we walked through to the court. It was fundamentally important to me that Patrick should believe me, how else could he convince anybody else if he himself wasn't convinced, no matter how smart a barrister he was? I smiled at the notion of plausible deniability which I was trying to use. I was telling the truth when I said that the police had planted evidence, that was why Patrick found me convincing. I had chosen my words carefully, lucky that Patrick didn't ask me which evidence. I paused in my stride, heart missing a beat. The questions would not be anywhere near as convenient or kind to me in the stand. Plausible deniability would not help me when Jeacock accused me of murdering the Budges, Phillips and Elmore. I would have to work on that one. The enormity of what was happening to me struck me full force as I entered the court room and my knees turned to jelly. Pretended to lose my grip on my briefcases and clutched at a seat, until my knees decided to obey the signals from my brain again. Felt like a man heading for the scaffold.

Patrick set straight to work. "Mr Sergeant, the court accepts you as an expert witness, as do I. I would like to take you through your evidence and, with your help, ascertain the truth. It is my client's contention that the deleted, but recoverable files, were planted on his hard disk after his computer was impounded by the police in Hungary. Are you absolutely sure that this did not in fact happen exactly as my client will claim when he gives his evidence to the court?"

Sergeant was mildly surprised and looked towards Jeacock who avoided his gaze. "Well, there is no way of telling when the files were actually written onto the hard disk or when they were actually deleted.

As I said earlier, when you tell the computer the time and date it believes you, so the data could have been put on at any time before I received the disk from Detective Jacey. "

"You received the disk from Detective Jacey and not direct from the Computer facility at West Mercia?"

"Yes. In my experience that's quite normal. The West Mercia people always hang onto the original, they never let it out of their sight. Everybody gets image copies so nobody gets the original. "

"Except for the people at West Mercia. What is there to prevent somebody at West Mercia tampering with the original disk before the copies are released for inspection?"

"West Mercia have a first class security system. It's impossible for an outsider to tamper with any computers in their possession. "

Patrick paused for a few seconds. "You say it's impossible for an outsider to tamper with any computers in their possession?"

"Yes. "

"Surely it must be possible for someone inside West Mercia to…. modify any hard disk. A computer, in this case Mr Huszár's computer, comes in to West Mercia under the strictest possible security. In order to copy the hard disk the staff must have to use the computer. It is obviously possible to modify the data on the hard disk, is it not?"

"It is possible. "

"Is it possible that my client's computer did not contain these deleted files when it arrived at West Mercia and they were added afterwards. ?

Sergeant trusted the integrity of the West Mercia system and had not considered this as a serious alternative. "Yes, it's possible. You would need to ask the staff at West Mercia exactly how their security system works. "

I handed Patrick a note. "How can you be sure that the disk handed to you is an exact copy of the original disk? Was it, for example, sealed in a tamper proof way?"

"No, it was not sealed. "

Patrick could see from Huszár's note that the copy sent to him directly had not had a special seal on it. "How do you know, then, that the copy handed to you had anything whatsoever to do with my client's computer? For all you know there could have been a mix up and this could be a copy of another hard disk, totally unconnected with this case, could it not?

"The disk had an identifying label stuck on it and the accompanying headed paperwork confirmed it as connected with this case. If the disk had been subsequently tampered with then the details would not tally with the details on the paperwork or with the original disk or with the disk handed to me…. I checked these points and was satisfied that the disk was as it was when it was released by the lab. "

I pulled out a sheet from a briefcase and handed it to Patrick who walked over to the stand and handed it to Sergeant. "Is this the sort of paperwork you are referring to?"

Reference OX 769 HUS. Hard Disk --Seagate ST3600A   1 lost allocation units found in 1 chains.
8,192 bytes disk space would be freed
536,616,960 bytes total disk spacee
  35,192,832 bytes in 611 hidden files
  21,725,184 bytes in 657 directories
463,124,736 bytes in 17,392 user files
  16,574,208 bytes available on disk
    8,192 bytes in each allocation unit
    65,505 total allocation units on disk
    2,023 available allocation units on disk

Sergeant took the sheet and studied it before looking up. "The details on this sheet match the details on the sheet that was sent to me and match the data on the hard disk, save for one thing?" I sat bolt upright and the court stilled. "The data on the sheet refers to the original model of hard disk which is no longer available and, in any case, West Mercia have standardised on a different brand of hard disk. The imaged hard disk itself is larger than the original so the capacity is different but in all other respects the data specified in this letter is identical to the data on the disk in my possession and identical to the covering letter in my possession. "

Patrick retrieved the letter and looked at it for a few moments. "I count more than sixty individual digits in this letter. How can you be so sure they match the digits in your letter, without checking?"

Sergeant drew himself up and after a few seconds, said with pride. "There are in fact sixty eight digits on that sheet, this is what I do. Those details match exactly. My original is at home and this can be easily checked. "

Patrick read a fresh note from me and turned to address the judge. "Your Honour, may I propose an adjournment to enable us to compare the original with the hard disk given to Mr Sergeant. I suggest, with all due respect to the police facility at West Mercia, that their system may have been abused and these letters and disks should be properly copared. Perhaps if we reconvened tomorrow morning?"

 "Very well, but I shall take a very dim view if this turns out to be a wild goose chase. "

"Thank you, My Lord. "

Patrick arranged with Jacey for Sergeant to bring his disk to Nick's house and joined them in the private room. "You think, you're hoping, that Jacey tampered with the disks he got from West Mercia and then passed them on to Nick and Sergeant. " I nodded. "Let's hope you're right. There are signs that the judge thinks he's given us more than enough leeway to make our point. If we come back from this empty handed he's not likely to be so accommodating in future. This could be our last shot over the fabricated evidence. Ring me as soon as you know, I shall be in my chambers till late this evening. " Patrick refused to have a mobile "posaphone" as he called it, far too common.

Magda drove as I studied the figures on the hard disk. It would be dead easy to add and subtract files to a disk and not affect these figures. As long as the total number of files tallied and the total memory tallied you could have anything you liked on the disk and these details would remain the same. It was surprising that an expert like Sergeant could miss this point, the list was really not much more than an index. Magda waited at the kerb, engine idling while I ran to the flat and came back with the hard disk in my briefcase. Wasn't going to risk dropping it.

Nick had his computers on when we turned up. "Coffee?"

"Later. Let's get this disk loaded, I'm busting blood vessels here. " Followed Nick into his workroom and placed the briefcase on top of the desk, opening it clumsily. My hands were shaking. Tried to steady my hand as I offered the disk to Nick who immediately connected two cable harnesses linking it to one of the computers. "Can you do that live?"

"It's rigged with a hot docking bay, very handy, you should get one. It's good for back up disks, you just plug them in. "

I wasn't listening to Nick, I was listening to the hard disk picking up speed until it was spinning at seven thousand two hundred revolutions per minute and then listening to it chatter away with the computer as it gave up its secrets. Please, I thought. PLEASE! A screen full of numbers flashed briefly on the screen and vanished before I could take them in, Nick was deftly tapping keys and manipulating the mouse. The virulent yellow, red and purple welcome screen for WinFax came up followed by the main programme. My eyes followed the mouse pointer as Nick pointed at Wastebasket. IT WAS EMPTY! I slumped into a chair as Nick came out of the programme and opened Undelete. "What are you looking for? There weren't any files in the WinFax Wastebasket?" What does that mean?

Nick's fingers were flying as he spoke. "There wouldn't be. That Wastebasket normally only holds deleted files until you shut WinFax down..... Here are the deleted files that you don't want to see. " A list of about a dozen files was scrolling down the screen. I recognised them as WinFax MailBox files and incoming WAV files. The hard disk direct from Roger Barker would be identical so my own hard disk still had these damning files. I shrank visibly in the chair as Nick turned round, the palms of his hands held upwards. "I'm as gutted as you must be Joe, I really thought we had them then. I really thought we had them. " Magda squeezed my shoulder, barely able to hold back the tears.

I stood up. "Have to revert back to plan Z. Is there absolutely no doubt? Is this an exact replica of the other disk? Maybe they had to doctor them and made a slip. Maybe the times don't match?"

"No, if you think about it, all the image disks will be identical because they were imaged at West Mercia. That's where yours came from.

No, if they doctored the disk before it got to West Mercia there is no way you can prove it. Their forging system is foolproof, if they managed to do the doctoring before it reached West Mercia. " Nick turned slowly. "They've got you, I'm afraid and there's nothing more I can do to help you. Check the two disks. You'll find they are a perfect match. "Magda burst into tears, I took her in my arms. "Joe, Joe. What will happen to you, to us?"

I took a deep breath, no point in frightening the women unnecessarily. Anyway, the burden of proof was still with the police and they had a very iffy case. "It's not as bad as all that, Magda. I was hoping this would prove them wrong and get them thrown out. They still have to prove that I did it, not that I might or could have done it. " I was surprised at how much better my own words made me feel. The hard disk defence was a blow because I thought I had them, but in reality, I was no worse off than a few hours ago. This was a chance that never was. I smiled at Magda almost convincingly. She smiled back, far more prettily but even less convincingly. "OO KK. Let us go get drunk. "

Nick came in with the coffees as I was printing out the details on the forged files from both disks. The expensive laser printer soundlessly spewed out the two pages. Even the print outs from the two disks were indistinguishable from each other. I raised my hot mug. "I appreciate your effort Nick. Thanks for trying. "

Nick raised his own mug. "I believe you Joe, maybe I can get that across in the box. I'll have a chat with Roger Barker and tell him what I think, you never know?"

"Nick, I'm shattered. Mind if I leave you to it with Sergeant? if you come up with anything let me know.

Nick looked sympathetic, the strain was showing in I's face. "Sure. See you in court tomorrow. "

We were on our third Pálinka when the mobile rang. I exchanged a look with Magda as I reached for it.

Hardly dared hope.

"Hope I didn't raise your hopes by ringing, Joe. I thought it would be kinder to let you know we found nothing, save you waiting for a call. . "

Switched the phone off without saying a word. The judge did a pretty good impression of having had a bad night and my head was pounding from the hangover. Dumb, dumber, dumbest. Patrick had had to announce that yesterday's adjournment had been fruitless and he apologised to the court.

"Approach the bench please.... Mr Eccles, I have given you the benefit of the doubt so far, mindful of the serious nature of the case and mindful of giving you every opportunity to defend your client. Now can we please get on and, perhaps, proceed without any further unsubstantiated references to the police falsifying evidence. I am of the opinion that you may well be achieving the opposite to your desired effect with the jury who may well decide that you are protesting too much. " He looked over his half glasses in a perfect caricature of a judge.

"Thank you, My Lord. I hear what you say. "

"Proceed!"

Patrick headed back to his desk and picked up a sheaf of papers. He seemed to me to be nervous. Yesterday's abortive episode had unnerved him. "Mr Sergeant, I thank you for your patience and help yesterday in helping us to establish that the hard disk in your possession and the original hard disk at West Mercia are an exact match. I have only one final question. As an expert.... are you able to say categorically that the accused's hard disk now in the possession of the police.... is exactly as it was when it was taken from his flat in Hungary by the Hungarian Police.... . some months ago.... . over one thousand miles away from here?"

"Assuming the police security worked properly, yes I am. "

"The question is, Mr Sergeant, are you able to say, categorically, without any qualifications whatsoever, that the accused's hard disk now in the possession of the police.... is exactly as it was when it was taken from his flat in Hungary by the Hungarian Police.... . some months ago.... . over one thousand miles away from here?"

"No, I suppose I'm not able to say that. "

"Thank you, no more questions. "

Jeacock stood up slowly. "In your wide experience in this field, Mr Sergeant, can you recall a single case where the computer evidence from the police was found to be FORGED (he almost spat the word out) by Her Majesty's Police Force?"

"No, I cannot. "

Patrick jumped up. "Given your wide experience Mr Sergeant, are you able to say categorically that no cases of forgery by Her Majesty's Police have ever been missed?"

Sargeant looked long and hard at his hands. "No, I cannot. "

Jeacock pulled a face. "No more questions, you may stand down. That completes the case for the prosecution, My Lord. "

"Very well. Call the first witness for the defence. "

Nick came to the stand and was sworn in. Suddenly in my eyes he looked far too young to be an expert at anything. I looked first at Julian and then at Patrick and back at Julian. Julian guessed what I was thinking and simply nodded towards the witness box, trying to look encouraging. Nick did look very young.

Patrick saw Nick through the jury's eyes and addressed the problem up front, impressing me no end. "Mr Hopkins, you are registered as an expert in computers with the Law Society?"

"Yes. "

"Do you know Mr Sergeant professionally?"

"Yes, he's very good in his field. "

"Is Mr Sergeant registered as an expert with the Law Society?

"Yes. "

"Has Mr Sergeant been registered as an expert for as long as you have?"

"Well, actually, no he hasn't. I've been registered for four years and in fact, I sponsored his application when he asked me for a reference. "

"How long ago was that, when he asked you for a reference?"

Nick cast his mind back. "About twenty months ago, maybe twenty two. "

"Were you surprised that a man some ten years your senior should ask you for a reference?"

"No, I never gave it a thought. I was more experienced than he was, that's all. "

Patrick glanced at the jury, satisfied that his point was made. "Mr Hopkins, you were asked for your expert opinion on the authenticity.... or otherwise.... of the allegedly forged files on Mr Huszár's computer hard disk.... and this is a copy of your report, is it not?"

Nick took the file and looked through it. "Yes, this is my report. "

"The court has already heard, in great detail, about the contents of this disk so I shall not test their patience by going through it all again. I have one question, Mr Hopkins. Is there any man alive who can categorically state that the contents of that disk are exactly as they were when they were taken from my client's flat in Budapest?"

"No, there cannot be. No matter how good the security, no matter how many people were watching and cross checking each other, there is not a single byte out of the five hundred and twenty million, forty two thousand, seven hundred and fifty two bytes on that disk that could not have been placed on that disk after it was taken from Mr Huszár.... .

and neither I nor any other expert could possibly tell if that had been done. "

"How so, Mr Hopkins? We're all given to understand that computers are so very clever, how can the computer be fooled so comprehensively and, apparently, so easily?"

"Simple. If you pick any file on the computer hard disk it's simply made up of binary digits, a one or a zero. These digits are placed there by the computer according to the rules of the programmes and they form a pattern. But, when it comes to checking out an expert computer forgery, it's like trying to find which digits are forged when in fact each digit is identical with the next. In this case all that would need to have been done to forge these files later was to lie to the computer about the date and time and then just plant the files. Easy, if you know how. "

"In your expert opinion, then, what creedence can be given to evidence from computer hard disks?"

"Without corroborative evidence, nil. "

"Nil?"

"The phrase used by professionals in the business is that computer records are not worth the paper they are not written on. "

"Your witness. " Patrick sat down with a smile.

Jeacock saw no advantage in labouring the point, best to drop this like a hot potato. "Mr Hopkins, is there any evidence that this hard disk which was removed from the accused's home, and sealed using established and reliable security methods, is not now in exactly the same state it was in before it was removed?"

"No. "

"Thank you, no more questions. "

Patrick stood up and addressed the judge. "My Lord, our next and final witness is the defendant himself. "

The judge looked at the clock. "In that case, it would seem appropriate to adjourn till tomorrow morning. Court dismissed. "

We adjourned to the Quill and Pen and Patrick insisted on getting the first round. "Vot u tink, Patrick?" This was a favourite question often posed by my father and my father suddenly figured heavily in my thoughts. For the first time in my life I felt disadvantaged, helpless, just as my father must have when he arrived in England at the end of the war. "Vot u tink?"

Patrick downed half of his pint in one draught. "Lucky we have a good judge, but you never know. We did well today, or rather, our expert did exceptionally well today. Well done, Nick. "

"It was easy. It's amazing how convincing you can be when you believe something strongly. You know, none of these points is new to me but I see them from a whole new angle. Computers are so easy to fool that they'll soon be worthless as evidence in their own right, worthless. This case has opened my eyes, do you know why in particular?" Nick looked around at Patrick, Magda and me. "Because in less than a weekend I could have any one of you forging these disks, untraceably. Joe could probably do it without any coaching at all, in fact he could probably teach you how to do it. "I downed my lager and headed for the bar, this was getting too close for comfort. "Same again?" I returned with a tray of drinks. "Vot u tink?"

"We're certainly not dead yet, if you'll pardon the expression. I never like to put odds on a case but if you are as convincing under Jeacock's cross examination as you were with us the other day…. then I am hopeful that the police will fail to make out their case for murder and they failed to take the precaution of lodging a lesser charge. They may well end up empty handed. "

Raised my glass. "So it's shit or bust as they say in the best of circles. " Downed my glass, thinking,   SHIT!

"One thing, Joe. Don't get too clever in the box tomorrow, don't respond to Jeacock's needling. He's a good deal cleverer than you give him credit for and he takes very good advantage of the fact that, to coin one of your phrases, he's an annoying little oik. " Patrick wagged his finger at me. "Whatever you do, do not let this annoying little oik get under your skin. Just stay calm and stick to the plain and simple truth and he'll just bounce off you, understand?"

"I understand and thank you, Sir. I shall picture him stark naked in front of the whole court and then he can't possibly annoy me, can he? Bet he's got knobbly knees, I'll try not to laugh. "

"Fine, just think of his knees, whatever it takes. I have to go, have a good night's rest and consider an abstemious night, you looked rather the worse for wear this morning. Sharp as a pin, nine sharp for a final chat in the morning. Goodnight. " He was off and out of the door.

I turned to Nick. "He's right, I've had enough for tonight. "

Nick looked surprised. "You won't need me any more?"

"You never know. Not a problem is it?"

"Course not, I'll be there. "

Took Magda's arm. Slept fitfully. Woke countless times with images of the Budges asleep in their chairs, Elmore's head framed in flames and Phillips' slumped body in the corner with the ominous hiss of gas loud in my ears like a bad attack of tinitus. Have to find some way of kidding my brain into thinking I was innocent or Jeacock would shoot me down in flames. Plausible deniability, but how? Miles away as Magda brought coffee and toast to me in bed. She kissed my forehead. "You did not sleep very well, József?"

Tried to smile but failed. "Troubles with my conscience. It bloody well knows I'm lying, and so do I, that's the problem. " She stroked my temple. "It vill be all right, you see. "

Still trying to convince my brain of my innocence. Thought back to the year and a half of the contract, of Elmore's smirking face as he said, "Tough being a builder, isn't it?". Thought of Phillips' self satisfied expression as he turned up an hour late to tell me he hadn't bothered to do a valuation because it wasn't worth the trouble. Of Budge's wooden empty features as he sat in his car licking his pencil before noting yet another fatuous comment in his site diary. My men had referred to Elmore as "The Gorilla" because of his huge no-necked head. Phillips had been "The Barrow Boy" because of his London accent and Budge was "Won't Budge" because he was so inflexible........ . I had murdered the Gorilla, the Barrow Boy and Won't Budge. I had no idea who Colin Elmore, Dave Phillips and Ron Budge were. From behind, head framed by the flames in his car, Elmore had looked like a Gorilla. Phillips, slumped in the corner under the stairs, did look like a Barrow Boy leaning back against his barrow, all that was missing was his flat cap. Budge certainly wasn't going to budge, boozed up on free whisky in his tacky chair. Gorilla, Barrow Boy, Won't Budge. I recited the lines in my head like a mnemonic, over and over and over again. I thought back to Huszár exacting his revenge, executing them for their crimes. If Elmore had not behaved like a Gorilla, I would not have executed him. If Phillips hadn't behaved like a Barrow Boy, I wouldn't have executed him. If Budge had been prepared to budge, I wouldn't have executed him. It was their alter egos that I had always dealt with on the contract, and then, finally dealt with afterwards when Huszár had enjoyed exacting his cold revenge. I came to with a start, sweat running down my back and down my forehead. Got out of bed. "I'm having a shower. " It was only seven, plenty of time for the pre meeting at nine. Checked my beard, it didn't need a trim. Picked out the nasal hair trimmer Lesley had bought me as a joke present one Christmas, a lifetime ago. Trimmed my nasal hairs and heard Lesley's riotous laughter in my head. Hadn't thought of Lesley for a while. "Love you, Lesley. " I said it softly to the mirror. Brushed my teeth and then showered, first with hot water and then warm, to cool my body down.

Wrapped in a towel, body still wet, I checked the wardrobe while the water evaporated off, making my body even cooler. Chose dark jeans and sweatshirt. My tallest black Spanish boots. Finally dried myself off, plenty of Right Guard and I was ready to get dressed. Felt like a Matador getting ready for the ring. Fully dressed, looked down at my boots, wiped off the dust that had accumulated on them by polishing them against the backs of my legs and went to the mirror. Had to bend my knees to see the top of my head because, with high heeled boots, I stood a hundred and ninety eight centimetres tall. Satisfied I turned to Magda who was ready and waiting. "Let's go kick some arses. " Magda drove as I sketched a picture of a Gorilla's head, a flat capped thin faced Barrow Boy and a donkey which wouldn't budge. Sketched a guillotine. The girls and Andrew were ready when we turned up and they squeezed into the back. I put the sheet of cartoons up in front on the dash. Nobody asked what they meant. As we went into the court I kissed them all, including Andrew, much to Andrew's surprise, and went off to the private room. It was five to nine, I was the first to arrive. Had a last look at the cartoons and placed the sheet in the back compartment of my briefcase.

Patrick, Julan and Nick came in together. None of them had any suggestions for me and Patrick simply explained that he would take me through my defence as quickly and simply as possible and then rely on cross examining me after Jeacock had finished, to repair the breaches, if any. "Bear in mind that this is not a high powered intellectual jury, avoid any smart comments or cutting remarks. Don't act aggrieved or affronted, just answer everything in a calm and controlled fashion. Think before you answer, don't leap in too quickly, it might look as if you are rehearsed, don't take too long, it might look as if you're making it up. Limit yourself to answering the question put to you, don't add anything, especially extra explanations or denials. Brief. Brief. Brief and even more brief. "

"That's a lot of briefs. "

Patrick pulled a face. "That's a good example of what I mean! Think twice but think fast. "

The court takes on an entirely different perspective when it's you in the dock. Ten times bigger and the crowd a hundred times larger. I stumbled slightly over the affirmation, wasn't used to reading out loud, it was surprisingly difficult, all two lines of it.

Patrick led me in gently, running me through a potted life history, my education and how I had ever ended up with my own building company. Then came the contract, with all its difficulties.

"And how did you react when you suddenly found that these council employees were apparently out to get you, Mr Huszár?"

"I was surprised but I didn't take it personally. Individually, all three of them were reasonable people. The contract had gone wrong because of their mistakes and they were trying to protect themselves, they were scared for their jobs. "

I turned towards the jury. " I saw Elmore as simply lazy and incompetent and from where he sat it was easy for him to decide it was all my fault. Budge had no mind of his own and Phillips was simply a dissatisfied man, he hated the work. He was brighter than the other two put together and had had a series of mind numbing jobs. He was simply passing through and everything was a chore. This contract was a chore, especially when it went wrong. "

"Subsequently, you sued the council and went to arbitration. Were you satisfied with the result?"

"No. I won, but it was a derisory award and I appealed. I got embroiled in a very large contract that tied up all my resources and was unable to pursue the appeal before time ran out six years later. "

"Then what happened?"

"My wife died in a road accident and I sold up and moved back to Hungary, which is where I live now. "

"You are accused of the premeditated murder of five people. "

"The police case reminds me of the council. A small number of people grinding away half heartedly for their pay, think they spot a connection or a story, and the next thing that happens is that they have convinced themselves that these tenuous connections are not only fact but that the contrary evidence does not exist. I was in Hungary at the time of the deaths of Ron Budge and his wife, Dave Phillips and Colin Elmore. I was in Edinburgh when Mike Taylor died. I didn't kill any of these people. At one stage the police were even trying to say that I killed somebody on a boat in Spain. All of these deaths were designated accidents by the coroners concerned. My only connection is that I sued them. "

"So you deny harming any of these people. "

"I have not harmed any of these people. " I did execute, I thought to himself, Won't Budge, Barrow Boy and Gorilla. It only occurred to me later that I had no alter ego for Mike Taylor and John Bull.

"Thank you, Mr Huszár. Your witness. "Jeacock made a show of shuffling endless reams of paper and notes. The speed with which Patrick had handed over to him had caught him napping. I waited. My device, renaming the victims and designating them as executed had worked, I really believed that what I said was true, it was true, after all, I hadn't harmed them I had executed them.

"Mr Huszár. You pride yourself on your abilities, don't you?"

"I'm competent at most things that I apply myself to. "

"The manners of the deaths of these five victims…. do you admit that they could have been murders as opposed to unfortunate accidents?"

"Of course. Unlikely, but presumably possible. "

"You know about the danger of inadequate ventilation in a room with a gas fire?"

"Yes. It is a strict Building Regulation and Gas Board requirement. "

"Are you not surprised then, that Mr Budge, an experienced Clerk of Works, should block up his own gas flue. ?"

"No. My company often fitted flues for clients and on our calling back clients had regularly blocked them up because of the draughts and because they wanted to save heating costs. "

"And what did you do about clients blocking up their flues?"

"I would remind them that the regulations demanded it for safety reasons. Most of our work was in draughty old houses and I didn't consider it to be an actual problem. "

"So you never insisted that they change them back?"

"No. It was entirely up to them, and, as I said I didn't consider it to be a problem. "

"Did you block up your own gas flues?"

"No. "

"Did you block up the Budges' gas flue in order to kill them?"

"No. " (I sealed up their flue in order to asphyxiate them.)

"But your technical and practical knowledge would have enabled you to understand the significance of doing so and would have enabled you to succeed in blocking up the flue?"

"Yes. A child could do it. "

"So you could have done it?"

"Yes, but I didn't. " (I didn't block the flue, I sealed it.)

"Mr Phillips. He was an experienced surveyor and yet he died apparently from an electric shock whilst replacing a large mains fuse in the dark and then getting gassed. Do you see any similarities in these two cases, Mr Huszár?"

"Both men would have been expected to know better. "

"Precisely. Does that not strike you as an odd coincidence? Two men, both of whom were enemies of yours, both died in silly accidents. Or were they accidents?"

"They were not enemies of mine. In thirty years of business I have crossed swords with hundreds of people. I've been threatened with sledge hammers, meat cleavers, physical beatings. Fundamentally they were scared, usually over money or that I would retaliate over some argument we were having. I don't consider any of these people to be my enemies, I have no enemies. I'm not that important to anyone. Most accidents, by their very nature, are odd. That's why they are accidents. I see nothing that I would term as odd in the way Dave Phillips died. "

"From the expert evidence put to the court, you understood how Mr Phillips died?"

"Yes. He got an electric shock and fell back onto a gas meter, loosening a pipe connection, and was gassed. "

"You have a good memory?"

"I'm noted for it. "

"Hypothetically speaking, could you have arranged Mr Phillips death to look like an accident?

"I cannot imagine how anybody could have persuaded Dave Phillips, on a planned basis, to attempt to replace an Electricity Board mains fuse and for him to get a shock. It is in fact very easy to replace such a fuse and the chances of someone like Phillips electrocuting himself in such a way must be hundreds to one. If, as you say, there was bad blood between him and me he would have run a mile?"

 "I put it to you, that by some means unknown to anybody but you, you persuaded Mr Phillips to attempt to replace that fuse and then you left him to be gassed. "

"I did not murder Dave Phillips. " (I executed the Barrow Boy.) I pictured the cartoon with the flat cap.

"Mr Elmore. Would you say his murder was particularly clever?

"If it was a murder, perhaps. "

"Isn't fitting a diesel bomb to a toy plane and dropping it by remote control a clever idea?"

"Ingenious, perhaps, hardly clever. "

" I put it to you, Mr Huszár, that you cleverly engineered Mr Elmore's death by dropping the diesel filled balloon in his path and then putting a can of petrol into the car and setting light to it. "

"I did not murder Mr Elmore. " (I executed the Gorilla.)

"Mr Taylor. His drowned body was found near Oxford and the police have shown that in spite of your alibi that you were in Edinburgh you could have driven to Oxford and murdered him between eleven at night and nine in the morning. Do you accept that?"

"From the figures and times the police gave I would have had to have averaged more than ninety five miles an hour on the main motorway.

 I would say that is impossible. I have never even managed that for more than an hour flat out on the German Autobahns. "

 "Your car is a Jaguar with a five point three litre engine, how fast can it go. "

"A hundred and forty. "

"A car with a top speed of a hundred and forty can average much more than a hundred on a motorway when it is empty at night?"

"Not in my experience. "

"How do you account for your car keys being found at the scene of Mr Taylor's murder?"

I thought to correct the word murder but then I realised I did think it was a murder, by Jacey. "I have never been to the site. I believe that Detective Jacey took the keys from my car and planted them there. Two forensic officers have testified that the keys were not there when they searched the scene. The keys were found at the scene after Jacey had an opportunity to steal the keys from my car and it was Jacey who found them. There is no forensic evidence that my car was ever at the scene but there is forensic evidence that Jacey's car was at the scene.

"It was only one officer that failed to find the key, and he said he didn't look properly because the site had been already searched. "

"I make that two officers that failed to find the keys. You forgot the first one who had already searched. I would like to hear his testimony. "

Jeacock turned towards the jury. "Sadly, that is not possible. Mr Jenkins died recently after a long illness, and, evidence has already been put before the court that he was not well on the day he was at the scene and his search was inadequately made - the keys were there all along. "

Thought fast, bastards might have me over the keys? "Nevertheless, the subsequent forensics expert did thorough tests for footprints and didn't find any. He didn't find any prints to match these!" Raised my right leg high and onto the front of the stand, three inch heels sticking out towards Jeacock. "These boots, and I have several pairs, are the only kind of shoes I ever wear. I will present witnesses who can say they have never seen me wear anything else. They are a trade mark of mine. "

Jeacock was not impressed. "Anybody planning a brutal murder would obviously not wear such distinctive.... boots, to the scene of their crime. You could easily have bought a pair of normal shoes and thrown them away. The police have presented compelling evidence that someone skilled with a computer could readily have arranged for the computer to make the calls that you claim you made from your home in Hungary. Are you suffciently skilled with computers that you could have programmed your computer to make those calls. The.... hidden files found by the police in your computer, the files that prove that the calls were made by your computer, do you not admit that their very existence, the very fact that they were hidden, proves that you must have had a good reason for hiding them?"

"They weren't hidden, they were deleted. Those files were planted in my computer after it was taken from me. Both expert witnesses, ours and the police experts, confirmed that those files could have been put in at any time. I repeat, those files were not my files and they were planted after the computer was taken away from me by the police. "

"These files, the ones you say were planted by the police, presumably the same police that you think planted your keys at the scene of Mr

Taylor's murder. The dates fit the dates when the murders were carried out, they fit them exactly. "

"Since they were planted in my computer for that very purpose, well they would, wouldn't they?" (Thanks, Mandy Rice Davies.)

"Or..... they fit so exactly because they were designed by you to provide you with an alibi for your murder trips to England. " Jeacock turned with a smirk towards the jury who seemed to be lapping it up.

"This is nonsense. I am an expert with computers, albeit self taught. I know that the computer evidence is false and I ask to be allowed to prove this in front of the jury. "

Jeacock looked back at me, turned leisurely towards the jurors and said. "I believe that what Mr Huszár, the self professed computer expert means to say is that he cannot believe that he was.... that stupid. Perhaps.... it was not stupidity but Mr Huszár's arrogance, an example of which you have just seen, that led Mr Huszár to be so casual about his computer files. Perhaps Mr Huszár thought himself to be so very much cleverer than us mere mortals, we idiots with computers, that he did not need to go to the trouble. Perhaps he kept these files to prove to himself what an incredibly gifted man he is. Thank you very much indeed, Mr Huszár, no more questions. "

Patrick shot to his feet. "Your Honour, I must speak with my client. At the court's discretion, may I ask that we adjourn until the morning?"

"Court will adjourn until the morning. Mr Huszár, in anticipation of a request from prosecuting counsel, would you please hand over your passport before leaving the court. Court dismissed. "

I looked up at Magda, Zsofi, Zsu and Andrew. Even Andrew had tears in his eyes.

Patrick was angry. "I warned you about your smart mouth! You all but said you did murder them all. "

"Don't do a Jeacock on me Patrick, don't extrapolate on what I said and don't misquote me to me. Nick, I need one of your computers here for the morning with both imaged hard disks fitted so I can play around with one of them. " I looked at Patrick and Nick in turn. "Those files were planted by the police after they took my computer. Anything to add, Nick? You're the real expert. "

"If I come up with anything, I'll let you know. I'll bring the computer with me in the morning. I can always be called in again to add to your evidence, can't I?"

"Biggest screen you've got, please. Patrick, anything positive to say?"

"Shame you can't give this presentation right now, in time to cancel the impression you left in the jurors' minds. I modify my previous advice by saying that tomorrow you must be as smart as you possibly can be with that computer, make it look like child's play, and don't forget, the computer is very daunting to the average lay man so make the explanation as simple as you can but you must be as smart as you possibly can be. Shame about Jenkins, that's as bad a blow as your outburst. Just don't rise to Jeacock again, he will be even more bumptious with you tomorrow. "

"Hasn't he had his go?"

"Your introducing the computer will enable him to argue that he should be allowed to cross examine you again. He'll be doing his best to get you to rise to his bait again, count on it. "

"Just like I did this afternoon. I know. I know. "

Joined Magda outside the court. The others had gone to the car, too distressed to stay out in the open. Magda had dried her eyes and was wearing a very brave face. "That was a bad mistake, yes?"

"Yes. " I explained my plan about the computer and asked to talk about something else. The girls had recovered their composure by the time we got to them. Andrew was slightly perplexed, he was the only one who didn't know the truth. We ate at an Indian restaurant but I couldn't taste the vindaloo, mind was elsewhere.

D I Reed was catching up with his paperwork. He looked at the five file boxes I had so meticulously prepared. Budge, Elmore, Phillips and Taylor, all dead. This was definitely a dead case, might as well let records have them since it wouldn't matter if they did get "definitely lost" this time. He put the boxes alongside the filing cabinet and returned to his desk. He passed John Bull's file to his out tray along with those of Budge, Elmore and Phillips. He opened a folder Jane had placed in his in tray. MATAV? Of course, Huszár's phone records. "Good try, Joe. " He'd heard about the deleted files being found at West Mercia. His eye ran down the lists, mainly local, regular calls to England, a handful to America. He mused about the international dialling codes, trust the Yanks to grab the number one code for themselves, leaving England amongst the also rans at forty four. He returned the lists to the folder, which file should he put them in..... . forty four...forty four...THIRTY FOUR! He opened the file again, thirty four? He had a friend with a time share flat in Spain, thirty four was the Spanish code. He ran his eye down the list until he came to it again. A nine second call to a number in Spain at the beginning of April last year, coming up for Easter. He took the files out of his out tray and opened John Bull's file, leafing through it. No information about his flat in Spain, just he died in Ibiza. He looked at the list and back at the coroner's report. He picked up the phone and dialled the Spanish number. "Hello, I am calling from England, who are you?"

"Non comprendo, Signor. "

"Ibiza?"

"Si, Signor. Ibiza. "

"Gratias. " He put the phone down thinking of how lispy the Spaniard sounded. Huszár had made a call to Ibiza a few days before Bull's accident. That was one hell of a coincidence. He looked at the phone lists, apart from a few calls shortly after the call to Spain..... . no calls until two days after Bull died. More coincidences. He looked at the five box files, meticulously prepared by Huszár and then set aside. He looked at the files on his desk, leafing through them, Bull, Budge, Elmore, Phillips, Taylor. Huszár hadn't set it aside at all, Huszár never set anything aside. Huszár had finished the job for himself! Reed picked up the phone records and Bull's file and went to Ducky's door. Ducky was surrounded by paperwork, he was in for a late night by the look of it. "Sir?"

Ducky looked up at him over his glasses. "You seem to have backed the wrong horse with that Hungarian of yours. I just heard he gave the game away in court today. Witts has just been crowing on the phone. He's accusing you of covering Huszár's tracks in your eagerness to get your own back on The Club. "

"Sir, this is about Huszár. Look at this. " He took Ducky through it. "They didn't charge Huszár with Bull's death, did they? Looks like they got him for the others anyway, just send a memo to Jacey. Might help show them we are on the same side after all. "

"Better still, Sir, I'll take this lot up to London with me tomorrow and pass it on to Jacey. Show willing, this case is personal for me Sir. I'd like to be there to see the end of it. "

"Go on then, can't do us any harm. "

Woke at seven, I had slept right through. There wasn't anything left to worry about. Today's presentation would be easy, I liked showing people what a computer could do. The final result was probably entirely out if my hands, gave himself fifty fifty at best. Looked at Magda, her eyes had opened as I showed signs of awakening and it was obvious that she had not slept well. "Sorry, Magda. Will you wait for me if....?"

"Yes, I love you. "

"I love you too and I'm glad you'll wait. Save me a wheelchair. "

Patrick stood up. "My Lord, my client asks that he be given the opportunity to demonstrate to the court, and in particular to the jury, that had he planned these murders as alleged by the crown and had he planned the computer alibi, as alleged by the crown.... then it would have been unthinkable that he would not automatically have fully erased these files. The files which he alleges were falsely put into his computer by the police. "

"What does this request entail. "

"My Lord, our expert has a computer ready. It would only be a matter of minutes to install the computer in the court. "

"Very well, proceed. "

Nick had done well. He had come armed with an extension lead and multi sockets so the computer was up and running in five minutes. Patrick walked from the screen to the jury box to satisfy himself that the jurors could see what was going on.

"Mr Huszár, you said yesterday that you would prove that your computere files had been tampered with. Would you please demonstrate to the jury exactly what you meant. "

I rose from the stand and headed for the computer. The key board and mouse were at a low level and I had to bend over to manipulate them, tried not to look clumsy as I did so. Turned to the judge. "May I please have a chair, it will allow me to keep clear of the jurors' line of sight and also I am having difficulty reaching down so low. " Still had my tallest boots on. The judge gestured towards the court usher who fetched a chair. "Some of the files found by the police were dated October last year and deleted in July this year. I changed the date in the computer to October 1996 and opened up WinFax, creating a MailBox, naming it ForgedMailBox. Turned to the jury. This is the type of file found by the police on my computer which I say was put there by them. This file can be set up to forward calls exactly as the police claim I did. Assuming that I did do that and having finished creating my alibi, they say that I then deleted the files like this in July this year. I changed the date to 12th July and deleted the file. It has now been deleted and apparently has gone for good. I changed the date back to the current date.

In fact (I opened up Undelete) the file is still in the computer and can be recovered by this Undelete programme. There alongside it, are the part deleted files the police claim they found. "I pointed to the screen. "They have different names but the dates are the same. None of the normal programmes can see these files once they have been deleted and that is how criminals have been caught and that is what I was referring to yesterday. This file is dated October last year and the programme confirms it was deleted in July this year. This file is a replica of the files planted by the police and found in my computer and I just created it for you, in minutes. The file I have just created is indistinguishable from the files I say were planted by the police. Any one of these files could just as easily have been planted by the police, the same police who planted my car keys at the site of one of the deaths. I submit that the police have not proved that I am the source of these files, it is just as likely that they are the source. "

As I turned back I saw Jacey leaving the court, following D I Reed out of the door. I had forgotten all about Reed, ever since Jacey effectively took over, Reed had been out of it. Turned back to face the jury. I selected the drive letter of the disk I was working on. "This disk, for example (I looked at the screen) was last defragged eighty five days ago. "

"Eighty five days ago??" I did a mental sum in my head.

"Eighty five days is a week after my computer was impounded by the police!"

"Eighty five days ago my computer was in the hands of the same police force that I say forged the incriminating evidence!"

"That was a week after my computer was removed by the police. "

Patrick leapt to his feet. "My Lord. . "

"Yes, Mr Eccles, I will call a recess for this point to be clarified by the experts. "

"No, if it please you My Lord, may we, instead, call the prosecution's expert witness back to the stand?"

The judge looked at Jeacock. "No objections My Lord. "

"Very well, call Mr Richard Sergeant. "

I looked up into the gallery at Magda, I could tell from her expression that she hadn't understood what had just happened. At that point Jacey was coming back into court with a knowing smirk on his face, he had missed Huszár's finale.

Patrick walked up to Sergeant as he sat down in the stand and pointed to the computer. "Mr Sergeant, unusually I have called you back because you are the expert computer witness for the prosecution. You are familiar with the crown's case that the deleted files which were left on the accused's computer prove an intent to provide a false alibi. They purport to prove that he must have had a reason to delete them and that he was not in fact in Hungary at the time the calls were made. " Sergeant nodded. "I would point out to you that the evidence clearly shows that the computer was defragged after it came into the possession of the police. "

Sergeant went over to the computer and looked at the information on it. Patrick went over to him and pointed to the computer box. "Mr Sergeant, are you satisfied that all the information you have been looking at concerns the accused's hard disk?"

Sergeant turned. "Yes, but I can hardly believe it. May I have a few minutes to consider what this means?"

"By all means, take as long as you like, Mr Sergeant, we want your considered, unrushed, expert…. prosecution expert…. . opinion. "

Sergeant sat at the computer for a few more minutes without touching anything and then turned towards the judge. "I'm ready. "

Sergeant took the stand and his face visibly cleared as he worked out the consequences of what he had just seen. "I can hardly believe what I have just seen. "

Patrick was ready for the kill, he raised his arms up towards the gallery, the sleeves of his gown billowing out like the wings of a bird of prey about to pounce. "Please, in your own words, as the expert witness for the prosecution, tell the court exactly what have you just seen?"

"Evidence of forgery on the part of the police!"

The court erupted and the Judge called out in a loud voice.

"Silence, or I will clear the court. Silence!"

Sergeant looked at the Judge. "What I have just seen is conclusive evidence of forgery on the part of the police. " The court erupted again and immediately lapsed into silence as the judge raised his gavel. The judge stared hard at the centre area of the court and meaningfully lowered the gavel in slow motion. Sergeant turned to look at Huszár. "What I have seen is proof that the computer files were altered by the police since it was entirely within their control when the computer was last defragged. "

Patrick turned to the judge with a flourish. "My Lord, In view of this incontrovertible proof of the police tampering with evidence I move that the case be dismissed and that the Crown Prosecution's attention be immediately drawn to the likely source of this false evidence. "

The Judge picked up his gavel and the court room resounded with the crash as he smashed it down. "Case dismissed!"

I looked up at Magda and raised my fist in a victory salute. Turned to thank Patrick and followed his stare, Jacey was scurrying out of the court doorway. "That was a close call, Joe. Congratulations. You just put forensic computer evidence back into the abacus age. "

"Tell that to Intel and Bill Gates. They cop the money for designing the systems, I'm just an unpaid, make that innocent, bystander.

Patrick stood up. "You always were good value Joe. You'll get costs anyway, but you should put in a claim for compensation. This forged evidence could be very lucrative for you and the police will want to settle out of court. "

Reed had come into the court and was standing a couple of metres from me. I gestured to Patrick. "D I Reed, Julian Hatton and Patrick Eccles, winning solicitor and barrister.... and I'm the winning defendant.

D I Reed was working on the forgeries case. "

Reed took Huszár aside. "I missed the decision because I was outside waiting to be called as a witness. Jacey came storming out, said I was to forget it and shot off. What happened?"

"Jacey doctored my computer hard disk. Made it look like I had fabricated my alibis. He got caught out because he did a sloppy job. You'll get to hear all about it when Patrick issues a summons.

Reed looked thoughtful as he opened the file in his hand. "I was wrapping up the forgeries case when I came across this, thought you might like to comment?" He gave Huszár a MATAV phone record with a single call highlighted in iricandescent orange.

Huszár took the sheet, the call leapt off the page like an old 3D movie. Huszár's mouth went dry, resisted the urge to swallow.

034 971 309480 April 4th 08. 33 09 It was Huszár's call to Bull!

"I don't recognise the number. "

"It's an Ibiza number. Know anybody in Ibiza?"

Huszár was thinking fast. "The only Ibiza number I ever recall having was John Bull's. " Must have dialled it by mistake, he was under Bull and my daughter is under BaBa, an old nickname. "

"I had just got myself new FAX software and I was still getting the hang of it. I must have selected his number. . . . . cut the call after nine seconds when I found it wasn't her.... don't remember making the call. "

Reed took the sheet back, still holding it for Huszár to see, still gauging his reaction. "Your computer seems to have played a very important part in all of this. " He placed the sheet back in the file, snapping it firmly shut. "Lucky for you that Jacey was trying so hard and went to the lengths he did, otherwise......you might not have discredited him. You might not have been able to discredit the keys being found at the gravel pit and.... this call to Bull just before his.... accident.... might have been very good news for Jacey's case?"

"Jacey overcooked his hand, just like Robert Shaw in the Sting. "

" I know the film. Which scene do you mean?"

"The scene on the train. Shaw is a big wheel gangster who runs a crooked card game for kicks. He uses doctored packs of cards but Paul Newman beats him by doctoring identical packs. Shaw knows he's been fucked but can't do anything about it because he can hardly complain that Newman was a better cheat than he was, which is what he would have to say because the only proof he has that Newman cheated is that Newman's winning hand wasn't the one Shaw had fixed for him. "

Reed looked back, stony faced and then gradually let slip a knowing smile. He knows, thought Huszár. He knows and he's letting it go?

"Joe, this is finished now, isn't it?"

"Yes it's finished. They just picked the Wrong Hungarian. "

"I've been through your records, Joe. I believe the phrase is "Wrong Hungarian Bastard. That is, if nobody has tampered with your birth certificate. "

"OK. They picked the WRONG HUNGARIAN BASTARD. "

"Shall we call it a day then?" Reed held out his hand.

Huszár shook his hand, felt like Reed meant it. "Call it a day. Thanks..... ?" I raised my eyebrows, looked at the file.

Reed tapped the file. "Not much I can do about it, you just got acquitted, and, I feel a responsible for leaving you in it the first time. Like your film said…the worst guy lost. Now, we're even. "

Huszár smiled at Reed's carefully chosen words. "You're a fair cop, Reed. I owe you. "

"I've seen what happens when you owe somebody, I prefer just even, thanks all the same…. By the way…. about your claiming compensation, you might think about quitting while you are ahead. " Reed turned and left, his mind already on another case.

Patrick had been watching. "What was all that about. "

"Reed was involved in the original forgery case and got pulled off it by the Black Hand Gang. He was keen to finish the job by taking the forgers to court but missed his chance because the forgers are all dead."

Patrick was an experienced barrister and Huszár's answer didn't fit the body language he had just witnessed, there was clearly more to it but his experience also told him that he was not about to find out what it was from Huszár. Might ask Reed sometime, if their paths ever crossed again. "Want me to handle this compensation claim for you?"

"No. Thanks. I've had a bellyful of legal hassle. "

I thought back to the last time Huszár had defragged the hard disk.

Must have got the date wrong???

www.ingramcontent.com/pod-product-compliance
Lightning Source LLC
Chambersburg PA
CBHW052032020726

47501CB00004B/1369